BAGATELLE

BAGATELLE

A NOVEL by
MAURICE DENUZIÈRE

TRANSLATED BY JUNE P. WILSON

WILLIAM MORROW AND COMPANY, INC.
NEW YORK   1978

Library of Congress Cataloging in Publication Data

Denuzière, Maurice (date)
    Bagatelle.

    Translation of Louisiane.
    I. Title.
PZ4.D416Bag 1978   [PQ2664.E616]   843′.9′14   78-655
ISBN 0-688-03316-4

BOOK DESIGN   CARL WEISS

Printed in the United States of America.

First Edition

1   2   3   4   5   6   7   8   9   10

A T THE TIME THIS STORY BEGINS, WHEN THE SOUTH
was ruled by the cotton aristocracy, a panama was the
natural headgear of a "cavalier."

On this particular morning—the tenth of May, 1830—
Clarence Dandridge was making prodigious use of his panama
hat. He was a tall, spare young man, and on this occasion he
was wearing a beige flannel frock coat opened to show off a
double-breasted brown silk waistcoat. He was doffing his
broad-brimmed hat every twenty paces. Sometimes it was
with a sweeping gesture, sometimes with the merest flick of
the brim, to indicate precisely the esteem in which he held
the person passing by.

As he left the Hotel Saint-Charles in New Orleans, where
he had spent the night, the first man he ran into at the corner
of Rue Iberville was Mr. Hopkins. The planter from Plaquemines was in a jovial mood but a little the worse for wear,
having probably spent a taxing evening at a cabaret. A little
farther along, in front of the Absinthe House at the corner
of Rue Bienville, he gave a curt greeting to Felix de Armas,
a well-known auctioneer who was no doubt on his way to
dispose of some mildewed cotton and a pair of slaves. As he
was about to cross Rue Saint-Louis, he took courteous note
of Mr. Briggs, a merchant and speculator associated with
Mr. Hermann, who was looking bemused, as if he were totting
up the profits from a deal he was about to bring off. Then,

as he turned into Rue Toulouse, he crossed paths with a church warden from the Cathedral, a portly and pretentious individual to whom he doffed his hat with particular application.

Mr. Dandridge also made frequent and gallant salutations to the several young ladies who, graceful gazelles in taffeta and muslin, used their ivory-handled parasols less to protect them from the sun than to avoid the gaze of those they did not wish to see.

In Clarence Dandridge's case, the parasols were raised in a most encouraging manner. To be sure, he was not a plantation owner himself, yet he belonged to their social class, a class that existed nowhere else in the Union and which the democratic and boorish Yankees in the North damned out of hand as "the petty tyrants of Cotton." In Louisiana's best circles, Clarence Dandridge was known as a sober and courteous man, a good dancer—and a bachelor.

Thus, to the ladies of New Orleans, the expansive salutations of the "cavalier"—for "cavalier" was the title given to gentlemen in the South at that time—were taken as marks of homage from a man of honor. Also, his rare appearances and the mystery surrounding his private life made these infrequent meetings all the more titillating.

Occasionally he saluted couples going by in carriages drawn by spirited English horses whose waxed hooves clattered on the newly laid pavement. Mr. Roman received a particularly elaborate flourish of the panama, for he was expected to be the next governor of Louisiana.

By 1826, the city's prosperity had reached the point where all its main streets had been paved with stones imported from Belgium. Wide sidewalks flanked both sides of the streets, their gutters carrying water from the Mississippi to cool the air during the torrid months. Clarence remembered well when the streets were either a sea of mud, or ankle-deep in dust which ruined the polish on his boots, even penetrating into the snuffbox in his waistcoat pocket.

On this particular morning, Clarence Dandridge's sense of

well-being was palpable. Although a man dedicated to country life, he greatly appreciated the growing amenities of the
urban scene, the great cluster of ships in the harbor and the
burgeoning commercial activity. Indeed, New York would
soon have to look to its laurels. Over five hundred shops and
more than four hundred restaurants and cabarets were ar-
rayed along the streets that ran off at right angles to those
laid down by Leblond de la Tour, the King's engineer.
Whether one walked along the streets parallel to the river—
Bourbon, Chartres and Royale—or those that ran perpen-
dicularly—Bienville, Conty, Toulouse and Saint-Pierre—the
power and wealth of the South were everywhere apparent.

Where, only five years before, whole sections of the city
were either desolate swamps or land dotted with rickety
frame houses ravaged alternately by rain or baking sun, there
were now rows of handsome brick houses. In the design of
its public buildings, shops and houses, each architect followed his own whim. Here, the influence of ancient Greece
dictated imposing columns; there, the earlier Spanish domination was reflected in wrought-iron balconies, galleries supported by slender columns embellished with scalloped motifs
and iron or wooden gingerbread, as well as the open patios
where tiny fountains played in jewel boxes of greenery. Then
again, imposing facades graced with large windows and fan-
lights bespoke the French influence. But whatever the style,
each was adapted—one might even say perverted—by the
colonial past and the quixotic tastes of its owner, whose overriding aim usually was to document the scope of his success
and the quality of his origins.

The great levee that protected the city from the river's floods
now stretched more than a league, the tightly packed earth-
works reinforced by layers of shells from Lake Pontchartrain's
abundant supply. Long arcaded stone buildings were beginning to rise on the levee; some people predicted they would
reach the incredible height of five stories.

A visitor in 1830 looking at the picture of the New Orleans
Garney had painted ten years earlier would have recognized

neither city nor port. Little by little, steam had won out over sail. Schooners, brigs and oceangoing vessels now hobnobbed with the shallow-draft river steamers propelled by side paddle-wheels that belched smoke from their huge brass-rimmed funnels. Every product harvested along the river's sinuous length eventually ended up in the generous curve of its arm, from which came New Orleans's original name of Crescent City. For good measure, the cargoes from its tributaries, the Ohio and the Missouri, joined the river traffic to reach the port where the Old World came in search of provisions. By the same token, the river and its tributaries brought to the hinterland the products of that same Europe which had taught it liberty along with agriculture and commerce.

On the congested quays, swarms of slaves maneuvered their wagons among piles of bulging cotton bales from which a white tuft projected here and there, loaves of indigo from the delta, molasses and sugar from Louisiana and Alabama, crates of dried beef from Arkansas, barrels of salt pork and triangular ingots of lead from Mississippi, thousands of hogsheads of tobacco classified according to their place of origin: "bright-leaf" from Virginia, "kitefoot" from Ohio, "sweated" from Natchitoches, "crossed" from Maryland. Also bundles of animal skins—beaver, bear, hare—too evil-smelling for passenger boats, hence carried down the river on log rafts along with lumber and tarpaulins from Kentucky, the rafts sold together with their cargoes.

Barrels of wine from Madeira and Bordeaux were piled next to cases of bottles bearing the names of France's noblest vineyards, labels reading Chateau-Margaux, Sauterne, Muscat de Frontigan next to casks of Old Whiskey of Konongahela, Absinthe, Julien, Medoc and Moselle. Elsewhere, gigs, cartons of books, music boxes, English saddles, fine shoes, porcelain from Limoges and Wedgwood, lengths of silk, kerseymere, cotton flannel, gloves, locks, clocks, earthenware pots from Lorraine, up to and including cloves and strawberry preserves —everything, in fact, that a refined people could possibly hope to eat, wear, fight with or be distracted by.

In the middle of the confusion, traders, agents and middlemen in frock coats, silk waistcoats, frilled shirts and high silk hats milled about trying to identify the merchandise unloaded from ships now riding at anchor in the river. Coming from Le Havre, Bordeaux, London, Liverpool and Lisbon, they had brought the best that Europe had to offer—the things less backward countries produced with greater skill.

With so many rich people avid for luxuries and competing for the latest arrivals in the shops along Rue Royale, business was booming. The moment a new shipment was announced in the columns of *L'Abeille* or the *Courrier de la Louisiane*, the rush was on.

To the city's seven banks three more had been added, one of them boasting seventy million francs in capital (about fourteen million dollars). The bankers reaped 6 percent on a three-month loan, 7 percent to 8 percent on longer terms. The exchange rate for the dollar—which Louisianians persisted in calling a piaster—was 5.85 francs. Although interest rates were legally pegged at 7 percent, local capitalists had little trouble getting 20 percent. Mr. Potinent, one of the city's leading hardware merchants, expressed it for all the town's businessmen when he said: "Buy intelligently in Europe and you can easily make a profit of 15 percent."

In the motley crowd on the quays, the ships' captains kept a sharp eye on their crews, for desertions were becoming a vexing problem. The prosperity of the Southern capital was all too tempting to men without ties. In an octoroon's smile or the glib talk of a smuggler, these would-be adventurers saw their fortunes made. In contrast to the sailors were the "roustabouts," the strongest blacks, who loaded and unloaded the ships and were always ready to do a little extra for a few "picaillons" slipped into the hand by a harried shipowner. The *Ceres*, a three-masted schooner loaded with cotton, was leaving for Bordeaux, the brig *Tristan* for Nantes, the schooner *Katherine* for London. Below their national colors, they all flew the "blue peter"—a white square on a blue ground—indicating that the ship was about to leave port; the Stars and

Stripes; and sometimes even the identification of a Louisiana merchant and a flag showing a soaring American eagle, a ribbon in its beak proclaiming the New Orleans motto: "Under my wings, everything prospers."

The sound of English, French, Spanish and Creole filled the air. From the strident tone of the voices and the heated bargaining, it was not difficult to guess that money and the pleasures it delivered were the great preoccupation. This was New Orleans, the city men had willed into being, where, in March 1699, Pierre Le Moyne d'Iberville and his brother Jean-Baptiste Le Moyne de Bienville had planted a cross and marked the trees in the belief that the place looked propitious for a city. Now, a century later, John Law's dream of a "Compagnie des Indes" was finally coming true.

If Clarence Dandridge was seldom seen in New Orleans, it was because his employer, the Marquis de Damvilliers, was always only too eager to hop on the next boat that would take him to New Orleans from his plantation, Bagatelle, at Pointe-Coupée. A dispute over a cargo of cotton that needed his intervention, a visit to his banker, or the state of the market in sugar, indigo or Indian wheat was all the excuse he needed to while away a week in the city.

But on this particular occasion, something very different had brought Clarence Dandridge to New Orleans. A ship from Le Havre was due into port, and on board that ship was a certain Caroline Trégan, the Marquis's godchild, orphaned a few months earlier. But for the fact that the Marquis's wife had died of yellow fever three weeks before, Caroline's godfather would have felt it both a duty and a pleasure to appear on the Quai Saint-Pierre to welcome the young lady.

Clarence, delegated to take his place, remembered little of the girl except that she had been by turns mischievous and sulky. The Marquis assured him that she had now become a real "Parisienne" and that the reason for the trip was to collect her inheritance.

Bagatelle's manager took the assignment with good grace,

if with little enthusiasm. There was nothing he wouldn't do for his employer, for the Marquis had plucked him—a mere adolescent—from a painful and humiliating predicament. Their affection for each other was deep, although it seldom found expression in words. On the other hand, alive or dead, the late Marquise had left Clarence unmoved. Dorothée had been a morose and malingering woman who, hating Louisiana's climate, had spent most of her time in Virginia where her father owned the largest plantation in the state. Barren as well, she left virtually no trace at Bagatelle. A bird of passage, she departed this life as discreetly as she had lived it, preparing her soul with the same instinct for order she used in packing her bags.

As for Caroline Trégan, the Marquis's godchild, she had left Pointe-Coupée in 1825 at the age of thirteen in order to continue her education with the Ursuline nuns in Paris. Her memories of her dead godmother must be faint indeed. The Marquise, who had been unable to conceive, detested the hullabaloo of children and only rarely invited Caroline to Bagatelle. Clarence recalled that the girl's single pleasure had been to play in the pigeon cotes which the first Marquis had built near the great avenue of oaks.

After his wife's death, Adrien de Damvilliers had immediately resumed the placid life of a bachelor and renewed the late afternoon ritual with his manager. The two men would sit in their rocking chairs, with glasses of fruit punch in their hands, on the gallery that ran along the front of the house. As they smoked their cigars, they would discuss the many problems of the plantation and its four hundred slaves, calculate the effects of the drought on the harvest, or talk horses. Politics was seldom mentioned. The only articles in the newspapers that interested the Marquis were those dealing with agriculture and commerce. Sometimes, the two men prolonged their conversation until after nightfall, when the moon caught the flight of the bats as they darted in and out of the Spanish moss that hung from the great oaks' branches screening the curve of the Mississippi River.

"Caroline's arrival may change some of our ways," Clarence said to himself as he directed his steps toward the port's administrative offices. There he learned that the *Charles Carroll* wouldn't be docking until the end of the afternoon. (The ship was known as one of the most luxurious in the fleet owned by Jerome Bonaparte's ex-father-in-law, with cabins paneled in mahogany inlaid with bird's-eye maple.) The news of its arrival had just come by lugger from the post at La Balise at the southeasternmost point in the delta, where ships' captains had to take on a pilot for the river trip to New Orleans.

Clarence knew all about the hazards of navigating the river's sandbanks, as well as the snail's pace of the port bureaucracy which suspected each and every ship of carrying yellow fever or contraband spirits. As the ship advanced up the river it also had to heave to at Fort Saint-Philippe so that its captain could present his manifest. Then, twelve leagues from the first stop and two leagues before the Détour des Anglais, he had to weigh anchor in front of the quarantine station, where an inspector and a doctor came aboard. Ever since the epidemic of 1817, officials had taken strict account of ships' "health certificates" and, on occasion, even examined the passengers. If nothing suspicious was found on board, they made out the certificate, which in turn was submitted to the authorities in New Orleans. It cost ten piasters for a three-masted schooner and six for a brig.

A fourth stop was required at the customs house on the Détour des Anglais, where another group of officials exacted "light money" and tonnage fees. Contention was the rule in these various transactions: There were petty inspections, innuendos and subterfuge, discreet bribes and tips. After weeks of heavy seas and near-escapes from Mexican pirates, the ships' captains viewed their entry into an American port as the ultimate test. And so it was with a light heart that they paid out the five piasters to the captain of the port, and another fee for the right to dock at the city's quays.

With more than two thousand merchant ships in and out of the port each year, the navigational complications in this bureaucratic ritual were awesome. In 1825, however, the city authorities, to whom the requirements of commerce came first, reluctantly decided to ease the bottleneck by eliminating the quarantine. The mayor declared that it was "inefficient, ineffectual, and a hindrance to the smooth operation of commerce."

Clarence had had the foresight to reserve two cabins on the *Prince du Delta*, the newest of the river boats which would make the trip back to Pointe-Coupée in three days. He hoped Caroline would enjoy the "river greyhound," advertised to make six miles an hour against the current, in addition to having "its hull sheathed and plugged with brass, its cabins elegantly furnished, its repasts abundant and of the finest quality."

The bells of the Cathedral of Saint-Louis were pealing ten o'clock as Clarence entered his bootmaker's. An advertisement in that morning's *L'Abeille* announced that Mr. Stuart had just received "a shipment of patent leather, polished calf and Moroccan leather in red, blue, yellow and tan." So, he would order some boots and at the same time see Mathias, a Bagatelle slave he wished to have freed because of his great skill at cutting and sewing leather. Thanks to his position with Mr. Stuart, the city's foremost bootmaker, the former sugarcane cutter had sloughed off some of the stigma of slavery while at the same time bringing his owner, the Marquis de Damvilliers, the tidy sum of thirty dollars a month, which Mr. Stuart paid punctiliously. The Marquis's transaction was therefore profitable. At that time a bank teller pocketed forty dollars a month and a hundredweight of finest quality cotton brought between nine and eleven dollars.

As Clarence Dandridge walked in, Mathias put down his tools and his sweating face broke into a wide smile.

"Mister Dandridge, it's a long time since you come to the city! How's the cane this year, and how's Master de Damvilliers's cotton?"

Clarence informed the slave of his mistress's death and Mathias expressed suitable condolences even though he had hardly known her. Dandridge quickly changed the subject and asked to see some samples of polished calf.

"Here they is, Mister Dandridge," Mathias said eagerly, wiping his large hands covered with cobbler's wax and bits of thread. "Mr. Stuart'll be right back, but I can show you what just come off the boat . . ."

"Just a minute!" came in a loud voice from the other side of the shop. "I don't believe that this gentleman is any more pressed for time than I am. I was about to make my choice. But perhaps there'll be enough left for a manager . . ."

Mathias stopped in his tracks and gave Clarence a tentative smile. Dandridge, coming in from the bright sunlight, had failed to notice a couple sitting in a dark corner of the shop. Taking off his hat, he turned toward the man who had just spoken. Bagatelle's manager had caught a hint of irony in the man's tone, and the last phrase with its accompanying laugh had been delivered for the benefit of the lady sitting next to him. He recognized the man as a shipowner of Spanish origin whose parents had come to New Orleans with Manuel de Salcedo, the last governor under his Very Catholic Majesty, Charles III. Large and portly, with long black side-whiskers and a lace ruffle cascading over his silk waistcoat, the shipowner had a commanding presence. Although he confined himself to the exporting of bones, cattle horns, and moose and deer antlers, which were dispatched to Marseilles, his fortune was considerable.

"I wouldn't dream of interrupting Madame's selection," Dandridge said with a small bow. "I have all the time in the world, Mr. Rámirez."

"Good. You go right on talking to the nigger. We have a large order to discuss."

The woman laughed again in appreciation of her companion's tone of authority. Then she stood on tiptoe and whispered something to him in Spanish. He let out a vulgar laugh. Mathias glanced at Dandridge. Dandridge raised his eyebrows and smiled.

"Why don't you show me some shoelaces," he said to Mathias, turning his back on the couple.

At that point, the shipowner addressed his companion in a loud and resonant voice. Clarence caught only the last part of the sentence: ". . . le falta la tercera pierna." (He's missing his third leg.)

Clarence went white, pushed away the box of shoelaces Mathias was handing him and, throwing his panama on the counter, strode up to the man. "I understand Spanish, Mr. Rámirez. And if I tell you that you have been vulgar in the presence of a lady, I think you'll understand my French."

Mathias hadn't understood the insult. But he had never seen Mr. Dandridge look so pale, his jaw twitching, his eyes steely—like those of the white men when they catch a slave fleeing into the forest. Rámirez let out another loud laugh.

"If I'm wrong, then prove it to this lady."

The slap on the shipowner's face sent his hat sailing across the counter. The young woman screamed and grasped her companion's arm.

"There's going to be a duel," Mathias said to himself, for he knew the ways of cavaliers.

"My seconds will be waiting on the porch of the Cathedral in an hour," Dandridge said. "They will await yours there. We will fight with swords, at noon, in the Pré Saint-Anthony . . . for I like to lunch at one o'clock."

The incident hadn't taken more than a few seconds but it had gone according to custom. Rámirez grabbed his hat from Mathias, who had picked it up off the floor as if the gesture would erase all trace of the altercation.

"Keep your dirty hands off my hat," he spat out at the black. "I'll take the whole piece of yellow Morocco. Besides, this gentleman here will no longer be needing boots."

It was obvious that he wanted to strangle Clarence then and there, but being a little winded and having accepted the challenge, there was nothing to do but wait until noon to pierce the cavalier's heart. He placed his hat back on his head and, forgetting his companion, headed for the door. Mathias, aware that Dandridge was not fully under control, had surreptitiously picked up his sharpest knife. As the Spaniard was about to leave, he turned and made a last retort: "I'm going to pierce you in the heart, Mr. Dandridge, and not a single lady in New Orleans will miss you . . ."

Dandridge showed no sign of having heard this last insult, but the knuckles of his fists had turned white. When Dandridge spoke again, his voice was calm—almost conversational.

"Unless of course, Mr. Rámirez, your own bones complete your next shipment . . ."

Then he turned toward the counter and picked out some leather for two pairs of boots. Trembling with emotion, the black managed to say: "You know, Mister Dandridge, he's a bad man. He can hurt you. I'm scared." Clarence took note of the knife sticking out of the black man's fist and gave him an affectionate pat.

"Don't you worry about me, Mathias. And try to have my boots ready by Easter. But don't *you* ever risk your skin for a white man, Mathias. There isn't a man in this country who's worth it."

The shoemaker was speechless. He couldn't have been more stunned if a bishop had told him that God didn't exist.

Everybody knew it but nobody dared admit the fact that duels, along with yellow fever, fire and the explosions in the river steamers' boilers were Louisiana's worst plagues. Even though duels counted the fewest victims, the number of deaths was still worrisome. The combination of overindulgence in alcohol and the heat tended to goad those with belligerent natures. They had an atavistic urge to fight and, like their pioneer forefathers, were always ready to mete out justice and wipe away the smallest insult with blood.

When Clarence appeared before his twin friends, Alexander and Louis Mertaux, Acadian descendants and lawyers of good repute, he had already been to see Mr. Balanger, the armorer on Rue de Chartres, and made arrangements for him to bring two Sheffield swords to the Pré Saint-Anthony behind the Cathedral.

Nicknamed Castor and Pollux, the two sobersided lawyers spent more time studying the history of French kings than pleading in Criminal Court. They wished to know the exact cause of the altercation. They belonged to the very small group of Louisianians who were aware of Clarence's past and were thus able to appreciate—without comment—the gravity of the insult he'd been subjected to. Hands clasped, their elbows on the arms of two chairs symmetrically placed on either side of a fireplace dominated by a portrait of Louis XIV, the brothers nodded their heads in unison.

Finally, Alexander let out a sigh and asked, "Why didn't you choose pistols?"

And Louis, who knew Rámirez's girth, added: "You certainly should have, with such a target . . ."

"When you're fighting on grass, only swords have the proper effect," the cavalier replied.

The lawyers rose reluctantly. Alexander glanced at the clock while Louis took their hats off the rack. They shook Dandridge's hand and suggested he remain in their drawing room and have a glass of port while waiting for the duel. Clarence declined.

"You need a cool head when you're about to fight a duel. Besides, I have some business to do."

The three men stepped into the sunlit street. The sidewalks were thronged, for it was the busiest time of the morning. Clarence and the Mertaux brothers went off in opposite directions, the latter heading for the Cathedral to meet Rámirez's seconds. On the way, they would stop and warn Dr. Berthollet that he must be prepared to stanch a wound or even close a dead man's eyes before lunchtime.

Clarence went straight to Pat O'Brien's, the famous restaurant on Rue Saint-Pierre where he was accustomed to lunch. He reserved a table for one o'clock in the patio next to the fountain, and ordered a plate of fried shrimp, scrambled eggs and crêpes Suzette. Mr. Jones, the maître d'hôtel, suggested a bottle of Medoc and Dandridge concurred. He then made his way to the Bar de Maspero which, along with several other bars, filled the role of cotton exchanges.

As he walked in, he was greeted by several planters, some reading newspapers, others feeling samples of cotton and talking shop with clerks in shirt sleeves and black kerseymere waistcoats. The back of the bar was a kind of club. There the men alternately discussed serious business and city gossip. If Clarence had told them that he was about to appear "under the oaks"—the expression used to explain that one was about to fight a duel on the Pré Saint-Anthony—all of New Orleans would have known about it in an hour.

The place was full of foreign buyers—English, French, Dutch—as well as millowners from the Northeast in town to buy the harvests not yet claimed as security on loans by New Orleans bankers. Dandridge learned that the first cotton sold—it was from last year's stock—had brought 1.36 francs a kilo or eleven and three-quarter cents a pound, which was reasonable enough for cotton of medium quality.

"How are things at Bagatelle?" Clarence suddenly heard someone say behind his back. The elegant round little man fanning himself with his silk hat was Abraham Mosely, a cotton merchant from Manchester, England. The Marquis, who was much impressed with his business acumen, liked to joke that he was a descendant, by way of camels, of the Biblical patriarch whose name he bore.

"I hope we have less rain than last year, Mr. Mosely. The new plants are coming up nicely. We should be able to make up twelve to thirteen hundred bales—enough to fill a 360-ton three-masted schooner, like one of the Quesnels'."

Mr. Mosely smiled ruefully at this allusion to his competitor from Rouen. The year before, Quesnel had snatched the entire Bagatelle harvest right out from under him. The Frenchman had offered 1.36 francs (26¢) a kilo, whereas Mosely had stubbornly refused to pay more than 1.34 francs (25¢). Naturally, he had ended up buying cotton of lesser quality.

"It won't be the Quesnels' ships that bring your cotton to Europe this year, Mr. Dandridge. I will have my own! Please tell the Marquis that I will be making my annual visit at the end of September."

A keen and conscientious buyer who also loved his food

and his comforts, Mosely preferred visiting his suppliers at their plantations. Most of the foreign buyers stayed several weeks in New Orleans, spending their evenings at the cabarets, gambling, being fleeced by the adventurers who thronged the city or by Creole courtesans who in a few nights made enough to see them through the entire summer. Toward the Louisianians, these buyers acted like emissaries to a land of disease-ridden savages who existed only for the benefit of European profits. They still cast Louisiana in the role of the young girl who, once saved from a rushing stream and now grown to robust womanhood, naturally wished to show her gratitude to her libidinous old protector.

The local people, in their new cosmopolitanism, welcomed the visitors and their old-fashioned notions as one would ignorant country cousins who must not be frightened, lest they keep a tight hold on the purse strings. And so they were coddled, enticed into licentious ways and offered every exotic delight. Then, one fine morning, mellowed by the climate and the city's joys, the buyers were presented with samples of cotton fibers of an immaculate whiteness and an incredible silkiness, at a price that allowed for the inevitable bargaining. What they eventually got were bales of cotton rusted by the wet leaves that had fallen on the open pods. Some of the craftier visitors had the bales opened to compare their contents with the sample shown previously. But most of them ended up hoodwinked.

Abraham Mosely was not one of these. He treated the citizens of liberated America as equals, accepting the fact that they had thrown off the British yoke (with the more or less disinterested aid of the French) and had no intention of being treated as colonials, no matter where the merchant came from. Separated by the Atlantic from the smog of the Midlands and the leprous outskirts of British cities, Mosely viewed Louisiana as a last outpost of Europe's vanishing civilization, which wars and revolutions were putting to rout. He loved plantation life. His sensual nature delighted in its aristocratic manners, the happy blend of British sportsmanship and

French taste, of virility and elegance, of the rustic life mixed with the refined. His pink face and chubby hands, the fat belly straining his waistcoat's seams, the protruding lower lip—all bespoke the epicurean. He cast the same appreciative eye on his dinner partner's décolletage as he did on the roast suckling pig on its bed of baked apples, or on a miniature by Joseph Boze.

Clarence Dandridge, who was familiar with his tastes, assured him that he would be most welcome at Bagatelle. He would not, alas, have the opportunity of seeing the Marquise, for she had died less than a month before. But perhaps the loss would be made up by the Marquis's young goddaughter.

Mosely offered his condolences and moved on to other subjects. He hated anything that reminded him that life, especially the good life, must inexorably end.

Mosely added: "Please tell the Marquis that my price this year will be high enough to discourage him from pulling up his cotton and replacing it with sugarcane, as too many Louisiana planters are now doing."

If Dandridge hadn't had a pressing appointment, he would have gladly continued their conversation. A well-informed foreigner like Mosely was much more interesting than his opposite number in New Orleans with his niggling local concerns. Abraham Mosely's reference to sugarcane could have kept them talking the entire afternoon—first over glasses of iced tea, continued over absinthe, deferred during the hour of Malaga and resumed after dinner over a bottle of brandy. For indeed there was a great deal to say about the collapse of the cotton market since the wild speculation of 1825. In its wake, it had brought on a crisis in credit, a drop in the banks' discount rate, and a rise in interest rates. To these financial woes, artificially created by a handful of Northern speculators, they now had to add Alabama's disruptive competition. Its production had been growing alarmingly and the cotton it was sending down the river from Mobile was undercutting Louisiana, Mississippi and Tennessee. The "middling" cotton of Louisiana was still the most highly prized, but it had been seriously affected by the drop in the price of inferior grades. To add to the planters' vexations, a string of bumper crops had depressed competition between Yankee and European buyers. King Cotton had recovered, but there were bad memories. The crisis was over, the market stabilized, common sense had returned, yet the planters remained nervous. Perhaps cotton would someday suffer the same fate as indigo, and thousands of bales would be left to mildew in the warehouses of New Orleans.

The planters with properties in the humid zones of the delta had been the first to diversify and plant sugarcane—the striped variety. The vast fields thrived and multiplied; also, the cane required less care than cotton. The improvements in its exploitation since Étienne de Bore discovered how to crystallize its syrup had turned sugarcane cultivation into a profitable enterprise. And in the last two years, they had found out how to make molasses right in the fields during the harvest. Over a hundred new sugar refineries had sprung up in Louisiana alone, producing more than a hundred thousand pounds of sugar a year. At seventy French "sols" a kilo (seventy-five American cents a pound), this was a good source of revenue for planters as well as for refiners. The Southerners were not going to let the Yankees exploit their sugarcane as they had their cotton. But here lay a part of the problem: The South's refusal to industrialize had meant that the cotton mills were all in the North, mainly around New York and Boston. As a result, on every dollar brought in by cotton, Yankee industrialists pocketed forty cents. The South was damned if it was going to let that happen to sugar. It had been foolishly contemptuous of factories, with its notion that working the soil was the only activity suitable to an aristocracy. The time had come to process what it had so successfully grown, and "in situ." That at least was what the younger generation thought, despite the fact that the cotton nobility viewed the idea as on a par with cholera.

"But goddamnit, what can you do?" Dandridge was saying to himself as he made his way up Rue de Chartres to the

Cathedral. "The Marquis de Damvilliers has cotton in his bones."

There were no two ways about it: Nothing pleased the eye of a Southern gentleman as much as a field of ripe cotton when the buds were exploding their snowy balls into the waiting hands of the blacks. It was altogether different from a field of sugarcane, for all the beauty of its stalks standing like a well-disciplined army.

As he approached the Pré Saint-Anthony, it occurred to him that he might well not be around to witness the next cotton harvest at Bagatelle. Rámirez might turn out to be a consummate duelist. Clarence knew himself to be a good fencer but it had been three months since his last bout with the fencing master. Nor did he like the idea of welcoming Caroline Trégan with his arm in a sling. As a cavalier, he wanted a clean-cut decision: He would come out of this duel in one piece—or dead.

On the third stroke of noon, he walked out onto the field of battle. Rámirez was waiting for him, leaning against an oak, a cigar in his mouth. The four seconds had finished their preparations. Mr. Balanger, the armorer, was standing off by himself with the two swords in scabbards of supple leather. Clarence greeted him, then joined his seconds. The Mertaux twins and Rámirez's seconds had already marked out the field and removed the larger stones to prevent any unfortunate missteps. The Spaniard was cultivating the air of a man whose time is being wasted.

Mr. Balanger was asked to come forward and present the swords. Louis Mertaux, as director of the duel, scrupulously reminded the protagonists of the French ceremonial, demonstrating that the blades were "smooth, straight, triangular, without nicks, and of equal length." As the participants were removing their frock coats, hats, waistcoats, and cravats, Dr. Berthollet hurried onto the field, his kit in one hand, his shabby silk hat in the other. Gasping for breath, he said: "This is my third duel of the week, but so far no one has needed me. The dead want a carpenter more than a doctor."

Louis Mertaux invited Mr. Dandridge and Mr. Rámirez to

take up their positions. The Spaniard wished to continue holding his cigar. The seconds asked him to dispose of it. Rámirez handed the cylinder of fine Natchitoches to one of his friends, bidding him not to let it go out. Pointing to his adversary, he said with a sneer: "That dandy isn't worth the loss of a good cigar!"

Clarence was well-dressed but no dandy. With his broad shoulders, well-developed chest and long supple muscles, he carried his twenty-three years and his six feet like a true cavalier—a distinction Rámirez was unable, or unwilling, to make. The Spaniard, older, and shorter by several inches, looked more like a buffalo, his small feet being the only reminder of his Andalusian ancestry. Blinking in a ray of sunlight that filtered through the oaks, Clarence suddenly saw what he had to contend with. His opponent was as solid as a piece of upholstered furniture, his legs as sturdy as old trees, and the sword in his large fist looked like a thin reed. A halberd would have been more appropriate for such a man— or a cemetery. Clarence took in the dark eyes under the thick black eyebrows, the square head framed by bushy side-whiskers resting on his shoulders as if his Maker had decided to dispense with a neck. How on earth would he ever manage to insert a blade into that compact mass of flesh and muscle?

Louis Mertaux's voice interrupted his reflections.

"Take your places, gentlemen, if you please." When they had done so, he added, "I assume we will want to stop at the first sign of blood . . ."

"With the last breath," Rámirez spat out and stamped his foot.

The director let the comment pass and called out: "Gentlemen, *en garde.* . . . Begin!"

On the last syllable, Ramón Rámirez charged, exactly like a buffalo. He took three steps, holding his sword at arm's length as if it were a lance. Dandridge dodged, but not fast enough to save his sleeve. The seconds heard the material rip. To Clarence the touch of the cold steel on his bicep felt like a glancing bullet.

The Spaniard was no stylist, but it was clear that for all his lack of elegance, he could easily impale his adversary up to the hilt of his sword. Clarence felt a tremor, but being quicker than Rámirez, he had already taken up a defensive position. This time Dandridge was on his guard and forced his opponent to fence according to the rules. The clash of metal on metal was reassuring to the Mertaux brothers, who had been disconcerted by the Spaniard's first thrust.

Yet such was Rámirez's power that Clarence felt the shock in his forearm. He realized that if he was going to continue to parry, he would soon grow weary and his adversary's spirit and endurance would win the day. He made his decision: To relax his muscles and establish a rhythm, he teased the Spaniard by making thrusts and blocking his attacks with a simple movement of the wrist. Twice he grazed Rámirez's elbow, like a fencing master correcting a bad position; then he broke and dropped his guard.

That was what the buffalo was waiting for. Annoyed by the steel tip that always seemed to be pointing at his face and bedeviled by the skillful economy of Dandridge's ripostes, he lunged wildly. With a quick cut, Clarence blocked the Spaniard's sword as he was moving forward to finish off his adversary. But Dandridge was more agile now. He pivoted out of the way and Rámirez's blade went past him. When the Spaniard resumed his position, it was too late. Standing at exactly the correct distance and before the buffalo could take in the movement, Clarence lunged, the tip of his blade ripping the Spaniard's face from cheek to chin. Keeping to the same trajectory, Dandridge's blade continued down the Spaniard's torso to the belly and, with a split second's hesitation, sank into his bulging genitals.

Rámirez let out a cry, dropped his sword, clutched his groin and sank to the ground. Clarence brought his heels together, placed his left hand on his hip, leaned on the hilt of his sword with his right, and waited for Dr. Berthollet to minister to the fallen. Then he walked up to the Spaniard's seconds, who stood looking aghast.

One of the two said: "I can understand the cut to the face, but the other one, sir . . ."

"He'll get the point!" Clarence shot back.

One of New Orleans's few enclosed carriages happened to be passing by, and the barely conscious Rámirez was placed inside. Dr. Berthollet reported on his examination of the victim.

"He'll be all right, but it will be a while before he's ready to enjoy the ladies' favors."

Clarence Dandridge smiled, put his clothes back on and thanked the Mertaux brothers, who seemed little elated over his victory. But that was to be expected of the dour pair.

The clock on the Cathedral's belfry rang out half after twelve. Clarence would be in good time for his lunch at Pat O'Brien's. As he vaulted over the fence at the far end of the Pré, he caught sight of Mathias peering through the palings, his face wreathed in smiles. Like an actor equally gratified with his own performance and the response of his public, Clarence gave him a sweeping wave of the hat.

The *Charles Carroll* arrived at six o'clock. From his seat in the gig he had rented for the occasion, Clarence watched as the ship approached the wharf and docked. In the fading light, the horizon beyond the river was touched with orange, ocher and madder red, as if the blue of the sky had been drained into a sorcerer's pot in which the colors of the setting sun were slowly simmering. Purple, gray and greenish reflections played on the river's surface, and through the haze of the river steamers' smoke their tall stacks looked like so many gutted candles. A few clouds which a moment before had appeared insignificant suddenly took on alarming proportions.

Realizing that he would probably have difficulty recognizing Caroline Trégan among the disembarking passengers, Dandridge had asked the customs official checking passports to tell her he was waiting for her.

After his duel with Rámirez, a good lunch at O'Brien's and a two-hour siesta at the Hotel Saint-Charles, Bagatelle's manager felt in splendid fettle. Although the role of chaperon was not to his taste, he couldn't help feeling a certain curiosity. Caroline Trégan would probably be pretty. At eighteen, well-bred girls usually were, and the fashions of the day saw to it that any imperfections were well disguised. Coming from Paris, she would of course be elegant. What else? Also she might be a little weary after forty-six days on the high seas. For all the ship's well-advertised comforts, the ocean had a way of upsetting stomachs and inducing pallor. She probably liked sweets, and hats trimmed with ribbons and perhaps even flowers. . . . She would know the family tree of all her schoolmates, and the pertinent details about those who had married. She would have a blue notebook in which she had inscribed the addresses of her friends, the best dressmakers, kitchen recipes and embroidery designs. She would be able to play the piano, recite at least two fables of La Fontaine and long sections of *Le Cid*, but would know nothing of Voltaire and would be incapable of adding four and five. And at teatime, she would wolf down six pieces of toast and most of the sponge cake . . .

Hands clasped between his knees, his head cocked under his panama, Clarence Dandridge went on piecing the girl together as his eyes followed the dipping and swirling of the gulls around the *Charles Carroll*'s masts. The smart tap of an umbrella against the side of the gig interrupted his thoughts. Looking up, he saw the freckled face of a young girl, a bunch of violets perched on the narrow brim of her hat. Two large and lively blue eyes gazed at him with assurance, and her full lips—a woman's lips—were smiling at him.

"Are you Mr. Dandridge?"

"You are Caroline Trégan?" Clarence asked, leaping from the gig.

"No, sir. I am Mignette, Mamselle Trégan's maid. She recognized you from a distance and asked me to fetch you. Please follow me, sir."

There was grace and authority in the bright young girl. Clarence followed her, catching whiffs of patchouli in her wake. Caroline had completed the formalities and was waiting on the quay, two large leather bags at her feet.

This was an altogether different woman from Mignette. As

he elbowed his way through the porters, the agitated family reunions and the shouting cabbies, Clarence Dandridge kept his eyes riveted on Caroline. That memory would remain with him always. Standing rigid like a madonna in a primitive painting, the young lady was supervising the assembling of her luggage. She was wearing a dress of black faille, wide of skirt and tight at the waist, a short vest of the same material with leg-o'-mutton sleeves and wide lapels outlined in silk braid. A loosely tied velvet ribbon whose ends floated over a starched ruffle of English lace was the only adornment on her otherwise correct orphan's garb. A small hat with a taffeta pouf completed the costume.

Was she actually beautiful? This was not the first adjective that came to mind as Clarence bowed, hat in hand, before the Marquis's goddaughter.

"A peculiar beauty," he said to himself. Her oval face was a little long, her brow a little wide between the severe loops of her copper-colored hair. "À la Sevigné" the hairstyle was called, in which the loops that curved over the cheekbones turned into a mass of ringlets known as "anglaises." Her nose was straight, the nostrils curving a little outward, but her mouth was her most interesting feature, combining two morphological elements seldom seen together: a thin flat upper lip that made her look dry, almost hard, with a full and well-modeled lower lip indicating a certain sensuality. Her eyes were almost turquoise, dotted with black specks which gave her glance a disconcerting sharpness. Under the arch of her sculptured eyebrows and a generous fringe of lashes, her mineral gaze bespoke power. But Clarence Dandridge, at that particular moment, saw only a talent for persuasion that might ease the path of an orphan without fortune.

As he was leading the two young ladies toward the gig—a porter would see that the bags were taken directly to the *Prince du Delta*—Caroline suddenly stopped.

"My goodness, Mr. Dandridge, how New Orleans has changed! I was only thirteen when I left for France, but I'm sure there weren't as many ships then. . . . I've never seen so many ships in my whole life. . . . And all these houses and all the people hurrying about. . . . Why, it's a big city!"

Her voice was melodious, her tone distinguished. Five years with the Ursuline nuns in Paris and in the big world had banished the singsong accent of the South. Nor was there any trace of the old-fashioned expressions dating back to the days of the pioneers and the Cajuns of the bayous. If one had social ambitions in Louisiana, it was best to pretend one didn't understand them.

"New Orleans has indeed grown, Miss Caroline," Dandridge said as he helped the young women into the gig. "They say it has about thirty thousand inhabitants now."

That was the end of the conversation. The gig had room only for two, so Clarence had to go on foot. Taking the horse's bit in his hand, he led the gig to the Quai Sainte-Pierre where the big paddle-wheeler, the *Prince du Delta*, the pride of the Mississippi's river fleet, was tied up. As she started up the gangplank, Caroline turned once more toward the city.

"I would have liked to spend a few days in New Orleans. It would be a pleasant transition between the hectic life of Paris and the quiet life I'll be leading in Pointe-Coupée."

Clarence caught a wistful note in her voice. He guessed that she had no intention of remaining long in Louisiana. Only the time necessary to claim her inheritance—which wasn't going to amount to much, from what he had heard.

Since he hadn't anticipated that Caroline would be accompanied by a servant, he had reserved only two cabins on the steamer.

"I don't wish to be separated from Mignette," Caroline announced. "Would you ask that a folding cot be placed in my cabin, please. That should do very nicely."

Clarence was a well-brought-up young man who respected a woman's comforts—even if she were only a servant—but he had not been eager to give up his cabin. He was therefore delighted with Caroline's solution and immediately went in search of the proper official.

The manner in which Caroline had speedily solved the problem made it clear that the Marquis's goddaughter was a woman of decision. Like all Southern gentlemen, he was used to the spoiled and lazy ways of its young women. Until they married and started running their own homes, they affected complete ignorance of the demands of daily life. The respect, even adulation with which these young princesses of Cotton were surrounded and the way they were pampered by their black nursemaids, who in turn reigned over a swarm of lesser servants, made it inevitable that they would be unable to cope with practical matters.

At the age of eighteen, Caroline Trégan had crossed the Atlantic with a servant barely older than she was. A month and a half on the high seas on board a boat at the mercy of nature's vagaries and in close quarters with total strangers constituted an adventure no planter's daughter would have dared face. Moreover, Caroline had arrived as fresh as a daisy, had declared the trip delightful, reported no storms, no alarums, not a moment's distress—to the point where Clarence was almost disappointed. Instead, she had read books, played cards, embroidered, and passed from one continent to the other as if she were crossing the street.

Mignette confessed that she preferred the steadiness of the river steamer and the fact that you could see land on either side. But that was the only remark Caroline permitted her to make. This was apparently another of her traits: to view past events as unworthy of mention. Not much of a talker, he surmised. The news of the Marquise's death was also greeted without emotion.

"I knew her so little that I can't imagine her dead or alive," Caroline said. "I do feel sorry about the grief it must have caused my godfather." She sounded worldly rather than afflicted.

"The Marquis is a strong man, both morally and physically," Dandridge observed. "The plantation demands so much attention that he hasn't really had time to give in to grief. But I know he will appreciate your coming."

Her smile made up for the coolness of her gaze. "I'll go see him often, of course, but I shall be staying at my father's house—that is—my house."

"I'm afraid your father's house no longer exists."

Caroline looked stunned. "What do you mean, it no longer exists? Did it burn down?"

"No, it was demolished," Dandridge said. "The Marquis took over Mr. Trégan's land and had the house torn down. It was almost in ruins and would have collapsed with the first strong wind."

"What right did he have to do that?" Caroline demanded. "I am my father's only heir and I did think my guardian would at least wait until I arrived before settling my affairs!"

Clarence was taken aback by her sudden outburst. He could have told her that the Marquis's quarter-century of generosity toward Trégan had cost him twice what her father's land was worth, that on the eve of his burial, the Marquis had paid off all his creditors, that her father's foolish speculations had been the talk of Pointe-Coupée and, to cap it all, at her father's deathbed, the Marquis had pledged that he would support and dower his daughter as if she were his own. But Guillaume Trégan's daughter waved him away as he started to speak.

"Let's not discuss it further. This is a matter between me and my godfather. The details don't concern you."

So, this insolent girl was reminding Bagatelle's manager that he was a mere employee of the Marquis, touting her self-confidence, and telling him in no uncertain terms that she would be expecting a reckoning from a "seigneur" who ruled over ten thousand acres and four hundred slaves, sat on the parish council and could, if he so wished, be a senator tomorrow! As the bell announced dinner, her smile weary but her voice conciliatory, Caroline said, "Mignette and I will have sandwiches in our cabin. We'll see you tomorrow, Mr. Dandridge, and many thanks for your warm welcome."

Clarence accompanied her to the door of her cabin on the top deck. The maid, who was beginning to unpack the bags, answered the knock on the door. Dandridge remembered to remind Caroline, "The big river steamers don't sail during the night. We'll be tied up to the wharf until morning. I hope the noise of our departure doesn't disturb you."

His warning earned him the smile a lady might give her butler when he predicted rain for the next day. Clarence spent a few minutes unpacking in his own cabin, then went down to the dining room where several passengers were already choosing their tables. They could have come aboard later in the evening, after dining at home or in a hotel, but such was the *Prince du Delta*'s reputation that the cotton snobs couldn't wait to sample its delights. The dining room in the stern of the boat was known to be the finest of any boat plying the river.

When Dandridge made his appearance, the crimson draperies edged with gilt braid had already been drawn. On each table, a small whale-oil lamp cast an orange glow. The silver service, the etched crystal glasses, the fine porcelain plates all impeccably set on damask tablecloths gleamed in the soft light. A battalion of black waiters—slaves picked as much for their ability to carry off their white waistcoats as for their skill at serving—moved about noiselessly under the eye of a tall severe *maître d'hôtel* with grizzly hair and a well-cultivated expression of disdain. Many a rich planter had tried to lure Sam Brown away, for his reputation as "the most stylish butler between Memphis and New Orleans" made him one of the most illustrious personalities on the Mississippi. He was tacitly allowed a certain authority, and it was said that when he ate alone in the ship's small messroom, he used a knife and fork —just like the gentlemen whose orders he took.

There was a story going the rounds that when another river-boat on which Sam Brown was working caught fire—not an unusual mishap—the order was given to evacuate the boat and to take as many objects of value as possible. But the big black had jumped into the water empty-handed. When his master scolded him later on, Sam smiled and said: "Aren't I your most precious possession? I hear I'm worth six thousand dollars!"

Of course Sam Brown knew Bagatelle's manager. He recommended a table in a corner and lauded the virtues of the ham cooked with turnips. Clarence also ordered an oyster stew, a chicken in aspic, a salad of dandelion greens with a vinegar and sugar dressing, and an apple tart. The *maître d'* nodded approvingly, nodding still more emphatically when his patron asked for a bottle of old Bordeaux.

Clarence had spent a fruitful day. He had risked his life on a point of honor, and he felt pleasantly satisfied with his lot. When he got back to Bagatelle, he would return to the familiar routine: the morning horseback rides to oversee the workers on the plantation, his visits to the slaves' village and to the hospital, where he would exchange a few words with Dr. Murphy, and at the end of the morning, his daily meeting with the Marquis. He would give him a report on his observations before moving on to the accounts and the day's mail. When he wasn't accompanying his employer on his visits to neighboring plantations, he used his leisure time to read or to ride along the riverbank. At the end of the day, he often headed for Barrow House on the other side of Fausse-Rivière to play a game of billiards. It had the only billiard table in the parish, and Clement Barrow, who had lost a leg and rarely left his plantation, was always glad to see his favorite neighbor. The planter's spinster sisters made marvelous buckwheat cakes which they served with Vermont maple syrup, and Clarence enjoyed gossiping with the old ladies, who knew everything there was to know about Pointe-Coupée.

In point of fact, Clarence Dandridge's chief occupation at Bagatelle was to write the history of the Damvilliers. The Marquis, the third to bear the name of Adrien, was very proud of his origins and more particularly of the success of three generations of Damvilliers in America. But it would never have occurred to him to set down their history if Clarence hadn't suggested it. For three years, Dandridge had been going through dusty archives and certificates of baptism, and corresponding with the parish priests of eastern France—to the extent that transatlantic exchanges permitted it. From the planters in the neighborhood he had picked up anecdotes and private family stories transmitted from generation to generation, gradually piecing together what in the Marquis's mind had become a Pantheon of the Damvilliers.

As he started on the ham delicately laced with Madeira sauce and the braised golden turnips that melted deliciously in the mouth, Clarence's thoughts returned to Caroline. He suspected she was not uninformed about her father, the last survivor of a family of pioneers who had at one time been enterprising but whose blood must have grown thin during the course of their colonial travails.

Mme. Trégan's death of puerperal fever a few days after her daughter's birth had been a blow from which Guillaume had never recovered. Eighteen years after her death, he still mourned her loss. It was a more pitiable than edifying sight. Worse still, he often reproached his daughter for having cost her mother's life. Lacking all paternal affection, Caroline had been raised by a black nurse who loved her tenderly while despising her master. When, in 1825, his deceased wife's sister and her husband made a visit to Pointe-Coupée, Guillaume asked the Drouins to take Caroline back to France with them and make a lady of her. Mr. Drouin was a wealthy shipowner from Nantes whose family had prospered in the slave trade. His wife was delighted at the prospect of taking her niece under her wing, especially as she was childless and lived alone for the most part in their house on Rue de Luxembourg in Paris. Common sense told her that it would be in the child's interest to remove her as promptly as possible from a father who was clearly heading toward demented mysticism.

The dandelion salad now before him, Clarence recalled what he had learned of the Trégans while doing his research on the history of Bagatelle. His curiosity had been whetted by the fact that the Trégans had probably arrived in America before the Damvilliers. In 1603, the manifest of the *Bonne-Renommée,* a ship owned by the governor of Dieppe and bound for Hochelaga (now Montreal), listed a carpenter named Trégan. He turned up again on a ship exploring "la baie Française" in search of silver mines believed to be near the Bassin des Mines. This area, together with its village of

Grand Pré, was especially dear to the Acadians of Nova Scotia. That is where Trégan, and the Dugas, Gaudets, Terriots and twenty other settlers from France established their colony.

The children of Louisiana had been brought up on stories of the Acadians, their unfailing virtues and their triumphs over adversity. They were hardworking trappers, peasants and fishermen, and their wives were prodigious breeders. They had done more than found a colony: They had brought to the New World a healthy and robust people who were not discouraged either by dispersal or by material disasters.

As the son of an Englishman, Clarence would have liked to find some justification for the enormous harm his paternal ancestors had inflicted on the peaceful Acadians after they became subjects of George III. But everything pointed to treason, abuse of authority, inhumane treatment, sometimes outright hatred for 'a people who believed in all honesty that their suffering and efforts had earned them a foothold on this continent. The Trégans had probably lived a pitiful existence in a log cabin in Port Royal, Acadia's little capital on the Bay of Fundy which, in 1700, numbered not more than forty houses. The Acadians' pathetic farms had been sacked by the Kirkes, two Scottish brothers and their henchmen, then threatened by successive waves of British privateers, Dutch freebooters and New England plunderers. Religious quarrels and clashes between countrymen added to their woes. In short, for over two centuries, the innocent and hospitable Acadians had known few moments of happiness.

A little before his death, Guillaume Trégan had shown Dandridge the pledge of allegiance that the British had exacted from the French settlers (Guillaume's grandfather among them) when they took possession of Acadia in 1713. The duplicity of the British government and its American representatives was all there in black and white. From 1720 on, the total eviction of the French Acadians became the new colonialists' sole aim. By 1746, the deed was done. The several thousand Acadians had been ejected from the lands they had cleared, the houses they had built. Some were deported to France on unseaworthy vessels without possessions or provisions; the more venturesome fled into the forests; the most recalcitrant ended their days on British hulks in Falmouth or Southampton; the lucky ones reached France and settled for the most part at Belle-Île off the coast of Brittany.

The Trégans, together with a number of other dispossessed settlers, scattered throughout the English colonies in America. They turned up in Massachusetts, in Maryland, Virginia and Georgia. It was from Georgia that Guillaume Trégan's father, then aged nineteen, decided to pull up stakes and move to Louisiana, then a French colony. After a horrendous journey, he arrived in Pointe-Coupée where he met up with the Hébert family who, like him, had come from Piziquid in Acadia. The Héberts had an only daughter. Like so many others, she had lost track of her fiancé during the course of their "displacement." Young Trégan caused her to forget the lost fiancé, and Guillaume was born of that union. Guillaume inherited a prosperous plantation from his father-in-law, and at long last, for the first time in two centuries, the Trégans seemed on the verge of finding peace and happiness. As Clarence drained the last drop of his Bordeaux, he wondered why lasting happiness appeared to elude this family, as if misery were the Trégans' lot—like some hereditary disease. Would Caroline, up in her cabin, someday come to the same conclusion?

He, Clarence, had never known unhappiness until in his adolescence, when, near the headwaters of the Platte River, he had an experience which left a stigma he would carry until the end of his days.

He thanked Sam Brown for his gracious attention and climbed to the top deck where, his back to the city, he leaned on the railing and gazed out over the river. In the clear May night, the masts of the ships silhouetted against the horizon looked like so many crosses in an old cemetery.

At daybreak, with the tender care of an English nanny pushing a sleeping infant in its pram, the *Prince du Delta* edged away from its berth to begin the slow voyage up the Mississippi.

Clarence Dandridge made his morning ablutions, dressed

with great care, then went up on deck to join the other passengers taking in the river scene. Moving majestically between the flat wooded banks like a displaced castle, the *Prince du Delta* crossed paths with large barges loaded down with merchandise, carried downstream by the current, and smaller barges maneuvered with heavy poles by powerfully built boatmen. Then there were squat little boats propelled by oars, with a single mast that could carry a large sail when the wind came from the right quarter. Sometimes the boatmen waved to the passengers on the steamer, whose large wheel at the stern riled up the water with the noise of a waterfall, leaving an undulating wake like the spine of some great, partly submerged monster.

"Aren't they fun!" a voice spoke up next to Clarence.

It was Mignette, pointing out the flatboats to Caroline. The girl seemed captivated by the activity on the river, especially these large floating huts that served as habitations for the nomads of the Mississippi. Entire families lived on them with their furniture, tools, and even domestic animals. Hanging on a line that stretched across the craft, their laundry flapped in the wind like freakish pennants. Dirty-faced children peered from the hatchway, pigs tethered by the foot snorted at inaccessible tidbits that floated by, lean men stripped to the waist sat hunched over the tiller staring vacantly at the elegantly veiled women and their silk-hatted escorts. On the flatboats, the hot May sunshine was welcome; on the steamers, the female passengers shaded themselves with fluttering parasols to protect their magnolia-like complexions—the pride of Southern womanhood.

One of the *Prince du Delta*'s cherished customs was morning consommé, and Clarence led the two young ladies to the forward deck, where the hot broth and biscuits were served at small wrought-iron tables painted a gleaming white. Caroline under her parasol and Clarence with his panama over his eyes tasted the moment in silence, refreshed by the cool breeze stirred up by the speed of the boat.

Clarence examined the girl between half-closed lids. She

was certainly different from what he had imagined, and last night's negative impression had completely worn off. He decided that she was in fact very pretty, and far from dumb.

From time to time, as they passed a large house half hidden behind the trees, its wide lawn rolling down to the river, Caroline asked: "Whose plantation is that?"

Clarence replied: "The one on the right is Elmwood, a Creole house built by La Frenière in 1762. He came over from France with Iberville and Bienville. The one on the left is Keller's, built by the Fortiers in 1801. It's a combination of French and Spanish styles you see quite often here."

"You seem to know everything about this country, Mr. Dandridge. You weren't born here and I was, yet I know nothing about the region."

"When you're the son of an army man, you're born wherever your parents happen to be. I was born in Boston because my father came to America with His Majesty's troops to put down the rebellious Yankees."

Caroline asked, "If your father was fighting the rebels, why did he stay on after they won their independence?"

"Because he loved the country, and after he'd been wounded and made prisoner at Yorktown, it happened that he was nursed back to health by a Frenchwoman, an Acadian like yourself. He married her, and gave up soldiering to become a lawyer in Boston. Which is where I was born. But my father wanted to end his days in England in the home of his ancestors. His fortune made, he left a few years ago. He is now a very old man."

A gust of wind blew Caroline's veil against her face. Then, after a moment's pause, she asked Dandridge if he would like to show her around the boat. They first went down to the main deck, a blend of comfort and elaborate decoration. The main hall, which served as a kind of grand salon, had the noble proportions of the lobby of a first-class hotel. By day, the "saloon" was lighted by large bay windows overlooking the river. At night, pale blue velvet draperies covered the windows and the saloon became the ballroom. Rugs were rolled up, chairs were pushed to the walls and the violins made their appearance.

"All it needs is a fireplace to make you forget you're on a boat!" Caroline observed.

There was another lounge in the bow. This one was reserved for the ladies who weren't interested in the passing scenery and wished to be out of the wind to do needlework or to gossip. Wing chairs and pedestal tables lit by silver candelabras were placed in small groups where the ladies could drink port and nibble on sweets as they embroidered or did crochet. As an extra touch, the architect had added a frieze of transoms between the windows and the ceiling, with tiny panes imitating agate. Caroline was so entranced that she sat down to watch the play of the sun through the colored panes and the tender glow it cast on the barometer on the wall, the marble of the tabletops and the silk of the ladies' dresses.

During lunch, Caroline expressed great interest in how the steam engines worked. That an eighteen-year-old girl should care about steam engines was mystifying to Clarence, but he was glad to oblige. She was astonished to learn that in the hold, slaves naked from the waist up worked in unbearable heat, throwing a continuous load of logs into enormous brass boilers. At regular intervals, the boat passed by the woodcutters' cabins mounted on piles along the riverbank, the men ready to heave logs aboard as the steamer moved past. Back in 1814, it took almost six days to make the trip from New Orleans to Natchez. Now, the *Prince du Delta* would need only three to reach Pointe-Coupée, a half day's run from Natchez.

Dandridge emphasized the dangers of travel by steamboat: the fog that sometimes shrouded the river, the sandbanks that shifted treacherously, the Mississippi's shallowness. But none of these compared to the threat of fire caused by collisions and, worse still, by exploding boilers.

"Captains love to race. But when you overheat the boilers, they can split open and then it's disaster! The *Zebulon Pike*—which we may pass along the way—is the fourth of that name. The first three exploded . . ."

"Good heavens!" Mignette exclaimed, fearful of a similar fate.

"It must be very exciting," Caroline said, her eyes glistening.

"What about the Indians? Are they really so bad?" Mignette asked, determined to know all the risks of river travel.

Clarence was reassuring: "In the past, they used to row their dugouts up to the sailboats, leap aboard and seize all the passengers' belongings. But they haven't done that for years. And they weren't nearly as dangerous as the river pirates— white bandits who stole silver, jewelry . . . and the prettier passengers," he added with a gentle leer.

"Oh, dear!" Mignette said, dropping a spoonful of sherbet down her front, which made Caroline smile.

"Don't be afraid," Clarence put in quickly. "We have the best pilot on the river. He may not know how to dance the quadrille but he knows every quirk of the river, its sudden risings, the eddies, the gusts of wind. He has the gift of predicting the weather. He can tell by the dampness on the spokes of the wheel if it's going to rain. In a fog he can tell where he is by the barking of dogs, and he never races another boat, for that was written into his contract."

On the first afternoon, Caroline happened to be at the bow when a sailor leaned out with a sounding line and shouted his findings back to the captain, who was standing on the bridge like a Neptune commanding the waters. The sailor spoke in a chant, like a tobacco auctioneer: "Mark four, half four, mark four, mark three, half three, mark twain. . . ." In laymen's terms, it meant that at that point the river was between twenty-four and twelve feet deep. The *Prince* was safe, for it drew only eight feet.

As the light began to fade, Clarence returned to the stern alone, to look out over the shifting landscape. It was his favorite time of day: the delicious moment when man and beast could give in to lassitude, the time of day when, with the shadows gone, everything stood out as it actually was, with its own precise dimensions. Sunsets on the Mississippi had a classical harmony that gave Dandridge a feeling of extraordinary lucidity. When he looked at the people around him, he believed he saw them as they really were. He saw, for example, that Caroline was desirable to others. He had noticed the way men looked at her when she walked by. Several of them he knew asked to be introduced to her. One of them was young Willy Templeton, on his way home to Pointe-Coupée from his studies at West Point. Caroline appeared to be pleased by the young man's attentions and demonstrated an ease she could only have picked up in the Paris salons. It amused Dandridge to watch the two young people making a first tentative pas-de-deux. To please seemed to be the overriding concern of most mortals. He did not share it. He went to great pains to be gracious to the ladies, but he was only following the dictates of Southern "civilization."

He was still leaning on the railing when Caroline appeared, a shawl over her shoulders, a book under her arm. In the evening light, her cool gaze had taken on a certain warmth. She too leaned over the railing, her thick ringlets falling as if to hide her face. A hint of honeysuckle and jasmine wafted to them from the banks of the river, enveloping her in its romantic essence.

"I finally feel as if I belonged to this country. Far from cities with their stone prisons. Here, there is space. The carefully planned vistas of London and Paris have their charm, but they don't awaken the desire to conquer forests and limitless prairies . . ."

"I agree," Clarence said. "The water, the sky, the land around us have more reality. The urban landscape is a penitentiary. Man is out of proportion to what he's built. Here you can feel tiny and divine at the same time."

The mockingbirds were returning to their nests, terrifying the cardinals with their noise and interrupting the chatter of the jays. Dandridge pointed to some turtles poking their heads above water as the great white ship floated by. "They're very rare now. Man has chased them into the bayous and the mouths of the rivers."

In the sky, a flock of flamingos headed for the swamps where thousands of frogs had set up a croaking chorus. Nearby, herons were picking their way through the reeds. Muskrats and water rats scurried about in the grass, and a few deer came to drink at the river's edge, then darted away in terror when the *Prince* let off a blast of its whistle. It was the captain's way of letting the woodcutters know that the ship was ready to dock for the night and take on firewood for the next day's run. The mosquitoes now arrived in swarms, forcing the passengers down to the saloons. Caroline showed Dandridge her book.

"I'm reading *Atala*. Its author, Chateaubriand, was here some years ago. It's the rage in Paris right now. It tells about the love affair between two savages and how their relationship is thwarted by religious laws. It takes place on the banks of the Mississippi. And he describes the buffalo coming out of the forest and swimming across the river, and the bear eating wild grapes, and herds of caribou . . ."

About love affairs among the savages, Clarence knew a thing or two, but he wasn't going to share his knowledge with Caroline. To change the subject, he asked her to tell him about Paris. Her eyes glowing, she told him about the shops, the restaurants, the many varieties of carriages, and Rue de Luxembourg where her Aunt Drouin lived.

"You can't imagine what our neighborhood is like! It's a wild mixture of terribly clever talented men, the lazy rich, tipsy foreign princes, adventurers, poor people pretending to be rich and rich men chasing after demi-mondaines." Of course she had been to the Théâtres des Varietés, to the Opera on Rue le Peletier, and had often dined at the Nicolet which imported many American delicacies and, in fact, operated a store in New Orleans. But most exciting by far was the premiere of *Hernani*. Marking the introduction of romanticism in the theater, it had caused a sensation. She had lost her hat in the excitement and clapped until her hands burned. Victor Hugo had patted her on the cheek and Alexandre Dumas sent them tickets to *Henri III*.

That historic evening was still vivid in Caroline's mind. She went on breathlessly: "You should have seen the art students and poets with their disheveled hair, bushy beards, wearing the strangest clothes—Spanish capes, smocks, waistcoats of every color! . . . People shouted, gesticulating wildly. All conventions were out the window. My aunt almost fainted because a student addressed her as 'tu'! Chairs were broken, tiaras crushed underfoot, but when Mlle. Mars said:

'Je me sentais joyeuse et calme, o mon amant,
Et j'aurais bien voulu mourir en ce moment . . .'

(I felt joyful and calm, o lover,
And would gladly have died at that moment . . .)

I started sobbing and a young man I'd never laid eyes on before took the rose from his buttonhole and dried my tears with it. Then he whispered in my ear: 'The most romantic tear for the most romantic of flowers . . .' Oh, Mr. Dandridge, what an evening that was! If my aunt hadn't dragged me away, I would have stayed all night, singing and laughing like a chambermaid!"

This was a new Caroline Trégan that Clarence hadn't seen before. Her cheeks were scarlet, her eyes feverish, and she spoke with passionate exhilaration.

"I'm afraid evenings at Bagatelle are going to seem very quiet after Paris," Dandridge suggested.

Suddenly calm again, Caroline looked at him with an expression of cool serenity, as if all the stage lights had suddenly been doused.

"You know, Mr. Dandridge, I believe that like many women I share Doña Sol's passion. There is no place in the world, no matter how quiet it may seem, where it can't be awakened."

"That is what you hope?" Clarence said with some trepidation.

"That is what I expect."

The dinner gong interrupted their conversation. That very

evening, Clarence would be a witness to Caroline Trégan's aptitude for provoking fate.

It was Willy Templeton who started the whole thing. At least, that is the way it appeared to Clarence when the young man woke him up at dawn with a rat-ta-tap of his signet ring on Dandridge's cabin door. Clarence put on his dressing gown and opened the window that gave onto the passageway.

"I see you haven't lost your West Point habit of rising early!"

"Mr. Dandridge," the young man said with the dignity that his declaration required, "I am about to fight a duel over the honor of the Marquis de Damvilliers's goddaughter."

"Damnation, Willy! And against whom, for God's sake!"

"Ed Barthew. He insulted her."

"How did he manage to do that?" Clarence asked with a frown.

Barthew was one of his closest friends, and one of the few people who awakened his sympathy.

"May I come in, sir?"

Seating himself in the cabin's only chair, the young officer described how the dispute began. Clarence could hardly believe his ears. Apparently, after he had retired for the night, Caroline had gone to the saloon, where two minstrels were playing banjos and singing old songs. Once the performance was over, Templeton invited her to his table where Barthew and another planter were seated. Their conversation turned to card and dice games, and Caroline confessed that she loved to gamble. Evidently she had learned to play whist and poker at her aunt's in Paris. The group started to play, but since gambling for money was not allowed on board, the rules had been relaxed to permit gambling for minor possessions—anything except jewelry. Templeton had thrown in a cigar case, Barthew a snakeskin pouch, and the planter an Italian lead pencil. As Caroline was trying to think of what she'd be willing to risk, Templeton suggested a lace handkerchief, but Barthew drew a round of applause from the spectators when he proposed she bet one of her ringlets. There were some protests, but to everyone's surprise, the Marquis's goddaughter agreed. Their entourage was stunned. Not only was a girl of good family gambling with men, respectable though they be, but to sacrifice a ringlet of her own hair! . . .

"It's indecent!" an older woman in a wig muttered to her husband. "Why doesn't she wager her chemise!"

"That's for next time," a gentleman standing by replied.

With regal presence, Caroline announced that she would proffer the ringlet only if she drew a bad hand. The restriction was accepted and the game began.

"Miss Trégan played very skillfully," Templeton went on. "She won both my silver knife and Mr. Aubron's pencil, but she was beaten by Ed Barthew who, for once, hadn't cheated. He collected his winnings and then demanded the lock of hair."

That was when things became heated. Templeton declared that Mlle. Trégan should be let off. No gentleman could permit a lady to give a lock of her hair to a stranger. They'd had their fun, but things should stop there. Barthew replied that gambling debts were sacred and refused to give up what was coming to him. A public discussion ensued, the majority approving Templeton's chivalrous attitude, the minority insisting that Barthew was right in claiming his due. Among these were several ladies who weren't averse to seeing the young lady with the French airs get her comeuppance. Captain Wangler was summoned to arbitrate the dispute. He was a cheery fellow who loved his gin, but he was little inclined to get himself involved with young hotheads deliberately asking for trouble. On due reflection, the captain stated that all contracts should be honored and therefore the young lady would have to abide by the rules of the game. What he didn't say was that with that abundance of hair, one less lock would make little difference.

"Mlle. Trégan was a good sport," Willy continued. "She said she had every intention of giving the winner his due. But that awful Barthew was lusting after it like some trophy."

Caroline then said that she would go back to her cabin to effect the amputation and see that the ringlet was delivered to Mr. Barthew. With that, she graciously offered her hand to Barthew and said with a dazzling smile: "Thank you. It's been great fun."

"Mr. Dandridge, she left that room with such dignity that we were all tempted to applaud her," Templeton added, his heart pounding at the memory of her exit.

"But I see no reason for a duel," Clarence observed, not unworried about how the Marquis would take his goddaughter's behavior.

"Well, in your absence, Mr. Dandridge, and my family being such close friends of the Damvilliers, I took it upon myself to uphold Mlle. Trégan's honor and to wipe away the insult that Ed Barthew was so shamefully perpetrating."

Willy Templeton paused and swallowed hard.

"I told Barthew exactly what I thought of him and invited him to meet me on deck. I said: 'Sir, I ask, no, I demand that you immediately give up that lock of hair and that you send Mlle. Trégan a note to that effect.' "

Clarence couldn't help admiring the young man's gallantry. "And, of course, Ed laughed in your face?"

"Not only that, he demanded that I remove my hat while I addressed him, and since I had no intention of doing so, he threw my hat into the river. A gray opera hat, from Paris!"

Clarence made an effort not to smile. "And, of course, you slapped him in the face."

"Precisely. We're going to fight at eight o'clock, with revolvers, on the roof of the top deck. Captain Wangler and an old man whose name I don't know who takes snuff are going to be Barthew's seconds. I've chosen Mr. Aubron and you for mine."

"I can hardly refuse you, my friend. I am in charge of Mlle. Trégan so I must willy-nilly take part in the affair. But I don't like it one bit. Such things can't help but harm her reputation. I hope Barthew doesn't kill you, Willy. I don't want you to end up inside an alligator . . ."

"Mr. Dandridge, may I suggest that when all this is over, you lecture Mlle. Trégan on our Southern ways. She doesn't seem to be aware of them."

"Willy, my friend, I think you'd better learn that Mlle. Trégan doesn't take to lecturing. As for our Southern ways, I'm not convinced they're always the best. Now get along with you, and good luck!"

Edward Barthew was not a cavalier in the proper sense of the term. In fact, had he spent more time on business and less on gambling, he would have been taken as a typical product of the democratic and commercial North. He had arrived from Boston one day with two suitcases and his lawyer's certificate, which he nailed to the door of an old house in Bayou Sara. He later hired two slaves to keep house for him, began to have a few clients—local types and minor planters mostly, who preferred discussing their problems with an outsider. There were strange stories about him going the rounds in Boston, but nobody knew anything specific. And since he made a point of avoiding the local society in Natchez, he was accepted for what he was, a taciturn and haughty man who didn't give a fig for what anyone thought of him. He made frequent trips to New Orleans, where he was seen in the company of women of questionable virtue. But those who had used him professionally were entirely satisfied, and the parish judges considered him both smart and eloquent. While the other local lawyers played politics, he carefully withheld his opinions. In fact, people wondered if he had any. His friends knew little more than the general public but were unanimous in extolling his courage. He had risked his life to save the local grocer's twin daughters when their house caught on fire; he organized the evacuation of an area when it was threatened by the great flood of 1828, and directed the construction of a levee to prevent future damage. He gambled away the better part of his earnings, yet he was admired for the way he broke up the fights that kept erupting on show boats, going so far as to use his fists or a handy piece of furniture to quell a riot. In every case, his economy of word and deed won the respect of all.

Ed Barthew was tall and dark, and almost always wore black. And because of his short black hair that shone like a raven's wing, one strand perpetually falling over his left eye, people thought he must have Indian blood. His voice was deep and intense, but he used it only when he had something to say. His well-shaped hands were not always clean and his shirts and cravats needed pressing.

Because he came from Boston, Clarence had retained him to clear up his father's affairs when the elder Dandridge left for England. He liked the way Barthew, unlike most of his colleagues, came straight to the point and avoided the wasteful and picayune procedures on which the fraternity fattened. The two men hunted together and often met at plantation balls where bachelors were always in demand. Barthew had good manners when called for, danced a correct if uninspired quadrille, but like Clarence, he preferred watching the others while he nursed a glass of whiskey.

This, then, was the man Willy Templeton was pitting himself against for possession of a lock of Caroline Trégan's hair.

As Clarence prepared himself for the event, he considered young Templeton's chances. At first glance, they weren't of the best. He had no idea what the marksmanship instructors at West Point had taught him, but he had hunted with Barthew and knew he had a quick eye and was fast on the trigger. Willy, to be sure, was the very picture of a Southern aristocrat with all the attributes that entailed. The Marquis had said it all, and the Marquis was very knowledgeable in such matters, when he nicknamed young Templeton "le Chevalier Willy."

Born sickly, the boy had worked hard to cultivate the manly grace of a pure-blooded Englishman, which in the South was considered the ne-plus-ultra of masculine beauty. Riding, archery, fencing and boxing with his older brother Percy, and later on, his military training, had given him a perfect physique much appreciated by the magnolia-hued heiresses of the region—not to mention their husband-hunting parents. His cadet's uniform suited him to a *T*, but for his trip aboard the *Prince du Delta* he had chosen to wear civilian clothes to prove that he knew the latest styles and could wear them with equal dash. Yet Willy was basically shy, and Clarence wondered how Caroline managed to make such a deep impression on him as to involve him in this imbroglio. Nor was Dandridge happy at the prospect—if things turned out badly—of explaining it to Willy's father. And what of the annual spring barbecue at The Myrtles if poor Willy wound up with a bullet in his head?

The duel was organized with dispatch. One of the combatants was to stand at the base of the smokestack, his back to the bow, the other at the foot of the mast flying the Union flag, his back to the stern. Mr. Aubron produced a pair of Elisha Cooliers he had just purchased in New Orleans. These weapons had automatic magazines and could fire five shots if the flintlock was working properly.

Captain Wangler of the *Prince*, appointed the duel's director, had to ask the passengers flocking to the roof to observe the spectacle to return to their cabins and remain there until further notice. He ordered the speed of the boat reduced, then he summoned a Memphis doctor who was honeymooning on the ship to come to the deck with his kit. The doctor demurred, saying he had no wish to witness a murder. The captain explained that in Louisiana, as in Virginia, when two men confronted each other with equal weapons and observed the rules, neither could be accused of murder. Nor was Wangler indifferent to the fact that henceforth the *Prince du Delta* could pride itself on being the first river steamer to stage a duel. He gave the doctor no choice: Either he fulfilled his mission or he and his bride could swim the rest of the way.

The captain was also worried about where stray bullets might land, and so the participants were ordered to wait until a passing steamer was safely out of shooting range. Ed Barthew appeared perfectly at ease, an unaccustomed smile on his face. For the occasion Willy had put on a clean shirt, its jabot flapping in the breeze, and a pair of impeccably creased black trousers. He looked very determined. To Clarence, he was a touching sight.

The revolvers were loaded; the captain marked out the twenty feet separating the contestants and asked them to take their places. Like true gentlemen, each asked to stand facing the sun which, at this hour, constituted a major handicap.

"Please accord me this pleasure," Barthew protested in his low voice. "It may be the only one you will ever be able to grant me."

Willy gave in; it would have been ridiculous to argue the matter. "It may well be the last, sir, but I have no wish to fire on someone blinded by the sun."

"The greatest distinction, my friend, and the one that makes up for all men's shortcomings, is to die with dignity," Barthew replied.

"Gentlemen," the captain interjected, "you are to shoot after the word 'three.' May the Father of Waters, who has witnessed so many unfortunate events, know that we here are resolving a point of honor!"

At that moment, a cloud of lavender muslin emerged from behind the bridge. Caroline stood in the morning sun as the men gaped, speechless.

"This is no place for a woman," the captain snapped.

"It does happen to be my place, Captain. Besides, I must give Mr. Barthew what I owe him."

She stepped up to the lawyer who, his revolver held against his thigh, was staring at her with a look of enraptured surprise. She handed him a lock of hair tied with a black silk ribbon. He slipped it inside his shirt next to his skin, then gave a deep bow. The presentation accomplished with cool grace, Caroline walked over to Dandridge and addressed him so that everyone could hear. "I shall be very sad if one of these two gentlemen can't join us at lunch to break the bread of friendship."

The captain was growing impatient. He shouted, "Gentlemen, please! One, two, three!"

Two shots rang out at the same moment. Templeton staggered, then fell to the floor, his eyes looking with disbelief at the blood spreading over his left thigh. At the other end of the deck, a trickle of gray smoke floated up from a hole in the side of the smokestack. Willy's bullet had missed Barthew's shoulder by a few inches and pierced the stack.

Prodded by the captain, the doctor ran to Willy's side. At the same time, Caroline rushed up to Ed Barthew and planted a passionate kiss on his lips. Few men, even under happier circumstances, could have wished for more. But no one heard what she whispered to the strangely troubled lawyer: "Sir, bless you for not killing the young cockerel. He is still so ignorant of life!"

The outcome of the duel was soon known to everyone on board. Several ladies went to Willy's cabin to coo over the wounded cavalier who had shed blood to save the honor of a young lady—even though her behavior might be questionable.

Clarence and Caroline met at the prow of the boat during the morning consommé hour. Dandridge was in a sullen mood.

"I hope you're satisfied, young lady. If it hadn't been for Barthew's cool head, we might have had an ugly situation this morning."

"Why shouldn't I be satisfied, Mr. Dandridge? Men love an excuse to fight. So I gave them one. Young Templeton got exactly what he deserved. Besides, I'm quite old enough to look after my own honor. I don't need the first man who comes along to defend my reputation."

"A man can die for so little," Dandridge replied with some heat. "Aren't you judging others by your own standards?"

Caroline gave him a wicked smile. "Mr. Barthew told me last night that you are no neophyte in this area yourself. What about the Spaniard you took on two days ago in New Orleans?"

Clarence was silent. So people already knew about his confrontation with Rámirez . . .

"Look, Mr. Dandridge," Caroline continued in a placating

tone. "Fighting comes naturally to men. We women are here to make them forget the one they've just fought and to prepare them for the one to come."

With that, she stood up. As she rearranged her veil, Clarence noted that she had changed her hairstyle. Her hair was now gathered into a chignon at the nape of her neck. Because of the missing ringlet, Clarence surmised. They were nearing Baton Rouge and the captain had just announced over the loudspeaker that all passengers must clear the forward deck so that the gangplank could be lowered. Musing over what she had said, Clarence went to the bar and ordered a glass of port. There he found Barthew sitting in front of a large glass of gin.

"Glad you came out of it so well, Ed?"

"What do you think, Clarence?"

"Those Coolier revolvers looked pretty deadly . . ."

"They certainly can be, and young Templeton could have gotten me with a second shot. I've been to see him. He may limp for a couple of days, but I gave him something that ought to speed up his recovery."

"What was that?"

"The lock of hair belonging to the young lady—whom you would do well to watch carefully, or Louisiana is in danger of many more such heroic exploits."

"So you gave Templeton the trophy you were so keen on winning!" Clarence laughed. From near tragedy to farce in the space of a few hours!

"The cavalier deserved it," Barthew said. "He can now carry it next to his breast as a souvenir of his first duel. I got something much better, something a man like me can really appreciate."

The two men exchanged knowing looks. Clarence said, "Caroline's kiss, I assume. If I do say so, it showed surprising competence, coming from a young girl. She must have learned it in Paris. Perhaps at her worthy Aunt Drouin's! . . ."

Barthew emptied his glass and rose to leave. "Excuse me, Dandridge. I'm getting off at Baton Rouge. I know a few ladies there who remove their chemises with more dispatch than their ringlets. And that's what I need at the moment."

The wisdom of his friend's impulse was not lost on Clarence. He gave him an affectionate tap on the shoulder.

"I'll arrange the lunch with Templeton. I know Mlle. Trégan will regret your sudden departure. What shall I tell her?"

"Nothing, I guess. She's a sharp customer. She'll understand."

Ed Barthew walked away, hesitated, and suddenly turned back. An impish expression on his face, he said with oracular gravity: "Watch out, Dandridge. That woman is a bird of prey!"

The Marquis de Damvilliers had barely touched his breakfast. The third Adrien to bear the name was a large sturdy man of forty with a chest designed for medals. Although he kept his razor sharp enough, he always seemed to be growing a beard. His face was square, his eyebrows so thick they had to be trimmed, and his large eyes were as gentle as a Jersey cow's. Mother Nature, in a gracious moment, had crowned him with a head of curly dark hair which he had long since stopped trying to tame. With his flat nose and large mouth, he looked a little boorish, but his general appearance inspired confidence.

The Marquis was eager to have his manager back, but the arrival of Caroline Trégan gave him pause. He remembered her so little, and visualized her as the blossom of a tulip tree falling on hard-packed earth. He had decided she should have the top-floor bedroom and he would put little Rosa at her service—the sprightly granddaughter of the black cook who had ruled over Bagatelle for more years than he could remember. At that moment, Mamma Netta appeared, a length of madras wound about her head like a deer's antlers. Hands on her hips, she stared at the untouched bacon and sweet potatoes with saffron sauce on his plate.

"The master isn't eating his breakfast?" she asked, rolling her eyes with anxiety.

"I wasn't hungry, Mamma Netta. But don't you worry. I'm perfectly well." To change the subject, he asked, "Have you prepared Miss Caroline's room? I don't know exactly when she's arriving, but I want everything ready."

"I've made up the bed with the embroidered sheets, there's flowers on her dresser, and I burned a handful of herbs to make the room smell nice."

The Marquis nodded his approval and, knowing the pride she took in her cooking, added, "We must have the very best meat, and sausages, and your cinnamon pudding for the young lady. They eat well in Paris, you know."

"You'll see, Master. I'll show her there's no better cook around. But, Master, you should take a leaf of mint steeped in cottonseed oil. It will do you good. Just because Ma'm the Marquise passed on is no reason you should let yourself go like this!"

Adrien de Damvilliers smiled at the good woman who had been counseling him "a mint leaf steeped in cottonseed oil" for at least thirty years.

"I don't need your medicines, Mamma Netta. I'd rather you brought me a cup of coffee with a bit of lemon rind into my study."

Mamma Netta bowed and in spite of her seventy years and two hundred pounds, stepped briskly back to her kitchen.

The Marquis was restless. Trying to kill time, he paid a visit to the stables, something he usually left to his butler. He inspected the gleaming harnesses, the bits, curbs and stirrups shining more brilliantly than the vermeil service that was brought out for important parties. He checked the suppleness of the saddles on their racks and whiffed the camphor on the blankets. His groom, Bobo, stood by eagerly.

"Bobo, harness the horses to the big carriage and drive over to Pointe-Coupée to see if Mr. Clarence and the young lady have arrived on the *Prince du Delta*."

"Yes, Master."

"I want you to wear your frock coat and white gloves."

"Oh, yes, Master!"

"I'm very pleased, Bobo. Everything looks well tended. You've been doing your work well. Now, we must pick out a mare for the young lady. Flassy, perhaps, and put the new English saddle on her."

"I'll have everything ready when the young lady comes," Bobo said. "But maybe the new saddle is a little hard for a young lady?"

"You be the judge, Bobo. For all I know, the young lady may not even ride."

"Or maybe she likes to ride sidesaddle, like Ma'm la Marquise?"

"We shall soon see, Bobo. You'd better get ready now."

Delighted to be wearing his best livery and driving the big carriage, Bobo rushed to his lodgings at the rear of the stables.

The Marquis whistled for Mic and Mac, Clarence's two Dalmatians, who had been wandering around like lost souls since their master's departure. He started off down the long alley of oaks to the path that followed the riverbank.

The oaks had just marked their hundredth birthday. They had been planted by the Marquis's grandfather on the day the house was completed. The year was 1730 and the first Adrien de Damvilliers was forty years old. And so he planted forty Virginia oaks on either side of a wide avenue, hoping no doubt that it would one day create an imposing approach to his house. Rooting in the alluvial soil of the Mississippi, the trees grew prodigiously. The trunks were thicker than a man's reach, and in summer their foliage made a dense shade that gave the simple white house at the far end of the dirt road the proportions of a castle. The third Adrien had grown up under these trees. He knew every trunk, all identical to the unobservant eye, but each with its own peculiar characteristics to his own. For example, the third one on the left had a large gnarl. He remembered resting his cheek on it and sobbing the day his father told him he would soon be leaving for the Jesuit school in New Orleans. The sixth oak on the right leaned toward its opposite number on the left as if they were exchanging confidences. The thirteenth on the left grew the largest acorns, and the Marquis's mother had prescribed them for pains in the legs. In 1825, under the first tree—the one nearest to the house—he had asked Dorothée Lepas to become his wife. The girl had walked the length of the alley and back, and when she returned to him, still waiting under the tree, she told him he could officially ask for her hand. As for the two oaks nearest the river, their roots had grown so large that they made great bumps in the road. When a carriage arrived at that point, the jouncing of the wheels sent painful spasms through its passengers' spines. It also announced that Bagatelle lay immediately ahead.

The second Marquis had preferred flowers to trees. Thanks to him, there was a rose garden and two flowering magnolias behind the house, flanked a bit haphazardly by giant azaleas and gardenias.

As he walked under the oaks, Adrien remembered how Caroline used to run down the alley, a little girl with eyes too large for her pale face, and long lace-fringed drawers showing under her pink dress. She would disappear behind the trees, then reemerge, her face stained with blackberries. Adrien didn't have a very high opinion of the girl's Aunt Drouin. Some disturbing rumors had come his way. It appeared that she cultivated artists, that she had lovers. For months on end, she and her husband didn't live under the same roof, Mr. Drouin either attending to business in Nantes or making trips to England. The child must have learned things in school that no planter's daughter knew existed. He wondered if she might not be intimidating and whether he would do well to send her back to France as soon as he had given her her inheritance—those pathetically few thousand piasters. He had reached the gate, which was always kept open. It was a glorious golden afternoon, the kind he loved best. The Mississippi was motionless, like a great mirror abandoned between the prairies and fields of cotton. He knew the river as well as he knew the oaks, and in its bend of the river where the water was as still as a lake, Bagatelle seemed rooted for all eternity.

With the two dogs sniffing about, the Marquis retraced his steps toward the house. There it sat behind the screen of trees, like a peaceful ark come aground in a green pasture. The lawn and flower gardens spread out like the flounces of a ball gown, the train trailing off into the distant cotton fields. For Adrien, to leave this place meant the pain of exile. Like his father, he had been born in the big oak bed the slaves had made for his grandfather. God willing, he would die in that bed. And there was no reason on earth why God shouldn't be willing.

At the end of the green tunnel, the house resembled a large rectangular box with a four-sided roof covered with mossy tiles, the long front line broken by four dormers, and on the ridge of the roof, two squat chimneys of red brick. A wide gallery enclosed by a fretwork railing ran the entire length of the house. Serving as both terrace and promenade deck, it was covered by an extension of the roof supported by slim columns. Every room had French doors opening onto the gallery, as did the main entrance. Come evening, during the hour for punch, the boards creaked under the rocking chairs. On rainy days, he sat on the gallery and listened to the tattoo of the rain on the roof and watched the water gush out of the downspouts into waiting barrels. The warm earth gave off the smell of a primitive jungle and the trees heaved and sighed. On summer nights he could taste the freshness.

The gallery rested on a series of brick piers like so many tree stumps. The clay had been molded by the first Adrien's own hands, then baked by his slaves—converted into masons between harvests of indigo. A broad wooden staircase whose treads bent under the Marquis's weight rose between plantings of myrtle, flanked by teak handrails worn to a glossy finish by three generations of sliding children—both white and black.

The first Marquis, an experienced builder with a well-founded fear of termites had, for lack of stone, fallen back on the most abundant wood available—wild cypress. Since his plantation had been a cypress grove, he had a wide choice of perfect specimens. Now a century old, and despite autumn rains and summer droughts, the wood had survived. Inside, lacking plaster, he had used a mixture of clay and dried moss which provided a much better insulation than the more modern materials.

Bagatelle may have been unpretentious, but the Damvilliers could pride themselves on having the oldest house in the region. There were more beautiful houses and certainly many newer ones along the river and further inland, but none had Bagatelle's peculiar charm. Their architects may have been eminent, but they had fixed ideas, and Adrien wanted no part of them. He knew the well-designed gardens and spacious drawing rooms at Oakley where John James Audubon sometimes lived, writing his books about birds and plants. He knew Cottage, a house in the Spanish style with four massive pillars of blue poplar. General Andrew Jackson, now President of the Union, had stopped there one night in 1815 on his way to Natchez after defeating the British near New Orleans. Adrien had a fondness for Olna, near Bagatelle, with its perfect proportions, and also Live Oak, whose proprietor's father had been killed by Andrew Jackson in a duel during a political campaign in Tennessee. But to all these more or less historical landmarks, he preferred Rosedown where, in 1810, at their first meeting, the parish planters had decided to repudiate the Spanish laws. On the other hand, he found The Myrtles, the Templetons' new house, ostentatious. With its hundred-and-ten-foot facade, its galleries with their cast-iron arabesques, the plaster ornamentation throughout the house, the silver doorknobs and the wallpaper in the hall in the Boston manner, it looked like a vulgar stage set.

While on the subject, Adrien recalled that the Templetons were planning a great barbecue for the end of May as a housewarming. He would take his goddaughter, for it would provide the ideal occasion for her to meet plantation society to which, in any case, she belonged by birth.

He hadn't been back ten minutes, eyeing distractedly his study shelves and trying to decide between *Les Voyages du*

Jeune Anarchis en Grèce and a book on botany by John Bartram, when he heard the sound of trotting hooves under the oaks. He pulled the curtains aside and peered down the driveway. There was Bobo, the feather in his beaver hat sticking straight up, driving the carriage as if he were approaching the White House. On the door of the lacquered landau, which sat high on its delicate wheels of varnished beech, the golden crown with eight rosettes—the Damvilliers's coat of arms— caught the slanting rays of the sun.

When Caroline saw her godfather standing on the bottom step of the front stairs, she vividly recalled the terror he had instilled in her when he pinched her cheek or cuffed her with his large hand. Now she embraced him warmly and they climbed the steps, arm in arm.

The Marquis ushered her into the drawing room, where James had laid a fire and Mamma Netta had set out the tea service, polished to a high luster for the occasion. After they sat down, there was a moment's hesitation. Caroline looked inquiringly at her godfather. "Would you like me to pour tea?"

"I'd be delighted," the Marquis replied. His goddaughter did the honors with grace while Mamma Netta passed a platter of buttered bread and little cupcakes lightly dusted with sugar. Caroline smiled indulgently at the big black slave and delicately picked a cupcake off the platter.

She and the Marquis were soon chatting like old friends. Clarence stretched his legs and watched the scene with amused relief. Adrien had expected a whimpering little snob. Instead, Guillaume Trégan's daughter turned out to be a straightforward young lady who expressed herself easily and without pretention. For her part, Caroline, who had dreaded the stiff welcome of a widower overwhelmed with grief, was gratified at his expansive laugh when she described briefly her life in Paris and the journey across the Atlantic. They quickly disposed of the mutual condolences, the Marquis saying simply, "It's our common lot," and Caroline managing a fugitive tear on behalf of her deceased father. She made it abundantly clear that she wanted to get to the subject of her inheritance as soon as possible. Her godfather went straight to the point: Caroline's father had left only debts, which the Marquis had just finished paying off.

"Isn't anything left of the plantation?" she asked, looking distressed.

"Nothing. Absolutely nothing," Adrien replied. "Your father had to sell everything. But since I didn't want to see him wiped out, I bought him out. We were able to get a good price for his best land. I'll show you the papers. I was able to hold back some of the money, for his creditors didn't know what your father had actually stashed away. I saw to it that this money was invested in cotton gins in which I have an interest. You, Caroline, are now the proud owner of four new machines made by Hodgen Holmes, which are bound to earn —in good years and bad—five thousand piasters each. That should take care of your ribbons and laces while you're under my roof."

"But I can't live here," Caroline wailed, determined to act out her role of orphan.

"And why not, please?" the Marquis asked. "It's a big house. You can do as you like. You'll have your own servant. We won't bother you in any way. Unless you wish to take your capital and return to Paris."

Caroline hesitated, still playing the poor waif without a roof to call her own. Then suddenly she sat up and said firmly, "Yes, please, Uncle Adrien, I'd love to stay for a while."

"I would be very happy to have you accept my hospitality, unless of course you miss Paris too much." Then gently, as if he were addressing a child, he added, "You know, we don't lack for distractions here. There are parties and balls, there'll be charming young men to dance with, their sisters will be your friends, you can help tend the rose garden, ride horseback—we've picked out a good-natured mare for you—and like all the other girls of good family, you can do embroidery, play shuttlecock, read."

Caroline thanked him and asked if she could see her room. She also wanted to examine the one hastily prepared for Mignette under the eaves. The Marquis summoned Mamma Netta and told her to find Rosa so that she could help "the young lady from Paris" with her unpacking.

"We dine at eight," Adrien said as they got to their feet. "Your servant can tell Mamma Netta or James where she'd like her dinner served."

The happier of the two was clearly Mignette. She was thrilled with her sunny white bedroom. From its dormer windows hung with flowered cretonne curtains she could just make out, through the branches of the oaks, the lake they called Fausse-Rivière. Despite the refinements she had picked up from her Paris employers, she was a country girl at heart. The plains of the Mississippi were much more vast and wilder than those of her native country and she was very impressed by the huge oaks lining the driveway to the house. Furthermore, she would be served by blacks as if she too were a young lady.

"That's what slaves are for, Mignette," Caroline told her. "All you'll have to do is look after my linen and my dresses. As for the rest, you simply give orders and they'll obey. Here, the whites are masters, no matter what their situation."

So, the slaves were just as she had read about them. They could be bought and sold like Pekingese dogs, and you could even beat them if they disobeyed. Mignette immediately put her authority over Rosa to the test by giving her shoes to polish and asking for a pitcher of hot water to wash with. And Rosa not only obeyed her instantly but addressed her as "mam'selle." Tomorrow, she would take on James, who had brought up her bags. She might ask him to move her dresser or sweep off the roof under her window.

"It's nice to have servants," Mignette said to herself, forgetting for the moment how her mistress had awakened her from a deep sleep to cut off a lock of her hair. Looking at herself in the mirror, she was still conscious of its absence. But Mignette was blessed with a happy disposition and felt pleased and proud of the way she had risen above her station. She couldn't wait to write her mother to tell her about her new life. If her old village friends could only see her now!

Clarence lived in a small one-story house connected to the main house by a covered walkway. He was glad to be back after his eventful trip, and as he unpacked his bags and handed his slave, Ilefet, the clothes that needed laundering, he wondered what effect Caroline would have on the peaceful routine of their lives.

She'll have to have a chaperone so that we're not always having to accompany her when she goes riding or makes visits, he thought. He also hoped that Willy Templeton would be discreet about the game of cards and the shipboard duel. As he dressed for dinner—the Damvilliers had long ago adopted the Anglo-Saxon custom now practiced at all the plantations—he compared Corinne Templeton with Caroline Trégan.

Percy's and Willy's sister was the epitome of a Southern heiress. Hers was a classic beauty, and although she was shy, gentle and modest in her comportment, she had much more personality than most of the tea-cozy dolls one met at plantation receptions and picnics. Yet the desire to grasp at life with both hands that he detected in Caroline was only a faint pulse in Corinne. Neither her nature nor her education had allowed her to give in to her impulses. With her, everything had to be filtered through authorized channels. First her mother, then the Ursuline nuns had taught her the virtue of discipline. Faced with a dilemma, she would sooner submit to a regulation than suffer the consequences of her own disobedience. This made her appear to be in retreat from life. Yet Dandridge knew she had a warm heart, a quality not much in evidence in a society that looked upon the foolish ways of adolescents as a form of charming impetuousness. How Anna Templeton had brought such a daughter into the world was a mystery, for she was one of those who, when the occasion presented itself, liked to pick the forbidden fruit. Naturally, the local aristocracy looked the other way. Such

weaknesses were not unknown after all, and the more indulgent viewed them as a kind of recreation, a compensation
for strict adherence to the conventions.

It took Caroline no time to adapt to the rhythm of the
plantation. She went riding every day, either with her godfather or Dandridge, she dutifully visited the cemetery at
Sainte-Marie to lay flowers on her father's grave, spent long
hours reading the serious works she found on the Marquis's
shelves, gave orders to the gardeners, and when evening came,
had Rosa brush her hair. She treated her servant exactly
as a planter's daughter should, which is to say with equal
parts of familiarity and disdain.

Mamma Netta sang Caroline's praises and laughed over
Mignette's comic ways. In exchange for gumbo recipes, the
girl taught her how to make her native Auvergne dishes. And
Caroline's reputation soared to new heights when she was
able to get the clock in the big drawing room working again.
It had been silent for ten years.

"All it needed was a good cleaning," Caroline said with
attractive modesty.

Ten days after her arrival, Caroline and Clarence set off
on a long ride around the plantation. She had asked to see
the cotton fields and Dandridge, always surprised at the almost
masculine range of her interests, headed for a field where
the slaves were cultivating the tender young plants.

The sun was already hot, but the moist earth and young
vegetation tempered its heat. In the prairies, the grass was
already high, and the Spanish moss clinging to the oaks with
its millions of tiny hands hung down in long pink festoons.
It was the oaks' way of shedding the parasitic growth that
threatened to strangle them.

The cotton plants were already poking their heads above
the furrows. Their pale green stalks looked like small grape-
vines, and their long, thin roots spread like tentacles in the
alluvial loam. In the axil of the branches, shiny plump buds

heralded the harvest to come. Clarence explained how in another forty days, they would burst into whitish flowers and gradually turn pink, then yellow or red. This splendor would last only three days. Then, when the corolla had dropped off, the boll would begin to grow until it reached the size of a gleaming brown egg with a pointed top. While the plant was growing into a three-foot shrub, the seeds in the egg would be ripening inside their covering of silky fuzz. Then, two months later, the tough shells surrounding the seeds would explode like stars. Resembling chicks without heads, these creamy pompoms would now be ready for picking.

"Did you know that the first slaves who were brought here from Africa by English and French slave traders thought that because of its downy fluff, cotton came from lambs born in the trees? Isn't that nice?" Clarence asked. Caroline agreed.

They finally reached the corner of the field where the slaves were working. It was the time of year for weeding and hoeing to keep the soil neat and clean for harvesting time. The older slaves who had thinned out the young plants now inspected the shoots for any sign of one of cotton's greatest enemies, the boll worm. And if, inside the bolls, they spotted the disease called "black arm," it would be a sign of imminent disaster.

The overseers stood languid in the spring sun as they watched the slaves inch forward, pulling on their corncob pipes and only occasionally slapping a young black girl's bottom to assert their authority.

Caroline frowned. "It seems to me that they work very slowly. Now in France . . ."

Clarence interrupted her with vehemence. "Miss Caroline, the Marquis is probably the most humane planter in the region. At this time of year, there is no need to speed up the work. That comes at harvest time. In the spring, he limits the slaves to ten hours a day, with no work on Saturday afternoons or all day Sunday. The children are allowed two weeks off to refurbish their houses under the supervision of the older slaves. The outsides of the houses have to be whitewashed to protect the slaves against malaria, yellow fever and cholera. He is very concerned for the welfare of his slaves. Bagatelle has a good reputation and he intends to keep it that way. Like his father before him, he forbids capital punishment. At Bagatelle, no slave is ever whipped. They are well fed and receive generous rations of corn and salt pork." Dandridge paused to give Caroline a sidelong glance. "Now, at The Myrtles, the Templetons' plantation, the overseers are free to use the whip whenever they have a mind to and even the paddle, which is the most painful and humiliating of all punishments."

"What's so bad about a paddle?" Caroline asked defensively.

"The paddle, young lady," Clarence said with some heat, "is a length of board with nails hammered through it. The slave lies curled up on his side, immobilized by a stick wedged under his knees and elbows, his hands tied tightly to his shins. He is then beaten on the buttocks with the paddle."

Caroline looked uncomfortable. "The slave must have done something dreadful. What was he being punished for?"

Clarence looked away. "Sometimes . . . often . . . for nothing at all."

Caroline fixed her eyes on the pommel of her saddle. "Oh," she said.

"Mind you, the Marquis doesn't let them get away with everything. He has his own way of punishing thieves, slackers or those who talk back. He simply sells them cheap, and the poor slave is bought by a worse master. As for runaway slaves, he puts a notice in the New Orleans and Natchez newspapers and makes a halfhearted attempt to find them. Sometimes one of them is picked up and the finder comes around for his reward. The Marquis turns the slave over to the judge and he's tried under our local laws. But the Marquis never attends the public bastinado. He can't stand the sight of a man handcuffed, dragging a heavy pole, being beaten twenty or thirty times on his bare back. Occasionally a runaway slave repents and returns to him after the beating, the skin on his back in shreds. The Marquis sends him to Dr.

Murphy, who visits the plantation hospital every morning, and once the slave is healed, he sells him for half what he originally cost." Clarence paused. "I don't suppose you hear about these things in the Paris salons, Miss Caroline?"

Caroline shook her head in silence.

"Well, I can tell you that your godfather gets plenty of criticism from the other planters. They think his 'weakness' encourages the slaves to rebellion. But Bagatelle is the best-tended plantation around, and at harvest time when the slaves have to work fifteen and sixteen hours a day, he gets good work out of them. It shows in our account books. A medium grade slave is amortized in less than six years. An average slave represents twelve hundred pounds of cotton a year. Bagatelle gets two thousand. And he uses one slave to only ten acres."

What he didn't tell Caroline was that the master of Bagatelle had never kept black mistresses and so far as anyone knew had never produced a bastard. The pretty young house servants at Bagatelle knew that they could take refreshment to their master's bedroom at night without ending up in his bed. There were those who justified these practices on the grounds that they "protected the virtue" of white women. As for the children born of these couplings, they simply increased the number of slaves—although their paler skin was no protection against the overseer's whip.

"Don't think the Marquis isn't aware of how foreigners feel about slavery—especially the French," Clarence continued, glancing at Caroline out of the corner of his eye. "He knows all about European notions of liberty, dignity, the right to determine your own life. But it doesn't work here in the South. Here we need hands more than we need brains. But you'll be glad to know that the British are the worst. They carry on about the sorry lot of the slaves when it was they who made fortunes tracking them down like beasts and transporting them from Africa to America. Mr. Mosely, a British cotton trader who comes to Bagatelle each year, tells us that in Manchester, sixty percent of the adults can't write their own names, that the people on the outskirts of London live in huts you wouldn't put a dog in, that thousands of young girls spend twenty hours a day sewing to earn enough to eat, that children less than ten years old work twelve hours a day in the mines, three hundred feet below ground level, without ever seeing the sun . . ."

From Caroline's expression, Clarence could see that she had taken in enough social history for one day. She was disturbed, but it was also evident that she was impatient to return to the waxed and polished comfort of the big house. That was all right too: just so long as she began to understand how the wax and polish and comfort were come by.

They turned their horses' heads and started for home. It was hot now, so Clarence chose the narrow shaded path that ran parallel to the river. He took the lead and let his thoughts continue from where their conversation had left off. Someday, perhaps, he would tell Caroline what was on his mind. But not yet. Besides, it might seem disloyal to the Marquis.

For Clarence was one of the few men who smelled change in the air, something that most of the planters refused to acknowledge. He had noted the first ripples of the evolutionary process stemming from the North. It revealed itself in their differing methods, in the rivalry of their interests, in their social animosities, and he was convinced that the day was not far off when these would become politicized. With the Ohio River as the dividing line, two conceptions of national identity—two ways of life—were ranged against each other. Thomas Jefferson had foreseen it at the time of the Missouri Compromise in 1821. The years that followed had proved him right. In the interval, the South had organized a "solidarity of thought and action" to give the planters ammunition against possible threats from the North. In fact, events were moving so fast that unless you were—like Adrien de Damvilliers—dozing in a haze of prosperity, you would have sensed the insidious penetration of Northern ideas and manners, especially in the Southern cities. To make matters worse, the industrialists in the North, looking toward eventual economic independence, were demanding tariffs to limit competition from British and French textile mills. The cotton planters were against protection, although the sugarcane planters—who also were not immune from foreign competition—were for the tariffs. Adrien had taken it very hard. One evening, over their glasses of punch, he had grumbled, "This system they're trying to impose on us is going to play havoc with our European buyers. It'll be fine for the North, but our profits will go up the chimney."

He, along with the other Louisiana planters, had backed Vice-President John C. Calhoun when he came out against the tariff of 1828 and expounded his doctrine of "nullification"—that any state had the same right to withdraw from the Union as it did to join it. Clarence argued that Calhoun's theories were a threat to the Union's integrity and were bound to encourage each state's particularity. States' rights should be protected, of course, but by less radical means.

Dandridge was still mulling over these irreconcilable ideas when they reached the alley of oaks. Both in deep thought, Clarence and Caroline didn't speak again until they reached the stables. The girl leaped off her horse, declining Bobo's hand.

"Thank you for a very instructive ride, Mr. Dandridge," she said with an enigmatic smile. "You've given me much to think about. Now I need a good wash more than anything else!" And she strode off toward the house, flicking her riding crop against her thigh.

That evening at dinner, the Marquis seemed a little put out and remarked on the long ride she had taken with Dandridge. Caroline laughed brightly. "Dear Uncle Adrien, you should be proud of me. Thanks to Mr. Dandridge, I received a very thorough education on cotton, your slaves, what a good master you are, and the different ways in which the North and South look at things. And it was so beautiful in the fields! Please don't be angry with me."

"My dear child," the Marquis replied, only partly pacified. "I was only hoping that you'd find time to pay some attention to the house. So much needs to be done. I never liked the Marquise's taste in furniture. It's too new, too modern. It comes from Boston, and although it's much admired by our guests . . ."

Dandridge, also anxious to appease his employer, chimed in, "I must admit I prefer the old family heirlooms. The sofas, the wing chairs, the bulging commodes, the red silk draperies—didn't you tell me the draperies dated back to Louis XV?"

"What did you do with all those things?" Caroline asked.

The Marquis sighed. "Oh, they were stored away somewhere and I suppose they're quietly rotting away. Goodness, it's been five years already."

"Could I look to see if any of it is still usable?" Caroline ventured.

"I'd like nothing better. But I'm afraid that none of it will be good for much more than stoking the furnace. In any event, I give you a free hand. From now on, you're the 'demoiselle de Bagatelle.' "

Caroline seized the opportunity, and for the next week, she appeared only at mealtimes, exhausted, but with her eyes glistening. Dandridge put some slaves at her disposal and she spent all her time in the storage room. Of her discoveries, she said not a word. Only Mamma Netta and James appeared to know anything. It wasn't until later that the Marquis and Clarence realized that Caroline had decided to bring off a revolution. They left in all innocence to spend two days in Natchez. When they returned, the revolution had taken place.

At the sound of the horses' hooves, Caroline stepped onto the gallery. Wearing a voluminous pink silk dress with a lace collar and flounces, she stood smiling on the top step as if she were welcoming the King of France. The two men stood transfixed. For the first time, Caroline was out of mourning clothes. The little orphan girl had turned into a great Southern beauty.

"Dear Uncle Adrien," she said, going down the steps with a rustle of skirts, "I have a surprise for you."

Her tone sounded a warning, but her eyes glittered like those of a girl who has spent hours preparing a gift.

During the several weeks since her arrival, Clarence's initial prejudice against Caroline had melted away. In her magnificent costume, she was a creature of grace and spontaneity. The Marquis, having no need to show his manager's discretion, found her irresistible and accepted her welcome as a gift from heaven. Forgetting the long and tiring ride, he raced up the steps—something Clarence had never seen him do before— took the girl's hand and swung her about as if in a dance.

"She's a princess, Dandridge, a real princess waiting for the return of the weary travelers!"

Clarence's Dalmatians had come running up to their master, then suddenly stopped, their noses sniffing the air, as if the charm of the girl in pink were working on them too. The group walked into the house and there spread out before them was Bagatelle as it had been before the Marquis's marriage.

The little devil was taking a big risk, Clarence said to himself. Then he looked at the Marquis. The master of Bagatelle was awestruck. All the Duncan Phyfe was gone. Back were the long, triple-arched Louis-Philippe sofa covered with beige Utrecht velour, the Boulle table with a brass and mother-of-pearl inlay, love seats and small armchairs, the "duchesse" day bed on which his mother used to recline with Creole languor, the "bergères" near the stone fireplace, the commode signed by Cressent with its leafwork of chiseled gilt bronze, the little tables of Brazilian rosewood on which Sèvres vases overflowed with flowers, and all of it cleaned, waxed, polished, shining, gleaming.

"My God, Caroline," Adrien exclaimed, "you've made me years younger! It's my mother's house, exactly as she arranged it!"

On the newly cleaned walls, he recognized the old pictures. Gone were the "school of Joshua Reynolds" landscapes and the dark Hogarth engravings hung by the deceased Marquise. In their stead were the portraits of the Damvilliers in their ornate frames, smiling at their return to a place of honor. A group of horses by George Stubbs, purchased by the Marquis and discarded by his wife, seemed to be snorting with triumph between two windows. On the other hand, a portrait of the pale and melancholy Marquise had been relegated to a dark corner. The Marquis made no comment about his deceased wife's fall from grace. The large chandelier with the crystal drops had been taken down, cleaned and rehung, and now, bristling with pink candles, it sparkled with reflected glory in the big mirror over the mantelpiece.

"This isn't all," Caroline said, now confident she had the master's approval.

She led the two men into the dining room where the long Adam mahogany table was back with its three triple-footed pedestals. Above the table, which could seat twenty guests, she had hung a large "punkah" of flowered salmon silk with a gold fringe to cool the room and discourage mosquitoes. The Marquis couldn't remember ever having seen it before. As in the drawing room, the wall sconces had been reinstated, and on the sideboard, silver platters and ewers had been restored to their former brilliance with loving applications of Spanish whiting.

Caroline's magic had even encompassed the breakfast room, the small room where they often took their meals, and the small sitting room adjoining it, although she apologized for not having time to furnish the latter.

"We must have a bottle of champagne," Adrien burst out, "and you, Dandridge, think up a toast to Bagatelle's presiding fairy!"

They passed a joyful evening unlike anything Bagatelle had seen in years. Mamma Netta, who had been in on the preparations, outdid herself. She brought out the old porcelains, crystal glasses, silver service and snowy table linen. The men dressed up for the occasion, and Adrien, in his black frock coat and ruffled jabot, looked like an expansive "seigneur" of olden times, as responsive to a lady's charms as to a bottle of good wine.

The master of Bagatelle raised his glass to his goddaughter, who wore just the right expression of pride mixed with becoming modesty.

"I drink to a reborn Bagatelle!" the Marquis said with an

enthusiasm Dandridge had never seen before. It was as if he were drawing a final veil over the memory of his dead wife.

Then he turned to his manager. "What do you drink to, Dandridge?"

Clarence, contemplating for a moment the bubbles of champagne in his glass, raised his eyes to Caroline who was waiting expectantly, her chin resting on her hands. Finally he said in a low voice, "I drink to the return of a Southern girl, to her good taste and to . . . to her intelligence."

"Bravo," the Marquis said exultantly, and they turned their attention to the chicken gumbo Mamma Netta was serving.

That evening, Caroline had trouble going to sleep. When Dandridge had mentioned her "intelligence," was he really trying to say something else? Had he substituted that word for another? Was he being ironic or hinting at some kind of complicity? Had he actually meant that she was clever, or ambitious, or even presumptuous? But what mattered most was that her Uncle Adrien hadn't questioned her motives in restoring Bagatelle to its former state. All the same, she had a long way to go before the house could be made to fit into her personal scheme of things. In a confused way, she felt certain that her destiny would be played out on the banks of the Mississippi. There at least a woman could still find power and wealth. But the cool and unresponsive Dandridge would force her to be patient. His skeptical eye might not yet take in the goal of her ambitions, but he would be following her every move.

While she tossed and turned in her lemonwood bed, the Marquis and Dandridge smoked their cigars on the gallery. Adrien's euphoria was due not only to champagne. Clarence guessed that it had quite a lot to do with Caroline.

"It's amazing," the Marquis said, shaking his head. "She put things back as if they'd been fixed in her mind since childhood. But she was just a harum-scarum child when she was here last. Dandridge, I tell you, children have a talent for observation that we don't suspect."

Clarence could have reminded him that Mamma Netta had spent half a century in the house and of course had been consulted. She couldn't help but know where the furniture had stood after polishing it all those years. But instead he agreed with the Marquis, who went on rocking dreamily in his chair.

Adrien had a last thought. "You have to admit, Dandridge, that it's very useful to have a woman around the house."

"Very useful, Adrien," Dandridge said with a laugh. "That's what God made them for, I suppose, that and a few other equally useful functions."

"And you think Caroline can fill all those roles, Clarence?" Adrien said with an insinuating laugh. "Whoever marries her gets a good filly, heh?"

With that, each of the two men went to his room.

"To have a successful barbecue," Anna Templeton once said, "the food must be plentiful, the girls pretty and elegant but in fewer numbers than the young men, so that the latter will be free to pay some attention to the wives while their husbands talk business. You must be able to sit on the lawn without staining your clothes. Then, away from the house, out in the park, there must be benches for courting tucked away in bosky nooks. And finally, you must see to it that the gentlemen find bottles of whiskey, which of course the ladies will pretend not to see, at the foot of an occasional tree."

When the three guests from Bagatelle arrived at The Myrtles, it was soon obvious that Mrs. Templeton had acted according to her principles.

Caroline was wearing a dress of white tulle with lavender flounces as a reminder of her recent bereavement, a bouquet of melancholy violets tucked into her décolletage. Perched on her head was an organdy sunbonnet tied with a ribbon to match the flounces of her dress. As Anna Templeton embraced her, she noted the girl's soft ivory skin and the absence of rice powder, which she herself had to apply to hide a burgeoning pimple.

When Willy saw the carriage drive up, he immediately joined his mother, his sister Corinne and his brother Percy, a glass of whiskey in his hand.

"I think you already know one of my sons," Anna Templeton said to Caroline. "This is my older son Percy, and my daughter Corinne. I'll have to introduce you to Mr. Templeton later. He must be down there somewhere," she said, pointing toward the lawn that sloped gently down to the river. The park was crowded with guests looking up admiringly at the large house squatting on the ground like an enormous and elaborately decorated meringue. Willy, in a pearl-gray frock coat, checked cravat and trousers with understraps, offered his arm to Caroline and the two set off. "Come. I want you to meet our guests. Everybody who counts for anything in these parts is here today." Percy, his face florid, his stance as solid as the overarching oaks, watched his brother and Caroline move off, appraising the young lady's retreating silhouette with a connoisseur's eye.

"How is your wound?" Caroline asked Willy gently as they approached a group of guests.

"It's not worth mentioning. Dr. Murphy took excellent care of me. And naturally no one knows the reason for the duel."

Caroline gave the young man's arm a squeeze and looked at him with a sad and tender smile. This encouraged Willy to reach into his waistcoat pocket and extract a small locket which he opened furtively. Inside, tightly curled, nestled the lock of Mignette's hair.

"Mr. Barthew felt he owed me his trophy, although I would have liked to receive it from your own hand."

Caroline tried to control her surprise. "That was very generous of him, and I'm gratified that you attach such importance to it."

Willy's audacity was repaid by yet another smile and more pressure on his arm.

The Marquis had joined a group of planters, and Clarence was talking to Corinne. The daughter of the house, in her gown of English lace and her long dark hair gathered at the nape of her neck, looked as fragile as a piece of Dresden china.

"The Marquis's goddaughter is charming, Mr. Dandridge,"

she said warmly. "And she seems so European."

"Yes, she is charming, and she's blessed with an easy assurance."

"We country girls are going to have trouble holding onto our swains, Mr. Dandridge. We're all such ignoramuses."

Clarence strained to keep up his end of the repartee. It was the price you paid for attending these receptions, he reminded himself.

"Come now, Corinne, you are not an ignoramus, and may I say that I find you devilishly seductive today."

He tried to put warmth in his tone, but the coolness of his gaze gave away his indifference to the young lady's charms. Corinne heard the tone; she didn't see the gaze. She smiled, revealing the dazzlingly white teeth which Mrs. Templeton likened to "Cleopatra's pearls," then closed her eyes, the better to savor the compliment. She had been in love with Dandridge for such a long time, and this was the first time he had ever paid her a compliment. Her hands grew moist in her silk gloves and her gown suddenly felt tight. But she knew the rules that governed a young lady's comportment and therefore said nothing.

Clarence suggested, "Won't you give me your arm? I think it's time we joined the others."

Clarence gallantly slipped his arm through hers, and they moved down the sandy path. Corinne gave him a sidelong glance.

"Mr. Dandridge, do you know why Willy fought a duel with a lawyer on the *Prince du Delta?*"

"I have no idea, Corinne, but I'm sure your brother had good reasons."

"Something to do with gambling, perhaps?"

"That's possible."

"Mr. Dandridge, he could have been killed for nothing, or killed a man he didn't even know!"

"That's the risk you take in a duel, Corinne."

"Oh, I know you men think nothing of it. But even if someone insulted me, I wouldn't want any man . . . my brother, for example . . . to risk his life under those conditions. There should be a law against such things."

"It's a question of honor, Corinne, not a sporting impulse."

"I think there's honor and courage in keeping yourself alive for the sake of those who love you. I know that not many girls talk that way, but I don't care. It's what I think."

Clarence was moved more by her tone than by her words, and patted Corinne's hand as if to calm an overexcited child. His touch threw her into such a tizzy that her knees almost gave way. Fortunately, her father crossed paths with them at that moment.

"Come on, Dandridge," Mr. Templeton said jovially, "come talk to the men. Don't let Corinne monopolize you. The women need us only during the ball, and that's already enough."

"I wanted to show him the house, Father," she said, pouting, for she had hoped to keep Clarence to herself a little longer. But Clarence excused himself.

"I'll come back to you later, Corinne. We'll eat lunch together, and tonight I'll ask you for the first dance."

"Oh, yes! I'll give you all my dances if you like."

She stood watching the two men she loved most in the world as they wandered off. The man on the left, her father, knew she loved him; the other man appeared to be totally unaware. Crestfallen, she went off in search of her mother, who might be needing her.

"Well, Dandridge, my daughter seems very happy today. I wish you'd come to The Myrtles more often. It would give her so much pleasure. It wouldn't surprise me if she weren't a little soft on Bagatelle's manager . . ."

This was his way of telling Clarence that even if he didn't belong to the planters' class, he would do for an heiress a little short on suitors. Corinne was already twenty, and in a country where young girls were betrothed at fifteen and married at sixteen, she would soon be considered "on the shelf." Mr. Templeton was well aware of his daughter's plight and if Dandridge made up his mind, he would make only token objections. Percy was a poor businessman, and it wouldn't be a bad idea to have a manager trained at Bagatelle as his second-in-command. But they hadn't reached that point yet, and although Corinne's father thought her a little insipid, she might still attract some planter's son whose wild oats were behind him and who was now ready to settle down with a good wife.

Clarence devoted the briefest possible time to a discussion of cotton and politics, then went in search of Willy. The young duelist was wandering from group to group, Percy having snatched Caroline away under the pretext that he wanted to introduce her to his wife Isabelle. The girl had been in the house at least fifteen minutes.

"Mr. Dandridge, I think I'm in love with Miss Trégan," Willy said in the tone of a man announcing he has just contracted the measles.

"It's quite obvious, Willy."

"What do you think?"

"I think she's very attractive and indeed capable of inspiring the sentiments you profess. But since my instincts lead me to distrust sudden infatuations, I would wait a little before making an open declaration. After all," Dandridge added with a hint of duplicity, "you should let others have a chance!"

"At West Point we were taught not to hold back before a bastion. You either take it or go around it!" Willy said solemnly.

"A blockade sometimes brings good results, Willy."

"That's Corinne's strategy with you, Dandridge, and so far the poor goose hasn't a thing to show for it."

Clarence dropped his bantering tone and said emphatically, "Corinne is not a poor goose, Willy. She is a shy and sensitive young woman who needs tenderness and understanding."

"Then why the devil don't you ask for her hand, Dandridge? That's what she's been waiting for for years!"

"Because I'm not the right man for her."

"But she's twenty years old and I know Papa will give her to you. She'll be rich one day, you know. Aren't you tired of being Bagatelle's manager?"

"That isn't the question, Willy. I'm not the right man for her, and that's all there is to it."

Willy pulled himself together. "This is a stupid discussion. Please forgive me, Dandridge. Let's go find some champagne."

As they were walking toward the buffet, Willy stopped in his tracks and turned to Clarence. "Are you in love with Caroline?"

"Not in the least, Willy," Clarence replied in a calm voice that contrasted sharply with Willy's. "I've been in love only once in my life and that was a long time ago. I doubt it will happen to me again."

"Why not?" the younger man asked, astonishment winning out over discretion.

"It's a long story. Perhaps I'll tell it to you someday, when you've gotten over the pangs of love—in other words, when you've either fallen victim or been healed."

"I know I can count on you, Dandridge," Willy went on, calmer now. "Please don't hold it against me for telling you all this. I can't confide in anybody around here. My brother is a bounder, my father thinks only about business, and my mother would go around babbling to everybody about the condition of my soul. She's so damn romantic."

"I think Corinne would understand," Clarence replied, "but perhaps it would be wiser to spare her this kind of problem. She's easily upset. But you can tell me everything. Just think of me as a reasoning mirror."

Willy caught sight of Caroline's coppery hair among a gaggle of brunettes and bolted away. There he goes, ready to storm the bastion again, Dandridge said to himself, and raised his glass to the retreating figure. And because he was fond of Willy and his boyish candor, he wished him luck.

It was a beautiful afternoon. The oyster stew was excellent, the roast turkey with its compote of fruit was done to a turn, and the Indian pudding called for a glass of the Bordeaux cooling in buckets under a damp cloth. Girls in pink and white were playing shuttlecock as the young men stood watching stiff-legged out of concern for their trousers' creases. As the girls leaped this way and that, their cavaliers sometimes caught sight of a lace ruffle on a pair of batiste drawers, a well-turned calf, a delicate foot, or a rounded shoulder suddenly peeking out of a disarrayed bodice. Their cheeks pink with exertion, the players tried to correct these innocent indecencies—but not before they had made sure the young men were watching. The older men had found refuge on the gallery and were eating and drinking in picnic style as they listened for the hundredth time to Mr. Templeton's tale of La Fayette's visit to Louisiana in 1824. It appeared that Washington's friend had taken the *Natchez* as far as Baton Rouge, where the local farmers acclaimed him as the French hero of the American revolution.

"And when he returned home," another man joined in, "he found a new king on the throne. Charles X may be leading the country into trouble, but people say he's a good man. La Fayette is opposed to him, which is a brave thing to do when you're his age and with his reputation."

"France is heading for a democracy, mark my words," a second man said, "even though the French have no aptitude for politics. In my opinion, La Fayette would make a very good president of a republic. It was Washington who taught him how to persuade men that liberty for all sometimes depends on the will of one man."

"Didn't I hear," Dandridge broke in, having just joined the group, "that La Fayette considered slavery an outmoded institution and that it was high time we got rid of it?"

There was a silence. Southern planters preferred avoiding this subject. Adrien de Damvilliers came to his friend's rescue.

"Monsieur de La Fayette had been in the North before he came to see us. His friends up there must have influenced him. But he would have quickly seen that the Negroes in our Southern states are far happier than the free workers in New York or Boston. Nobody there guarantees them food and shelter. They're slaves without masters. And that's the worst thing that can happen to you when you belong to an inferior race."

Dandridge gave a wry smile. It was a familiar argument. Templeton took advantage of the pause in the conversation to suggest a game of whist in the drawing room. The betting was fixed at two cents a point, cigars were passed around, and Anna Templeton, although opposed to any form of gambling, saw that card tables were set up and drinks were served to the players, and ordered a slave to work the "punkah" to help clear the air of smoke.

Dandridge didn't play cards, so he set off to examine the decorations in the new house. He glanced at a few paintings, then stopped before the wallpaper in the hall—Mrs. Templeton's greatest pride. It had been made by Joseph Dufour in Paris and was an imitation of a tapestry showing an episode in the life of Charlemagne. Under a vast canopy, a queen dressed in white—probably the emperor's fourth wife, Louitgarde L'Alamane—sat watching a tourney unfortunately taking place out of the picture's range.

"What an artist! Don't you think so, Mr. Dandridge? What a remarkable feeling for composition. And look at Charlemagne's beard. How would you describe it? Isn't it positively . . ."

"Blooming . . ." Clarence suggested.

"You have it! Blooming like our cotton plants!"

The comparison was perhaps farfetched, but it was all that Mrs. Templeton could think of. A plump and vivacious little woman, Corinne's mother had velvety eyes and a sensual mouth. It was rumored that she had initiated a goodly number of young men into the pleasures of sex, and very skillfully too. Among the guests, there must have been not a few husbands who owed their proficiency to her inspired teaching. She offered Clarence her small hand.

"Have you seen my boudoir, Mr. Dandridge?"

"Not yet, madam, but wouldn't it be indiscreet?"

"Not in the least, Mr. Dandridge. Follow me."

It was a cozy little room. A large mirror hung above the gray marble mantelpiece on which stood a bronze clock flanked by two paired statuettes of black Venuses and two crystal candelabra. An ottoman covered in pale blue silk filled the space between two windows covered with tulle over which heavy draperies matching the silk of the ottoman fell in soft folds held back by silver cords. A few small chairs were grouped around a pedestal table of gilt wood. Against one wall, a large mirror above an ornate console reflected a portrait of Madame de Pompadour on the opposite wall. With the pale blue silk wall covering and the frieze of darker blue above, the room looked like a candy box. Dandridge's attention was drawn to a handsome harp with a sculptured pillar, a small stool sitting beside it. He brushed the strings with his fingers, setting up a melodious hum. Then, looking up, he realized that Mrs. Templeton was waiting for him to say something. Bagatelle's manager had no illusions about why he had been invited into the room. Mrs. Templeton sat down on the ottoman, rearranged the folds of her dress and cast a meaningful glance at Clarence to pave the way for the session she had plotted.

"Dear Clarence, do you know why my Willy fought that duel on the *Prince*? You were there, weren't you?"

Dandridge sighed. How he disliked these people who had to know the why and wherefore of everybody's actions. As if she had guessed at his displeasure, she quickly added, "I am his mother, after all, and I have a right to know why my son risked his life. There was a woman behind it, I assume?"

"Other reasons are equally possible, madam. I think some altercation over a card game is the more likely one."

"So, you don't know exactly, is that it?" Willy's mother covered her irritation with the most seductive of smiles.

"Not exactly, no. I was reading in my cabin when the incident took place."

"Then let's say no more about it," Mrs. Templeton said with finality. "Nobody seems to know. Yet it's hard to believe that Willy would have risked his life for nothing."

Clarence was silent, his eyes fixed on the floor. "That's a handsome rug, Mrs. Templeton. Where did it come from?"

"From India, Mr. Dandridge. An officer in the British Navy gave it to Corinne but she didn't like the design. She has very strong opinions, you know."

Ah, here comes the second subject, Clarence said to himself. He wasn't wrong.

"Tell me, Mr. Dandridge, what do you think of Corinne?

She appears to be so very fond of you. Do you realize that she has turned down several offers with no explanation?"

"I feel great affection for her too, Mrs. Templeton. Corinne is both gracious and sensible. I suppose she will marry when she's absolutely sure of her feelings . . . and besides, she must be very happy in such a family as yours."

Anna Templeton looked dejected. "No, Mr Dandridge, Corinne isn't happy. A twenty-year-old girl without a suitor cannot be happy. She feels . . . how shall I say it . . ."

"Thwarted? I don't believe it!"

"I'm afraid that she cares for someone who isn't aware of her feelings, someone who is either blind or doesn't care for her, Mr. Dandridge."

Oh, Lord! Clarence said to himself. Mrs. Templeton was trying to corner him with her not-very-subtle machinations and he must brave it out.

"Some men are shy and even frightened," he said. "In those cases, it's better not to rush things."

"But she's twenty years old, Mr. Dandridge. Twenty years old! I married at fifteen. People will think she has some kind of blemish."

Clarence laughed. "My dear Mrs. Templeton, you're getting worked up over nothing. There are plenty of young men in Louisiana who . . ."

"But she doesn't like the young men. She thinks they're superficial and stupid. She's interested only in mature men, somebody like you, Mr. Dandridge . . ."

A winning smile on her face, Corinne's mother gave Clarence the full benefit of her large dark eyes. It was time to bring this embarrassing conversation to an end. Clarence got to his feet and went over to the harp. He twanged two chords, and in a ringing voice declaimed a verse from Racine's *Andromaque*:

> "But have I sought to please her?
> Wouldn't one say, on seeing instead
> Your charms all-powerful and hers disdained,
> That she is the captive here while you reign."

Mrs. Templeton, ignorant of the verse's source, could only conclude that Mr. Dandridge was making her a proposition. She felt a double pleasure: that a woman over forty could still inspire desire, and that she had suddenly been catapulted into a romantic situation.

"Oh, Mr. Dandridge," she said, pretending confusion as she smoothed the folds of her skirt. "How can you say such things . . ."

She rose to her feet and held out her hands. Clarence felt obliged to take them, ridiculous though the situation had become.

"We must go now," she said. "The ball is about to begin . . . " and, pink and panting, she held up her cheek as if expecting a kiss. "You will dance with me, Mr. Dandridge?"

Clarence nodded and waited for her to recover from the emotional turmoil he had unwittingly provoked.

While Mrs. Templeton and Clarence were closeted in her boudoir, Caroline had held court under a magnolia tree. The young ladies had spirited her away from Willy and the other aspiring admirers to question her about the latest news of Paris. They wanted to know about her life there, the balls, the court, the salons, what the shops were like, night life on the boulevards. They asked about the latest word in fashions, how the young men behaved, what music was being played, what books read, and was it true that Parisians treated Americans like semi-civilized "redskins." Caroline had to show off her shoes, produce her tiny bottle of toilet water by Guerlain, explain how hairdressers created chignons, and promise to reveal the contents of her wardrobe when they came to visit her at Bagatelle. When she suggested she teach them the waltz, a dance their parents considered a "lascivious circular flight danced only by Germans," there were squeals of delight. In addition to all her other paraphernalia, the girl from Paris had brought them a forbidden pleasure.

At the Templetons', as with most planters' families, the quadrille was the only dance allowed. Brought over intact from France, it was an old country dance made up of five figures: the promenade, "moulinets," the wooden horses, the basket, and the final farandole. In groups of four, the couples made identical movements to the accompaniment of violins, a piano—the Templetons' was naturally a Chickering from Boston—and a few woodwinds. There was no contact between dancers except for one hand resting on the partner's arm. To clasp a dancer around the waist would have created a scandal.

"Take your places for the quadrille," Mr. Templeton boomed out as the musicians tuned up their instruments on their corner platform.

In conformity with the rules of etiquette, the master of the house invited the wife of Senator Calvy, the oldest member in the assemblage, for the first dance. The Marquis de Damvilliers found himself with Corinne, Willy with Caroline, and Mrs. Templeton with old Fontaine, one of the richest planters in the region. With Willy as her partner, Caroline displayed the grace of a gazelle. She was as supple and precise as a trained dancer, and her relaxed smile showed that she knew every step of the dances. Willy wanted only to show off his partner's virtuosity. They made a handsome couple. Everyone commented on it.

A little later, having led the strenuous Mrs. Templeton through a dance, Dandridge went in search of Corinne. She had been waiting for this moment. He asked her to dance three times. For Clarence, who danced seldom, it was a gallant gesture. Corinne was very appreciative.

"I know you don't like this type of distraction, Mr. Dandridge. Please don't feel you have to ask me again."

She said it softly, like a woman who willingly gives up her own pleasure for the well-being of the man she loves. For the first time, Clarence felt something approaching tenderness for the girl. She lowered her eyes in excited confusion. He made a vow that he would try to avoid Corinne in the future. He was encouraging false hopes which would inevitably bring her pain. The most he could muster was a feeling of affection, the same emotion he felt in front of Gainsborough's "La Perdita." This absence of response was confusing to the women he attracted. Some put it down to arrogance; others to an undying love for some far-distant or inaccessible lady; the more racy had him involved in a homosexual relationship. Those who knew him best interpreted it as plain misogyny. His cultivation, his intelligence, his courtesy, his sense of honor and his gallantry with the female sex made it easy to overlook this oddity in his character. Whatever his inclinations, the parents of unattached girls were convinced that Clarence Dandridge's fate was already sealed: Corinne Templeton clearly had the lead. So they turned their attention to what hapless men remained.

The evening finally came to an end. Toward eleven o'clock, the carriages began to file down the road and back to their various plantations. While the men dozed, the mothers listened to their daughters' whispered confessions. No conversation went without a mention of Caroline Trégan. She was unanimously declared charming. The young men tried to extract more information about the exciting new arrival from Paris; they had looked with envy as Dandridge took his place beside her in the Marquis's landau.

The soft warm night exhaled the perfume of spring flowers. Above the dark mass of the forests beyond the cotton fields, the sky was flecked with stars, a new moon suspended in their midst like a silver comma. Caroline, nodding in her corner, observed: "There is no sky in Paris."

The Marquis yawned. "If this weather lasts, the cotton will be ready a week early . . ."

Clarence, his eyes half shut, remembered other similar nights when, as a young Bostonian in search of adventure, he had marched, farther up the river, toward his extraordinary destiny.

The distant barking of Dandridge's Dalmatians announced that they were nearing Bagatelle. Bobo straightened up in his seat. During the party, he and the other coachmen had taken a few swigs of whiskey in the slaves' quarters. Now he felt like a bale of cotton coming apart at the seams.

* * *

Caroline was soon convinced that life at Bagatelle was the most agreeable of all possible forms of existence. When she compared the worldly pleasures of Paris and London to what she had now, the South always won out. Of course she knew that this civilization was based on the exploitation of blacks. She had learned it in Paris, long before her ride with Clarence. But was that any reason not to enjoy the privileges that came with her situation? Wasn't that the divine will?

She had no trouble understanding how those who had never known a different life could view plantation life as another Eden. Under the authority of a benign master, the slaves worked the fields like the humble caretakers of nature's amplitude, while the Great White Planter's wife and children tasted the rightful joys of the elect. The blacks, like domesticated animals in human form, filled the role the Creator had assigned them. Because they withstood the humid heat and the malaria that killed whites, they seemed expressly made to cultivate cotton—proof that God's designs were not all impenetrable. Slavery was actually a form of adoption. Besides, if you looked carefully, justification for it could be found in the Bible. Wasn't this another expression of the divine will?

In exchange for a roof, board and lodging, and the elementary care a farmer owed his livestock, the slaves gave themselves body and soul to the Great White Planter. He, in turn, casting aside for the moment the question of whether "eternity was available to Negroes," taught them to love God and saw to it that their children were baptized. The slaves gave themselves to these pious exercises with good grace and considerable zeal, even though they had a way of corrupting the hymns with strange syncopated rhythms. This distressed the Great White Planter who saw in it a pagan manifestation carried over from their days in the jungle. But, since he was a just and good man, he blessed these unfinished creatures. For wasn't this yet another expression of the divine will?

Life on the plantation was gradually taking on a tropical rhythm. Everything moved more slowly. Caroline spent long hours on the gallery or taking aimless walks along the river-bank. But what she loved best were the long evenings on the gallery after dinner. For her sake, the Marquis and Clarence forswore their usual plantation talk and discussed more general topics. One night, Caroline asked her godfather to tell her about the early history of the Damvilliers at Bagatelle.

"I'm sure I was told it as a child but I've forgotten most of it."

"My dear child," the Marquis replied, "young ladies aren't supposed to be interested in dry subjects like history."

Caroline gave him a sharp look. "But Uncle Adrien, I *am* interested in history—it was my best subject at the convent. Besides, I happen to be interested in your family's history."

Adrien turned to Clarence and with a deprecating wave of the hand, said: "Clarence, you're the family's official biographer. You tell my nosy goddaughter about our origins. But be brief. I don't want you to abuse her patience."

Clarence, astonished as always by the range of Caroline's interests and not a little suspicious of her motives, started tentatively.

"Well, where shall we begin? Perhaps in 1699. That was the year that Le Moyne d'Iberville sailed up the Mississippi from Baton Rouge and found himself at a large elbow of the river where an island had been formed by two arms of the river. They named it Pointe-Coupée and moved on. From 1700 on, settlers began to arrive, encouraged by agents of John Law's 'Compagnie des Indes.' Among the settlers was one Claude-Adrien de Damvilliers, your godfather's grandfather, to whom Louis XV had given ten thousand acres of land for services rendered."

Caroline stopped him: "What were those services, Mr. Dandridge?"

Clarence knew perfectly well what they were. And although he was certain that Caroline would have liked the story, he deferred to the Marquis's sensibilities and said blandly, "It may have had something to do with his brilliant performance at the battle of Fontarabie in 1719."

The truth, naturally, lay elsewhere. The first Marquis was indeed a brave soldier, but he owed his Louisiana plantation not to his sword but to his wife's amorous exploits. This lady had often shared the king's bed and must have put in a good word for her compliant husband. When he learned that he was a widower in 1740, he expressed his gratitude to his late wife by naming the plantation after the small castle in the Bois de Boulogne where the king conducted his amours. And now that he was a free man, he immediately married the daughter of a neighboring planter who had borne him a son three years earlier—which regularized a situation that might have become embarrassing. Everybody at Pointe-Coupée chose to overlook the fact that the second Marquis, Marc-Adrien, was born well before term—to say the least.

There was a skeptical grumble from the Marquis, then, shifting in his chair, he said: "Go on, Clarence, get on with your story."

"As time went on, some families—like the Damvilliers, the Ternants and the Audubons—made small fortunes from indigo, later cotton and occasionally rice. But many more settlers died, leaving their children a miserable shanty and a patch of earth good for little but Indian wheat.

"All those gray-shingle houses you see by the side of the road belong to the descendants of those first settlers. For all that they lived meager lives, few took advantage of Napoleon's invitation to return to France when he sold Louisiana to the United States for that famous twelve million dollars. And so, three thousand miles from their native land and its grasping despot, the French became partners in the young democracy."

Clarence paused and peered into the dark to see if he still had his audience's attention. Caroline was inexhaustible: "Do you really think Louisiana will stay French, Mr. Dandridge?"

"Louisiana has become American in its political institutions, but I think it's safe to say that it will always keep its French ways. Even the Americans—and the occasional English who settle here for business reasons—gradually take on French ways."

"Is this a good thing?" Caroline asked.

Clarence hesitated for a moment.

"Look, the American nation is young. It will soon be powerful. Its democracy is being constantly strengthened by the waves of immigrants who come here to exploit its riches. But a country is like a tree. In order to grow and to be able to withstand the buffeting of the wind, it needs roots that go deep into the soil—or into the past. In the North, they have British, Irish, Dutch roots; in the South, French and Spanish. A century from now, the new buds will have both the distinct and the mixed characteristics of the original plants—the same way you find traces of forgotten ancestors in young children. But the day is coming when there'll be a true American character."

"What do you think will hold this mixture of races and nationalities together? Interest or love?"

"Faith, Miss Caroline. Perhaps not the faith that moves mountains, but the faith that binds men together."

"Well spoken, Dandridge," came from a gruff, somewhat sleepy voice. "But I think that's enough for one night. At the rate you're instructing my goddaughter, you'll be turning her into a Northern bluestocking. We can't have that, Dandridge!" Adrien let out a small snort, rose to his feet and ushered Caroline into the house. Clarence headed for his own lodgings, where the yapping of his Dalmatians announced his arrival.

As the days grew hotter, Caroline spent the afternoons in her godfather's study. It was not only the coolest room in the house, but she had also been pleasantly surprised by the variety and quality of the books on its shelves. Her most exciting find was a collection of harpsichord music. Was there perhaps a harpsichord hidden away in one of Bagatelle's crannies? She asked Mamma Netta but the old cook couldn't remember. So she and Mignette started on a minute exploration of cellar, attic, closets, any space large enough to conceal the instrument. At last their efforts bore fruit. They found it in a corner of a storage room completely covered with layers of old sheets and blankets. Tense with excitement, Caroline gently removed its swaddling clothes and there, to her joy, was a magnificent instrument in the French style, with baroque legs, a scrollwork rail, the underside of the cover beautifully painted with a scene from the legend of Orpheus, as was the sounding board with a garland of flowers. And all of it in perfect condition.

Caroline knew enough about harpsichords to recognize that this one had a particularly wide keyboard—about sixty notes. As she ran her fingers over the two keyboards, she made a face. The instrument might be in splendid condition, but it was in dire need of tuning.

"Where on earth am I going to find a harpsichord tuner?" Caroline exclaimed. Remembering that her mistress had mentioned a piano when she told her about the barbecue at The Myrtles, Mignette said, "People who own pianos are bound to know, Miss Caroline."

"Of course, Mignette. Let's get the buggy hitched and ride over to The Myrtles. Corinne Templeton is sure to know."

Corinne did indeed. The local tuner was the organist at Natchez. She would get word to him to stop off at Bagatelle on his next rounds. While Mignette helped Mrs. Templeton prepare tea, Corinne and Caroline took a brief walk in the park.

"My brother Willy will be very sad to have missed your visit. You've made a big impression on him, you know. He's asked me so many questions about you," Corinne confided breathlessly. "He wants to know if you're going to stay at Bagatelle or if you intend to return to Paris."

Caroline pondered what she would say. Even though she had made up her mind to remain at her godfather's, it might not be a bad idea to keep Willy guessing. It would make him all the more eager.

"Corinne, I don't know what I'm going to do. I'm an orphan, and I've had no indication that my godfather wishes me to stay with him. On the other hand, my aunt wants me back in Paris, and the city does have its charms."

"But couldn't you be happy in Louisiana? Everybody here

loves you. And I'm so happy to have a new friend who knows so much."

Placing her hand on Corinne's arm, her eyes half closed, Caroline murmured, "How can there be happiness for an orphan without money? It's embarrassing to be under obligation to a generous man like my godfather. He's already done so much for my family."

"Oh, Caroline, please don't talk that way! There's nothing to stop you from being happy among us. And Mr. Dandridge has told me confidentially that the Marquis is delighted to have you in his house."

"Did Mr. Dandridge really say that?"

"Yes, and many more nice things about you. I hope I'm not being indiscreet, but I want you to know how much people love you."

"Thank you, Corinne," Caroline said, her voice heavy with feeling. "Thank you! You do me so much good!" And she kissed Corinne, who blushed with pride at the success of her good deed. Then, guessing at what her new friend most wanted to hear, Caroline said in a confidential tone, "Mr. Dandridge has a very high regard for your family and speaks of you with special warmth. He says you're much the most accomplished of all the girls he knows . . ."

"Did he really?" Corinne said, unable to hide her lively interest in these observations. "What else has he said, Caroline?"

"He told me"—this was pure invention now—"that you are very beautiful, and that you're not at all like the rest of the giddy girls who think only about clothes and flirting. But, you see, Mr. Dandridge is very shy and he wouldn't like it if he knew I'd told you these things. Men are like that. Their pride makes them dissemble the way they feel until they can't hide it any longer."

"Oh, Caroline, thank you. You are my true friend. Even though we've known each other such a short time, you knew how anxious I was to know . . . that I'm not . . . that he doesn't find me displeasing."

"He certainly doesn't find you displeasing, Corinne. You

may be sure of that. But you must act as if I hadn't told you anything. Men don't understand women's ways . . . our little plots."

"I know!" Corinne said gaily. "We'll plot together. You'll teach me the waltz and how to dress, and you and I will play music together."

"My dear, dear Corinne," Caroline said, trying to calm the girl's exaltation, which, later on, when the time was ripe, she would turn to her own advantage. "You do make me want to stay in Louisiana."

"Oh, do please stay. I already love you like a sister."

It was her turn to embrace Caroline, then she took her arm and led her back to the house where her mother and Mignette were becoming impatient.

That evening, Corinne took Willy for a turn in the park. He had spent the day at the new sugar refinery his brother Percy had just built. She told him all about Caroline's visit, how understanding she was, how mature, and encouraged him to court the delightful girl who, being an orphan, was in such desperate need of true affection. The occasion would come soon, if he cared to accompany her to Bagatelle where she had been invited. That, as Dr. Murphy would have said, was like asking a patient if he wanted to be cured.

Then, one morning, the cotton was in bloom.

A slave came running in with the news while the household was at breakfast. He stood breathless at the door of the house, twisting an old hat with a ragged brim, a broad smile on his face.

"Masta, the flowers has come! . . ."

Adrien de Damvilliers walked up to the slave with the expression of a man who has just been told that his wife has borne him a son, and thumped the slave on the back by way of appreciation.

So, once again, as it had for so many years, the white gold was about to shower its wealth on Bagatelle. What greater proof of the divine benediction?

The Marquis summoned Mamma Netta and asked her to give the messenger a large cake and a jar of maple syrup to take to his family. To these he added a gold piece, thus carrying on a tradition begun by his grandfather. Every spring, the first slave to bring the news that the cotton was in bloom received a gift. Only heads of families could compete. This spring's champion was named Telemaque. He had been born on the plantation and his wife had given him ten children. He sang the Gloria admirably at Sunday Mass, and worked hard.

Adrien and Clarence immediately jumped on their horses and rode off to the fields. Caroline and Mignette were invited to follow in the gig. The men set off at a gallop and waited by the edge of the field for the girls. The four contemplated in silence the vast sea of green now dotted with white, yellow and pink buds. Hour by hour, thousands of buds would open, and in less than two days, the fields would be an ephemeral ocean of bloom representing the prodigious smile of nature responding to man's will. It was the earth's way of telling men that once again she was ready to share her bounty.

Adrien moved down between the rows, the blacks greeting him with respect—and also grateful for a moment's respite from work. Then, with great care, Adrien picked two flowers and presented one to Caroline, the other to Mignette.

"The first cotton bloom brings good luck for the rest of the year," he said with a stiff little bow to each.

The two girls returned to the house while Dandridge and the Marquis stayed on to consult with the overseers. The head man was a red-faced German, a corncob pipe stuck permanently between his teeth. The slaves feared him because, although he didn't carry a whip—as did most overseers on the other plantations—he could give a kick in the rear that left a mark for a week. The Marquis was pleased to note that there wasn't a weed in sight, an indispensable ingredient to a good harvest. From now on, every inch of soil would have to be watched for any sign of predators. Adrien discussed the necessary precautions with the overseers, then left with Dandridge to see how the indigo was faring.

As Adrien and Dandridge rode back to the house, the Marquis told his manager of Caroline's decision to stay at Bagatelle.

"I think it's a good thing, Dandridge. I was afraid she'd find us boring. We're not a very lively pair, you and I, but I'm happy to see that she doesn't think so. She has made friends, she's invited everywhere, and I've noticed that several young men are paying her court. What I'd like to do is give a barbecue to pay back all our friends who've been so kind to her. Do you think she'd like that, Dandridge?"

"By all means, if you don't think it's too soon after your wife's death."

The Marquis was a little taken aback.

"To tell you the truth, Dandridge, I'd forgotten all about it. You and I have always been honest with each other. Sometimes I think of you as the brother I didn't have, sometimes as my best friend. What a brother might not be able to admit, a friend can. To you I can confess that I very seldom think about my poor wife. Sad to say, Dandridge, Dorothée barely touched my life. She left me with fewer memories than a good cotton harvest."

Clarence was touched by the Marquis's confession, but a stubborn sense of decorum forced him to say, "Of course, your wife was away so much that, if I may say so, we became used to not seeing her."

"True, but even when she was at Bagatelle, it was as if she weren't really here. All it took was Caroline's putting back the old furniture to wipe out five years of a life that was barely conjugal." Then he added after a pause, "She was a gentle creature, but the only thing we had in common was our upbringing, which was apparently not enough to make us into a couple." He was silent again, then he blurted out: "I don't give a damn what people say, Dandridge. We're going to give Caroline a barbecue. Bagatelle isn't a cemetery!"

Clarence admired Adrien for his straightforward ways and his ability to come to a decision—qualities he did not share. The Damvilliers's motto "Go beyond" perfectly suited this man of the soil who knew how to take drastic measures when called for and with no thought for hypocritical conventions. Such men were rare in plantation society. They spent most of their time debating what was "done" and "not done," without reference to their own convictions or personal tastes but only out of fear of social opprobrium.

Their conversation brought home to Clarence how important Caroline had become to Bagatelle. No domestic decision was taken without her advice. She planned the menus with Mamma Netta, visited the slaves' hospital, kept an eye on the tradesmen, played hostess to the occasional guest, and tried to spare the Marquis the nagging concerns that were the lot of a man without a wife. As for Mignette, the Marquis had virtually adopted her. He very soon stopped treating her like a servant. As suspicious as a peasant faced with the unknown, he was at first discomfited by Mignette's behavior toward her mistress. But as he began to understand their relationship, he came to realize that in Paris, relations between master and servant must be very different from those in the slave states of the South. And when his goddaughter, with an oratorical flourish, likened Mignette to "a confidante in a Molière play" and asked if she mightn't take her meals at the family table, he immediately agreed. In fact, he asked Mignette to consider herself an "honored guest." Caroline was overjoyed, for she had suffered to see her faithful companion demoted to a status that bore no relation to her merits. It had also lowered her esteem in the eyes of the blacks, who paid great heed to the social hierarchy of the whites.

Dandridge, remembering with a twinge of irony Lord Byron's description of Mrs. Charlemont's rapid elevation from attic to the master's table—and its consequent ill effects on the relationship between the poet and his wife—went out of his way to make Mignette comfortable in her new station. From the start, the girl had been intimidated by the manager's cold gaze; now she felt her natural spontaneity return. Meals at Bagatelle were much livelier as a result.

A few days later, Clarence asked Mignette if she would like to learn to ride. She was thrilled, and from then on, she, Clarence and Caroline were often seen trotting along the riverbank.

The cotton bolls had barely attained the size of a large nut when the news reached Bagatelle that yellow fever had broken out in New Orleans. Each year the humid heat of a summer brought back the dread disease, which played havoc, especially in the South's larger cities. When, toward the end of June, the first deaths were announced in the newspapers, the wealthier citizens abandoned their city houses for the healthier climate of the plantations.

Caroline, with her usual aplomb, had forbidden Mignette to mention the disease, so the poor girl spent hours discussing the latest news with little Rosa. To keep her mind off the fearsome topic, Mignette helped her mistress prepare the wool for a tapestry she had just begun. She had also become a passionate horsewoman and had made great friends with Bobo, who added his groom's lore to Dandridge's lessons in horsemanship. Now the two rode togther to Sainte-Marie when a horse needed shoeing. That is how Mignette came to know the burly Alsatian blacksmith who was to play such an important role in her life.

There was only one death in the slaves' quarters. After a week of high fever, a very old woman died as discreetly as she had lived. Dr. Murphy promptly declared that she had died of old age. But the slaves knew better. She was the first victim of "dengue," the name they gave yellow fever, and their superstitious practices reappeared.

The day after the funeral, the rain came and lasted for a week. It fell in buckets, sometimes with the violence of a hurricane. It shattered the leaves, flattened the azaleas and rhododendrons, smashed the magnolia and tulip-tree blossoms, and turned the paths into quagmires. One evening, as Dandridge and the Marquis were taking off their muddy boots under the gallery, the sound of music reached them from the small sitting room.

"Good God, it's my mother's harpsichord," Adrien blurted. "I haven't heard it for twenty years. Do you believe in ghosts, Dandridge?"

"No, Adrien, I don't believe in ghosts. But I do believe in the talents and . . . intelligence of your goddaughter."

"Let's go see," the Marquis said, and quickly put on the shoes James was handing him.

Caroline had sat down at the harpsichord when she heard the horses' hooves in the driveway. The tuner had done his work well: The tone was mellow and true. She had never played an instrument of this quality. Because the house was built of wood, the notes reverberated with particular brilliance, the phrases taking on an almost sensual smoothness. She started with a gigue from Rameau's "New Suites for Harpsichord." Over a century old, the music was still as fresh as the play of fountains at Versailles when it was composed. Adrien and Dandridge waited in the doorway before making their presence known. Caroline, who knew perfectly well they were there, played with elegance, making the medium and high registers scintillate, bringing forth solemn warblings and cascading triplets with equal virtuosity. Occasionally, the folds of her gold silk dress moved imperceptibly as she worked the pedal. Swaying over the keyboards, she looked like a dreaming sylph singing with a supernatural voice.

When she had finished, the Marquis cried out: "Bravo! Bravo!" and rushed up to the girl, who turned to him with an expression of confused surprise.

"I haven't felt such joy in a long time. You are a magician, my girl. Let me embrace you."

More used to petting horses than women, Adrien gave her a bear hug and three big smacks on the cheek, peasant-style, and crushed her breast to his hard chest. Over her godfather's shoulder, Caroline caught sight of Clarence, who was still standing in the doorway, his hands behind his back, surveying the scene without visible emotion. She read a vague look of contentment in his eyes, those of a gambler who suspects he's about to win a bet.

The Marquis, absorbed by this new happiness, was asking Caroline where she had found the harpsichord, how she had had it tuned. While he listened to her modest recital, his rough hands caressed the sides of the instrument as if to bring back lost sensations.

"Caroline, play the second rigadoon, the one in the major key that goes. . . . How does it go? . . . Ah, yes! Tra la la la, you are the one I love. . . . Tra la la la, I'll love you always. . . . It was my mother's favorite. Do you think you can find it?"

"I know it by heart, Uncle Adrien."

And she launched into the lively and wry musical dialogue that evoked the happy pursuit of a shepherd after his shepherdess in a Watteau painting.

"Play it again," the Marquis said as soon as the last note died away.

When she had finished the second time, Dandridge noticed a tear run down the Marquis's cheek. It was the first tear he had ever seen on his employer's face. His wife's death had produced only a sigh of resignation.

From that day on, the sound of the harpsichord could be heard at all hours of the day and night, coinciding with the end of the yellow fever epidemic and the explosion of the first cotton bolls in their fields. The harvest was in full swing and looked to be a good one. When the weather was fair, the slaves spent their long days stuffing the silky flakes into bales. When it rained, they—less willingly—plucked the wet leaves off the down to ward off the dreaded rust. From daybreak to sundown, every man, woman and child on the plantation lived for the harvest, and the roads along the riverbank saw a constant shuttling back and forth of wagons carrying baskets of the white gold from Bagatelle to the cotton gins.

The Marquis was in perpetual motion, as if he thought he

could speed up the picking by his own frenetic pace. He spent his days in the fields, watching over the slaves, excoriating them when a puff of fibers was plucked prematurely, making them pick up any fibers that fell from their baskets, swearing at the sun when it failed to dry the wet plants, constantly demanding a reckoning and bullying the overseers. Then he'd gallop over to the cotton gin, pick up a fistful of seeds and berate the slaves for leaving too much lint on the seeds.

One day, Caroline asked to be taken on a trip to the cotton gins. If her money was to be invested in gins, she wanted to see how they worked. With Dandridge as her guide, she watched, fascinated, as the cylinders, some with small saws, others with brushes, passed back and forth over the seeds, the first plucking the fibers, the second brushing them off the saw teeth. Her uncle had several machines and added to his—and her—profits by renting them out to other planters once his own harvest was processed.

When Caroline reported her visit to the cotton gins to Corinne Templeton, her new friend was amazed at the idea that a woman should be interested in such things—a subject discussed only among men. The friendship between the two girls was now solidly established. No week went by without one visiting the other. Warned ahead of time by his sister, Willy was always present when Caroline came to The Myrtles, and often accompanied his sister to Bagatelle. They played music, drank tea, giggled and chatted.

Willy persevered in his courtship, unaware that behind Caroline's prattle lurked a steely mind that never let the conversation range beyond the most harmless topics. They would discuss other friends' love affairs, heroes in novels, the famous passions of ladies and their cavaliers in olden times. Willy took these as reasons to nourish his hopes; Caroline used them as a subterfuge to keep him at arm's length without discouraging him. In point of fact, she was beginning to find Willy a very dull young man.

Percy was something else again. A womanizer of long standing, Willy's older brother had divined the passionate nature behind Caroline's controlled facade. He concluded that she was more well-bred than virtuous. Thanks to a chance encounter with Captain Wangler in Natchez, he had learned the reason for the duel on the *Prince du Delta*. He also knew the manner in which the prim Caroline had kissed Ed Barthew. She had simply behaved like a female, and this led him to the conclusion that the Marquis's goddaughter needed only a match to set her aflame. On two occasions, in his brother's absence, he had escorted her partway home, and his instinct told him that he had only to wait for the propitious moment to bring things to a head. He wouldn't have dared admit that this woman, who was by turns arrogant, clever at small talk, and capable of putting you in your place with a look, was far more intimidating than all the women he had seduced. A Don Juan excited by resistance and at the mercy of his animal impulses—those of his heart were seldom involved—Percy decided to play a waiting game. One evening, when he had been helping Caroline into her gig, he ventured to hold onto her hand. She promptly withdrew it with a small click of the tongue that signified: "Come now, Mr. Templeton, this isn't done!"

Percy reflected that a truly innocent girl would have pretended not to notice. The small rebuff was proof that Caroline knew how to handle men's desires. This fired him all the more but he saw that he would have to be circumspect.

True to his word, Abraham Mosely arrived at Bagatelle as the cotton harvest was coming to an end. He had just finished a several months' tour in the North and Canada to buy skins for the Hudson Bay Company. He made no attempt to hide his relief at being back in "civilization." Bagatelle, its vegetation rampant in the slanting light of summer's end, offered the delights of the good life. Mamma Netta's refined cooking and the cozy comfort of a well-run house made for all the elements of perfect hospitality.

"Goodness, Mosely!" the Marquis remarked as he welcomed his friend, "you don't look at all well. We'll have to do something about that!"

"If you'd been eating salt cod and dried venison and dried

beans and sleeping in a log cabin with evil-smelling men for two months, you wouldn't look well either."

Mosely wasn't indifferent to Caroline's charms nor to her lively mind and her talents as mistress of the house, but Mamma Netta's cuisine was even more to his liking. "A woman's beauty," he once said, "cannot be eaten for breakfast." In a matter of days, he was his old pink self and his waistcoat had regained its former fullness. One evening he regaled the company at dinner with his recent business trip to New York.

"You cannot imagine what a filthy city it is! They speak every language under the sun but they bargain in an English no Englishman can understand. The place is filled with garbage, which is fine for roaming pigs and dogs—and that may be the way the city figures to keep its streets clean. The moment it rains, you wade around in a sea of mud and it's worth your life to cross Broadway with all the landaus, coupes, phaetons and even buses that barrel up and down at wild speeds. The women look vulgar in their garish colors and ostrich plumes. The men wear brass buttons on their frock coats like coachmen. And the best houses serve dried beans and mashed squash, and tell you it's better than Lucullus! The only thing worth eating is the clam chowder—even though it's served in chipped plates."

"What a picture you paint! Is that what they call progress, my dear Mosely?" the Marquis said to needle the Englishman.

"Progress! Do you know that at the Astor Hotel I saw men blow their noses with their fingers and spit out their tobacco juice wherever they liked, just like Welsh miners? They gargle the water in their finger bowls, wave their napkins around as if they were flags, talk at the top of their voices, gulp down their food as if it were their last meal, and drink out of their soup plates. They seldom wash and they go to the theater in their shirt sleeves. Hah, what a splendid civilization they're preparing for us! Do you realize that the wage earners are in a revolutionary ferment and that the Workers' Party won a third of the vote in New York two years ago? One of their leaders actually told me: 'The rich should be divested of their fortunes just as you'd take a knife or revolver from a thief.' And everywhere you go, slatterns made up like puppets eye your watch chain."

Taking his cue from the Marquis, Dandridge added more fuel to the Englishman's fire.

"But Mosely, aren't the Northerners very enterprising and, I'm told, extremely cordial?"

"It's a false cordiality, Mr. Dandridge. On Wall Street, they think only of fleecing the foreigners. They're all talking nothing but railroads, and since the Baltimore & Ohio went into service, men who haven't the money to buy a railroad tie try to get you to become a shareholder in their companies. If you're to believe them, the railroads will soon become a vast network covering the whole country because that's what commerce and industry want. . . . Marquis, I wonder if I could have some of your old port?" Abraham asked, as if a cordial might blot out the dreadful Yankee world he had evoked.

"And let's not forget," he added, watching the amber liquid flow into his glass, "hypocrisy has an important place in this new society. The orators of the American Society for the Promotion of Temperance couldn't care less about the immoral activities of streetwalkers, but they promise eternal damnation for anyone who drinks a glass of gin."

Leaning toward his host, Mosely became insistent.

"Watch out for those Northerners, Marquis. They're determined to take over the wealth born of other people's work. They're going to submit the aristocracy of the South to the rule of the majority. Which means them. Your way of life exasperates them. They think you're backward tyrants because you buy slaves the way you buy a hat. But you should see the contempt with which they treat freed slaves. In their eyes, liberty is salary enough for the poor buggers, who sleep in the streets and earn their bread doing jobs too menial for whites."

"That's exactly why we're not afraid of the Yankees, Mosely. They don't know how to grow anything. What would become of their weavers without our cotton? What would they eat without our sugarcane and our rice, our beef and pork, our wheat and corn? And what about the factories they're so proud of? How can they produce anything without England's steel and Missouri's lead?"

"Just give them a little more time and they'll be making all kinds of things, Marquis. They know how to manipulate money and make other people work for them. I've been to the textile mills in Massachusetts. At Francis Lowell's mill—he's the man who invented the new power loom—they have over five thousand workers. They've begun mining iron ore in Pennsylvania, and in Boston, a hat-maker earns six dollars a week. The day is coming when America won't be needing Europe's products. The North has already discarded European traditions and manners. They don't think the South is American enough, so the South is going to be forced to fall into step, aided and abetted by the federal government."

"When this happens, if it does happen," the Marquis said solemnly, "we'll put our faith in the Tenth Amendment of the Bill of Rights, which proclaims that in certain areas, state sovereignty remains inviolate and the authority delegated by the states to the federal government has its limits. If no single state can resist the federal government, perhaps a group of states can."

"I know all about Mr. Calhoun's theories," Mosely retorted. "But it's equally possible that one of these days, using the pretext of doing away with slavery, they will resort to force to impose the laws voted by the majority."

"Only financial interests count, Mr. Mosely. Men's ideas, memories, habits, even prejudices differ from state to state. The federal government has to keep this in mind. The Union exists only by mutual consent. It cannot be done by force."

Then, to bring the argument to a close—for the Marquis didn't like to discuss these matters with a foreigner—he said, "Should it ever come to a confrontation, I feel certain that the South will carry the day because we share the same sense of honor."

Abraham Mosely looked dubious.

* * *

All the Englishman's dire forebodings were forgotten in the preparations for the cotton festival.

At Bagatelle, the Marquis had harvested fourteen hundred bales of top quality cotton—white, silky and without a trace of rust. Mosely, without further discussion and even before the cotton was ginned, bought the entire crop at his host's price, which would bring the Marquis a profit of $75 a bale weighing 478 pounds. In other words, the Marquis would be richer by $100,000. Without a thought for his goddaughter's sensibilities, he gave her a present of $5,000 as a gesture of gratitude for the way she had run his house. She went through the act of protesting, then scolding him. Finally, blushing prettily with lowered lids and insisting that it was she who should feel obligated to him for all his many kindnesses to a poor orphan girl, she accepted the gift. When she added the profits from her own cotton gins, she would end the year with over $25,000 of her own.

At all the plantations, the cotton festival represented summer's apotheosis. Caroline had been put in charge of Bagatelle's preparations and was determined that theirs be sumptuous.

First, the date had to be set. To avoid any conflict with neighboring plantations, the ladies of the parish met every year to set up a calendar. This year's gathering was at Mrs. Templeton's. As the ladies met around the tea table, Caroline did her best to fill the role of Bagatelle's mistress. There was general rejoicing that the Marquis's goddaughter had seen fit to resume a tradition neglected by the late Marquise. Everyone was impressed with the girl's air of authority, which she carefully tempered with deference and humility. Playing on her lack of experience, she even managed to garner the best date—the one winding up the series of parties. This would permit her, she told the ladies, to gain some much-needed experience by observing how the others were done.

Since the Damvilliers's house was not very large, Caroline had the idea of erecting a platform at the end of the alley of oaks where the dancing would take place in the light of lanterns hanging from the branches. She engaged the best orchestra from Natchez, and assigned a dozen slaves to help Mamma Netta in the kitchen. Two overseers were dispatched to New Orleans to buy the wine, champagne, whiskey and candles. The paths were spruced up, the lawns watered and mowed, the entrance to the house freshly painted. Carpenters made benches and long tables which, for lack of large enough tablecloths, would be covered with sheets. Caroline was very careful in choosing the slaves who would wait on table, and had three tailors in the slaves' quarters make up crisp white uniforms. Mignette was assigned the task of training the slaves. Everyone who performed well would be given a dollar the day after the party. This innovation was greeted with enthusiasm, and all the blacks worked with renewed zeal. Caroline also thought up the idea of making two hundred boutonnières out of the last cotton blooms, to be presented to the male guests as they arrived. As he viewed these preparations, the Marquis was thrilled at the prospect that Bagatelle would once again be the scene of a lavish entertainment.

When Caroline asked him to check the guest list, he found nothing amiss except for the inclusion of a certain Mr. Edward Barthew. Who was this man?

"He's Dr. Murphy's closest friend," Caroline said. "I met him on the *Prince du Delta* as I was coming here. He was extremely kind to me."

"Splendid," the Marquis replied. "I look forward to making his acquaintance."

To escape the frenetic activity at Bagatelle, and because the plantation's harvest was insufficient for his needs, Mosely, accompanied by Dandridge, made a tour of the neighboring plantations. As he should have known, little cotton was still available: what hadn't been spoken for by brokers was owed the banks in payment for loans. This prompted the Englishman to launch another tirade against Southern fecklessness, to which Clarence lent only half an ear. He had heard it all before and besides, it had been a long day.

They were riding along a dusty path bordered by bare cypresses. On their left, vast cotton fields spread out, now abandoned and brown under the hot sun. To their right, the Mississippi flowed between obsequious willows, their branches caressing the river as it flowed by. On the opposite shore, through copses of nettle and sassafras trees, the whitewashed huts of a slave village looked stricken by the heat. In a nearby field, a herd of cows huddled under the shadow of an oak, their tails flailing the insects on their dirty flanks. After the effort and sweat of the harvest, nature seemed to have given up. Birds flew more slowly, and in the stagnant light of afternoon, the landscape seemed trapped in a kind of vegetal apathy—like a scenic wallpaper hung on the transparent air. Everything hummed with indolence and irresolution. Summer was almost over.

While Mosely's horse stopped to nibble a tuft of grass, Dandridge led his under the shade of a tree and took off his panama to cool his forehead. His hands folded on the pommel of his saddle, he addressed himself to Mosely's diatribe.

"You see, Mosely, we're like this country. These large spaces we inhabit, inhabit us in turn. Our point of reference is this endless landscape. As with wild animals, we need our own territory in order to live, where we can hunt, gallop, feel the wind in our faces, give vent to sudden feelings of exaltation that insulate us from our tendency toward melancholy. We can never be happy in the man-made world of factories and offices, and the artificial life they entail."

Abraham Mosely mopped his neck with his handkerchief. "You Southerners aren't made like most people."

"We belong to a very old race, Mosely, and we still listen to what nature has to tell us. We are rooted to our soil like these oaks. Because we seem passive and reflective, the Northerners think we're lazy. Because we spend our money on aimless pleasures, they think we're frivolous. Because we believe we're an aristocracy independent of Mammon, they despise us. This place," Clarence made a sweeping movement with his arm, "is one of the happiest in the world, and in another century, the people of the Union will be grateful to us for preserving it."

"Maybe you're right, Dandridge, maybe you're right. But a lot of people in the North—the politicians, the Quaker bankers, the churchmen, the journalists—think of you as either sinners, idiots or despots, depending on the case. And they intend to reform you, perhaps even to punish you!"

"What a fine bunch of missionaries," Dandridge said with a sneer. "They take us for Seminoles," and he dug his spurs into his horse's flank.

Their conversation was interrupted by the sound of galloping hooves. The two men turned in their saddles and saw Caroline and Mignette bearing down on them in a cloud of yellow dust. Both men took off their hats.

"Bravo, Mignette," Dandridge called out. "You're becoming a first-class horsewoman."

The girl thanked him with a smile as she straightened her riding hat. The furious pace that Caroline had set had brought fire to Mignette's cheeks. Mosely's gaze took in the small heaving breasts under the tight riding jacket. Next to her, Caroline looked like a dignified "grande dame." Not a hair was out of place under the severe tricorn, there was not a wrinkle in the somewhat masculine jabot tucked into the black velvet jacket and her gray kid gloves looked bandbox-new. Sitting erect in her saddle, her eyes cool and steady, her color unchanged by the exertion, the Marquis's god-daughter had what Mosely would call class.

"What a beautiful day," Dandridge said. "We won't be having many more like it."

"A little hot for my taste," Mosely countered, fanning himself with his hat. Caroline looked at him askance.

"Really, Mr. Mosely? You don't like the heat? I think the temperature today is ideal!"

Dandridge, who had learned to interpret her every intonation, translated this to mean: "Only vulgar people perspire."

The group headed back to the plantation in the hope of

arriving in time for tea. Mignette and Mosely rode in front, while Dandridge curbed in his horse to keep pace with Caroline's.

"Everything is ready for Sunday's party, Mr. Dandridge. But I've just had a terrible thought. What if it rains? The house can't hold all the guests!"

"When the Negroes want to make sure of the weather's cooperation—for a marriage or some other ceremony—they bury a gold piece at the moment the sun sets on the eve of the event."

"Superstition!" Caroline said scornfully.

"Of course. But our slaves believe that gold is a component of the sun. They hold that the sun is attracted by the gold which some greedy god stole from it. By burying the gold piece at the moment the sun is about to disappear, you catch its attention and it will return the following day to reclaim it."

"It's a charming legend, Mr. Dandridge, but I have my doubts about its efficacy."

"As always, Miss Caroline, it's a question of faith. If you accept the fact that faith can move mountains, you can equally believe that a ten-dollar gold piece will make the sun shine."

"I have faith in . . . in my luck, Mr. Dandridge," the girl replied rather sharply. As she turned toward Clarence, there was a look of peculiar intensity in her eyes.

"I too have faith in your luck," Clarence said with an odd smile. "But my faith is based on the way you have of pressing your luck."

Caroline didn't find the remark impertinent. It was a statement of fact. Just then, Dandridge's horse sidled up to Caroline's and the two riders' thighs almost touched. She looked straight at Clarence.

"Mr. Dandridge, will you stop calling me Miss Caroline? Can't you simply call me Caroline?"

Clarence was a little taken aback. It was flattering, of course, but it could raise problems of protocol. However, to refuse her would have been rude, so he acquiesced.

"Thank you, Clarence," the girl said, taking immediate advantage of the right she had just given. "I think our tastes and aspirations are sufficiently alike so that we should be real friends."

"Of course you may count on my . . . respectful affection."

"You make me very happy, Clarence. I know I behaved very stupidly on the *Prince du Delta*, but I think you understood that it was a passing moment of foolish pride. Your discretion proved it to me."

Had these solemn words been aimed at Willy Templeton, he would have been plunged into a transport of joy. Clarence Dandridge, however, accepted them all as an expression of simple gratitude and, with unaccustomed spontaneity, held out his hand to Caroline. She touched it lightly, and as he so often did when he was at a loss for words, he resorted to a suitable quotation: " 'The virtue of a young woman who has momentarily forgotten herself is more difficult to conquer than the virtue of a woman who has never been seduced.' . . . A Chinese proverb, I believe." He smiled sheepishly.

At last Caroline felt certain she had overcome the only resistance she had encountered at Bagatelle.

As the path narrowed, the two riders had to go single file. Riding behind, Clarence kept his eyes on the slender figure in front of him. What is that girl's real ambition? he wondered. Whatever the means she uses, it will be very interesting to watch her ascent. Even if she resorted to ruse or treachery, he would support her as far as his honor permitted, for she was undeniably the ideal mistress for Bagatelle—especially if the storm clouds Mosely predicted threatened the South.

Of all the cotton festivals held at the various plantations, Bagatelle's was by far the most successful—although an unforeseen incident came near to ruining it. Without Ed Barthew's cool head, it could have turned into a tragedy. The sun had set and the couples were dancing in the light of the lanterns when a slave in charge of replacing the burned-out candles accidentally set a tree on fire. It immediately became a flaming torch. The girls fled, screaming, while the men stood rooted, not knowing what to do.

"Bring me a horse . . . and a lasso!" Ed Barthew shouted, peeling off his frock coat.

Bobo, who was helping at the buffet table, ran to the stables. Dandridge immediately grasped what Barthew had in mind. Hurling his coat at Corinne, who stood by petrified, he grabbed the rope from Bobo's hands and as Barthew leaped on the horse, he looped one end around the trunk of the tree and threw the other directly into Barthew's hands. Then he snatched a cane from an old man, who almost collapsed with the loss of his support, and whacked the horse's flank. The horse neighed, reared back, and spurred on by Barthew, galloped at full speed through the oaks toward the river. To the sound of breaking branches and with a great shower of sparks, the burning tree finally yielded. As slaves, egged on by the Marquis, brought pails of water, Barthew could be seen in the distance, up to his waist in water, the flaming tree in his wake. The next moment the fire was extinguished. When Ed returned, drenched from the waist down, his horse's eyes starting out of their sockets, the crowd broke into a roar of applause.

"Come change your clothes at my house," Dandridge called out. Barthew had a bad rope burn on his hand from the lasso. Dandridge applied some ointment and made a passable bandage. "I think that will hold," he said.

"Well done, Dandridge. A shot of gin will do the rest. I have to admit I was scared. With all those girls in lace dresses, I saw myself pleading some tragic cases."

"Don't forget that you specialize in fires!" Dandridge said with a laugh.

"I specialize in fires that yield me something, not in accidental fires . . ."

Barthew knew only too well that insurance companies often refused—with good reason—to honor their contracts when, as frequently happened, traders maintained they'd lost everything, including their account books, in disasters that had a way of occurring at the end of the season. By the time the volunteer firemen had stirred from their beds, everything had gone up in smoke. The victims claimed there was no way of establishing the extent of the loss. That was when Ed Barthew came on the scene, finding witnesses and interested parties. He usually won his cases, whence his reputation as a clever lawyer with the victims, and that of a scoundrel with the insurers, who were less easily fooled than the parish judges.

Dandridge wasn't fooled either, but such was his affection for Ed that he accepted the often questionable verdicts when they went against the big Yankee insurance companies. As Barthew liked to say: "My client's word is every bit as good as that of the insurance company, which accepted the risks when they pocketed the premiums."

Although Dandridge was a scrupulously honest man, he delighted in Barthew's cynicism. In contrast to those who went to church and hid behind the appearance of virtue the better to fleece their fellow man, Barthew made his accommodations and profited from human frailties with a clear conscience. He knew that the big crooks couldn't be touched, and that by laying it on the little man, a greedy society was able to salve its conscience.

Were they generally known, the views shared by Bagatelle's manager and the ethically unconventional lawyer would have raised a number of eyebrows. But Dandridge knew exactly how far Barthew would go.

"I haven't seen the beautiful Caroline yet," Barthew said as they walked back to the party. "I trust her hair has grown back."

Dandridge was tempted to tell him how the Marquis's goddaughter had fooled everyone. But he held his tongue. When Caroline regaled him with the tale on their initial ride from Pointe-Coupée to Bagatelle—"Come, Mr. Dandridge, do you think a person of quality would spoil her coiffure for a stranger!"—Clarence had been censorious. But with the passage of time and her exemplary conduct since her arrival at the plantation, he had put it down to yet another example of women's cunning ways. Happily, the silly game had turned out well for everyone concerned, and poor Willy Templeton, still wearing the locket containing the lady's maid's hair—an uncommon lady's maid to be sure—was more to be pitied than Barthew.

"I wonder why she invited me, Dandridge. The Marquis would never have done it."

"She's a clever filly, Barthew. She's much more of a person than she appeared to be on the *Prince du Delta*. It's my guess that she'll make a rich marriage before the year is out."

"With the little soldier?"

"That would surprise me. She belongs to the soil and I think she'd prefer a real planter."

"May it do her good, my friend," Barthew said. "But between you and me, I prefer her companion. She has eyes and a mouth that promise much."

A while later, as the lawyer and Dr. Murphy, both a little the worse for wear, were comparing the relative merits of whiskey and gin, Caroline appeared on Willy Templeton's arm. In honor of the event, the young lieutenant was wearing his dress uniform—blue tunic, gray trousers, gilt epaulets, and a sword belt with a large buckle.

"Mr. Barthew," Caroline said, "I'm sorry I missed your heroic exploit. It all happened so fast . . ."

"It's well that it did," Barthew said with a small bow. "You might have lost another ringlet."

Caroline appeared to miss the allusion and went on, "I wanted Willy himself to tell you that the wound you inflicted on him is completely healed. Healed and forgotten. Isn't that true, Willy?"

The young officer with the pink cheeks and the carriage of a soldier on parade held out his hand to the lawyer. Barthew held out his bandaged hand.

"Be gentle, lieutenant. I'm the wounded man now."

"My goodness, are you badly burned, Mr. Barthew?"

"It's nothing, Miss Caroline," Dr. Murphy broke in. "The

lasso was hard on his tender skin. A rope is dangerous only when it's around your neck. Isn't that so, Barthew?"

Turning to young Templeton, Barthew said a little thickly: "Brave defender of the Union, do join us in a drink! Where will you be serving?"

"In the 15th Kentucky artillery. They say it's a fine regiment, sir."

Dr. Murphy put in: "To be a military man when there's no war in sight would seem to be the best possible employment for a young man of good family."

Murphy had taken care of Willy's measles along with a dozen childhood illnesses which justified his easy familiarity.

"Si vis pacem, para bellum . . ." Ed murmured as he refilled the glasses.

"What do you think of that girl, Murphy?" Barthew asked as the young couple moved away.

"Lots of good things, my friend," the doctor replied. "She visits the slaves' infirmary almost every day. She often asks to come with me on my rounds. She has a warm heart. Believe me, she's a real Southern woman."

"What do you mean by that?"

"I mean that she can lead a man by the nose without his even knowing it. I'd keep my distance, believe me."

"Keep one's distance?" Ed repeated. "I think I agree with you, doc."

Munching on pecan cookies, the two men turned to watch the ball. In the light of the lanterns, the spectacle had undeniable charm. A ball was the only occasion where the young could decently exhibit their bodies and indulge in sensual movement. The girls in their pastel gowns danced with their heads thrown back, as heedless as newborn babes. The young men, slim and elegant in their tight frock coats, executed the steps of the quadrille with practiced precision. Necklaces and bracelets sparkled in the soft light, and there were bursts of laughter from the groups gathered around the edge of the platform. Further back, in the shadows of the oaks, other couples strolled, exchanging confidences. The Marquis was in his element as he wandered from guest to guest, making sure everyone was happy, his hand running through his mop of hair grown even more intractable in the humidity.

He had danced the first dance with his goddaughter so that everyone would know she was the evening's heroine. To anyone who would listen, Mosely said: "This night marks the South's apotheosis." Percy Templeton had come alone—his wife was expecting a baby—and frequently stole Caroline from Willy with the authority of an older brother. Emboldened by the champagne, he straightway entered the lists, showering her with compliments that few proper cavaliers would have dared pronounce. The way he clasped her hand when a step in the quadrille warranted it, or held her elbow as he guided her off the dance floor spoke volumes for the relationship he hoped to establish. She made no attempt to discourage him, enjoying the power she had over this strong male animal. Unlike the romantic young prudes dancing with their self-conscious partners, she laughed, talked back, gave as good as she got, and accepted with nonchalance his ambiguous words and looks. She promised him nothing, but it crossed her mind that this Templeton with the racy reputation and arrogant bearing who ogled her décolletage and ran his eyes over her body would undoubtedly make a splendid lover.

"Did you know that Willy is joining his regiment next week?" Percy said as they executed a turn.

"Certainly. An officer has to do his duty."

"You'll be coming to The Myrtles less often?"

"Why do you say that, Percy? You know how fond I am of your sister."

"Who will accompany you home when you come to visit Corinne?"

"Good heavens, I can take care of myself! Besides, I have Mignette."

"May I offer my services as an escort?" Percy replied, showing the teeth of an affable ogre.

"We'll see about that," Caroline said, laughing. "If your wife is willing . . ."

Percy raised his eyebrows as if that were a detail of no importance. At that moment, Caroline's hand seemed to grow soft in his. The final gallop in the quadrille was over, and he was left with an equivocal impression. Other partners came to claim her and Percy didn't see her again until it was time to say goodnight.

"It was a wonderful party," he said, as had everyone else. Then he added, looking into her eyes, "Corinne tells me you're coming to The Myrtles in a few days. You must take advantage of the last of the good weather."

"I'll be sure to do so, Percy."

The older Templeton was left with a lively and inadmissible hope.

Corinne was also in raptures. Clarence Dandridge had been a dutiful cavalier and invited her to dance several times. Now he was standing off to one side smoking a cigar. The Marquis joined him.

"What do you say to our going over to the slave quarters, Dandridge. I promised Telemaque I'd stop by the village to see their festival." They were soon joined by Dr. Murphy, Ed Barthew, Mosely and Mignette, who also wanted to see the "Negro dances."

Telemaque welcomed the group warmly and summoned the singers and drummers back to the circle. A strange plaintive music began to fill the air, the dimly lighted white huts forming an exotic background. First the slaves sang the legend of the "lamb-tree," the traditional homage to King Cotton, whose serfs they were. Then they started to dance, beating the earth with their bare feet as a lone drum thrummed under the brittle fingers of an old man with eyes closed, his thoughts perhaps wandering back to his native tribe on the banks of the Senegal. A lively voice poured out a song incomprehensible to the whites. Composed for the occasion, it mixed Creole and Caribbean words and their own dialect.

There was a round of applause at the end of the first stanza, with the Marquis clapping the loudest. A few of the blacks watched the whites' reaction with apprehension, but the group's spontaneous applause reassured them. They could now give free rein to their own enjoyment.

Mignette, realizing she was the only white woman at the black sabbath, hung back between Mosely and Barthew. Telemaque, superb in his red cotton tunic, brandishing a pole crowned with antlers and a sprig of cotton, offered his guests stools to sit on and gourds containing a strange drink made of fermented cane juice mixed with ground pecans. The liquid burned the throat like alcohol. It may also have explained the frenzied movements of the dancers who, eyes glazed, were going into weird contortions as they circled the fire. "Dansé Calinda, boudoubi, boudoubi," the voices rose again, filling the night with African echoes.

Ed Barthew clapped his hands to the rhythm of the drum, Dr. Murphy sipped his drink in silence, while Adrien and Dandridge chatted with the children who were looking bug-eyed at the glittering gold watch chains that looped across the white men's silk waistcoats. Meanwhile, Mosely was explaining to Mignette how these blacks had been shipped from the African coast by British and French slave traders.

"Believe me, they're happier here. The Marquis is a good master. He feeds them and takes care of them. And look how happy they are!"

Mignette agreed, not daring to admit that their raucous expressions of joy gave her a curious feeling of sadness. Rosa had told her a lot about these people, and how they were divided into two very different categories. There were the house slaves—about twenty at Bagatelle, counting Mamma Netta, James, the chambermaids, the waitresses, the laundress, the seamstress, the gardeners and stable boys. Then there were the slaves who worked in the fields. The first group were like members of the family and lacked for nothing. Their flights of fancy and their laziness were tolerated, their advice was sought, their naive sayings were repeated, they were addressed by name. The others were confined to the village. Those now dancing before their master made up the anonymous crowd of field hands—those who lifted and carried, hoed and pushed wagons, and the masons, carpenters and joiners. Theirs was the hard work, supervised by overseers, and they envied and often hated their brothers who worked in the big house.

How can these simple people be truly happy? Mignette wondered. They live with the permanent threat of separation, their families scattered to the four winds. The only happiness they have is working together until they die.

Ed Barthew noticed the girl's distress.

"What do you think of this fine festival, Mignette? Isn't it much more interesting than the other one?"

"I'm not sure," she replied, moving her knee away from the lawyer's. "I wonder if these people aren't dancing to forget their condition."

"That is the reflection of a 'Parisienne.' They forgot all about it a long time ago. They live from day to day and accept their fate like an ancestral destiny."

"I don't think freedom is something you forget, Mr. Barthew." And she added: "All you need to do is ask them."

"Ah, that is not a question you put to a Negro."

"Why not? Is it forbidden?"

"No, but they wouldn't understand. You see, in their eyes, freedom is a white man's word."

The Marquis rose to his feet and gave the signal to leave. Telemaque took a torch and led the group back to the park, where the planters' festival was drawing to a close. Adrien made suitable thanks, then spoke the words the big black was waiting for.

"When my guests have gone and it's daylight again, I want you to come and take what food is left for your family—everything except the alcoholic beverages, of course."

Mignette felt a sudden contempt for the Marquis. Like throwing a dog a bone, she said to herself. But Telemaque, full of gratitude and made bold by the cane juice, bowed low and kissed his master's hand.

Mignette turned away. The scene was too revolting.

Work had started again when Dandridge learned through

Bobo that Mignette had an admirer in Pointe-Coupée. The man in question was Albert Schoeler, the local blacksmith, an Alsatian and former sailor who had deserted to stay in Louisiana. The French consul had tried to locate him, then forgot about him, as happened to many sailors. Schoeler came by his living honestly. He didn't drink and was putting money away so that eventually he could buy his own plot of land. He already owned two slaves. And his smithy, on the town's main street, resounded to the sound of the anvil from early morning until night. Easygoing and a man of few words, he now had the necessary five years' residence and had just become an American citizen, which would give him the right to vote at the next election.

On her frequent trips with Bobo when a horse needed shoeing, Mignette had taken a great liking to the sturdy blacksmith. He in turn had become smitten with the young French girl. They had exchanged smiles, then small talk, and finally had arrived at avowals and marriage plans. But any public announcement was put off, Albert Schoeler not being certain how the Marquis de Damvilliers would take the news that a member of his household was contemplating marriage with a lowly blacksmith.

"Next to Bagatelle, my house is a hovel, Mignette. You may miss the comforts you've gotten used to. Wait until I've made enough money to buy some land and become a real planter."

His ambition was laudable, but the clumsy yet tender kisses he lavished on Mignette when they met on Saturday afternoons in a small beech grove between Bagatelle and Pointe-Coupée filled the girl with nuptial impatience. As good Christians and respectful of conventions, they could not consider lovemaking without marriage. Mignette told her betrothed of the desire in Mr. Mosely's eyes, that Mr. Barthew had tried to put his arm around her waist, and that therefore the best way to protect her from these assaults was to announce their engagement. Albert counted on happenstance to convey the news to Bagatelle. Bobo, who was both naive and indiscreet and more observant than Mignette gave him credit for, told Mr. Dandridge and the secret was out. One morning, Clarence entered the smithy, a broad smile on his face.

"Well, Albert, you're about to carry off a young lady, I hear?"

The blacksmith placed his hammer on the anvil, put his iron back on the fire and tried to look unruffled.

"So you know, Mr. Dandridge. But believe me, I have the most honorable of intentions."

"I'm sure of it, Schoeler. But why wait and hide in the bushes like two fugitives? The Marquis and Miss Caroline would be hurt if they learned it through . . . gossip."

"What if they're against it, Mr. Dandridge?"

Clarence looked astonished.

"Why would they oppose your engagement, Albert? You're quite good enough to marry Miss Mignette, and she is entirely free to accept you as a husband. She's not a member of the Damvilliers family . . . and she's not a white slave!"

Then, because the blacksmith remained silent, Clarence said, "Would you like me to tell the Marquis and Miss Caroline?"

"Well, I must admit that it would make things easier for me." The blacksmith looked very relieved. "You see, Mignette, that is, Miss Mignette is beginning to say that I don't love her enough, that I'm ashamed of her position as a servant. Can you imagine, me, a blacksmith!"

Clarence gave a small smile.

"It's because she's impatient, Albert. She wants you to make up your mind. Let me handle it."

Dandridge did, and very effectively. The Marquis made a few jokes; Mignette blushed. Caroline asked that the blacksmith come to her, and that Mignette inform her mother, who would probably be upset to learn that her daughter had suddenly decided to marry an unknown man thousands of miles from home.

* * *

Toward the end of October, Dandridge accompanied Abraham Mosely to New Orleans where the Englishman was to board ship for Liverpool. The date for Mignette's marriage had been set for the following May. Generous as always, the Marquis announced that he would give Mignette a dowry "as if she belonged to him." For the blacksmith and his betrothed, the path to happiness was opening up before them, smooth and free of all obstacles.

"I would be glad to have that girl bring me my infusion at bedtime," Mosely said, knowing the ways of the South.

Dandridge didn't care for the joke. "She's far too good for that, Mosely. Mignette has more virtues than most of the women we know."

"A little too much virtue for my taste. My approaches weren't very well received, and without the nice little servant the Marquis gave me, I would have had to practice abstinence —which isn't good for a man my age."

Clarence wondered how many young slaves at Bagatelle could be laid at the Englishman's door.

The two men parted on the Quay Saint-Pierre in New Orleans. Mosely had bespoken Bagatelle's next two crops, which one of his agents would ship to England. So he himself wouldn't be back for another three years. Dandridge watched his plump figure head for the gangplank, followed by a dozen porters. He took off his panama and waved him a final farewell.

The city was deep in mud. The autumn rains had swollen the Mississippi and it had spread into the city's outskirts. The paved streets were bare, but the rest were covered with a yellow ooze that clung to one's feet. Gigs and landaus, now covered, could barely move, and the horses often slipped and fell between their shafts.

From the Mertaux brothers, Dandridge learned that Señor Rámirez, now fully recovered from his wound, had been the laughingstock of the local prostitutes, who had lost many a piaster from the effects of Dandridge's sword. To anyone who would listen, the Spaniard swore that he would cut the Marquis de Damvilliers's manager to ribbons on the first propitious occasion.

"Next time, I don't nick him. I slice him in two," Clarence answered back.

The two lawyers nodded in unison and opened the files the manager had come to consult.

It was during his stay in New Orleans that Dandridge learned of the events that had shaken France during the month of July. It appeared from the newspapers that the Deputies had invited the Duc d'Orléans to become lieutenant-general of the kingdom and that La Fayette had demanded a promise of liberal guarantees. The overthrow of the Bourbons and the accession of Louis-Philippe left Dandridge unmoved. But he was amused to read that the king had chosen to go into exile on the *Great Britain,* a sister ship of the *Charles Carroll* and therefore owned by the same Mr. Patterson, ex-father-in-law of Jerome Bonaparte. As a good son of Albion, Clarence liked the idea that a Bourbon should be sent packing on a ship associated with a Bonaparte.

Dandridge was still in New Orleans on November 1 when all the French ships anchored in the Mississippi lowered the fleur-de-lis and hoisted the tricolor. That night, there was many a drunken French sailor in the city's cabarets.

At the Maison de France, the French consul, M. Guillemain, showed Dandridge a letter he had just sent to M. de La Fayette.

"In their admiration for the heroic population of Paris, the citizens of New Orleans, their hearts forever tied to their former country, have hastened to open a subscription for wounded Parisians, and the widows and orphans of those who fell in the glorious battles of July. I take this occasion to offer to Washington's great friend, the hero of '76, a generous Frenchman and the wise patriot of 1830, the tribute of my sincere admiration, as well as the personal assurance of my high esteem."

Having read the document, Dandridge had to add his own

contribution to the fund. Count Molé, the new Foreign Minister in Paris, would certainly be gratified by the zeal of the counsel who had served the government of Charles X with the same devotion.

Dandridge stopped by his bootmaker to say hello to Mathias and pick up the boots he had ordered the spring before, then visited a few "bar-exchanges" to discuss the news with various planters in town to conclude the last cotton sales of the season. Then he ordered winter provisions from Perret's. He learned that salt beef cost seven dollars a barrel, whiskey $3.77 a gallon, that Natchitoches tobacco was unavailable, and furriers were paying two dollars for a beaver skin.

Clarence boarded the *Zebulon Pike* in a driving rain for the trip back to Pointe-Coupée. As always at this time of year, the trip was slow and difficult. The muddy waters at flood tide were full of tree trunks torn from the banks, adding yet another hazard to river navigation. The ship resonated with a dull thud when the heavy flotsam banged against its hull. It took all the captain's skill to keep the river wreckage from getting caught in the ship's paddle wheel. It could chew up branches, but tree trunks threatened to block its movement and cause serious damage. A few miles from Baton Rouge, those aboard were astonished at the sight of a steamer sitting in the middle of a field, now become a swamp. The swollen Mississippi had taken it off its course and abandoned the boat there when it dropped back to its normal level. Out of its element, the large vessel looked like the aberration of a mad architect. Further up the river, the *Zebulon Pike* had to come to the aid of a steamer stuck on a sandbank. To add to all its other difficulties, the wind was blowing from the northwest, thus slowing the boat even more. As a result, it took four days to reach Pointe-Coupée.

Once back at Bagatelle, Clarence picked up his winter habits. He loved the season of sedentary pleasures. With a roaring fire in his hearth, he would spend whole days at his desk with his documents and files, piecing together the "History of the Damvilliers." Mic and Mac, who hated getting their paws wet, seldom left the fireside. In the big house, Mignette was preparing her trousseau and Caroline was finishing her tapestry depicting the village of Damvilliers-sur-Meuse, Adrien's ancestral fiefdom. Dandridge furnished her with the family's escutcheon, which she embroidered in a corner of the sky. Adrien, infuriated by the cold weather that kept him confined to the house, shuttled aimlessly between his library and the gallery. In the evenings, he badgered Caroline to play the harpsichord. Only the occasional visitor or a reception broke the monotony of their restricted lives.

Willy Templeton had received permission to write to Caroline, and so she received yearning letters describing his life in the 15th Kentucky artillery regiment. He apparently spent more time at balls than in maneuvers, he missed The Myrtles, and bemoaned the fact that Percy and Corinne saw her so often.

At about the same time, Mamma Netta fell ill. The old woman, who lived in a hut near the main house, had been stricken with a fever that Dr. Murphy was powerless to cure. She refused all nourishment and was fading rapidly. Adrien and Caroline visited her regularly, and the Marquis, an optimist by nature, was visibly troubled. He was deeply attached to his old nanny: She had listened to his prayers morning and night, and often covered up for his transgressions to avoid paternal punishment.

"Murphy, you've got to get her back on her feet. Can't you see that she's itching to start her gooseberry jam?"

"The poor woman's worn to the bone, Marquis. She's going out like a lamp without oil. There's nothing to be done. Bleeding only makes her weaker, and poultices do her no good. You must resign yourself to seeing her go."

Mamma Netta's children and grandchildren instinctively knew that death was near. Rosa told Mignette that her grandmother was crying because she missed having her favorite daughter—Rosa's mother—at her bedside. Anna had been sold reluctantly during the hard times in 1824, but to keep her in the neighborhood, the Marquis had placed her with the Barrows. Mignette, convinced of the rightness of her cause, asked Dandridge to accompany her to Barrow House on the next clear day. Clement Barrow and his aged sisters confirmed the fact that Anna was still with them and that she worked in the laundry. The slave was summoned.

"That's Mamma Netta's daughter all right!" Mignette exclaimed when she saw the large woman climb the front steps.

"How can you be so sure?" Adele Barrow asked, still hesitating over whether she should offer the girl a cup of tea. After all, it was only because of the Marquis's generosity—or was it his weakness?—that the girl had been elevated from the servant class.

"It's because she looks so much like her mother," Mignette said firmly.

"All slaves look alike, my child," the old spinster said with asperity.

When Anna was told that her mother was dying, she broke into sobs and threw herself at Mignette's feet.

"Take me to her, miss. Please take me to her."

Adele Barrow dismissed the slave with a wave of the hand. "We will think about it, Anna. Go back to the laundry while we consider the matter."

Leaning on his crutches, Clement Barrow wheedled: "I think it would be a good idea to let her spend a few days at Bagatelle, Adele. The request has come from Bagatelle, and Anna's daughter is Miss Mignette's maid, after all."

Clarence had said nothing so far. He was noting Mignette's dismay at the lack of humanity in people who were considered good masters.

"I have a suggestion to make, Clement," Clarence put in. "Since we'll be needing a woman to replace old Netta, I wonder if you'd let us buy Anna."

"She's not a very good laundress," Adele said crisply. "She's lazy, surly and dirty. I'm warning you. But we'll give her up if it's the Marquis's wish—and this young lady's here," she said with a nod toward Mignette.

"Well and good. What's your price, Barrow?"

"Oh, I have no idea . . . let me see . . . how about. . ."

"Three thousand piasters," Adele Barrow broke in.

"All right," Clarence said, "three thousand piasters it shall be. I'll bring you the money in a few days."

"And we'll send you Anna tomorrow," Adele added.

That was the price of a healthy, diligent slave. At a slave trader's, poor Anna wouldn't have fetched twelve hundred piasters. Mignette knew nothing of current prices and was embarrassed by the tenor of the conversation. They were bargaining over a human being made of flesh and blood—as were this dried-up old spinster in the lace cap and the pale-faced cripple.

"If you don't mind, Miss Barrow, we'd like to take her with us now," Mignette said smartly. "Her mother may die at any moment."

"How will you take her? In your gig?" Barrow asked with surprise.

"Why not? We can all squeeze in," Dandridge said. Adele Barrow and her sister sighed between pinched lips. It wasn't done to travel with a black in a narrow gig. Slaves were supposed to go on foot.

"Would you like a cup of tea?" Adele Barrow finally got around to asking. After all, she had just brought off a coup: She had gotten rid of Anna, who wasn't worth the pork and corn it took to feed her.

That day, the buckwheat cakes laced with Vermont maple syrup tasted bitter to Dandridge. But not to Mignette. She not only found them delicious, she had also made the discovery that the manager's heart was warmer than she had thought. And his idea of buying the slave was an inspiration. Little Rosa would lose her grandmother, but she'd get her mother back instead.

Mamma Netta was buried in the slaves' small cemetery, and Anna, a mediocre laundress but a good cook by inheritance, took her mother's place at the stove. Before she relinquished her soul to God, the old woman had passed on to her daughter the secrets of some of her best recipes. It was her way of perpetuating herself.

Mignette was taken aback by Caroline's anger at her having acted without her consent, and getting Mr. Dandridge mixed up in something she could have taken care of herself. Her mistress wanted to know how much Anna had cost but, frightened that the cost might appear high, Mignette kept her own counsel. The Marquis's goddaughter planned to put the question to Dandridge at the earliest opportunity, but when she received an invitation to spend a week with Corinne Templeton just before the New Year, her curiosity evaporated in the excitement of packing.

When Caroline had gone, the Marquis didn't know what to do with his evenings. The harpsichord was silent, the game of trictrac abandoned, the big drawing room empty. He actually came to regret that, unlike most planters, he didn't have a house in New Orleans where he could take in the theaters, concerts, receptions and its many other diversions.

"Clarence, would you believe me if I told you that I miss our Caroline?" Adrien said one evening. "The fact is that the house seems deserted without her. She is always thinking up ways to distract us, and Mignette is so full of preparations for her wedding that she can't talk of anything else."

"The sun and womankind have divided up the world between them. The first gives us our days, the other makes them worth living," Clarence said, quoting an obscure Frenchman.

"That's quite true, you know," the Marquis said thoughtfully. "What about uncorking a bottle of old port, Clarence? Maybe it will help us see things more clearly."

The wine loosened Adrien's tongue.

"I want to give Caroline a really nice Christmas present. I was considering a gold chain that belonged to my mother. Do you think she would like that?"

"Is there a woman in the world who doesn't like jewelry, Adrien?"

"She's no ordinary woman, Clarence, and I have to confess I don't know her tastes very well. Since she arrived at Bagatelle, she's concerned herself with satisfying mine. Her father was a curious man, gentle but stubborn, and he seldom expressed his true feelings. Caroline seems to have inherited his character in some ways."

Clarence added, "Along with a clear head and the will to bring off whatever she takes on, a quality that was sorely lacking in Father Trégan."

"Clarence, don't you think I should be thinking about her future? Will Willy Templeton make her a good husband? I've been told he's very smitten with her."

"Willy would certainly make a good husband for any girl in our society, Adrien. But if you really want my opinion, I think Caroline needs more than just a good husband—in the lackluster sense we give it here. Caroline needs a man . . ."

"Oh?" Adrien said, taken aback by the subtle distinction he didn't altogether understand. "You don't think Willy is a man, Clarence?"

"Let's say that young Templeton's personality seems a little pale next to Caroline's. She needs someone less amiable and more domineering."

"Oh?" said the Marquis again.

"But I also think that you needn't torment yourself over your goddaughter's future. She'll decide it for herself."

The two men were silent. From Dandridge's remarks, the Marquis was trying to piece together a girl hitherto unknown to him who now seemed much more difficult to assess and far less amenable than before. He was used to accepting people as they were, without any regard for hidden complications. Clarence, on his side, was puzzled by the Marquis's deep preoccupation, which must have something to do with ill-defined feelings. Caroline remained a paradox susceptible to diverse and even contradictory interpretations. One thing, however, was certain: They must expect the unexpected.

Two days before Christmas, Dandridge had his proof. Caroline had said she would be returning from a visit of several days at The Myrtles the night before Christmas. Now she was back a full day early. It was pitch black outside. The rain had stopped but a cold wind was blowing in gusts. Clarence had just put out his light after a long night of reading when

Mic and Mac pricked up their ears and started growling. He hushed them, but his curiosity led him to open his door onto the covered walkway between his apartment and the main house. In the dim moonlight that occasionally broke through the passing clouds, he made out the vague shape of a buggy that had stopped under the trees, then a light-colored dress puffed out by the wind like a phantom's shroud, with a dark silhouette beside it. For a fleeting moment, the two shapes became one, then the woman started running toward the steps and the man returned to the buggy. He just made out a voice he recognized to be Caroline's, speaking in a loud whisper. "Good-bye. Remember that today never happened."

Then, in answer to a deeper voice he couldn't quite catch, he heard Caroline say, "Never again, you hear! Never again!"

The pale dress disappeared up the steps as the buggy, to avoid the noisy gravel, turned around on the lawn, which brought it close to where Clarence was standing. The man in the buggy was Percy Templeton.

Clarence closed his door silently and got into bed, his head churning with disquieting thoughts. He had just discovered a new Caroline, no less disturbing than the one on the *Prince du Delta*.

Early the next morning, before the house was fully awake, the Marquis's goddaughter appeared on the gallery. A pale sun had brought Dandridge out with his dogs and the two met in front of the house.

"What a surprise? We weren't expecting you until the end of the afternoon."

"I came home early to get things ready for Christmas Eve. Percy Templeton was taking the boat at Pointe-Coupée and dropped me off at dawn. Didn't you hear the buggy?"

"I did hear my dogs growl but I thought it was still night. True, with the shutters closed and the curtains drawn, it wasn't easy to know what time it was."

Caroline leaned down to stroke Mac's head and remarked, "Dogs sometimes have dreams, like people. Too bad they can't tell us their dreams."

"It is too bad," Dandridge agreed, walking toward the breakfast room. "They might have much to teach us."

The Marquis was delighted to see his goddaughter back and made no attempt to find out when and how she had returned to the plantation.

"Our house fairy is back," he exclaimed. "And Christmas will be sunny! Hallelujah! Hallelujah!" he shouted, running his hand through his hair.

With the return of dry weather and the Mississippi back to its normal bed, the first order of business was to repair the levees. While groups of slaves set to work mending the winter's damage, others began preparing the soil for the spring sowing of cotton. The days seemed to grow shorter as master and slaves shook off the lethargy of the rainy season.

Clarence noted that Caroline had been avoiding The Myrtles since Christmas. Of course it could have been because Corinne was spending the winter months at her uncle's in New Orleans. Most planters' daughters spent the winter in town to take advantage of the opera season and the many parties scheduled for January and February. But wasn't there perhaps another reason why the Marquis's goddaughter had made so few visits and issued so few invitations? There was little doubt in Clarence's mind that Caroline was avoiding Percy. Clarence knew the older Templeton son well and reckoned that he and Caroline must have had a brief and illicit adventure.

Corinne wrote her every week from New Orleans, describing the balls, receptions, plays and concerts she had attended. From Willy Templeton she heard that he would be home for Easter. What she didn't pass on except to Mignette was that he wished to use the occasion to ask the Marquis for his goddaughter's hand, if she so agreed. Although her mistress appeared to give the matter some thought, Mignette was convinced that in the end, she would decline the proposition. Conscious of the delicious sensations her future husband awakened in her, the blacksmith's fiancée detected no similar feelings in her mistress where Willy Templeton was concerned. Mignette, straightforward as always, put the question to her mistress: "Miss Caroline, everybody agrees that Mr. Templeton is a charming young man, handsome, rich, a man of the world. People are bound to wonder why you're so cool to him. They'll think you're interested in someone else."

"Don't you play games with me, Mignette. There are too few marriageable men in this parish for you to talk that way. I'm not interested in marriage just for the sake of being married. I may be nineteen but I'm in no hurry. To me, marriage isn't an end, it's a beginning."

"And you don't care to 'begin' with Mr. Templeton?"

"No, I don't."

"What about Mr. Dandridge? Would you consider him?"

"Good heavens, Mignette! What makes you think Clarence Dandridge is interested in women? He's the bachelor type if I ever saw one."

"Oh, Miss Caroline," Mignette said with a mocking tone, "he may look cold, but he notices you . . . and he's a very handsome man."

"If he ever marries, he'll choose Corinne Templeton. You know that."

"Oh, she's nice enough, but it's my impression that she irritates him, with her patience and fluttering eyes. I think he wants a very different kind of woman."

"Oh?"

"A woman with more authority, more presence, more real charm. Someone more complicated. How should I say it? . . . a woman with brains."

"Well, Mignette, you certainly know a thing or two."

"I know enough to wonder if you and Mr. Dandridge aren't watching each other to see who plays the first card."

"You're out of your mind, Mignette. Clarence is my godfather's manager, and just because I'm not disposed to marry Willy Templeton is no reason to leap to the conclusion that I'm interested in 'someone else,' as you put it."

"Between now and Easter when Lieutenant Templeton

returns, a lot of water will have flowed down the Mississippi . . ."

"You mean?"

"That those who've been silent will begin to talk, and suddenly a third man will appear."

"You're an impertinent girl, Mignette. But I like your impertinence. When you see this 'third man,' let me know."

A drama was about to unfold that would be bringing the young lieutenant home sooner than expected.

One February afternoon, while the Marquis was making a tour of the plantation to check on the spring's labors and Caroline and Mignette had gone to pay a call on the Barrow sisters, a man covered with mud, haggard of eye and pale as death came running up to Bagatelle. Clarence was greasing his guns in a shack behind the house when his dogs suddenly started barking and leaped out the door. As he followed them out, he noticed the stranger talking to James, who had appeared on the gallery to see what the commotion was about. The man was gesticulating wildly.

"Quick, for God's sake. Go tell your master. The *Rayon d'Or* has just exploded about three miles down the river. We must get help right away. Please hurry!"

With these last words, the man collapsed on the steps. James shouted for Dandridge, unaware that the manager was striding toward him at full speed.

"You can see the smoke there, between the oaks," the man said, lifting his head. "It's terrible. People are badly hurt. Some are drowning."

These accidents had become too numerous to count. Only two years before, the *Saint-Louis* and the *Bison Blanc* had collided in a bend of the river at Pointe-Coupée and both ships had gone up in flames. There were over a hundred dead.

Clarence, who knew what this meant, immediately summoned Bobo, had him hitch up the landau and three gigs and ordered him to follow with all the slaves he could muster. He also sent a groom to warn Dr. Murphy and the sheriff of

Pointe-Coupée. Then he leaped into his saddle, leaving Rosa to revive the stranger with a glass of brandy.

When he reached the path that skirted the river, he could tell from the smoke where the boat was and the extent of the catastrophe. At the location of the accident, the river was almost fifty feet deep and a mile wide. If the passengers on board hadn't had time to put on their life jackets, many would have drowned by now. Crawling on his stomach under the heavy foliage, he could see the ship a quarter of a mile away, lying on its side athwart the river. Its black metal funnels were aimed at the riverbank like huge cannons, belching great clouds of black smoke. The flames rose straight up from the upended decks, devouring the cabin partitions and sending red tongues of fire through every aperture. White steam hovered over the water where the exploded boilers were spilling their contents into the Mississippi.

As he came closer to the scene of the disaster, Clarence heard the screams of people engulfed by the flames. Exhausted bodies lay on the riverbank as others, pleading for help, tried to clutch their way up the levee.

Disheveled women, their wet clothes clinging to their bodies, staggered about chattering unintelligibly. Men gasping for breath, their clothes dripping water, were breaking off the lower branches of the willows and holding them out to survivors struggling to reach the shore. Heads bobbed around the burning ship from which men and women kept dropping off like so many marionettes. An occasional arm flailed the air. Voices called out in encouragement or in despair. Hanging over the scene was the acrid smell of burning paint. Now the ship was breaking up like a big log on hot coals. Sections of railing and pieces of deck splashed into the water with a hiss and an explosion of sparks.

Riding past the wounded on the bank, Clarence spurred his horse into the river, seizing a hand here, another there, dragging onto the river bank exhausted men and women vomiting up water. He had gone back and forth twenty times when the carriages from Bagatelle finally arrived. Directed by Bobo, the slaves carried lengths of rope into the river and threw them wherever they saw a hand. Meanwhile, other blacks, the better swimmers, swam to the ship and brought back the few who were still afloat.

A moment later, the half-consumed skeleton of the ship disintegrated like a collapsing scaffolding, one of its paddle wheels emerging out of the water like a wheel of fortune at a country fair.

Alerted by the smoke that was covering the sky, men began to arrive from nearby plantations. Elbow to elbow, blacks and whites thought only of saving the victims the muddy river was trying to claim. Bodies were lined up under the willows, some already dead, disfigured by ghastly burns, while the wounded lay moaning, their heads rocking back and forth, their eyes staring at the impervious sky.

It was while he was walking among the wounded, surrounded by the sound of weeping and incoherent babble, that Clarence happened on Corinne Templeton.

The girl had been stretched out on a small hillock. Motionless, she seemed unhurt, like a doll rolled up in wet rags. Clarence leaned down and she gave him a small reassuring smile.

"Where do you hurt, Corinne?"

"I don't hurt anywhere," she said in a strange voice. "I don't hurt, but I can't move my . . . my legs."

Corinne Templeton had never said the word "legs" before. It would have been as indecent as to mention belly, breasts or buttocks.

"It's the shock, Corinne. I'll go find Dr. Murphy. He's somewhere around here. Then we'll take you to Bagatelle."

When he returned with the doctor, who had been trying to resuscitate a drowned man, Corinne had grown paler.

"Please find out what's wrong with her, Murphy. I want to know if I can get her as far as Bagatelle."

Grumbling like an old nurse, the doctor knelt down beside the girl while Clarence turned away in deference to the girl's modesty. When he heard Murphy heave himself back on his feet, he looked at him questioningly.

"She'll be all right," the doctor said in a loud voice. "But she must be carried flat, absolutely flat. Her spine has been . . . injured."

Then, tugging at Dandridge's sleeve to move him beyond the girl's hearing, he said, "Her back is broken, Clarence. She can't move her arms or legs."

"Is she dying?"

Dr. Murphy never prevaricated: "Yes, she's going to die . . . soon. Take her to Bagatelle and have word sent to The Myrtles. I'll stop by later. I still have work to do here."

"Is she in pain?"

"No, I don't think so. It's as if she had no nerves."

Bobo managed to find a wet mattress among the debris drifting to shore. With infinite care, Clarence placed Corinne on the mattress, then four blacks picked up the improvised stretcher and carefully stowed it in the landau. Clarence stood on the running board, constantly warning the driver to watch out for bumps in the road while keeping an anxious eye on Corinne. But she kept smiling at him, her face serene, her hair spread out around her head. She had never seemed so beautiful, so gentle, so free of this cruel world.

When Caroline, who had learned of the disaster from Anna and James, saw the big landau slowly drive up, she ran to the carriage to find out who was inside.

"It's Corinne," Clarence said, getting off the running board. "She's worse off than she looks. We must send somebody to The Myrtles right away."

Standing on tiptoe, Caroline placed a trembling hand on her friend's forehead.

"She must be taken to my room," she said in a toneless voice. "Clarence, go change your clothes. You're shivering. Leave everything to me."

Murphy stopped by during the evening, numb with fatigue. He was immediately attacked by Mrs. Templeton, her nerves at the breaking point.

"You must save my little girl, Murphy," she screamed. "Do you understand? You must save her!"

Mr. Templeton sat prostrate in an armchair with the dazed

expression of a man who was experiencing his first brush with misfortune. The Marquis, not knowing what to do or say, stood near his neighbor, his hands clenched behind his back. In Caroline's room, the servants moved about in silence, careful not to attract the attention of death to what remained of life lying among the lace pillows.

The doctor, with Caroline at his side, examined Corinne again. His earlier diagnosis was confirmed.

"Soon she won't be able to talk or hear. If anyone wants to say something to her, there's still a little time. Then she'll go without even knowing it."

While the doctor was preparing the Templetons for the inevitable, Caroline went in search of Clarence, whom she found walking slowly back and forth on the gallery.

"Go see her, Clarence. It will be her last moment of happiness."

Dandridge went into the room and up to the bed.

"Can you hear me, Corinne?" he asked, taking the hand lying on the sheet.

She tried to say yes but no sound came from her dry lips. Instead, she slowly opened and closed her eyes to let him know she had heard him.

"If you are willing, Corinne," Dandridge said, choking with an emotion he had never experienced before, "if you are willing, we will marry the moment you are well."

His words stunned her. She tried to say "thank you," then her eyes looked at him questioningly.

"Yes, Corinne, I love you, I've loved you for a long time. I want you to be happy!"

At this moment, the Templetons stormed into the room. Caroline held onto Corinne's mother to keep her from flinging herself on her daughter's bed. The group stood silently, looking at the motionless body. Only the eyes showed intensity. They moved from Clarence to her parents as if pleading with them to enter into a conversation. Only Clarence understood.

"Mr. Templeton," he said so firmly that he startled the man, "Corinne and I have decided to marry. I should have told you sooner, but since we're all here together, will you tell me, sir, if you accept my proposal?"

"Say yes," Caroline whispered in the ear of the old man, who appeared nonplussed by the oddly timed request.

"Why yes . . . certainly . . . ," he said, finally pulling himself together. Then, accepting his role in the strange drama they were playing before Death, he added, "The minute she's back on her feet, Dandridge. We'll all be very happy . . ." He couldn't finish for the sob in his throat.

"We'll be so happy, my darling," Mrs. Templeton said, swallowing her tears.

"We're going to be happy, Corinne," Clarence said—the only one speaking the words with true conviction. He thought he detected a glimmer of joy in her eyes, the same joy he had seen—not without embarrassment—the night of the cotton festival when he invited her to dance.

A moment passed during which the tick-tock of the clock sounded like a beating heart. Clarence bent down and very tenderly kissed the half-opened lips. Then he straightened up. Her eyes riveted on his, a lone tear trickled down her cheek.

An instant later, Corinne was dead.

Informed by a courier of the Louisiana Express, whose members rode in relays for hundreds of miles, Willy Templeton arrived in time for his sister's funeral. Since an officer must stand straight and maintain his dignity at all times, he kept his grief under control. Percy felt no such compunctions, which prompted several of the people attending the burial to observe that "the older brother loved his sister more than the younger one, who never took his eyes off Caroline Trégan, even in church!"

The *Rayon d'Or* disaster had caused sixty-two deaths and countless injuries. Many a planter's family was in mourning, for the boat, like many others at this season, was bringing home its wealthier passengers from their winter's stay in New Orleans.

It wasn't until several weeks after the tragedy that the

Marquis de Damvilliers dared discuss with Clarence the subject of Corinne's death. Casting discretion to the winds, he said straight out, "Did you really love the girl, Clarence?"

"You know the answer to that one better than anyone else, Adrien," Dandridge said dully.

"What I was trying to say," the Marquis was spluttering now, "were you really sincere when you offered to marry her?"

"At that moment, yes, of course. But I don't think she was taken in, Adrien. I sometimes wonder if my sudden declaration didn't persuade her that she was about to die. Now that I think about it, I wonder if I wasn't playing a dubious game . . ."

"You're wrong, Clarence," Caroline put in. "Corinne believed you. She was convinced that someday you'd ask her to marry you. She told me so herself. She was just waiting for the moment. Death gave her what she was hoping for."

Clarence was silent. From the gallery where the small group was sitting after lunch, he saw the cotton festival once again under the spreading oaks. But that canceled life would not reappear with the rush of spring. The memory of Corinne, timid and a little contrived in her impeccable dresses, could always be summoned back, but the reality, never.

The only conception of eternity available to men is in contemplating the emptiness left by death, the sensation of absolute absence. For those scattered by the vagaries of life, there is always the chance of meeting again even when separated by oceans and continents. Death makes them inaccessible to each other. They dissolve.

The Marquis and his goddaughter respected Clarence's silence. Dandridge, his coffee cup in his hand, rocked slowly back and forth, the boards of the gallery floor creaking under his weight. Caroline knew that of all the people who had loved Corinne—parents, brothers, friends, even she herself—Clarence would remember her with the greatest intensity. The Marquis was limited to a simple regret for any life cut down so soon. Burial was something concrete and sad, but his Christian faith gave him the assurance that there would be a meeting in the hereafter, in the indefinable reaches of the Good Book's sky. He remembered mentioning Corinne's love for Clarence the night of the cotton festival. When Dandridge had been unable to answer him, he had said: "God will provide a solution." Well, God had done so.

"Come on, Clarence," he said, trying for a bantering tone. "Thanks to you, Corinne died happy. Like a fiancée. The Templeton family is grateful to you, and Murphy tells me that the poor girl passed away without knowing it."

"A poor sort of happiness," Clarence said bitterly. "At that moment, I would gladly have exchanged my life for hers. But God, your God, Adrien, has never accepted these bargaining arrangements. He keeps his miracles for more edifying occasions."

"Because," the Marquis said, sitting up, "because he doesn't subscribe to men's selfish motives. He chooses those who will have an easy death and those he leaves with a difficult life. I fear that you, Clarence, got the worst of the bargain."

"I envy your certainty, Adrien, and your admirable faculty for accepting a superhuman will, an infallible wisdom. My personal God is Doubt, a kind of gaseous Janus who represents both everything and the opposite of everything and is amused to watch us play heads or tails over the bottomless pit."

"You're a blasphemer, Clarence," the Marquis said, shaking his head sadly. "You're revolted by Corinne's death because you doubt . . . even your doubt."

"It's not that I'm revolted by her death, Adrien. It's that I feel ashamed because I sustained her with a lie."

"That's not true," Caroline said with a passion that surprised both Clarence and the Marquis. "Corinne's death fills you with shame because it's delivered you from a dilemma without bringing you peace."

Clarence gave her a scathing look and, as he rose from his chair, said, "To each his peace, I suppose. Some find it by following their nature, others by opposing it."

His abrupt departure left the Marquis nonplussed and Caroline incensed.

"You were a little hard on him," Adrien said to Caroline. "There are many things you don't understand about the man."

"That may be. But what I do know," Caroline snapped back, determined to justify her lack of tact, "is that that man is arrogant beyond belief."

"Perhaps so, Caroline, but believe me, arrogance is a quality that you in your youth are unable to appreciate."

The scene left no visible mark on Dandridge's comportment, but during the days that followed, he made certain that he was never alone with the Marquis's goddaughter. He suspected she would have liked to go on with the discussion, and maybe offer some sort of apology, but he wanted to spare her the effort at humility. For, in his heart, he knew that her view of his response to Corinne's death was correct.

Mignette's marriage to Albert Schoeler took place as the cotton was just beginning to bloom. The Marquis, always generous, had resolved that the girl, so far from her own family, should have a real wedding. He escorted her to the altar in the church at Sainte-Marie, just as seigneurs used to lead the village virgins in olden times. The entire white population of Pointe-Coupée was present—artisans, overseers, tradesmen, farmers. Even a few of the rich planters had come to honor the Marquis de Damvilliers, casting aside for the moment the social prejudices of their caste.

"All these swells scare me," Albert confided to Mignette, she in a white gown, he a little awkward in his new frock coat and polished boots.

The wedding breakfast was served at Bagatelle, and Anna outdid herself to please the young woman who had made her return to Bagatelle possible.

A ball in the parish meeting house brought the festivities to a close. The Marquis and Dandridge stopped by for a moment, giving Caroline a chance to demonstrate that she was no snob and could dance a reel as well as a quadrille.

Mignette shed a tear at the moment of parting. The Marquis discreetly slipped an envelope into the blacksmith's hand;

its contents would go a long way toward fixing up their apartment above the smithy.

At a tea party given soon after by the Barrow sisters, Adele voiced the opinion that the Marquis had demeaned himself by treating his goddaughter's servant like a member of the family. His generosity was attributed to obscure reasons, implying that perhaps Mignette had permitted him certain liberties whose consequences the poor blacksmith would now have to assume.

The ladies who shared these innuendos included aging spinsters, the leavings of rich families, and heiresses either too demanding, too prudish or too ugly to catch suitable husbands. Fortunately, Adele's snide remarks found no echo and the Marquis's reputation remained above suspicion. Besides, the Marquis was about to provide the gossips with a new topic of conversation.

With the return of spring, Bagatelle moved outdoors. Breakfast was now served on the gallery outside the big drawing room. Caroline had always taken her breakfast upstairs with Mignette. After her companion's marriage, she asked if she might join the gentlemen on the gallery. The Marquis replied that they were indeed flattered by the prospect of a feminine presence at such an early hour. So, every morning at seven-thirty, Caroline found herself sitting between Clarence and the Marquis, savoring the appetizing aroma of warm bread, steaming tea and hot chocolate served in Queen Anne silver pots. Caroline had found the silver service in the cellar; Abraham Mosely assured the Marquis it had been made by Joseph Ward. Adrien took great pride in his silver with the Damvilliers arms engraved on its polished surface.

"Eating is a vulgar necessity," he stated. "It takes the proper appointments to give it elegance." Then, taking a spoonful of gooseberry jam, he added ruefully: "This is the last of Mamma Netta's jam. I wonder if Anna will make it as well as her mother."

Caroline usually wore a long dressing gown of crimson

velvet. But one morning, the temperature having gone up several degrees, she appeared in a robe of white dotted Swiss. Without her appearing to be aware of it, the morning sun shone through the sheer fabric, revealing to the Marquis, who was sitting in the shade, every curve of her body, liberated at this early hour from the confines of corsets and thick petticoats. The Marquis seemed transfixed.

While Caroline was going through the motions of pouring tea and passing buns, the Marquis's eyes followed her every move, relishing his goddaughter's innocent indecency. Clarence took note of his employer's appreciation of these unexpected transparencies.

"Aren't you afraid you'll catch cold?" he asked. "It's not summer yet and you're very lightly clad."

The girl caught the veiled irony in Clarence's tone.

"This material is warmer than you think," she said casually. "And it's such a beautiful morning and I feel so happy that I wanted to show off my new dressing gown to Uncle Adrien."

As she spoke, she flung her arms wide like a bird about to take flight, threw her head back, and with the glee of a little girl, exclaimed, "On days like this, I feel like running barefoot through the fields, spinning my hoop around the pigeon house and singing roundalays."

Her exuberant gesture brought two firm young breasts into relief, the pink nipples showing through the sheer material. They seemed to offer themselves without shame, Caroline unaware—or was she?—that her veiled nudity was more suggestive than the real thing.

Poor Adrien, who had never dared ask his deceased wife to remove her flannel nightgown during their infrequent conjugal embraces, tried to look away but couldn't. His cup of chocolate shook in his hand and his cheeks suddenly turned a deep pink, indicating to Clarence that he was under the magician's spell. The girl's disquieting candor, her uninhibited beauty, the mixture of dissembled licentiousness and ingenuous grace reminded him of a painting by Bernardino Luini he had seen long ago in a palace in Lugano, depicting Salome's seduction of her uncle Herod. Hadn't that doubtful virgin with her languor and false innocence won—according to legend—the head of John the Baptist?

As opposed to the Lydian bacchante, Caroline didn't move, although a trill on a flute might have been enough to impel her, quivering, into the whirl of a bewitching dance. If, at that moment, Clarence had heard Adrien stammer like Herod: "Ask me what you want and I will give it to you," he wouldn't have been a bit surprised. When Caroline had finished her last cup of tea and disappeared down the gallery, chasing after Mic and Mac who had come for their usual crumbs from the breakfast table, a strange silence fell between the two men. Adrien thrust his hand through his hair and in an odd voice Dandridge had never heard him use before, said, "Beautiful morning, heh, Clarence! A little canter in the countryside would do us some good, don't you think?"

The scene was repeated for more than a week. As Clarence observed his employer, he was increasingly reminded of the planters who sat alone in the front row of New Orleans cabarets ogling the dancers' garters. It was clear that Adrien couldn't wait for his goddaughter's apparition each morning and the way, in the play of light and shade, she changed from irreproachable young lady into provocative odalisque.

It was Rosa's intervention that put an end to what Clarence called (only to himself) her dance of seduction and the Marquis's inadmissible pleasure. One morning, Caroline appeared in a dressing gown that not even Adele Barrow could have faulted.

"Did you know that I got a scolding from Rosa?" she said with the disingenuous air of a little girl who has decided to confess that she has been into her mother's paint pots. "She says I shouldn't wear my dotted Swiss outside my room!"

The Marquis being tongue-tied, Clarence came to the rescue. "That's too bad. I thought the dress very becoming. It revealed all your . . . impulsive beauty. I'm sure Adrien enjoyed your magic spell as much as I did."

His lightly ironic tone told Caroline that once again, Dandridge had seen through her game.

"Enough of that," she said brusquely. And, turning toward

the Marquis, who stood stricken like an unmasked voyeur, she asked, "How is the cotton this morning, godfather? Will the crop be as good as last year's?"

The words spilling out of his mouth—for he was nothing if not voluble on this subject—the Marquis launched into a technical discussion as if to hold at bay a carnal world that reeked of sulfur.

A few days later, the mail brought Caroline a proposal of marriage from Willy Templeton. She found the wording simpleminded and syrupy, and spent a long afternoon considering how she should answer him. Sitting on the gallery, she leafed through a book with vacant eyes. As she wound and unwound a ringlet, she tried to sort out her feelings.

Dandridge returned before the Marquis, so it was to him she addressed her quandary.

"Clarence, I received a letter from Willy Templeton this morning. He has asked me to marry him."

She spoke with the same tone she might have used to announce that a bay mare had foaled or the priest from Pointe-Coupée was coming for dinner. Now, lying in ambush, she waited for Clarence's reply.

"Well, may I offer my congratulations, Caroline. Young Templeton is a fine young man. He'll end up a general." Then he added, "And now I have news for you. Percy Templeton is the father of a splendid baby girl!"

"His wife wanted a boy," Caroline observed, "but it will make Papa Templeton happy. Since Corinne's death, there's been no girl in the family. As for Willy's proposal, I don't think I'll accept it."

Clarence, his panama on his knees, raised his eyebrows and pretended astonishment. He pulled down his waistcoat, crossed his long legs and looked at Caroline.

"I suppose you have your reasons."

"He's too young, too stupid, and I have no desire to marry into the military. I belong to the soil. Willy is full of charm, a perfect cavalier, rich and serious-minded, but he really doesn't appeal to me as a husband. So, I fear I must cause him some pain."

Having said this, she sat intent, a mocking smile on her lips, her senses as alert as a wild animal's.

"In short, you don't love him. It's as simple as that," Clarence suggested. "At least you're honest. But maybe he misunderstood the interest you seemed to show in him. The young men around here sometimes don't understand the feelings they inspire. They're both too timid and too sure of themselves . . . and the girls are too shy."

"Willy is a romantic, but marriage is a lifelong affair. I don't want to be caged up with him. By nature I'm more attracted to mature men, decisive men with—let's admit it— more moral authority than Willy has."

"Evidently so," Clarence said with a malicious edge. "His brother Percy has a different temperament, but he's married now and the head of a family."

Caroline was caught off guard.

"Why do you say that, Clarence?"

Dandridge hesitated for a moment. But it was too good an opportunity to test her and to prove that there could be no circumlocutions in their relationship.

"Because, my dear girl, I witnessed your return two nights before Christmas, and it left me with certain impressions . . ."

"You think I had an affair with Percy Templeton?"

"Yes. Am I wrong?"

"That is my business. Do you think that only men look for passing pleasures? I've learned at Bagatelle to act like a man. I'm responsible to no one."

Clarence guessed that her anger was feigned.

"Don't be upset, Caroline. I'm no moralist. But, you see, Southerners are not as liberated as Parisians. In plantation society, people have few distractions, so they spend their time observing each other. The smallest misstep is enough to ruin a woman's reputation."

"That's pure hypocrisy. Men, whether bachelors or not, are permitted to have black mistresses."

"I admit it's hypocrisy, but to be without hypocrisy is a social sin here, Caroline."

She waved away these considerations as meaningless. Clarence, shifting his ground, turned amicable, full of understanding, not a little conspiratorial.

"I think you have the gift to become a great lady, Caroline. You have a strength lacking in most of the women around here, a desire to live life to the fullest—and damn the consequences. Now, in the South, women don't live with intensity. Their destiny is laid out for them. It follows an unchanging course, just like the river. Any stretching of the rules is condemned out of hand. Your lack of prudence has worried me more than your affair with Percy Templeton. I was afraid for you, as I was earlier, on the *Prince du Delta*."

It was immediately clear to her that if she was less than candid she would only succeed in alienating a man who seemed to understand her.

"Do you like me, Clarence? Or do you think me a loose woman or a flighty fool?"

Clarence leaned forward and put his hand on Caroline's arm.

"I feel great affection for you. Besides, who could resist your charm? That is why I don't want to see you spoil your chances by doing something provocative, tactless . . . or by rushing things."

Caroline looked at him for a moment, weighing the meaning behind his words. But under his skeptical logician's stare, she lowered her eyes.

"Clarence, I don't reason. I vibrate. I want to possess everything, not just what life wants to give me but what I can grab. I have no desire for the quiet little happiness Willy Templeton offers me. I want to find my place and make each new day a great blossoming. You too wanted no part of the happiness poor Corinne was ready to give you. Actually, we're not unalike, are we, Clarence?"

"I used to be like you, Caroline, and that may be why there's a certain complicity between us, why I understand the things you do, your boldness . . ."

"But you abdicated?"

"Yes, by force of circumstance. But that's a painful story.

Perhaps I'll tell you someday. When we're old!"

"I like talking to you this way, Clarence," the girl said with impulsive abandon. "I'm like a chess player who knows he has a good board but doesn't know which pawn to advance to win the game."

"Which pawn are you thinking of playing just now, Miss Trégan?" Clarence asked with a bantering smile.

"The Marquis de Damvilliers," she whispered, her face radiating covetousness.

"Your transparent dotted Swiss, dear Salome," he said, taking a perverse delight in their game of truth and consequences, "gained you several points. You may well become the Marquise de Damvilliers, but do please spare John the Baptist!"

They were both laughing when Adrien came on the scene. Weary and covered with dust, he sank into a rocking chair, which creaked and shuddered under the sudden weight.

"Get me something to drink, for sweet pity's sake! All the time you young people were laughing, the boll worm was attacking my cotton. We're going to have to destroy so many plants. It's a disaster. How I envy you, Caroline, for not having these worries!"

"But, Uncle Adrien, your worries are my worries. What can I do to distract you?"

"Play me that rigadoon I love, girl. Maybe music will make me forget my overseers' stupidity and my slaves' laziness."

Caroline disappeared into the house and a moment later, the twanging sound of the harpsichord wafted through the open French doors. The Marquis let out a sigh of satisfaction and stretched out his legs for James to remove his boots. Then he gulped down two glasses of water flavored with lemon juice and rubbed his head with the artlessness of a dog shaking itself.

"By God, Dandridge, it's good to be home among the people you love. I could eat a wolf and drink the whole Mississippi."

During the days that followed, neither Clarence nor Caroline alluded to their conversation on the gallery. But from then on, their thoughts moved in tandem, like two partners accustomed to playing together, who understood each other's signs and how the game is to be won.

Dandridge, now privy to the girl's ambitions, gave them his full approval. He knew there were risks in it for Adrien, but it was more important that his friend be happy, with a beautiful woman in his bed, a woman who had already given ample proof of her capacities as mistress of the house. Also, he counted on Adrien's combination of moral strength and rugged tenderness to keep the mettlesome filly within prescribed bounds. He felt quite sure that once Caroline had reached her goal, she would settle down and behave exactly as she should—and all the more readily because, knowing the value of everything, she would observe the rules in order to reap the fullest reward.

The weeks passed uneventfully. Caroline finished the tapestry she had begun the year before and presented it to Adrien on his forty-first birthday. It represented the Damvilliers's original demesne in France as it appeared in an old engraving. In an upper corner, she had embroidered the family's crest—"a fucule banded with gold, crowned with a halved fleur-de-lis also in gold with a silver bud, with three 'pheons' [arrowheads with widely spread barbs] also in silver, resting on the orle [the edge of the escutcheon]." Under this, she had carefully embroidered the heraldic device "Passer Outre" (Go Beyond).

The Marquis was beside himself. He kept embracing his goddaughter with, in Clarence's view, more fervor than the occasion warranted. She stroked his cheek and the contact with her soft skin made Adrien unusually playful. At dinner and during the rest of the evening, he couldn't keep his eyes off the provider of so much joy.

Caroline went to her room early that evening, and the two men took their accustomed chairs on the gallery, a bottle of port between them. They lit their cigars and sat back to enjoy the warm night and the rasping song of the frogs.

The Marquis broke the silence. "I wonder what keeps young Templeton from asking for Caroline's hand. Because they're still in mourning for Corinne? What do you think, Clarence?"

"There will be no proposal, Adrien."

"What do you mean? I thought . . . I understood . . ."

"You didn't understand me. Caroline doesn't wish it."

The Marquis sat up with a jolt. "She doesn't want to get married?"

"Not to Willy Templeton, at any rate."

"But she couldn't do better, Clarence. I don't understand. Does she love someone else?"

"Possibly."

"But who? She goes almost nowhere but to the Templetons. Maybe it's you, Clarence . . . yet again."

"Ah, no, Adrien! It isn't me. It's you, godfather," Clarence said with a roguish grin.

But for the dark, Dandridge would have seen the Marquis's cheeks, already pink from dinner and the wine, turn a deep crimson.

"What are you trying to tell me, Clarence? For heaven's sake, I've known her since she was so high. In her eyes I'm almost an old man."

"You've just entered your forties, Adrien. You're at your peak. Caroline likes men who are strong and sensible. She likes you, I tell you, but how the devil is she to let you know it?"

"She's told you all this?"

"Yes and no. But I gathered that if you'd stop playing the affectionate godfather and treat her like a woman instead of a little girl, you'd make her very happy."

"How funny, Clarence. God, how funny! I'm attractive to this beautiful girl, to this princess who dropped out of the sky?" Adrien kept shaking his head with disbelief. "She'd certainly make a ravishing Marquise! But what would people say if I married a twenty-year-old girl, me a widower and a Mississippi peasant? We're dreaming, Clarence, we're dreaming."

"All you have to do is offer her the station and happiness she deserves."

"Well! If I'd known that . . . I can't get over it! Girls have the strangest ideas."

The Marquis suddenly turned practical. He drained his glass and settled himself in his chair.

"If I ask her to be my wife, people will say that she's acting out of gratitude for all I did for her family. That she is poor and gave herself to me to pay off her family's debts."

"Who would dare say that, Adrien?"

"The Barrow sisters, for example—and some other rancid ladies I don't wish to marry."

"You are the master of Bagatelle, and I should think that was enough. Especially since Caroline is not the sort who would sacrifice herself to honor debts she had nothing to do with."

"It's too much. Me and Caroline, Caroline and me. What a team, heh, my friend! What a team we'd make!"

"Not a team, Adrien. Just because you like to play the lone bull doesn't mean that you and Caroline can't make a very presentable couple."

"You really think so? I think you've had too much port. Come, let's go to bed. I expect I'll have some pretty curious dreams tonight."

As they crossed the drawing room, their candlesticks in their hands, Adrien turned to Dandridge. In the flickering light of the candle, his nose cast a large shadow on his face and his dark brown eyes glowed. With his mane of wild hair, he looked like a lion.

"Clarence, if she can't find anything better, I'll gladly take her, by God! But all the same I find it hard to believe . . ." Then, with his heavy tread that made the bibelots shake and the old waxed floors creak, he went off, his head buzzing with tantalizing fantasies.

On the spur of the moment, Dandridge decided to leave for New Orleans early the next morning, although he had actually been meaning to go for quite a while. He left a note for Adrien, apologizing for not having told him of his plans earlier, and woke up James to ask him to tell Bobo that he would be needing the gig at dawn for the trip to Pointe-Coupée. His real reason, of course, was that he didn't wish to be around when Adrien and his goddaughter had their confrontation, or, what would be worse, avoided the confrontation.

As the boat moved down the river, it passed the grim remains of the *Rayon d'Or*, now hauled up to the bank at a curve in the river. All the salvageable wood had been removed by slaves to use for roasting their pork and corn. Soon, nothing would be left but doorknobs, a few old engravings that had escaped the fire, knives and forks, tin plates, rusted screws, melted pulleys. All these would eventually turn up in the blacks' huts or on scavenging boatmen's barges, the innocent plunder of yet another Mississippi mishap.

Leaning on the railing, Clarence's gaze rested on the green hillock where Corinne had lain, little suspecting her end was so near. He closed his eyes and tried to summon her gentle face and candid eyes. He wanted to bring back the sound of her voice, the singsong accent of the South, and the weight of her body as he placed her on the waterlogged mattress. But he could not do it. The dead refuse to conform to their survivors' wishes. It's their way of aggravating our feelings of remorse, of sharpening our regret. They like to make us uneasy, perhaps even to avenge themselves by suddenly returning unannounced, in an unexpected place, in a word spoken by a passing stranger.

He felt a hand on his shoulder and turned to find Dr. Murphy standing by him. The doctor had waited until they had passed the scene of the accident.

"You were thinking about the Templeton girl," he said, his hat on the back of his head, his tie askew. "I was too. Among all the dead I attended that day, she was the one who came back to mind. But I have no desire to see again the people I've watched die. It would take all my time . . ."

"It's odd. I was trying to remember her as I saw her there on the bank, and I can't do it."

"It happened too recently. You have to give the dead time to blossom in their new domain. Her face will come back to you in all its freshness and serenity when you've had time to absorb your grief."

"Let's go down to the bar and have a drink," Clarence suggested. He'd had enough of these sad reflections.

"Good idea, Dandridge. It's beginning to get hot."

In New Orleans, Clarence registered at the Saint-Charles as usual, made his customary visit to the Mertaux brothers and stopped off at various "bar-exchanges" to learn the news of the day and how the cotton crop looked for the coming year.

The city was bursting with construction, especially in the American sector, which was mushrooming with new arrivals from the North. Land speculation was forcing prices sky-high. A house worth 5,000 or 6,000 dollars in 1830 was now fetching 30,000 to 40,000, and the immigrants couldn't find anyplace to live. The banks were bloated with capital, and credit was easily available for those in good standing. Local businessmen were realizing fortunes and backing each other without asking for collateral. A new bank could be launched with a capital of ten million francs. A good slave who cost between 1,200 and 1,600 dollars before the yellow fever epidemic now got a third more—"with no talent and plenty of vices." Mulattoes could be hired as housemaids for 20 to 30 dollars a month and a black girl for between 13 and 16 dollars.

The wealthier classes—traders mostly—had at least 5 household servants, the rich Creoles 10 or 12. This was highly profitable for the slave dealers, who conspired with the captains of freighters to import blacks from Dahomey—the slaves preferred by the French colony in Louisiana. The importation of slaves had been illegal since 1807, but the profits from "ebony" were such that shipowners were willing to run the risk of having their ships confiscated in order to smuggle in cheap labor. Ever since a Dutch warship landed with the first 20 blacks in Jamestown in 1617, the slave trade had become a business like any other, and the Southern colonists cursed the politicians in the North for refusing to recognize their economic needs, preaching the abolition of slavery instead.

What concerned New Orleans more at the moment was the deportation of the Choctaws, who were being forced across the Mississippi to new territories which had been reserved for them—or so it was said. The Cherokees, Chickasaws, Creeks, Enchees and Seminoles were suffering the same fate. Naturally they were leaving unwillingly, for why should they give up their rich and fertile lands for the barren soil of the West? Also, the building of Fort Gibson in Oklahoma in 1824 had failed to attract the whites, for they too preferred the Indians' land to taking their chances on the western frontier.

New Orleans had just learned that a regiment of dragoons and some infantry troops were being dispatched against the Indians, and the town was full of stories of white massacres. Dandridge, who knew the tribes involved, suspected they were exaggerating the Indians' "savagery," of which he had had personal experience in his younger days.

On each visit, he liked the city less. The bars were crowded with interlopers attracted to the bustling city. Adventurers sidled up to respectable men with wild schemes for instant wealth. Deserting seamen, starving immigrants, prostitutes, men from God knows where speaking no known language thronged the streets and bawdy houses. And the police couldn't keep up with the thefts and assaults. A sheriff told Dandridge that John Murrell, a famous bandit who used to seize barges on the Mississippi and abscond with their cargoes, was walking the streets of New Orleans and frequenting its whorehouses with impunity. The well-dressed braggart loved to show off his thumb, on which the letters "H.F." (for horse-filcher) had been branded.

So it was with little regret that Clarence got aboard the boat for the return home. Among his purchases were a carton of books that included three novels of Sir Walter Scott, two books of Keats's poetry and Byron's *The Vision of Judgment*.

The enforced idleness of the trip gave Clarence a chance to ruminate on recent events. He spent most of the day in a deck chair protected from the wind, avoiding all conversation with his fellow passengers. He read or watched the passing landscape; its monotony gave free rein to his thoughts. He pondered his ambivalent feelings toward Caroline, the odd mixture of confidence and distrust which he feared could well break a man. Their conversation on the eve of his departure had been a duel of minds waged with unspoken duplicity. He was the intermediary observing the acting out of a drama in which he played two roles. His deep friendship for Adrien had not prevented him from feeling a kind of love that wasn't love for Caroline, and this troubled him, for he needed both these people to help buttress his life.

He classed Caroline among those women who instinctively know when a man is at his most vulnerable. While the ordinary run of women were the docile instruments of fate, these exceptional women knew how to get around the ironic goddess. Their complicity earned them pleasures and power, the same way a rich patron gives money and glory to the artist he supports.

Caroline will get more from Lady Luck than most mortals, Clarence said to himself. She might even be capable of stealing some of fate's occult powers. Sometimes she seemed as corrosive as acid, sometimes as delectable as nectar, yet she was always consistent. She never prevaricated. At once one and multiple, she could change as quickly as lights transformed a stage. Of this particular quality she had given ample proof. She could make Adrien happy, but her own happiness she would have to find herself. Through the simple pleasures of life, she was reaching out for a kind of peace that excluded neither violent passions nor intellectual satisfactions. Above all, she was prodigiously alive.

From these reflections, Clarence gained a certain reassurance, for he was only too conscious of his responsibility for pushing his master down a path where an ambush had been lying in wait for some time.

When the boat docked at Baton Rouge, he dispatched a courier to Bagatelle to make sure that Bobo was waiting for him when he arrived at Pointe-Coupée. Then he dismissed Caroline from his thoughts and opened his Byron to reread a passage in *Childe Harold*:

> Still he beheld, nor mingled with the throng;
> But view'd them not with misanthropic hate,
> Fain would he now have join'd the dance,
> But who may smile that sinks beneath his fate?

Contrary to Childe Harold, Clarence had accepted a life without happiness, content with an entomologist's interest in observing other people's agitations.

Bobo was waiting for him on the dock.

"What news, Bobo?"

"The cotton is going good, Mister Dandridge. Though folks be saying it's a little dry. But there's other news, Mister Dandrige. Miss Caroline and the master is goin' to git married. Anna say so."

The coachman had the gift of divulging secrets unless expressly told not to.

"That's very good news, Bobo," Clarence said, climbing into the gig.

Caroline had obviously lost no time. He couldn't wait to hear Adrien's version.

Dandridge had barely set foot on the ground when the Marquis, who had been impatiently awaiting his arrival, came bounding out on the gallery.

"Did you have a good trip, my friend?" he asked, pretending interest in his journey.

"Just give me time to clean up, Adrien," Clarence said as he headed for his apartment, Mic and Mac racing to give their master a noisy welcome.

But Adrien couldn't wait. He strode across the walkway separating the two houses and was at Clarence's door before him.

"Clarence, I can't wait. You don't know how happy I am.

You were right. She's accepted me. Isn't it unbelievable!"

In his excitement, Adrien stepped on Mac's paw and the poor dog let out a yelp of pain.

"My congratulations, Adrien. I wish you all the happiness in the world."

The Marquis continued breathlessly, "And do you know what she said? She said that if I hadn't made up my mind before summer, she was going back to her aunt's in Paris."

"You're a lucky man, Adrien," Clarence said, observing that his employer's joy had made him look ten years younger.

"It's all your doing, Clarence? If you hadn't opened my eyes, I would never have dared . . ."

"Didn't you ever think about it in secret, Adrien?"

The Marquis had the guilty look of a schoolboy. "Well, you know, you can think about things without being sure you really want them. You gave me the prod I needed."

The two men laughed, Dandridge caught up in the Marquis's delight.

"We have some champagne cooling, and Anna is preparing a special dinner for tonight. Caroline didn't want to celebrate without you. She's very fond of you, you know."

"Did you mention to her our conversation of two weeks ago?" Clarence was a little apprehensive about the way the Marquis might have broached the subject to Caroline.

"Of course I did. I told her—please don't hold it against me—I told her, 'That nosy Dandridge told me you didn't want Willy Templeton, and what you needed for a husband was a man more like me.' Then I said, trying to make a joke of it, 'Dandridge has some pretty funny ideas.' " As he recalled the scene, Adrien assumed the air of a crafty peasant.

"What happened then?"

"She didn't say anything. I didn't know what to do. I felt like a damn fool . . . then she started to cry. She stood very straight, looked very unhappy and said, 'You shouldn't joke about such things, Adrien.' She called me Adrien!"

"Then what?"

"Then I kissed her . . . and we talked . . . and I didn't

close my eyes that whole night. The next morning, *she* kissed *me*. I'd told myself that she'd changed her mind. Not at all. That night, we became engaged. Just like that. My head's been in a whirl a whole week now. Maybe it's love, Clarence," the Marquis added timidly. "I'd forgotten it had such an effect."

"When do you plan to be married?"

"Well, it's over a year since Dorothée died. The mourning period is over. I wanted to wait until the cotton picking was over, but Caroline is impatient. Yes, my friend, Caroline is actually impatient. The sooner the better. There's no point postponing happiness, is there?"

"You're right, Adrien. Happiness must not be made to wait."

Adrien decided to announce their engagement at a barbecue at Bagatelle. This way, he would be observing the local custom which decreed that all happy occasions be a pretext for a party. After all, distractions were few. He also wanted the news of his remarriage to be known before the gossips started yammering about the briefness of his mourning. So everybody at the plantation was warned not to divulge the secret before the event.

Once the date was settled, the Marquis—as a good Southerner—wished to resolve a small problem to which he attached great importance. Caroline had been living under the same roof with her godfather without raising any eyebrows. In her new position as his fiancée, this cohabitation might appear a little ambiguous. All the more since, with Mignette gone, no other woman lived in the big house. Inevitably, people would find this a curious state of affairs and suggest that the Marquis and the pretty orphan girl had anticipated their nuptials.

First he thought of sending Caroline off to stay with a neighboring family—the Barrows, for instance, as the prime arbiters of local morals. But Adrien was much more in love than he let on and was reluctant to deprive himself for purely conventional reasons—even for the briefest time—of the woman who would be sharing his bed before summer. So he thought up a scheme which would keep her at Bagatelle without raising any suspicions about their relationship: He would provide Caroline with a chaperone. The lady chosen for the role was the mother superior of the Ursuline convent in New Orleans, a cousin of the Damvilliers many times removed. Born Marguerite de Bonnifet, she had become Mother Jean-Philippe du Saint-Sauveur when she took her vows, and was known everywhere as a paragon of virtue. At the time she received the summons to appear at Bagatelle the lady was nearing seventy, but she had kept her pure complexion, gentle manners and the gaiety appropriate to the saintly. Also, she loved good food. The prospect of spending a few weeks at Bagatelle, therefore, enchanted the woman. So she set off with a light heart, including in her luggage an edifying book by an anonymous Capuchin—more pious than competent—entitled *The Saintly Happiness of a Christian Marriage.*

Caroline declared herself satisfied with the solution even as she exchanged knowing smiles with Clarence. The girl laughingly recalled her brief sojourn as a child at the old convent on Rue de Chartres whose dark hallways smelled, like all convents, of a mixture of warmed-over food, disinfectant, trimmed candles and incense.

"That is the odor of virtue, my dear," Adrien said, giving his fiancée's hand a shy caress.

"I hope the reverend mother doesn't bring it with her," Dandridge said. "I much prefer the smell of the vetiver and eucalyptus that Anna spreads around."

Caroline spent a busy spring. The hundred-year-old house had always been well maintained, but the rustic inclinations of its proprietors had made them pay greater attention to its solidity and resistance to weather than to its outward appearance. A weak beam, a clogged gutter or a buckling column was of much greater concern than a broken railing or crooked step. Replacing a rotting cypress board, yes; patch-ing up some peeling paint, no. So, during the course of the years, the house had retained its sturdiness but lost some of its grace.

Caroline had the floors scraped and polished with Mamma Netta's own homemade beeswax. The rugs were washed in tepid water with soap softened with wood ashes, the rocking chairs were recaned, and potted plants hung from the gallery beams. Inside, the heavy lace curtains were replaced with sheer cotton.

"The outside and inside painting can be done while we're on our honeymoon," Caroline said to Dandridge one afternoon over tea on the gallery.

"Where will you be going?"

"To Europe."

"You are actually going to get Adrien off his duff?" Clarence was astounded, for the Marquis had never set foot outside Louisiana, protesting that he hated all travel.

"He's the one who suggested it. While we're gone, dear Clarence, it will be your job to supervise the remodeling of Bagatelle. I'm determined that by this time next year, Bagatelle will be the handsomest house in the parish."

Caroline spoke with a new authority, confirming Clarence's opinion that she would indeed be a perfect mistress for Bagatelle. Since she seemed in an expansive mood, he asked her, "Are you happy, Caroline?"

"I am, and I'll be even happier later. You can't imagine what stability and the responsibility of a home mean to a woman. Under his rough and ready ways, Adrien is the most sensitive man I've ever known. And he has such strength. He seems indestructible. I think we'll make a good pair. Without being vain, I think I can honestly say that I'm exactly the woman he needs."

"And that Bagatelle needs. Will you be gone long?"

"About six months. Adrien wants to meet the spinners in Liverpool and the brokers in London. And I want to introduce him to Paris, which he's convinced is a sink of iniquity."

"Isn't it?"

"You can fall from grace anywhere, even in Louisiana. It's a question of knowing how to avoid danger before it strikes." Was she perhaps alluding to her adventure with Percy Templeton? This put Clarence in mind of Willy.

"Have you told Willy about your marriage to Adrien?"

"No, Adrien doesn't want a word said before he makes the formal announcement of our engagement. All I did was write him that I didn't want to marry him. I gave no explanations."

"He'll be very unhappy when he learns that your choice fell on your godfather."

"He may be unhappy, but I think he'll understand that it's precisely because I'm marrying Adrien that I wasn't the right woman for him. It would have been too easy to be Willy Templeton's wife. I don't like born worshipers, or men who can be dominated simply by a woman's wiles."

"But you're dominating Adrien with those very same wiles. You only need to look at him to know that's true."

"You're wrong, Clarence. Adrien can't be dominated. He is a man and a master. The man in him can be made happy or made to suffer, and he can be led up to a certain point, but the master remains inviolable. He's been in the habit of commanding too long to obey even out of love. I'll take care of the man. As for the master, I'll do my very best to serve him."

Caroline said all this with apparent sincerity and conviction. Yet, Clarence was yearning to ask her an indiscreet question. Perhaps this was the moment.

"Are you in love, Caroline?" he asked gently.

Not the least offended, she answered simply, "I'll have to tell you that later."

He admired her frankness and was gratified at this new proof of their complicity. At this point, he said to himself, she's closer to me than to Adrien. And he recalled how the Marquis had told him one day: "You're the kind of man whose whole life is lived in his head." Clarence's way of loving people was to understand them. They sat in silence, watching the black storm clouds gathering over the Mississippi.

"Adrien will be soaked to the skin if he doesn't come home soon," she said.

The words were no sooner spoken than they heard the sound of a galloping horse on the river path.

A minute later, in a gust of wind heralding the coming storm, the master appeared. Caroline ran down the steps to meet him. Clarence whistled for his dogs. As he was about to enter his apartment, he turned to observe the pair. They were walking toward the house, Adrien's large hand on Caroline's shoulder, and they were looking into each other's eyes as lovers have done since the beginning of time. Large gentle drops began to fall. Clarence went in, lit a cigar, and examined the Damvilliers's family tree tacked on his wall. He took it down, picked up a ruler and pen and drew a horizontal line after the name Dorothée Lepas flanked by a black cross. Where the line ended, he carefully wrote in "Caroline Trégan."

Upon her arrival, the reverend mother quickly became a very pleasant companion for Dandridge. Knowledgeable and cultivated, she was also an avid botanist and student of natural history. In her view, the contemplation of nature was ample proof of the existence of God. She was discreet in her performance of her duties as chaperone, well aware of the fact that she was there for the sake of appearances. And she approved of Caroline without reservation.

The cotton was already tall and vigorous when the two hundred invitations went out for the first Saturday in June. The ladies showed off their new dresses, the young men resumed old flirtations or started new ones. Even the Barrow sisters lent their presence, accompanied by Clement on the arm of an old retainer. For the Templetons, it was their first public appearance since Corinne's death. Percy came with his wife Isabelle. And Willy most unexpectedly was able to get a two days' leave. His look of sorrow was interpreted as the solemnity becoming a military officer.

This time, because of the threat of sudden rains, the dancing would take place indoors. The buffet was laid on tables under the oaks. The Marquis appeared relaxed in his new dove-gray frock coat, a mauve silk cravat over his starched white shirt. Caroline's gown of English lace was applauded by the mother superior for its simplicity. Framed by her ringlets "à la Sevigné," her porcelain skin and green eyes perfectly evoked the ideal of Southern womanhood as painted fifty years before by Joseph de Salazar, whose pictures adorned many a planter's home.

When Caroline saw Willy, she suppressed a look of astonishment. The young lieutenant smiled at her gravely in a manner that combined resignation and good breeding.

"I hope you don't find my presence unwelcome."

"Of course not, Willy. I am and will always be your friend." Then, to prepare him for what she knew would cause him further pain, she added, "Be on hand for an announcement coming very soon."

Ed Barthew had caught the end of the conversation and turned to Mignette, who was walking up to Caroline on her husband's arm. "What's to be announced? Aren't you in on the princess's secrets, Mrs. Schoeler?"

"Not in the secrets of the princess," she said with a sly smile, "but in the Marquise's perhaps . . ."

"You mean that Caroline may be marrying the . . ."

"Shhh. Don't be in such a hurry . . . and keep your assumptions to yourself, my dear Ed."

With most of the guests present, the Marquis decided it was time to make his announcement. Standing on the gallery, he clapped his hands to get their attention. Ed Barthew was one of the very few who had guessed what was about to take place.

"My friends," Adrien said in a loud clear voice, "I want you to be the first to learn what I hope will meet with your approval." He paused to scan the upturned faces. "I am about to marry . . ."

A murmur of surprise traveled through the crowd. Clarence looked around him and caught Willy's unsuspecting gaze. "The poor boy hasn't the faintest idea . . ." The Marquis waited a brief interval, then continued with the grandiloquence of a hawker at a country fair: "And now I wish to present my fiancée!"

With that, the front door opened, Caroline appeared on the gallery and took her place next to the Marquis. There was a general intake of breath, looks of astonishment were exchanged, then everyone broke into noisy applause.

"You all know Caroline," he said, taking her hand as she blushed prettily with downcast eyes. A consummate performance, Clarence had to admit. She then made a tiny curtsey, which brought forth more applause.

"Give her a kiss. Give her a kiss," a group of men shouted, soon picked up by a chorus of voices.

The Marquis hesitated, then kissed her with tender clumsiness. Caroline returned the kiss with just the right amount of impetuous enthusiasm.

"I now invite you to celebrate with us. Glasses in hand!"

As the excitement subsided and the guests repaired to the buffet table, Clarence stood marveling at the perfection of the little scene he had just witnessed—no doubt choreographed and thoroughly rehearsed by Caroline. But his thoughts now turned to Willy, for something told him he should look after Caroline's rejected admirer. He finally found him standing with Dr. Murphy, emptying glass after glass of champagne. Ed Barthew, who was looking for his habitual drinking partner, found himself walking next to Dandridge. The lawyer was in high spirits.

"Astonishing, isn't it? This sudden engagement?"

"Astonishing to whom?"

"Not to you, of course. But to the rest of us. And especially for poor Willy, who seems determined to get drunk. I thought young men learned how to drink in the army. Or is he so damned unimaginative that he has to drown his sorrows in wine?"

"He seems to be doing it pretty spontaneously," Clarence observed.

As the two men neared the buffet, Willy called out, his eyes glittering, his tone combative:

"Come drink to it, Dandridge. Caroline Trégan, Marquise de Damvilliers. What a love story, heh?"

The champagne was obviously taking effect. No one had ever seen the dignified Willy so unbuttoned. Murphy handed him a fresh glass so that he could drink with Barthew and Dandridge. Willy emptied it at one gulp, wiped his mouth with the back of his hand—a surprising gesture for him—and continued with increasing belligerence, "Dandridge, did you know that I offered her my hand and she refused it? The Templetons are only descendants of a British majordomo. The Damvilliers are something else, heh? They were cuckolded by the King of France!"

The people crowding around the buffet looked at each other with surprise and amusement. Some smiled, others appeared shocked. A few of the women inched toward the group in the hope of further revelations. Dandridge smelled trouble.

"Come on, Willy, calm down. This is neither the time nor the place to display your disappointment. Nobody here has done you any harm."

"I'm only mad at myself for behaving like a fool. I should have known that Miss Trégan had higher ambitions, just as Corinne should have known it about you."

Dandridge paled. But for the lieutenant's condition, he would have answered him sharply—even at the risk of provoking a duel.

"You don't know what you're talking about, my boy," Murphy intervened. "Here, drink this,"—and he gave him a glass of water spiked with gin.

"Don't you think you've had enough to drink, Willy?" Clarence said between pinched lips.

Barthew had been following the altercation with misgivings. While the young lieutenant was conscientiously sipping his drink, he whispered in Dandridge's ear, "Leave it to Murphy. He'll finish him off, then we can stretch him out in a carriage somewhere . . ."

Unnoticed by anyone, Percy suddenly appeared, probably

warned by a guest that his brother was "talking nonsense."
Angry, he took his brother by the arm.

"You come with me before you find yourself fighting another duel."

As he tried to drag him away, Willy shook him off savagely.

"I'll say what I want to whom I want and I'll fight with whomever I like when I like." Then he lapsed into hiccups, his bleary eyes wandering over the guests with a show of defiance.

Around the group, conversation had come to an abrupt halt, but Willy's thick voice could be heard at thirty paces. The Marquis, who had been talking with Clement Barrow, straightened up and peered over the guests to see where the noise was coming from.

"I must find out what's going on," he said with concern.

Caroline wanted to follow him but he waved her back.
"You stay with our friend, Caroline. I'll be right back."

His tone was clear and categorical. An order. She obeyed.

"What's going on, Willy? You don't like my champagne?" The sight of Bagatelle's master disconcerted Willy. He said apologetically, "I have nothing to say, sir, not about the champagne . . . or anything else. I wish you happiness . . . I'll go now."

If Barthew and Percy hadn't been there to support him, the poor lieutenant would have collapsed on the ground like a rag doll.

"Take him into the house and let him rest. And ask Anna to make him a cup of strong coffee." Having given out his orders, the Marquis returned to Caroline and the Barrows.

"One man's happiness may be another man's grief," Adele Barrow said with a simper. Adrien gave her a look that cut off further observations.

"The incident is closed," he said. "Willy is drunk. They don't know how to drink in the artillery."

Percy had taken his brother behind the house. Meek and limp, Willy was trying to restore his dignity with exaggerated earnestness. His brother stretched him out under a tree and borrowed a cushion from a landau to place under his head.

"Poor Willy, you don't know the first thing about women," he said gently. "Believe me, consider yourself lucky to have escaped Caroline Trégan."

"But I love her," the handsome lieutenant said in a stricken voice.

"What rubbish!" Percy said over his shoulder as he walked away. The sight of a Templeton with trembling lips and tears in his eyes was more than he could bear. He had been on the verge of telling him that he had slept with his idol, but he held his tongue, partly to spare his brother's alcoholic chagrin, partly because he didn't like to think about it. The iron in Caroline's soul had frightened him, and the memory of the episode was still painful.

Caroline had been at The Myrtles two days, flirting with him slyly, when Corinne came down with a cold and had to stay in bed. Caroline, left to her own devices, asked Percy to show her the guest cottage—a pretty little house his mother had done up as her Louisiana version of the Petit Trianon. He had intimated to Caroline the actual motives behind his mother's remodeling of the cottage, and a wicked gleam had come into Caroline's eyes.

"Dear Percy, I must see your mother's hideaway!" Then she added, with a look that set Percy's heart aflame: "But I want you to be the one to take me there."

Percy had been in a quandary over the request. Certainly he had entertained ideas of testing Caroline's provocative ways, but he was unprepared for the directness of her challenge. Southern girls of good family did not act in this manner.

They walked down a leaf-strewn path and finally came upon the house, tucked away in a woodsy enclosure. They entered the house (Percy had availed himself of a key) and as she beheld its ingenuous charm, she exclaimed: "Why, Percy, what a perfect setting for a seduction!"

With that, she put a match to the fire in the hearth and removed her cape. Fixing him with a teasing look, she said:

"Each time I take off a garment, you do likewise. But since I have no maid here, you will have to unhook my dress."

Once the dress was off, her eyes never leaving his, she shed every layer until she stood in front of him naked. Flinging her arms wide, she said with a lilting laugh: "And now, Percy, what do you suppose your mother would do next?"

At the sight of the opulent young body, Percy, down to his underwear, was abashed. No woman had ever challenged him thus; he had always been the aggressor. And the girls he had seduced were servants, anonymous females he never feared to see again.

Caroline moved toward him and took his hand. With a tone of impatience, she said, "Come, Percy, if you wait any longer, I shall catch cold—or change my mind."

He had led her into the bedroom and this Amazon without modesty or scruples had immediately taken the initiative. Removing his undergarments, she coolly examined his body from head to foot. "Very good. Yes. But you have a tendency toward fat that bears watching, dear Percy."

The next moment they were on the bed. Caroline played him like a kitten, teasing him, licking and biting him, then retreating with a rebuff when he thought he had the upper hand. When she saw that the gallant cavalier was at the end of his tether, she allowed him to take his pleasure. But hers was the greater. Not only was her young passion satisfied, but she had also humbled proud Percy and made him do her bidding.

An hour later, they were seen crossing the lawn toward the main house, Caroline prattling away, pointing out vistas and handsome plantings, while Percy walked beside her, head down and strangely silent.

Later that night when the household was asleep and his wife was snoring gently at his side, Percy had gotten up and tiptoed down the hall to Caroline's room. This demon girl might have won the first round; he, Percy, would dominate the second. He opened her door. Pale moonlight flooded the room. When Caroline saw his silhouette in the doorway, she sat up and exclaimed in a loud whisper: "What are you doing here, Percy?"

Percy closed the door behind him. "I'm sure you can guess, Caroline. I'm here to even the score."

"You stay in this room one second longer and I'll scream. I'm not your whore, Percy Templeton. You can't have me whenever you feel like it."

"Oh yes I can, Caroline," he said as he advanced closer. Before she could say another word, he had thrown back the covers, flung himself on top of her and covered her mouth with his hand.

He whispered urgently into her ear: "I'm going to show you how a man makes love, you hellcat." Removing his hand, he pressed his mouth against hers, pulled up her nightgown, inquisitive hands kneading her body, and with a mighty lunge that made her wince, began his assault. It was a lucky thing that the bed was against an outside wall; otherwise its loud rhythmic creaking would surely have awakened Corinne next door.

A few moments later, Percy's triumph was complete. With a deep groan, he collapsed on Caroline with his full weight. When he had caught his breath, he put his mouth to her ear: "You liked that, didn't you, hellcat?"

"You hurt me, Percy," she said with a whimper.

His voice muffled by her hair, Percy was insistent: "But you liked it, Caroline. I know you liked it. You were with me all the way. You can't deny it."

Covering her embarrassment with anger, she spat out: "I hate you, Percy Templeton. You're not a man, you're an animal."

Then she shoved him aside, sat up and announced: "I want to go home. I want to go home right now. I can't face you or your family tomorrow. Especially Corinne." She prodded the recumbent figure. "Go get dressed and hitch up the buggy, Percy. I'll meet you by the stables in twenty minutes."

Percy stretched lazily. "So the hellcat wants to go home and lick her wounds," he said with a malicious grin.

"Get out!" she hissed.

Percy calmly picked his dressing gown off the floor and walked to the door. Before opening it, he turned and said unctuously: "Hellcat is an animal too."

A half hour later, Percy sullen and Caroline sitting ramrod straight beside him, they started back toward Bagatelle.

Six months later, the volatile Marquise-to-be still gave him pause.

Caroline only learned of Willy's behavior at the barbecue the following day—from Clarence.

"What a stupid fool," she said with contempt.

"I think I heard him say something about volunteering for a regiment fighting the Indians."

"He can have all the glory he wants, so long as he leaves me in peace."

"The Cherokees' arrows are just as effective as Cupid's," Clarence said, sighing with sympathy for the unfortunate lieutenant. "But he'll do better on the field of battle than in a lady's chamber."

"Physical courage is no proof of intelligence," Caroline said crisply. "Good soldiers are often imbeciles."

Dandridge found the remark cruel—and self-serving.

At the beginning of autumn, the Marquis and Marquise de Damvilliers sailed for Liverpool aboard a clipper known for its speed and comfort. With them they carried the memory of a glorious wedding, a high-water mark in the annals of Pointe-Coupée's social history. The most sumptuous gift was undoubtedly Abraham Mosely's: a clock and pair of candelabra in vermeil from, according to his accompanying note, Queen Anne's bedroom at Warwick Castle. "This last of the Stuarts occupied the throne of England before the Damvilliers took up residence on the banks of the Mississippi, but knowing that the English silver brought from France by the first Marquis was from her reign, I hope that my gift will fit in with the decor of your dear Bagatelle." When he sent him his warm thanks, Adrien added that he would like to visit him in England at the beginning of November.

The bride and groom sailed into Liverpool on a cold damp day, the sky a leaden gray with heavy clouds weighing down the rooftops. For the first time in his life, Adrien put on an overcoat and a thick felt hat. Caroline taught him how to use an umbrella. Such was his happiness that the elements didn't faze him—although anyone else coming from a sunny climate would have found the environment unbearably lugubrious. He simply observed that nature had overlooked this harbor, and that the Mersey with its stony banks was a piddling river compared to the Mississippi. But he was profoundly impressed by the bustling port, its docks with their enclosed basins, its granite quays, the grime on its warehouses, and most of all, by the forest of masts that made it look as if every ship in the world had dropped anchor in Liverpool's harbor.

They spent the night in a hotel on Lord Street and the following morning, while Caroline was dozing on a shabby sofa, Adrien set off in search of a bank on Dale Street to present his letter of credit. In passing, he glanced at the Town Hall, built in 1754 and therefore contemporary with Bagatelle. He found it pretentious and in much worse shape than his own house.

The banker received him graciously, for wasn't the Marquis de Damvilliers one of those who were making Liverpool rich, whose cotton arrived by the shipload every year? And hadn't his ancestors added to the city's revenues when the slave ships returned not only with their exotic cargoes but the profits of the slave trade as well? The good bourgeois folk of Liverpool had never set eyes on a black, yet it was to the blacks that they owed a large part of their wealth. They preferred not to know how the slaves had been abducted from their tribes in Africa to work in American fields. Nor did they wish to know under what atrocious conditions these passengers had made the Atlantic crossing. Besides, it would have been depressing for their wives, who knew Africa only as the place that produced ostrich plumes and coconuts.

"Let's get out of here, my love," he said on returning to his wife at the hotel. "I don't like the people and it's raining soot."

So they rented a carriage driven by a coachman who swore in an unintelligible English and took the road to Manchester. Adrien noted that the highway was in worse condition than the meanest road in Louisiana.

Manchester on the Irwell, a small tributary of the Mersey, looked as gloomy and inhospitable as Liverpool. Adrien had never seen so many ill-clothed people, trudging like spent beasts toward grimy factories where they converted "his" cotton into cloth. He glanced at Caroline huddled in a corner of the carriage, swathed in shawls, trying not to wince at every jolt. He took her hand and kissed it tenderly. At the sight of each other's discomfiture, they both burst into laughter. They tried to picture their refined friend Mosely in this dismal landscape with its morose population. The fact that he lived on Mosely Street, named after his family, was reassuring. His house must surely be more comfortable and cleaner than their Liverpool hotel. Adrien wondered about the bed.

Since their marriage, Caroline had revealed herself to be the perfect spouse. Adrien often looked at her, as he was doing now. It was a look full of tenderness and veneration. He was literally awash with a sense of well-being. Caroline was always attentive and full of happy inspirations. Not a day went by that she didn't dream up something to surprise him with and bring him joy.

And their nights. Adrien thought about these a great deal. From his wedding day on, instead of finding ways to extend his after-dinner chats with Clarence on the gallery, he seized the earliest opportunity to join Caroline in their big tester bed where she offered up her admirable body with abandon.

Brought up to distrust the claims of the flesh, Adrien had long believed that the pleasure it gave corrupted men's souls and amounted to little more than a fleeting and shameful reward for the sacred act of procreation. The Marquis owed most of his amorous curiosity to some drawings he had found on a top shelf in his father's library. As a result, he viewed the sexual act with a mixture of prudishness and unconscious lust. The late Dorothée had revealed little of the female anatomy, submitting with closed eyes, in silence, and in total darkness, to his confused assaults.

Caroline offered a love that inspired his art and the multiplicity of its practices, their bodies naked and unashamed in the soft light of the opaline lamps. Without in any way raising his suspicions, she guided his initiatives, suggesting preliminary caresses with feigned timidity. As he grew bolder, she began to imitate his gestures, then played variations on them, each time with greater subtlety, greater audacity, more competence. Gradually, she taught him to perfect his lovemaking to the point where she took equal pleasure. Her young woman's sensuality found its response in her husband's vigor. In no time, she had succeeded in disciplining his peasant-like virility and improving the rudimentary techniques of his desire. Like an orchestra conductor bringing out the best in a score, Caroline managed in a few nights to turn her husband into an acceptable lover who left her exhausted yet as light as a cloud.

After their lovemaking, Adrien trembled with gratitude, caressing her nipples and marveling that he could encircle her waist with his hands. Then, once she had lapsed into sleep, he pulled up the sheet with the care of an antiquarian packing Sèvres china, covering the body so gloriously his.

Sometimes, when Caroline was gasping and moaning in her climax, he tried to quiet her with a kiss, whispering "Shhh," as if he still felt the vestiges of his old shame. But he no longer asked her, as he had during their first night, "Did I hurt you?"

Actually, his only frustration—and it was a small one to be sure—was that he couldn't share his nocturnal ecstasies with Clarence. When Adrien was preparing to leave the plantation, Clarence asked, "Are you happy, Adrien?"

"Yes, very happy, Clarence. Completely happy. In every way . . ."

Clarence smiled, understanding perfectly what his diffident employer was trying to convey. But at least he now knew that Caroline had acquitted herself well on every level.

Because of the thinness of the walls, the servants were also well aware of the couple's ardor and the success of their union. Those who were still virgins tried to imagine the delights experienced in the big bed, which every morning showed the telltale signs of love's effluvium.

Would they experience these ecstasies in Manchester? the Marquis wondered.

Mosely lived in a brick house mellowed by smoke, like an old pipe. Narrow, two storied, with a fan-shaped porch, it was approached by four steps leading up to its polished oak door. The carriage came to a stop with a screech of brakes. The coachman pulled on a bell that started a faint peal far inside the walls, while the Damvilliers, fatigued after fifteen hours of travel, stretched their legs on the sidewalk. Adrien sniffed the night air.

"Funny odor. A mixture of damp soot and hot sulfur. I suppose it's the way all factory towns smell."

At long last, a tall, unsmiling butler made his appearance. Informed of the visitors' identity, he went back into a dimly lit hall and, without saying a word, waved his arm like a cavalry officer commanding a charge. Two footmen in striped vests came rushing from the house and seized the luggage. Then, as stiff as a poker, the butler again waved his arm and beckoned the guests into the house.

They entered a large hall with gleaming floors, a tan fabric on the walls, a large mirror flanked by hooks for hats and coats, a marquetry pedestal table and a green velvet settee. No sooner had they taken in the decor than Abraham Mosely emerged from a neighboring room ablaze in a red silk dressing gown with black frogs, a broad smile on his doll-like face.

"I wasn't expecting you so late. I could have sent you my

carriage to fetch you here from Liverpool if you'd only told me!"

There were apologies all around, then Adrien's heart sank when his host said, "Parker will show you to your rooms," for this meant that he would be separated from Caroline. His bride was led to the second floor and shown into a vast room furnished in Chippendale and dominated by a large mahogany bed with a muslin canopy. The Marquis had an adjoining room almost entirely filled by a huge brass bed that creaked like the carriage that had brought them from Liverpool. With a wink, Mosely indicated a connecting door, then waited until the Marquis discovered the watercolor of Bagatelle he had painted himself. Filled with emotion, Adrien thanked his host, suggesting, however, that the artist had flattered his house. His enthusiastic brush had given it the dimensions of a Florentine palace set down in a virgin forest.

Caroline was exhausted, so she went to bed right away. Out of courtesy to his host, the Marquis accepted his invitation to join him in the drawing room, where he was brought a slice of York ham and a glass of claret. As they sat in their wing chairs on either side of the fireplace, Adrien felt he was at last in a civilized country. Everything in the house exuded refined comfort. The gleaming mahogany furniture, the polished paneling, the rare objets d'art, the deep rugs, the sculptured bronze sconces, the cut crystal in which his wine sparkled like rubies, bespoke the good taste of a baron at ease in his castle.

"Do you realize you could have come from Liverpool by train?" Mosely said expansively.

"By railroad? You have railroads?"

"Ha, don't we though. For the past two years, Mr. Stephenson's locomotive has been pulling five passenger cars between here and Liverpool. If nothing goes wrong, you can do the thirty-four miles in two hours and fifteen minutes, including stops. Isn't progress a marvelous thing, Marquis?"

The Marquis looked doubtful. He had heard that the railroads had been transporting coal in Virginia since 1830 and that the Delaware and Hudson had done the same between Honesdale and the Carbondale mines. Mosely, with a touch of British chauvinism, expatiated on what he called "the great adventure of the rails." "Railroads are the future, believe me, Marquis. I've put a bit of my own money into a steel mill manufacturing rails. The companies need capital to make cars and locomotives. Parliament has been besieged with requests for more railroad lines, and there's wild speculation in easements for roadbeds and railway stations."

"I know we have large projects for railroads in America. In fact, you told me about it at Bagatelle, remember? But I'm afraid they're nothing but traps for the unwary. Besides, I've heard that railroads are unhealthy, that their speed leads to suffocation—and Lord knows what else. Not to mention the danger of explosions in their boilers. We people in Louisiana know all about boiler explosions from our river steamers. It was in just such an explosion that poor Corinne Templeton met her death."

Mosely didn't like to be reminded of such things. He quickly interjected, "I'm going to show you our railroads. I'll even introduce you to George Stephenson and his son Robert, if you like. You'll see. They're neither fools nor utopians."

When they parted for the night, the Marquis went upstairs, then quietly opened the door connecting his room with Caroline's. His candlestick in his hand, he tiptoed to her bed. His wife was sound asleep, her lips parted, the fringe of her eyelashes outlining her closed lids. He stood admiring the perfection of her face, then drew the sheet over her bare shoulder and left, happy and supremely confident of the future.

Mosely organized their stay with tact and a sure instinct. The very next day, he gave a party in their honor so that they might meet Manchester's leading businessmen and industrialists. While Caroline attended tea parties given by oddly dressed ladies in stuffy drawing rooms and ate inedible cakes, Adrien visited textile mills and spinning factories. As he followed with rapt attention the processing of cotton into cloth, sheeting and shirting, it still remained in his mind a product of the soil.

Carlyle had recently declared: "Work is healthy. All work, even cotton spinning, is noble; work alone is noble." And people worked hard in Manchester. The indolent ways of the South would have seemed decadent here. Brokers, traders, bankers and agents were at their offices at the same early hour as the thousands of workers hurrying to their factories. The sight of all this activity made Adrien dizzy. Walking arm in arm down one of the city's principal streets, Adrien addressed his concern to his host.

"These people don't take the time to live, Mosely."

"But, my dear Marquis, everybody here works freely. That's the beauty of it. We don't have black slaves. These people may spend fifteen hours in their offices and factories but they earn a fair salary and spend it as they wish."

"When I look at their faces and watch them trudging along the street, it seems to me they're less happy and more tired than our Negroes. And what do they do when there's no work for them?"

"There's always enough work to go around. Only the lazy suffer. The master here, like everywhere else, is money. In order to have money, you have to earn it."

"But what about the weak, the disabled, the sick, the old? What happens to them? Who takes care of them? With us, they're assured of a roof, and pork and grits until they die. Even if they're not up to much."

"Here, those people are taken care of by their relatives . . . and there's the hospital. We haven't the time to worry about those who can't work."

"It seems to me that the slavery your philosophers love to condemn offers greater security. In the end, liberty is fine for those who have the means to use it. These people only appear to be free. I can sell my Negroes to another planter who'll take them over and put them to work. Your industrialists are free to lay off their workers and leave them to starve. In my view, these people aren't free at all. As we say at home, they're slaves without masters."

"There's one thing you've got to understand, Marquis," Mosely said solemnly. "These people's freedom is hope. There's no way your slaves can change their condition. They die as they were born, whereas our workers can work their way up, like all our citizens. They can earn more, become foremen, and if they save their money, eventually own something. Look at Mr. Stephenson. He was a little clockmaker; today he's an industrialist."

"But all these people who hold out their hands at street corners, totally dependent on public charity, and all these women in rags, and the one-armed or one-legged sailors, and the old men leaning against the walls, what hope can they possibly have?"

"They're the rejects, the refuse of our society. They usually get exactly what they deserve. We can't concern ourselves with them. England is growing, we have progress here, we're getting richer. The deadweights and foot-draggers have to look after themselves. That's the law of the new world!"

"It's not a very just law," Adrien said, pointing to a child of ten, bent under a load twice his weight. "I'd never dare ask a black child to carry anything that heavy!"

"You're being sentimental, Marquis. You know perfectly well that this goes on on many of your plantations. Nobody forced the boy to carry that load. Nobody forced him to do that kind of work. He could go off and shoot marbles if he liked . . ."

"Of course he could shoot marbles, but if he didn't do this work, he wouldn't eat, would he?"

"All right. Why don't you ask him?" Mosely said brusquely.

The Marquis walked up to the child, who stopped, resting his burden on a barrier.

"What's your name?"

"Timmy."

"What are you carrying there?"

"Sheets for the Hotel Bertram."

"Is it heavy?"

"Not too." The child looked suspiciously at the well-dressed man who had taken off his silk hat and was passing a gloved hand through his curly hair.

"How much do you earn?"

"Fifteen shillings a week, sir. I'm a messenger."

"What do your parents do?"

"I don't have any. I've got to be going, sir, or I'll get caught."

"Let me feel the weight of your bundle, Timmy. I want to see how strong you are."

The child reluctantly let him heft the bundle.

"Why, it's heavier than you are," he said with an ingratiating smile.

"I don't know about that, sir, but if I don't get going, I'm going to lose my job."

"All right, Timmy, you can go. Here, take this. It's an American silver dollar."

The child put the money in his pocket without looking at it, settled his bundle on his back and trotted off on spindly legs.

"You see, Marquis, he wasn't complaining. And he's conscientious besides," Mosely said as he watched the child disappear down the street.

Mosely wondered what Adrien would say if he saw the children working in the mines. But he guessed correctly that this man who lived in open country in a sunny climate wasn't ready for such a sight. He therefore didn't include a visit to the colliery in which he had an interest.

"I'm taking you to the Trade Club now," he said, putting his arm through the Marquis's. "I'll give you a good glass of sherry and you'll meet people who really count."

"All the same, I'm glad I met a child who doesn't count. I'll now know what to say to the Boston Quakers when they come to us with their lessons in liberty." Then he added, unaware of his seeming impertinence: "If I were British, I'd be a Socialist!"

Mosely was startled. "You're saying that only because

Timmy has a white skin and you're not used to seeing whites do hard labor."

"You may be right, Mosely. Blacks are different."

As Adrien walked around the city, which already boasted a population of three hundred thousand, he revised the opinion he expressed on his arrival. The gray streets seemed less depressing; also, the designs on the factory chimneys had a certain originality. But why were there so few trees? The only ones he saw—in private gardens and public squares—had the same sickly look as Timmy. Like Adrien, they probably had trouble breathing the polluted air that soiled a jabot in a single morning. The better houses looked solidly built, but why were they so narrow? Mosely explained that with the high price of land, houses had to be built tall. Behind their sturdy walls, however, the rooms were cozy and full of fine furniture, rugs and paintings.

"The English don't like to display their wealth. They keep it for their private lives."

Adrien and Caroline exchanged their impressions each evening before dinner. Both agreed that so much brick and stone was oppressive. They were therefore delighted when Mosely offered them his carriage and a valet for the trip to London, including an itinerary through Britain's garden—the Cotswolds.

Out of anxiety for Mosely's splendid horses, they moved slowly down the narrow valleys until they reached Stratford-on-Avon. Avoiding Birmingham with its factories and collieries, they reveled in the autumn landscape, the gently rolling hills, the villages with their thatched roofs, and particularly in their host's comfortable carriage with its smell of new leather. Adrien's disposition improved the moment he put the cities behind him. At Stoke-on-Trent, they stopped at a coaching inn named "Crown and Anchor," discovered the Staffordshire potteries and made love in a big bed whose coarse sheets smelled of open fields.

When they finally entered "Shakespeare Country," Caroline was beside herself, for she had read the Bard's every word.

It was an especially mild November, alternating between occasional light rains and periods when the warm sun broke through innocuous clouds, bathing the gentle landscape with autumnal glory. Some mornings there was a hint of winter when the sun hid behind a curtain of thick fog, but by mid-morning, it reappeared with all its summer warmth.

"I now understand why Clarence sometimes feels nostalgic about this country," Adrien said. "We should have tried to look up his father. He would have liked that."

"He didn't ask us to," Caroline replied curtly.

"My dear, haven't you noticed that Dandridge never asks for anything? He's the most discreet man I know. Without him, I never could have left Bagatelle for as long as this. He has to supervise the cotton picking, the shipping of the molasses, and all the restoration you asked for. I suppose he plays billiards at the Barrows or spends his evenings reading in the big empty house. Maybe he misses us. We should write to him."

The Damvilliers decided to stay in Broadway, tucked away among the rounded hills, and only fifteen miles from Stratford. Mosely had told them that it was an ideal spot from which to visit the area, and that the "Lygon Arms" was one of the best inns in England.

The round little innkeeper quickly recognized the quality of his guests. Besides, they had been sent by Mr. Mosely, the well-known trader from Manchester who always stayed there on his way to London and never failed to order a jugged hare. He showed them into his best room, which not surprisingly was the one where Cromwell had slept before the Battle of Worcester.

"I feel as if I were in a museum," Adrien said, feeling the bed of dark wood that looked like a coffin. They were equally impressed with the dining room, which was hung with antlers, armor, crossbows and heraldic devices. A huge fireplace in which a massive oak log crackled took up one whole wall. Adrien had loved the old tales of chivalry and now felt a childlike joy to be dining under the heavy beams that once resounded to the laughter of feasting barons. When a wagon covered with a silver dome was rolled up and the dome was removed, revealing a roast saddle of lamb, Adrien reached for Caroline's hand.

"What a wonderful trip this has been. I feel as if I were living a dream. We're all alone, you and I, navigating in another age. I wish this moment could last forever!"

His wife was not accustomed to such outbursts of lyricism. Perhaps the claret had loosened his tongue. Actually, ever since they left home, she had been feeling a growing tenderness toward her husband. As she took in the intense look in his eyes which promised a voluptuous night in Cromwell's bed, she remembered Clarence's question: "Are you in love, Caroline?" Tonight, had Dandridge been so indiscreet as to ask her again, she would have been very close to answering "yes."

They spent a few days visiting historic ruins, then headed for Stratford and spent the night in a rustic inn remarkable only for its lack of comfort. The rats that made free with their room were not at all put out by the presence of the Americans. They had obviously occupied the room for many generations. Caroline, who, unlike most women, didn't scream at the sight of a rodent, suggested that one of them, a scraggly old rat who could barely move, might be a contemporary of Shakespeare's. While she lay buried in her husband's arms, he kept a cane within arm's reach, like a Mars watching over his sleeping Venus.

At the end of November, they finally set off for London, a cold wind heralding winter, stripping the trees and denuding the copses. Thanks to Caroline's old London friends, they spent a hectic week attending luncheons, dinners and receptions. The men found the young Marquise pretty, clever, sprightly and much less dull than their friends' wives.

Adrien aroused special curiosity. The ladies took great interest in this slave-owning planter with the curly hair and powerful voice who, unlike their husbands and lovers, had neither paunch nor wattles, took the stairs four at a time, yet kissed a lady's hand with a particular grace. If the Tories avoided all political discussion with the Marquis—ever since the Marquis de La Fayette, all marquis' who had gone to America were suspect—the Whigs and Liberals were constantly asking him about America. Adrien found himself sloughing off his Southern antipathies to Northern ideas and painting a portrait of American democracy that would have pleased the staunchest Yankee.

As they were packing their bags for Paris, he summed up his impressions of their English stay: "Those English landowners, those fat heirs of earls and dukes understand nothing, want to see nothing. It's their arrogance and stupidity that cost them the American colonies. Their ignorance of how ideas are changing, and their damn class system is going to lose them their privileges and power. A new world is on the march, Caroline. Mosely's right. We may not like it as well as the old one, but without necessarily believing in those principles of liberty, equality and fraternity the French are always spouting, it's in that direction that Europe is moving. America could provide the example; it's a free world where no class is ignored or without a voice."

"But, Adrien, how does all this apply to our slaves—something the English never tire of bringing up?"

"That's altogether different, Caroline. We treat them better than the British treat their workers in Liverpool and Manchester . . ."

"But perhaps these revolutionary ideas will someday infect our Negroes, especially if the Northerners show them the way. What will we do then, Adrien?"

"We'll send them back to Africa, my dear," he said with a hearty laugh. "And since the British will have no cotton, they will have no shirts! Their splendid lords and ladies will be bare-assed like our Iroquois!"

On the other side of the Channel, the Damvilliers found Louis-Philippe's France going through the same convulsions they had witnessed in England. The Revolution of 1830 had left the Republicans with a sense of frustration. Born out of the people's anger at Charles X's suspension of freedom of the press, his modification of the electoral law and the dissolution of the just-elected Chamber of Deputies, the revolution had broken down the Bourbons's resistance after three days of bloody riots. Now the French were waiting for a profound transformation in their political life while the deputies were satisfied merely to take the measures necessary to safeguard their own rights from a royal coup d'état. The new monarchy and its "Citizen King" were intent on following an increasingly conservative course to the point where Casimir Perier, in response to a left-wing deputy, said: "The trouble with this country is that people like you think there's been a revolution in France. No, sir, there has been no revolution. Only the head of state has changed."

Mme. Drouin, Caroline's aunt, was a typical member of the *haute bourgeoisie*—the rising class that controlled all the money. Like many women in her position, she thought of herself as literary, but politically she belonged to the genus ostrich. She welcomed the newlyweds with great demonstrations of affection and the knowing sighs of a survivor from marriage's perils.

Mme. Drouin's décolletage, which the Barrow sisters would certainly have declared indecent, presented two firm rounded breasts, while her velvety eyes, ringed with the dark circles of a night owl, glided over the men. Now in the full flower of her forties, she devoted herself unstintingly to the pleasures of the flesh, which a convenient sterility had rendered innocuous. Either in the throes of melancholy over a recent rupture or in hot pursuit of a new lover, she ran her salon partly to give minor and reactionary poets a hearing, partly to find new recruits for her bed. In contrast to Mme. Recamier, who had far more illustrious admirers but never succumbed, Félice Drouin always did.

Adrien felt a retrospective jealousy when he conjured up the adolescent Caroline living among these unbridled ladies. Her intimate relationship with her aunt troubled him, although he would have felt better had he known how strict the good woman was with the young ladies who sought her advice. She enthusiastically explained the theory of love but strictly forbade its practice.

The Marquis de Damvilliers was not happy in this atmosphere of concupiscence. He felt useless and out of his depth, and was homesick for the broad reaches of his plantation. When night brought Caroline back to him, sated with the day's worldly entertainments, his ardor was boundless. He made love with a vengeance; she was not displeased.

The Damvilliers had thought to stay in Paris until February, but Adrien was consumed with impatience. He had received a letter from Clarence telling him that the cotton harvest had been good, although of inferior quality to the preceding year's. "The work on Bagatelle is at last finished; your house looks brand new. Willy Templeton was wounded by a Seminole's arrow; but the Indian did him a good turn, since the incident earned him the rank of captain."

Three days before Christmas, a small drama speeded up their leavetaking. As Adrien was returning from a service at Saint-Sulpice, he found Caroline, alone, holding hands with a redheaded poet.

"Damn it, Caroline, what do you think you're doing?" he bellowed, setting the crystal drops in the chandelier to jingling.

"Madame doesn't feel well," the young man stammered as he straightened up.

Caroline was in fact sitting slumped in a chair, looking pale and limp.

"It's probably your poems that made her sick. It would be well if you left the premises as fast as possible."

"But, sir, this house belongs to Madame Drouin."

"But my wife's hand belongs to me."

With that, he bore down on the impeccably tailored young man and grabbed him by the collar with one hand and the seat of the trousers with the other. Carrying him across the room as if he were a barrel of molasses, he ordered the butler to open the door, walked out onto the stoop and threw the poet onto a mound of snow scattered with dogs' feces.

When he returned to the drawing room, the Marquis was glowering. "So, about this illness of yours, madam? Can you tell me what caused it? Do you want some fresh air? It's stifling in here."

His wife seemed more happy than disturbed. Her color had come back.

"Sit down, Adrien. I have something to tell you."

The serene tone of his wife's voice was perplexing.

"Stop rubbing your head and listen to me. First, thank you for getting rid of that importunate young man. You could have done it with less vigor perhaps, but anger becomes you and I'm gratified to know that I have a husband who doesn't mince words when his wife's virtue is at stake."

"That's all very well, Caroline, but what's this illness about?"

"Well, Monsieur le Marquis, I wish to inform you that you're about to become a father. I happened to feel faint when that young idiot came to call. That's all there is to it—and it's perfectly normal, you know."

"My God!" the Marquis said and leaped to his feet, setting up another clattering of bibelots around the room. "You mean it? You really mean it? Oh, Caroline, how happy I am. What a Christmas present!"

He took her hands in his and kissed her with such violence that it brought a grimace of pain. Then he dropped to his knees.

"You're going to give us a little marquis?"

"Or a little marquise, Adrien."

"Of course," he said, a little put out by this possibility.

Caroline ran her fingers through her husband's hair. He seemed quite overcome. Then his face suddenly took on a tragic cast. "Does that mean we will have to stay in Paris until . . ."

"Why on earth? I intend that our son shall be born at Bagatelle."

"But the crossing at this time of year can be very uncomfortable."

"So, our child will have sea legs. If you really want to please me, Adrien, let us pack our bags now and head straight for home."

Everything was conspiring to make Adrien happy. He was about to become a father and he would be leaving this city which he heartily disliked. He broke into a Scottish reel with the grace of a bear, and the chandelier drops tinkled once again. The noise brought Mme. Drouin rushing into the room.

"*Mon Dieu*, what is going on? First I find one of my friends shivering on my doorstep and whimpering for his coat, then I find you dancing before my niece like a satyr."

"Madam," Adrien said, interrupting his dance in midair, "I'm happy because my family is now assured of descendants. And without in any way making light of your hospitality, I am about to take my wife home."

"Is that all? That's hardly worth your shaking my floors, terrorizing my servants and throwing out a gentle poet in whom I have a certain interest."

"Your handsome redhead was flirting with my wife, taking advantage of a passing spell due to her condition. Yes, madam, I threw him out. But don't you worry. He'll be back as soon as we're gone."

Mme. Drouin shrugged her shoulders and sat down among her cushions.

"Is it really true, Caroline? A child already? Anyway, I'm glad he was conceived under my roof."

"No, dear aunt, not in your house. Probably in Cromwell's bed in England."

"Oh?" the lady said. "In any event, he'll be born here. We'll have a real celebration."

"No, madam," the Marquis interrupted, "not in your house but in Bagatelle. In Louisiana. Like his father and grandfather before him. We are leaving Paris."

Defeated on all fronts, Félice Drouin adjusted her bodice and smiled.

"Don't you think an Atlantic crossing might be dangerous for a pregnant woman?"

Caroline walked over to her aunt and kissed her.

"Our minds are made up. We're going home. The sea air is stimulating—and I won't be the first to travel in my condition."

"But did not Monsieur de Damvilliers plan to visit the lands of his ancestors?" the good woman tried again.

"Our lands are on the banks of the Mississippi," Adrien said, more composed now. "I feel like a stranger here. I'm anxious to get back to my home and my cotton."

"Well, if you've really made up your minds."

"We have, dear aunt. We'll spend Christmas and New Year's Day with you, then take the first boat leaving for New York."

"I'll write Clarence as soon as we have our reservations," Adrien said with the glee of a soldier who has just been given an unexpected leave.

He left the two women to their gossip, took his overcoat, hat and cane, and raced down the stairs. While he was waiting for the carriage, he picked up a piece of paper that must have fallen from the poor poet's pocket. It read:

> Goddess of the Missisippi,
> Love awaits you in Paris,
> At a sign from you he picks up his lyre
> To sing what the gruff voice of a crude
>   husband cannot say and
> For whom tomorrow is of no concern.

"For God's sake!" Adrien fumed, hurling the poem on the same mound of snow where its author had landed. "That puny Don Juan can't even spell."

"Excuse me, sir?" asked the coachman, removing his hat as Adrien climbed into the carriage.

"I was saying that Mississippi is written with four *s*'s, and your weather is damn cold!"

*   *   *

During the Damvilliers's absence, Albert Schoeler and his wife Mignette had decided to take their chances in the West. Because of the high price of land, they could not afford to buy a plot in Louisiana. So they joined the exodus into the unknown which federal officials who had never set foot west of the Atlantic coast proclaimed to be miraculously fertile. In the hopes of populating the region beyond the Missouri and the Osage, the federal government was offering concessions at $1.25 an acre. Besides, the journey into Apache and Padouca territory appealed to Mignette's sense of adventure.

"If I'm going to end up my days the dull wife of a blacksmith, better I should return to France," she said. In the evening, while her husband was smoking his pipe, she read him Fenimore Cooper's *Last of the Mohicans*. Placid Albert immediately saw himself hunting bears, trafficking with the Indians, and setting up his smithy in the middle of a pioneers' village.

They straightway ordered a Conestoga wagon. Into their red and blue Conestoga with its white cover, Albert Schoeler stashed all his tools, including his anvil, trunks containing their clothing and household utensils, bags of flour—a hundred pounds for each—barrels of salt pork and ham, coffee, tea, sugar, dried beans and fruits, rice, spices, axes, a saw, spades, and of course two guns with several hundred lead bullets which he had spent days making. To these essentials, Mignette added her Parisian fripperies, hardly necessary to a woman braving the prairies but as important to her as the bicarbonate of soda in her pharmaceutical kit. After all, her silk gowns, laces and hats, handed down to her over the years by Caroline, were the only tangible proof of her past existence.

Before their departure, Mignette and her husband got into an argument over the fate of the blacksmith's two slaves. Albert had taught them their trade. Selling them would bring in at least four thousand dollars, and appreciable sum for a couple without much in the way of savings. But Mignette wouldn't hear of their turning Clovis and Armand over to the slave trader in Pointe-Coupée. They were cheerful men and good Christians, with muscles of iron. She wanted to see them freed so that they could continue to run her husband's smithy on their own.

One morning she took the little ferry over to Bayou Sara on the opposite bank to consult with Ed Barthew. Ed's office was on the second floor of a ramshackle building which also housed the local newspaper—the *Time Piece*. Ed gave her a warm welcome and launched into an explanation of how emancipation worked.

Louisiana law permitted all citizens who owned slaves to free them under certain conditions, among them that they be at least thirty years old and that no complaint had been lodged against them in four years. This last condition was not necessary if the slave had saved the life of his master, or of the master's wife or children. The master who wished to emancipate a slave had to declare his intention before the district judge. Then the judge published a notice detailing the request so that any citizen who wished to lodge a complaint could do so.

If there was none, the judge made out the emancipation form and exacted a deposit of a thousand dollars for each liberated slave. The master was also required to guarantee that the slave would leave the state within a month. A conditional clause stated that anyone finding that the slave had not left in time could pocket half the deposit, the other half going into the state's treasury.

"That's a stupid law," Mignette said, outraged. "Albert will never be willing to spend two thousand dollars on Clovis and Armand. I've had trouble enough convincing him not to sell them."

Ed pushed the rebellious lock out of his right eye with a tobacco-stained finger.

"There are certain arrangements possible. If the master wants to free his slaves as a reward for unusual service and if this reason is accepted by the parish jury, the liberated black may continue to reside in the state. On condition, however, that three quarters of the jury, at two successive meetings, give their consent in writing. This doesn't eliminate the usual deposit, but the master has to answer for his black's good conduct before the jury. Oh, and another thing. The master is enjoined to feed the freed slave, to take care of him in case of illness, old age or whatever might cause the slave to be unable to look after himself."

"That doesn't make things easier," Mignette said, discouraged. "But I absolutely refuse to sell my husband's workers as if they were so many farm animals. If Albert had been able to find a blacksmith to take his place, Clovis and Armand would have changed masters without its changing their lives. But nobody wanted to buy the smithy."

The lawyer suddenly brightened.

"It might be possible to tell the jury—I'd be glad to do it for Albert without its costing him a cent—that with Schoeler gone, there won't be anyone to shoe horses in Pointe-Coupée. The planters will have to cross the river to Bayou Sara. If your emancipated blacks—and I'm sure Albert would answer for their honesty and competence—promised to take over your husband's work, we might be able to bring it off. It would be the 'unusual service' to the community, slightly modified, as prescribed by the law."

"That's a very good idea. Albert could even leave them some tools."

"Wait a minute," Barthew interjected to quiet Mignette's enthusiasm. "Even if the jury accepts this argument, you'll still have to find the two thousand dollars, for the jury won't let you out of that one!"

"Oh!" Mignette said, stricken. "So the problem of the money remains. Albert is a good man, but he's very close-fisted. And besides, we have so very little money."

Ed lowered his voice.

"You're insured, aren't you? You carry insurance on the smithy and your apartment upstairs?"

"Of course. And with the constant risk of fire, it costs us a great deal."

"All right. We'll get your insurance money, Mrs. Schoeler.

It may be a little irregular, but the rightness of the cause makes up for the means used to bring it about."

"What do you have in mind, Mr. Barthew?"

"You don't need to know for the moment, Mrs. Schoeler. When you've packed the Conestoga the night before your departure, I'm going to ask Dr. Murphy to give you a farewell dinner. I suggest that your two blacks be elsewhere that evening. Why not send them off to Bagatelle to pick up a wheelbarrow or something. You understand what I'm driving at?"

Mignette placed her hands on the lawyer's.

"I think I do. But if Albert ever suspected anything, he would bring his hammer down on my head. Albert respects the law, you know."

"I've learned to respect respectable laws, Mrs. Schoeler, and to disobey the others, without, if possible, doing my fellow man any harm . . ."

A little later, he pulled his curtains aside to watch the blacksmith's wife disappear down the main street. She was walking at a quick pace, her head held high, her parasol pointing straight up. As a connoisseur of women, he took in her slender waist, the gracefully swaying walk. What a splendid little woman! Exactly what I should have had, he said to himself. Then he lit a cigar and poured himself a glass of whiskey, which he drained in one gulp. As good a way as any to warm the heart when it feels a chill.

In the middle of autumn, when the cotton ginning had begun and the slaves had started the fires under the pots of molasses, Clarence decided the time had come to resume his own activities: to read and to think.

For a man without ambition and with no social responsibilities other than those that went with his job, there was only one inexorable prospect: death. He thought about it often, but without fear or curiosity. Would it come suddenly, like a storm felling a cypress? Or would he see it in the distance as he walked his solitary path? While waiting, he enjoyed life in his fatalistic way, not lifting a finger to change its course.

Clarence was consumed by a universal doubt. In creation he saw only an intelligent overlapping of chance and necessity. Although he was conscious of being an element in a a great Whole, as the leaf belongs to the tree, he felt like a stranger in the human anthill. As an individualist, he believed that each human being must live according to his nature, and that any constraints, whether freely accepted or imposed, only perverted the play of forces that insured the world's equilibrium. That was why he distrusted philosophies, religions and morality as yokes designed to replace harmony with order and the unknown with the preconceived. Only contemplative people were really trustworthy, because in their serenity and freedom from attachments, they saw signs and portents invisible to others. As a tolerant man, he refused to use the words "always" and "never" because they expressed the presumptuousness of the human vocabulary. That is why his favorite hero remained Childe Harold, "that doomed and suffering genius hovering between the mysteries of mind and matter." But, unlike Byron, he did not look upon life as "the perverted smile of evil," but more as the manifestation of all the forces countervailing against the void.

When he sat in his rocking chair of an evening, his dogs at his feet, he was ready to believe that the indefinable energy that made a magnolia grow, a cardinal fly, the Mississippi flow, men move and think, came from the same unique source that distributed life's interchangeable parts in accordance with a subtle recipe.

The only man he could discuss these subjects with—to Adrien de Damvilliers, they didn't exist—was Edward Barthew. So, when Ed invited him to a dinner at Dr. Murphy's on the eve of the Schoelers' departure for the West, he accepted with alacrity. Barthew added: "I also suggest it would be a good idea if you checked all your equipment at Bagatelle. You're about to lose the only blacksmith on your side of the river."

At his urging, Bobo and the overseer responsible for the wagons on the plantation agreed to have the blacksmith or his apprentices make sure everything was in good working order. That was how Clovis and Armand happened to be away on that particular evening.

The fire at the smithy in Sainte-Marie was quite a show. It started without warning and spread with astonishing speed, the flames devouring everything with demonic hunger. All that was left was a pile of cinders and a few charred beams. The siren sounded just as the guests were about to sit down to a roast suckling pig prepared by Dr. Murphy's black cook, Céline. The volunteer firemen raced from their homes to the hand pump stored near the courthouse and dragged it in the direction of the glare that lit up the sky at the far end of town. When they saw that it was the blacksmith's house, standing isolated and therefore no threat to other houses, their zeal evaporated. Besides, the fire was beyond the point where they could hope to extinguish it. But they did their best.

Schoeler's closest neighbors, who knew he was leaving at dawn the next day, made straight for his Conestoga, loaded and under cover in the barn, guarded by his big yellow mongrel.

"It's a good thing they packed it in time," the local priest commented to one of the bystanders. What the good father didn't know was how Mignette had had to insist that everything be ready before they went to Dr. Murphy's party.

The two horses had also been spared, having been let out to pasture at a neighbor's. In short, the fire, whose cause was hardly worth investigating, was not too serious after all. And besides, weren't the blacksmith's house and its contents insured?

"I could have sworn I put out the fire in the smithy after I sent Clovis and Armand to Bagatelle," Albert Schoeler said when he arrived on the scene. He shook his head. "I don't understand how the fire could have started."

The firemen, for whom this wasn't the first unexplained blaze, suggested that maybe a gust of wind had blown through the smithy's shaky door and rekindled the dying embers. This explanation was generally accepted by all.

When the siren began to wail, the Schoelers had just finished accepting farewell gifts from the dinner guests. Murphy had assembled a traveling medicine kit, the Pernoud sisters had presented them with two straw hats they had woven themselves, and Fernand Poygras, the schoolmaster, donated a book on astronomy, since they would henceforth be sleeping out of doors. When the guests learned the location of the fire, Albert Schoeler left precipitously. Mignette, who had been acting oddly all evening—understandable in view of their momentous departure the next day—was eager to accompany her husband. Dr. Murphy opposed it.

"Let your husband go alone. While we wait for his return, we'll start on a bottle of claret to whet your appetite for dinner—and your journey west."

Mignette was given the place of honor, next to Clarence Dandridge, whose presence was much appreciated. Ed Barthew, who arrived late as usual, was prepared to enjoy himself —and particularly the wine. He complimented Mignette on her dress, and heard from Judge Claiborne, who was also present, that the parish jury would certainly authorize the freeing of Clovis and Armand so that they could remain in Sainte-Marie.

The blacksmith returned pale and out of breath.

"It was our house, Mignette. . . . There isn't a thing left, but the Conestoga is all right."

"Here, drink this," Barthew said, handing him a glass of wine. "I hope your blacks had nothing to do with it."

Dandridge spoke right up. "They're at Bagatelle until tomorrow. Bobo needed them in the barns. So I don't think you can pin the fire on them."

Mignette had begun to weep softly. Her husband put his arm around her shoulders.

"I know it's sad to have your house burn down, but we've lost very little since you were so determined that we pack the wagon in time."

"We were insured, weren't we? I hope the insurance covers the damage."

"I doubt you'll have any difficulties, Mrs. Schoeler," Barthew put in. "The judge is witness that neither your husband nor you nor your slaves could have set it. It was just an accident."

Dr. Murphy was the eager host. "I hope this hasn't spoiled your appetites, my friends. Céline's piglet can't wait any longer. To table, everyone."

When it came time for leavetakings, Mignette was particularly affectionate toward Ed Barthew. The lawyer had speedily concluded all arrangements with her husband. The money from the insurance would be held by Barthew until Schoeler returned, or would be sent to him when he had an address in the West. Out of that money, Barthew would be repaid for the two thousand dollars he had had to put down as guarantee for the two slaves' emancipation. Mignette also asked that out of the insurance money, Clovis and Armand be given a loan of three hundred dollars to install a new smithy on the ruins of the old.

"Everything is possible between honest and courageous men. You are all exemplary citizens," Judge Claiborne said sanctimoniously.

As the Schoelers were undressing in Dr. Murphy's guest room—because of the fire, they had no home to go to—Albert gave his wife a small flat object.

"Look, I found this in the rubble near the house. It's a snakeskin cigar case. It must have belonged to one of the firemen. Shouldn't we leave it with Dr. Murphy? He may be able to find the owner."

With the self-control she had learned from her mistress, Mignette did not tell her husband that she recognized the cigar case as belonging to Ed Barthew.

"I'm sure Dr. Murphy will find the owner. I'll give it to him tomorrow morning." And she tucked it deep inside her bag.

Three days later, when the Schoelers' wagon had just waded through the Red River, Mignette opened her bag to take out a mint candy.

"Good Heavens," she said. "I forgot to give that cigar case you found to Dr. Murphy. I'll keep it until we get back to Pointe-Coupée—if we ever do go back . . ."

Clarence had just received a letter from Adrien by clipper ship. It cost him two dollars, for the British company that insured transatlantic mail obliged the recipient to pay a part of the cost. The missive, typically brief, announced that the Marquis and his wife would be returning in mid-February. They must have sailed on the *Borcas*, one of the fastest ships of the Le Havre–New York Line, which averaged thirty-eight days on the high seas.

Therefore, when Captain Templeton stopped off at Bagatelle knowing the Damvilliers were absent, Clarence was able to tell him that the honeymoon was reaching its end.

War, even the inglorious war American soldiers were waging against the Indians, had matured Willy. He was very proud of his captain's insignia, won as a result of a minor wound on the arm during a particularly unheroic encounter. In addition to his promotion, it also gained him a convalescent leave which he used to show off his new rank at balls and receptions. Many a pretty girl had offered him her dance card, and there were many occasions when Willy recounted the charge that had won his honors—but without embellishments, for Willy had a limited imagination. Certainly he seemed more virile with his tanned skin and strong muscles, and he had at long last outgrown the pink doll-like look of the well-fed adolescent common to most planters' sons.

After dinner, while they shared a bottle of port in front of the fire, Willy pulled a locket out of his tunic pocket.

"Would you be good enough to give this back to Mrs. de Damvilliers? Discreetly, of course. It contains the lock of hair the Marquise forfeited in our game on board the *Prince du Delta*. You must remember the incident. Now that she is married, and after my foolish behavior at the barbecue when the Marquis announced their engagement, I don't think I should keep it."

Clarence slipped the locket into his pocket.

"I shall do it with the utmost discretion, especially since the locket shouldn't be given back to Mrs. de Damvilliers in any case."

"What do you mean?"

"Simply that this hair doesn't belong to Caroline."

"I see what you mean," the captain said with a knowing laugh. "It belongs to her husband, like the rest of her person."

Dandridge looked at Willy with the expression of a schoolmaster who realizes that his pupil hasn't understood a word of the lesson. War may strengthen the body, but it does precious little for the brain, Clarence said to himself. Aloud, he was very precise. "No, not to the Marquis either. This hair belongs to a young lady named Mignette, now Mrs. Schoeler, who is presently heading west with her husband."

If an Indian chief brandishing his tomahawk had suddenly burst into the room, Willy could not have been more stunned.

"Are you telling me that Caroline was making a fool of me as well as of Ed Barthew?"

"It's a kind of female joke, Willy. But you mustn't hold it against her. The episode is over and done with."

Willy was silent. He didn't know what to say. That lock of hair that had never left him, that he placed next to his watch on his night table every night, that had earned him so much kidding at West Point, that hair belonged to a servant. He went from surprise to shame to anger.

"What kind of a woman would act that way with gentlemen about to risk their lives for her? She's nothing but a . . ."

"Shhh. Be quiet, Willy. You're under her roof. Don't say anything you may regret. I hesitated for a while before telling you my little secret, but since you were getting rid of it anyway, I didn't think it mattered any longer. There comes a time in every life when you must render unto Caesar . . ."

"To Caesar or to Proserpine. Give me back that locket!"

Willy spoke with such authority that Clarence complied. Certain of what would happen next, he stretched out his legs and folded his hands like a spectator about to watch a drama unfold. His expectations were confirmed: Willy seized the trinket and hurled it into the fire, then emptied his glass of port in one gulp.

"There comes a time when you burn what you once adored," Clarence said with an ingratiating smile.

"Anyway, I'm glad you set me straight, Clarence. It's as if I'd had a bad tooth pulled. Let's talk of something else."

When the bottle of port was empty, Willy put on his heavy overcoat and asked for his gig. A cold wind was agitating the Spanish moss on the oak trees and pushing the clouds toward the south. Dandridge watched the jouncing lantern disappear, then returned to the drawing room. When James had gone to bed after locking the doors, Clarence picked up a poker and scratched around in the ashes until he found the now-blackened locket. When it had cooled, he cleaned it with his handkerchief and saw that the glass had broken, but inside, the lock of hair in the shape of a question mark was intact. He put it in his pocket and went to his quarters. Perhaps Barthew would appreciate this souvenir which at long last would have the right recipient.

The Damvilliers were back at Bagatelle a week sooner than expected. The captain of the *Borcas*, a fearless seaman and enthusiastic gambler, had decided to shorten the crossing by taking the most difficult route by way of the Grand Bahama banks. Five times the ship had hit the reefs. The European passengers complained vociferously, but the Americans on board were full of admiration for the captain's daring, egged on the crew and looked with contempt on the fainthearted. But when they finally sighted La Balise at the mouth of the Mississippi, there was a general outpouring of hurrahs that could be heard all the way to the tower. Some cheered in gratitude to Neptune for bringing them into safe harbor, the others—among them Adrien and Caroline—as an ovation to their captain for giving them such a memorable experience. The future mother had revealed only one symptom of her condition: Even in the foulest weather, she had eaten voraciously, causing great unease among the already seasick ladies.

Adrien said, "I'm so glad to be back in my own house and to see you again, Dandridge. Europe was terrible, like a hag tormented by vices for which she's too old. Everybody talks about revolution and uprisings without having any notion of what to put in the place of what they want to destroy. The British want a monarchy dolled up like a republic, and the French a republic governed by a king. As for the Dutch and the Poles and the Belgians and the Germans, they're prepared to imitate anybody . . ."

"I'm very glad to see *you*, Adrien," Clarence interrupted. "Every so often, on winter nights, I found myself wandering around the empty house like a lost soul."

To Dandridge, Caroline looked like a new woman. She was blooming, she was happy, and her pregnancy made her even more beautiful, even more desirable. In his euphoria, Adrien announced to the delegation of slaves who came to greet him that he was granting everyone on the plantation a two-day holiday.

"Dandridge, there really is such a thing as happiness. I feel as strong as a bull. Bagatelle is going to see some beautiful days, beautiful years. If Caroline gives me a little marquis— as I expect she will—I'm going to build a hospital for the poor whites in Sainte-Marie. I can't be happy unless I do something for those who've been less fortunate than I."

The Marquis's joy seemed to be contagious. The entire area was going through what later historians would call "the golden age of the South." Louisiana and Mississippi together had produced 132,363 bales of cotton the preceding year, which had sold so well that only 7,000 bales remained in the New Orleans warehouses. The state of Louisiana had taken in a record $507,291, and despite its many expenses, there still remained $167,235 in the public treasury. A new hospital costing $17,000 had been built in New Orleans, and new parish schools to the tune of $41,000. True, the prosecution of criminals and the maintenance of prisoners in state penitentiaries had cost Louisiana's citizens $35,000, but the treasury had had to spend only $900 to indemnify the proprietors of slaves executed for their crimes.

To be sure, not all the South's inhabitants profited from its prosperity. Among these were the poor whites Adrien had singled out for his largess—should God grant him a son. They worked tiny plots of land in the "henhouse," that area once encircled by the Mississippi and now lying between the river and the man-made lake called Fausse-Rivière. Just like the blacks, they labored with picks and shovels; they rented a slave or two for twenty or thirty dollars a month—if they could afford it—lived in mean huts and drank only water, their only luxury being a small patch of melons and gooseberries. Very touchy about their liberties, they grumbled about paying their taxes and failed to send their children to school. Only a few whites were worse off: men without homes or families who lived in the woods or bayous as trappers; hunters of muskrats, alligators and nutrias; men who made charcoal; and herders or fishermen whose only advantage over the blacks was the color of their skin. The planters' aristocracy pretended they didn't exist; when they did acknowledge their existence, it was to complain about their ways and their evil influence on the slaves. The slaves envied them only their guns and, like their masters, referred to them as "rednecks" or "woodpeckers."

In the middle of an August heat wave that made the cotton leaves droop and the spindly stalks bend under the weight of their buds, Caroline summoned Dr. Murphy to her room. The child stirring in her belly was nearing its term.

"Things look very good," the doctor told the Marquis. "And I wouldn't be surprised if your wish came true. It sure is an active little brat. I'd say it would be around the end of the month."

For weeks now Caroline had been the center of attention. The future Marquis's layette was ready, and the seamstresses on the plantation had put new lace on the big cradle shaped like a ship in which Adrien had spent his first months. The servants, ruled by Anna, had a religious respect for maternity. In their eyes, the mystery of birth was the highest sign of the divine will.

Adrien, feverishly excited as the great day drew near, would rush in from the fields to find out "if everything was all right." Dandridge happened on him in his library one day, leafing through a treatise on anatomy to learn how a baby was born.

"Childbirth is the most natural thing in the world, Adrien. You mustn't worry."

"But it must be terribly painful. It would appear that the more slender the woman, the more difficult the birth. I can't help thinking about the risk she's taking. Thank God we have Dr. Murphy—unless he's drunk when we need him. I wonder if I shouldn't keep him right here and make him toe the line from now on."

"Murphy has to look after his patients. And having a baby isn't a disease, Adrien. It would be very selfish of you to keep him here for no good reason."

"Of course I'm selfish. Where Caroline is concerned, I want all the luck on our side."

When Caroline went into labor on August 15, Dr. Murphy was nowhere to be found. Couriers were sent to all the plantations, and Bobo was directed to canvass Sainte-Marie. It was reported back that the doctor was at Port Hudson on the opposite side of the river, a good two hours from Bagatelle.

"Go find a boat and bring him here," Adrien shouted at Clarence while Caroline, under Anna and Rosa's watchful eyes, chewed handkerchiefs steeped in vinegar.

"If the doctor don't come," Anna said firmly, "I'm goin' to git Planche. She helps all the Negro women."

"I won't hear of it!" Adrien shot back. "Murphy must be found and brought back here."

Clarence had already gone to find a boat and rowers to take him to Port Hudson. Adrien was pacing back and forth around Caroline's bed. She seized him by the wrist as he was passing by and said imperiously, "I want Planche brought here, and you, Adrien, are to leave this room. You're making me dizzy."

As her husband was about to object, she said, "I'm made exactly the same as other women. Now go!"

Planche, whose name came from her extreme thinness and the driftwood-color of her skin, was the slave quarters' midwife. She was also something of a sorceress: She knew the healing herbs, but was also suspected of casting spells on people, which made her an object of fear. It was better to be on good terms with her. She talked little and lived alone in a cabin near the river. With her long, dry, supple fingers, she was one of the best cotton ginners. And her pale eyes and skin hinted at a trace of white blood.

When Rosa ran to the ginning house to fetch her, Planche stuck out her scrawny chest. "I knew they'd be needing me."

The midwife silently followed Rosa into the house. Adrien, now pacing the gallery, acknowledged her presence but said nothing. Planche went into the kitchen, washed her hands and arms with great thoroughness, and demanded a clean towel to dry herself.

"I want lots of boiling water, girl, and take lots of towels to the mistress's room, hear?"

Then, from a leather pouch hanging from her neck, she extracted a small bouquet of herbs which she put to steep in a glass of wine. These ritual motions were executed as if she had all the time in the world. At long last, she asked to be taken to the Marquise's room, but not before she had requested a five-dollar gold piece and a pair of silver scissors, which she dipped into the wine and again wiped on a clean towel. Rosa followed her preparations wide-eyed, all the time praying to God that Dr. Murphy would arrive in time, for the Marquis had made no attempt to hide his distrust of the old gray woman. When Planche reached the mistress's room, she dismissed poor perspiring Anna with a wave of the hand and closed the door. The house became as silent as a tomb.

Adrien kept wandering into the drawing room and from there into the kitchen.

"Isn't anything going on?" he said to Anna. "It would be nice if someone told me something. I'm going to go see for myself."

"You mustn't go in there, master. Planche don't want anyone near her. The Marquise don't either."

Finally, the sorceress opened the door a crack to ask for a basin of water. Then she shut it and the tension mounted. Adrien took up a position on the gallery next to the window with the drawn curtains. Behind them he could hear Caroline's moans indicating that labor was well underway. Why in God's name didn't Murphy arrive with his reassuring science?

A moment later, Planche walked up behind him on her cat feet. He almost jumped out of his skin.

"It's a beautiful boy, master. A very white boy."

"How is your mistress?"

"She's just fine," Planche said with professional calm.

Dr. Murphy arrived three hours later, a little the worse for wear. He found Adrien leaning over the crib, in which lay a reddish baby with wrinkled skin and vestiges of brown hair —as ugly as the rest. Caroline, her hands behind her neck, her hair carefully combed by Rosa, smiled as her husband kept repeating: "He's so tiny . . . he's so tiny."

Dr. Murphy examined both mother and child. He found the first in perfect condition, and the second as clean as a new penny. Planche had cut the umbilical cord after tying it up with a bunch of herbs. Then she attached the five-dollar piece to the baby's navel with two strips of gauze so that "the little Marquis will have a pretty belly."

"All the same, Murphy, you should have been here. Turning Caroline over to this Negress put me in a cold sweat."

"I couldn't have done better, and probably not as well. I've seen Planche perform more than once, and if I ever had a wife about to give birth, I'd get Planche. I'll bet Caroline didn't suffer at all. That sorceress has secrets . . ."

Caroline put in, "She gave me some herbs to chew and after that my mind went blank. It was as if someone else had suffered in my place."

"When she cut the cord, didn't she say anything?" the doctor asked.

"Yes. She said that the little Marquis had the sign of fire."

"What does that mean?" Adrien asked brusquely. "More of that sorceress nonsense?"

"I think it means that your son will have his father's fiery temperament. Isn't that right, Dr. Murphy?"

"You're probably right," he replied thoughtfully. Despite all the whiskey he'd drunk, he had enough sense to hold his tongue. The last time Planche told a new mother that her baby had the sign of the snake, the child died of a snakebite in its crib. Planche's training was very different from that given in Northern medical schools.

The future Marquis de Damvilliers, third of the name born in Louisiana, was baptized Marie-Adrien because he came into the world on the Virgin's holy day. Later, when he inherited the title—which would now be nothing but a title—he would drop the first name and become Adrien de Damvilliers like all the other Damvilliers who had preceded him. In the meantime, he turned out to be voraciously hungry, noisy, and with a vitality that delighted his father but gave his nanny, Imilie, more trouble than all the six children she had borne the German overseer.

Eighteen thirty-two, the year of Marie-Adrien's birth, was marked by a relatively poor cotton crop. The number of bales was down 97,000 from the preceding year, which pushed prices up, bringing nice profits to the speculators. But of much greater importance was the new tariff under discussion in Washington, which would raise the price of manufactured goods imported from Europe, thus bringing great hardship to the South.

The planters and businessmen of Louisiana were looking to President Andrew Jackson to, if not entirely reject the tariff, at least lower it substantially. As a military man, he had prevented the British from taking New Orleans in 1815, a victory that was celebrated every year. But Jackson was also a slave-owning cotton planter in Tennessee. This was a most encouraging sign. As soon as he was elected, the new President had declared himself hostile to the monopolies, and the industrial and commercial middle class whose influence was growing apace in the Northeast. But they were soon disappointed. First, because Old Hickory had instituted the "spoils system" which distributed all the federal posts of any importance to members of the winning party. Its first result was to create a new class of citizens—the professional politicians—who were greatly distrusted in the South.

In his annual message to Congress in 1832, Jackson had asked for a tariff reduction, thinking to appease the South and its intransigent spokesman, Vice-President John C. Calhoun. When Calhoun learned that the President was actually considering a new tariff to appease Northern voters, he resigned and ran for the Senate, where he went into open battle against the federal government. He defended the sovereign right of states to secede, at the same time insisting that "nullification"—which permitted a state to reject legislation that went against its interests—was a way to avoid the Union's dissolution.

A convention was held in South Carolina. It adopted "nullification" and passed a whole series of measures defying the spirit of federal laws. To the Northerners, this was an outright act of rebellion against the Union's sovereign authority. Jackson, his temper always at the boil, threatened to send federal troops against South Carolina. No other Southern state followed South Carolina's example; their representatives preferred compromise, which eventually won them a gradual tariff reduction.

The Marquis de Damvilliers, basically a reasonable man, backed Jackson's position. Without in any way involving himself in politics, he was able by sheer example to influence a great many planters. One December evening, when a few friends had come for dinner, Adrien found himself delineating his argument:

"The idea of nationhood can only be based on respect for the Union's laws. Americans don't exist as a people yet. We have to wait several generations before we have a race of true Americans attached to the soil. I learned in Europe that foreigners who've been here are astonished that we have no community of interests, or religions, or traditions, or manners and morals. They meet Englishmen in New England and

Georgia, Germans and Irish in New York, Spaniards in Florida, Frenchmen in Louisiana. Yet all these people call themselves Americans, the way members of the Reform Club in London call themselves reformers. I heard a Frenchman say in all seriousness that the only true Americans were the Indians we were driving from their territories! We're no longer pioneers selfishly exploiting exotic lands, but citizens living off our land by our sweat. That's what the Old World must begin to understand about us. The people of South Carolina are still acting as if they were pioneers. I know all about how their businesses suffer on account of the tariff. I suffer too. I have to spend half again as much for my Bordeaux, and I'll suffer even more when I have to pay the thirty or forty dollars that will come due when Mrs. de Damvilliers's Pleyel piano arrives from France. But is that any reason to push for 'nullification'? Certainly we have interests to protect, unjust regulations to fight, but we also have to convince the people of the North that our reasons are valid instead of automatically treating the North as the enemy. For we're all Americans, you know."

It was very unusual for Adrien to talk so long and so categorically. Clarence suspected Caroline's influence, for he had heard her speak disparagingly of planters' wives whose chief complaint against the tariff was its effect on the price of ostrich feathers, Malines lace and Limoges china.

"You'd make an excellent senator . . . in a Northern state!" said old Mr. Templeton in the silence that followed. "My son Willy risked his life for the Union when he went to fight Indians who have no respect for treaties. You talk of convincing our enemies. Why don't you go and convince the savages who put paint on their faces and worship sticks of wood."

"But the people who want the tariff aren't savages, Templeton," a planter spoke up.

"I sometimes wonder—when I see how they insult us in their abolitionist papers which, don't forget, are supported by the money they take from us. They behave like enemies jealous of our prosperity. I'm not the kind who turns the other cheek. One of these days," and old Templeton raised his arm and shook his fist, "we're going to have to fight to survive, to defend the values of the South." With his white mane, bony face, sunken eyes and old-fashioned cravat, he did look like a prophet of old. As the elder of Pointe-Coupée's planters, he deserved respect. No one, therefore, thought to contradict him —except his host.

"I hope God gives us the wisdom never to arrive at that point!"

Clarence smiled. In Adrien's mind, God was a Southerner.

Andrew Jackson's reelection and the defeat of his opponent, Henry Clay of Kentucky, caused the Southerners to tighten ranks. At Pointe-Coupée, planters remembered Mr. Templeton's prophecy better than the Marquis de Damvilliers's reasoned discourse.

When Adrien and Caroline had returned to Bagatelle from Europe, Clarence told his employer that he wished to build himself a small house of his own because his two-room annex left him too dependent on the Damvilliers.

Adrien was taken aback. "Why do you want to change things, Clarence? You're a member of the family. Our house is your house."

Dandridge protested that a couple needed privacy. It must be especially hard for Caroline to have the plantation manager present at every meal and always in her drawing room—never to have her husband to herself.

"I'll talk it over with my wife. But I don't like the idea at all," the Marquis said.

One morning after breakfast, when Adrien had hurried off because of some problem at the gin mill, Caroline stated her position.

"I hope you'll continue to live here, Clarence. Adrien wants it that way." After a moment's hesitation, she added, "So do I. You have no idea how important your presence is. To my husband, you're the brother he chose for himself. As for me, you're my loyal friend. More than that, you are in a sense a trusted witness."

Caroline was wearing a garnet-red velvet dressing gown which set off her pale skin. Dandridge flicked a crumb off his waistcoat and contemplated the young woman.

"All right. If Bagatelle's happiness is in need of a witness, a witness I shall be."

Caroline caught a hint of bitterness in his voice. "Adrien and I want you to be happy too, Clarence . . . with a home of your own, something to care for besides Bagatelle."

"What you mean is you'd like to see me get married?"

"Why not? There are dozens of girls who'd like nothing better than to be Mrs. Dandridge. But you don't make much effort."

Clarence was silent.

"Perhaps you're still thinking about Corinne Templeton, Clarence. But life goes on, you know."

"I often think about Corinne, but not the way you think. Besides, I'm hardly God's gift to women, whoever she may be."

Caroline laughed.

"Come on, Clarence. The handsome cavalier, learned, with what I assume is a healthy bank account. Quite the contrary, my dear. You are seduction personified. But perhaps you're being too difficult?"

"I suppose I am. But for entirely personal reasons, I have no intention of getting married. And that's that."

The firm way in which he spoke gave Caroline to understand that he wished the subject closed.

"If that's the case," she said simply, "please don't change anything. Adrien would be unhappy, and he'd think your desire for a separation was a kind of snub."

"All right. Let's say no more about it. But I depend on you to tell me when you're tired of having me around."

"Don't depend on it, Clarence. You belong to Bagatelle more than I do. I was only grafted on. This house casts a spell. You can't leave it just like that."

"True enough," he said, his eyes wandering past the gallery to the old oaks. "Bagatelle has a soul and maybe even magical powers. This is where my life found its first anchorage."

"And mine its meaning," she said quietly.

After their talk, the subject of Dandridge's move was never broached again. Adrien and Clarence spent their mornings on horseback as usual. And when winter came, the Damvilliers returned to their apartment at the Saint-Charles and their box at the opera. During their absence, Clarence took over the running of the plantation, going to New Orleans only when the Damvilliers were back at Bagatelle. At the balls and receptions, the women—following the dictates of London and Paris—had shifted from bonnets to hats, from taffeta to tulle, and wore airy Watteau-like peignoirs in the privacy of their homes. The men ordered their cravats from the Place Vendôme, their saddles from Rue de Richelieu, hunted with English rifles, and relinquished the frock coat for the long jacket with rounded tails.

From time to time, Abraham Mosely turned up at Bagatelle, as round and rosy as ever and always bearing carefully selected gifts. When, on May 3, 1834, Caroline gave birth to her second child, a girl named Félice in honor of her Aunt Drouin, Mosely agreed to be her godfather, adding without a trace of a smile that he reserved the right to marry her when she turned sixteen, just as the Marquis had married his own goddaughter. At Caroline's request, Planche presided over the birth, with Murphy in attendance. This time, the midwife saw no sign on the child, who soon showed herself to be sweet-tempered and pretty.

Among the planters, the Damvilliers family was accepted as conforming perfectly to Southern ways. But there were differences. Thanks to Planche's mysterious ministerings, Caroline had retained her youthful figure despite two pregnancies. And every year, Bagatelle was refurbished while other planters abandoned their wooden houses for vast stone manor houses with columns and porticoes. While the "nouveaux riches" immigrants tried to embellish their family trees with European titles, and searched Europe for "family heirlooms," the Marquis and Marquise de Damvilliers received their guests under portraits that had crossed the Atlantic a hundred years before.

When Caroline, in her white tulle dress with mauve festoons and black silk frogs, sat playing Rameau on the harpsichord or the now-authorized waltzes on her Pleyel, she was fully conscious of the envy she inspired. She knew she had at last achieved the only station befitting her, the station for which she was destined—the top.

Clarence knew he had had a hand in her ascension. The Caroline he had welcomed in New Orleans was a conqueror, capable of using devious means to achieve her ends. What more can she possibly want? he asked himself as he wondered at the seeming lack of new ambitions in a woman he had thought insatiable. He had been afraid that the lady of Bagatelle might suddenly throw off her conjugal ties and veer off into a new passion. But instead, Caroline had turned into an irreproachable wife and exemplary mother who gave every sign of finding in her husband all the satisfaction her temperament craved. So Dandridge felt a great relief when he left Pointe-Coupée for New Orleans at the end of March, 1835.

It was an unfortunate period to be in the city. An early heat wave had engulfed the town, and an outbreak of cholera was taking ten lives a day. The traders were in a funk because cotton prices had plummeted, sending a wave of fear through the stock exchange. The artificially high price of houses and land in some parts of town tumbled by 50 percent; in others, not a buyer could be found. The speculators put the blame on President Jackson. Despite two resolutions for censure submitted by Henry Clay and approved by the Senate, the President had kept the House of Representatives behind him. On the strength of their support, he announced that he would not renew the charter of the Bank of the United States. In his view the Bank was dangerous to the country's democratic institutions, and "great evils to our country . . . might flow from such a concentration of power in the hands of a few men irresponsible to the people."

In New Orleans, the bank was forced to pay its bills like any commercial enterprise and to recall all the debts owed it in order to pay off its creditors. This was manna to the moneylenders, who made as much as 20 percent on their loans.

During his stay, Dandridge was witness to an incident that left an unsavory mark on Louisiana's history and furnished ammunition to the abolitionists. As he was strolling up Rue Royale after lunch one day, he noticed a cloud of smoke hovering over the rooftops. When he reached Rue du Marché, he saw that a house was on fire and recognized it as Doctor Lalaurie's. The doctor, born a Frenchman, enjoyed a very good reputation. His wife, twice widowed, did not. Born Delphine MacCarthy, the daughter of a rich trader, she had first married the Spanish consul, Ramón de Lopez y Angula. Her second choice was less auspicious, being part banker, part lawyer and suspected of dealing with pirates and contraband. Few wept at his passing. The lady's third marriage restored her to her place in society. She gave splendid receptions, was an arbiter of fashion, and lent her name to good causes. Only her treatment of her slaves gave rise to criticism.

Among those watching the fire was the French consul, Mr. Gailliard, who always turned up when a Frenchman was in difficulties. Dandridge greeted him.

"I am here out of duty, not sympathy, Mr. Dandridge. I know all about these people and how they torture their servants, beat them, withhold their food. Ghastly!"

"Unfortunately they're not the only ones."

"Perhaps not. But do you know that this barbarous woman has tortured her blacks with her own hands—men whose lives were given over to her by the law of a republic that pretends to teach liberty to the rest of the world!"

A few years earlier, Mrs. Lalaurie had been brought to justice by a relative. Accused of mutilating her slaves, she appeared before a jury which was expected to deal her a heavy sentence. But, following her lawyer's advice, she swore under oath that she had never committed these acts and that they were attributed to her by people who wished her ill. She gracefully placed her hand on the Bible and was acquitted. Cleared of all misdeeds, she thereafter indulged her evil ways with increasing ferocity. Several times, her slaves had been driven to jump out of the windows to escape her. Her neighbors began to wonder about the strange goings-on in the doctor's house. Now these same neighbors were about to see their worst suspicions confirmed.

While the firemen were at their work, a group of men entered the house as Dr. and Mrs. Lalaurie watched silently. Hearing groans coming from a closet in the attic, the men opened the door and found seven slaves chained and near death. One of the men ran out onto a balcony and called down, "Sheriff, come up here and see how these bastards treat their Negroes!"

The sheriff, who was gossiping with some bystanders, dispatched an underling. But the summons had aroused the crowd's curiosity. Dandridge and the consul exchanged glances, and the Frenchman, using the prerogatives of his office, went into the house, Dandridge following close behind. They had penetrated no farther than the courtyard when a scene of unspeakable horror stopped them in their tracks. A group of blacks, some with broken necks, others with their legs torn by iron rings and their bodies covered with infected sores, lay on the ground where their rescuers had left them. Ravaged by fever and thirst, one of them was drinking the water that had poured off the charred walls.

"If we hadn't arrived in time, they would either have been roasted alive or asphyxiated by the smoke. And this bitch of a woman didn't even tell us they were there," a fireman said.

Someone else added: "Nobody has the right to treat men like that—not even niggers."

Sick at heart, Dandridge went back to the street. As the tortured slaves were carried off to the hospital, the crowd, indignant but silent, began to disperse. Clarence approached Mrs. Lalaurie, who was standing unconcerned next to the sheriff, and gave her a long, hard look. She coolly answered his look, although her husband appeared uncomfortable.

With a loud and clear voice, Dandridge addressed the sheriff: "I trust this woman will be brought before the Criminal Court. You saw the state in which her servants were found?"

"What you don't know, sir, is that the fire was started by a black housemaid. She's the one responsible for the fire. We'll get our hands on her, never fear."

Dandridge turned on his heels. Suddenly, out of nowhere, came a group of sailors, liberated blacks, and ordinary men and women. Horrified by what they had either seen or heard, they rushed into the house and started smashing everything the fire had spared. Some attacked the walls with pickaxes as if to erase all vestiges of the malignant house. The militia made no attempt to stop them. They knew the people's anger was such that representatives of the law would be wise not to try to protect the Lalauries' possessions. As the couple removed themselves from the scene, Mrs. Lalaurie was threatening the sheriff with legal action if the authorities failed to take proper measures to safeguard her property. The next day, Dandridge learned that the Lalauries had fled to Mobile out of fear for their lives.

While Bagatelle was basking in domestic felicity, unrest was brewing on several fronts. A pamphlet published in Boston had just found its way to Louisiana. A New England writer named Lydia Maria Child had previously written *A History of Women* in which she inveighed against the masculine domination of women. It raised a few titters among Southern men, but that was all. This time she had published *An Appeal for that Class of Americans called Africans* where she likened the subordination of women to the cringing submission of slaves. In this tract, Southerners saw the hand of the Northern abolitionists aiming to plant in their wives the notion that everyone should share the same liberties, regardless of race or sex. This was a veritable engine of war masking Northern economic interests under the guise of a humanitarian cause designed to trouble the soft-hearted.

Not long after, another incident occurred to put Southern nerves on edge. Cotton picking was just getting underway when a disturbing piece of news reached Bagatelle. Dandridge, more observant than his employer, had noticed that the slaves in the fields were occasionally meeting in small groups which dispersed abruptly as soon as he appeared. The blacks seemed to be singing less, joking less. Something was wrong. On a visit to the plantation hospital, on the pretext of learning if any cases of yellow fever or cholera had turned up, he asked a few questions. In the end, he got his answers from Armand and Clovis, the two liberated blacks now running the smithy at Sainte-Marie.

Through mysterious channels, the slaves had learned what *L'Abeille* in New Orleans hadn't seen fit to print until much later: that a conspiracy of slaves had been discovered in Baton Rouge and fourteen blacks accused of taking part had been arrested. In the same issue of the newspaper, an editorial reminded its readers of the governor's proclamation delivered the previous month, to wit:

> Whereas it has been conveyed to the governor that a band of vagrant blacks has been traversing the country with the aim of exciting people's minds,
>
> And whereas it has also been brought to the governor's attention that some of these individuals have made confessions such as to excite fears of the existence of a widespread conspiracy that demands unswerving vigilance on our part and all the energy of which we are capable,
>
> The governor invites all citizens to suppress insurrectional movements and arrest the suspects. In case of need, the State will provide the people with weapons.

Clarence warned Adrien, "That's why our blacks are frightened. There are always excitable people who see conspiracies everywhere. I think it would be a good idea if none of our slaves left the plantation for a while."

In the next few days, word got around that a cache of fifteen hundred rifles had been discovered in New Orleans. The population instantly readied itself for battle without bothering to find out if the story was true. "Our awakening will be as the lion's!" chimed the bellicose *Courrier de la Louisiane*. One reporter who had "spoken ill" of the militia, whose excesses were frightening the townspeople, was almost hung without a trial. Abolitionist sympathizers were hounded like heretics in the Middle Ages. An expression of pity for blacks suspected unjustly, or the word "liberty" cropping up in the most innocent sentence was enough to put a man behind bars.

And again, there was a public outcry when a large bundle of antislavery brochures mailed in the North was discovered in the post office at Charleston, South Carolina. When, at year's end, President Jackson forbade the postal service to distribute the abolitionist literature, the Damvilliers—along with the other Southern planters—approved this abuse of authority which, as good democrats, they should have decried.

The day the newspapers announced that a fire in New York had destroyed six hundred and seventy-four houses, Caroline asked for a second helping of pork and turnips. Adrien, who had been expressing concern for the victims of the fire, gave her a quizzical look. She smiled serenely and addressed herself to her overflowing plate. When, at the end of dinner, she asked for more cake and a glass of madeira instead of coffee, Adrien raised his eyebrows. Were these perhaps the now-familiar symptoms?

"Am I to understand that you are expecting a third child?"

Caroline looked at him slyly. "How did you guess? Yes, I have reason to believe that he'll be born next July. If it's a boy, I hope, Clarence, you will agree to be its godfather?"

"I would be proud."

"It would be a good way to keep you permanently at Bagatelle," the Marquis observed. Then, feeling expansive over Caroline's news, he ordered up a bottle of champagne in celebration.

It was in fact another boy. He came into the world with an

admirable instinct for patriotism—on the Fourth of July, 1836, the sixtieth anniversary of the country's independence. Adrien thought his head with its few silky reddish hairs oddly shaped, but declared that a boy born on that day couldn't help but grow up an exemplary American. Caroline had an easy delivery with Planche's now-authorized assistance; the old woman saw on the child "the sign of water."

"He's going to be a sailor," Adrien said with boyish enthusiasm. "He'll take the cotton to Europe that Marie-Adrien grows here."

Murphy and Clarence exchanged glances over the crib. Neither had a liking for the midwife's enigmatic prophecies.

Pierre-Adrien, an additional guarantee to the family's name, came into the world when the South was going through a new time of unrest. Texas was in ferment, and the Indians in Florida appeared unwilling to move to Arkansas where the federal government wished them to go. Ever since, in the wake of the original Spanish settlers, the American colonists had succumbed to the attractions of Texas's fertile lands, Southern citizens thought it should become a part of the Union. In 1835, the already numerous colonists rebelled against the Mexican authorities and sought their independence. The following year, one hundred twenty-seven besieged Texans under the leadership of William Barrett Travis held off 4,000 Mexican soldiers at Fort Alamo before finally surrendering. Among the victims were David Crockett and Jim Bowie, soon to become national heroes. In spite of this defeat, the settlers became landowners and grew corn, sweet potatoes and sugarcane. They then demanded membership in the Union. The Northerners refused, for they didn't want the proslavery South to grow in influence, so Texas proclaimed itself an independent republic. While the French and British coveted its wealth, the Mexicans threatened to reclaim the territory forcibly taken from them.

On the other hand, hounding the Indians in Florida from their ancestral lands troubled few consciences. In 1836, the Seminoles finally rebelled. They took Fort King, defeated the federal troops and ravaged Florida. Their chief, Osceola, killed General Thompson with his own hands and invited the Creeks to join his tribe in their struggle against the Union.

The government put down the rebellion, and New Orleans society delighted in visiting a camp just outside the city where twenty-four hundred Creeks were penned in like livestock. The chief attraction was Chief Neah Emath, an old man of ninety as proud as an eagle, and an erstwhile thorn in General Jackson's flesh.

In the city proper, land speculators had hired architects to plan new streets, squares, buildings and to lay out whole new sections—as if they anticipated a population of one million. The growing number of banks and the inflated value of produce had brought business to fever pitch. Old-fashioned lawyers like the Mertaux's kept their heads and discouraged their clients from being sucked into extravagant schemes. The French consul wrote his government: "It takes only a short stay in the United States to see how the spirit of conquest and encroachment is at work in this society. Insatiable greed and arrogance—the vices common to all upstarts—mean that everyone is fighting for the same space when, in fact, they are surrounded with thousands of acres of empty land. Always avid for better land, they desert Kentucky and Tennessee for Texas."

The results of these excesses were not slow in coming. Suddenly, merchants stopped payments and it was rumored that cotton planters were twenty million dollars in debt. Brokers who usually gave a year's advance on the next season's crop admitted to overdrafts of seventy-five million dollars. Cotton's sudden plunge in European markets caused these men sizable losses and the planters' incomes fell by 50 percent. The New Orleans banks didn't dare confess that they had only about fourteen million dollars' reserves against sixty million in deposits. Flour, which was worth fourteen dollars a barrel in January, 1836, had dropped to six dollars in May. Speculators facing ruin not infrequently resorted to suicide, like the Swiss consul, Theodore Nicolet, who put a bullet through his head. By August, as the yellow fever was again making its appearance, money was so scarce that it took $114 in bills to buy $100 in specie. New Orleans's sixteen banks had stopped payments.

Most Southerners blamed Andrew Jackson for their troubles, for hadn't he dissolved the Bank of the United States and thus strengthened the Wall Street bankers? Martin Van Buren's accession to the Presidency promised little improvement, as he had announced at his inaugural that he intended to follow in Andy Jackson's path. In addition to the financial crisis, racial tensions were causing terror and anger in various parts of the South. At Bayou Rapide near Alexandria in Central Louisiana, a widespread insurrection was planned for the night of October 7, 1837. Luckily for the whites, some slaves exposed the project two days before the fateful day and it was therefore quickly suppressed. Louisiana's official newspaper announced that over fifty blacks had been arrested, nine of the principals hung, among them some emancipated slaves. About forty men were in jail awaiting sentencing. In its next issue, the paper was able to add that eleven Negroes were executed in Alexandria on October 10 and fourteen more would suffer the same fate the next day. Two whites implicated in the affair had managed to escape but were being tracked down. It was later learned that the revolt had been planned to start in Alexandria, then move on to Natchitoches, and reach its climax in New Orleans "where the whites would be finished off for all time." On one of the blacks sentenced to corporal punishment, a letter was found from the philanthropist Arthur Tappan of New York which was very damaging to the abolitionist cause.

The news always arrived at Bagatelle mellowed by the passage of time. The Marquis sold his cotton and molasses for cash; therefore, he was little concerned over the crisis. The slaves in the parish of Pointe-Coupée showed no tendency to revolt—not even to disobey. Texas was far away; so were the Indians. The only thing that really upset him was the arrogance of New Orleans's elite in proposing that English be the only official language.

"English is the language of traders and businessmen; French is still the language of people of sensibility, of diplomats, of all those who despise profiteers and barbarians. It's the language of people who think!"

Dandridge, who had learned both languages simultaneously, French from his mother, English from his father, did not share Adrien's views.

"You think English is the businessman's language because you learned business from the English, and you think French is the language of sensibility because your parents taught you to look, love and feel in French. But you can't pretend that Shakespeare, Milton, Byron or Shelley expressed themselves like tradesmen!"

"All right—quote me a single Yankee poet or writer of prose! The language they mean to impose on us isn't Shakespeare's or Milton's. It's the English of the bankers in the City and the dockers in the port of London."

At this point in the discussion, Clarence judged it wise to change the subject. He knew that all the English writers put together wouldn't change Adrien's opinion.

One rainy, windy October night, Clarence and Barthew were discussing the nomination of a Louisiana man to be U.S. ambassador to the Republic of Texas. Suddenly, the wind and rain took on hurricane force. Rocking chairs banged on the gallery, the walls vibrated with the impact of the rain. The big oaks swayed convulsively, shedding great sheets of Spanish moss which sailed toward the river. Windows and doors were sealed in with heavy wooden shutters. Like a ship in a, storm, Bagatelle began to creak and shudder. The Marquis turned to Barthew. "You can't go out in this weather. Besides, they've probably stopped running the ferry to Bayou Sara. Please spend the night here."

Caroline, who was expecting their fourth child, ordered

that a room be made ready, and they spent the rest of the evening listening to the wild pounding of the elements. At dawn, when the hurricane had moved on, Adrien set forth through the fallen leaves and broken branches to check the damage done. The pigeon house had lost a few tiles; the roof of the stables, where Bobo had spent the night quieting the horses, was askew like a pot top; and a dozen huts in slave quarters had caved in as if a giant had stepped on them. He had seen worse.

"We had only the tail of the hurricane," the Marquis said to Barthew when the lawyer was about to leave.

New Orleans suffered far more. Several buildings were demolished, the colonnade in front of the Citizens' Bank collapsed. Six steamboats had to be written off, one blown up on land like a dead whale. The houses on either side of the railroad linking Lake Pontchartrain with the city were reduced to a pile of wood and bricks. The lake itself had overflowed into the outskirts, turning the cemetery into a vast swamp with a dozen corpses floating on the water, set adrift from where they had been left awaiting burial. Damages exceeded one million dollars. Adrien felt a wave of gratitude.

"Thank God we didn't go to the city this year! I would have been terrified for your child, Caroline. One scare and you might have lost the baby!"

"It takes more than a hurricane to scare me, Adrien. Remember when we crossed the Atlantic and I was expecting Marie-Adrien? He isn't any the worse for it."

"True enough. You're a brave woman and I thank God every day that I chose you for a wife."

Caroline glanced at Clarence, who was sipping his coffee, and he returned her look. Adrien missed the exchange of knowing smiles. They both had the same thought: It wasn't Adrien who had done the choosing and they both knew it.

"What's the difference?" Clarence said to himself as he drained his cup. "She knew enough to take her happiness, he to receive his. The marriage of ambition and love sometimes shows good results."

That night, Dandridge couldn't sleep, wondering if Caroline really loved her husband. Nothing in her behavior indicated the contrary, yet the very fact that she dared remind another person of her past follies revealed a strange clearheadedness. He arrived at the conclusion that the Marquis possessed only that part of Caroline she was willing to give. It was obviously enough to satisfy Adrien, but Clarence would have given anything to know what part of herself she had held back—something her pride would probably never let her reveal. In Clarence's eyes, to love profoundly meant a kind of unconscious abdication of self. Well, Caroline had not abdicated.

Contrary to the two older Damvilliers children, who were healthy and growing apace, Dandridge's godson was born listless and without appetite. Amalia, his nurse, wept to see him so skinny. Imilie, whose charges were always famished, said to her colleague:

"He won't live. We'll never see him grow up. One cold and, pffuit!, he'll be gone. The little Marquis and his sister are as solid as the master. The little one is pale like his mother, which isn't good for a boy."

All the same, the baby survived each minor setback and appeared to have righted himself by the time the old cradle was readied for Caroline's fourth child. This delivery was far more difficult than the others.

Planche had shut herself in with the mother. Adrien, nervous and apprehensive as always, paced the gallery, watching the rain fall through a curtain of fog. Night was approaching. He was waiting for Dr. Murphy's arrival from Sainte-Marie, where Dandridge had gone to fetch him. Finally, he saw Dandridge's gig under the oaks with the doctor sitting next to him. Adrien breathed easier and the small spasm that afflicted his heart every time he was emotionally moved quieted down.

"Thank God you're here, Murphy."

"What's the hurry, Marquis? Planche is here, I assume. You should be used to becoming a father by now."

While Dandridge took the gig to the stables, the two men went into the drawing room. Murphy collapsed into a chair, dropping his kit at his feet.

"Perhaps a little drink while we wait?"

Adrien signaled to James to bring the whiskey. Murphy was pouring himself a glass when Planche appeared at the door.

"Is it over?" Adrien blurted out.

The old woman didn't answer. She looked at Murphy and made him a sign to follow her. The doctor emptied his glass and picked up his kit. "So they need a doctor this time." And without waiting for Adrien's anxious questions, he hurried off to Caroline's room.

Planche pointed to her mistress. She was covered with sweat, chewing frantically on the midwife's pain-killing herbs, a greenish foam on her lips. Her eyes closed, her face contorted with pain, she was making a prodigious effort to expel the child, whose slimy body could be seen emerging between her thighs.

"The umbilicus, heh?"

The black woman nodded. He threw his coat on the floor, rolled up his shirt sleeves, rinsed his hands vigorously in the basin of hot water and leaned over the bed.

Caroline's panting and moaning merged with the doctor's heavy breathing as he tried to free the baby from the cord that threatened to strangle it.

"It's another girl," Murphy said, still working feverishly, for the baby was turning blue.

Wide-eyed, Planche followed the doctor's every move, full of admiration for his assurance and dexterity. A moment later, Caroline's efforts had slowed, then stopped altogether.

"There she is. Now you finish her off, my good woman," he said, handing Planche the infant. "Give it a good wallop to start it crying so that its lungs fill with air, then cut the cord. You know, do what's necessary."

As he washed his hands, Murphy turned to Caroline, who was lying, head back, exhausted.

"Rest now. All is well."

Planche was holding the baby by the feet, head down. The infant started to howl.

"You hear that? She's angry before she's even opened her eyes," Murphy said. He put his coat back on and told Planche to give her mistress some hot coffee. Then he left the room.

Caroline, trying to get her breath back and still unable to speak, looked at him with gratitude. Murphy grumbled something unintelligible. They had skirted disaster.

Murphy found the Marquis and Dandridge leaning against the drawing-room mantel.

"What happened, Murphy? It didn't go well?"

"Everything's all right, Adrien. It's a girl."

"But . . ."

"Nothing, I tell you. Just a little difficulty that Planche could have handled by herself."

"But what about Caroline?"

"She's tired. It's perfectly normal. You still don't know a damn thing about deliveries."

The doctor found his glass and filled it again.

"I need a drink too," Adrien said. "I was scared."

"This is how the pangs of paternity lead to alcoholism," Dandridge said with a benign smile.

During the night, Caroline suddenly started running a high fever. Terrified, the Marquis sent Rosa in search of Murphy.

"Puerperal fever. It's one of the risks you take," Murphy said as he hurried to Caroline's bedside.

For two days, Bagatelle held its breath. Adrien constantly badgered the doctor, without so much as a glance at his second daughter.

"Don't be frightened. I have no intention of dying like my mother," Caroline said when she saw the look of dismay on Adrien's face.

When the fever finally subsided and the Marquise had recovered her magnolia tint, Adrien dropped to his knees by her bedside, buried his head in her quilt and cried like a baby.

"We're not having any more children, Caroline. I was too

afraid I'd lose you . . ." Then he collected himself, ran a trembling hand through his hair and went off to order a new wing built on the hospital at Sainte-Marie, the one he had commissioned when the "little Marquis" was born.

Planche did not disclose the sign on Julie. She simply told Anna a few days later that the baby had "a transparent heart."

Dandridge also breathed easier when the young mother was finally out of danger. The crisis had given him the occasion to measure his attachment to the woman. At twenty-five, and after four closely spaced pregnancies, Caroline seemed to have no weaknesses. She belonged to that rare breed of females who make the weak feel protected.

Bagatelle was inundated with presents and congratulations. Isabelle, Percy Templeton's wife, who had had nothing but girls, said to Caroline: "What luck! Two sons and two daughters. How happy you must be!"

"I am. With my four, Bagatelle is certain to last. I'll bring them up to be men and women worthy of carrying on their father's name." Then, remembering the criticism leveled at her own father, she added: "You see, Isabelle, the blood of the Trégans isn't as weak as people think."

The Barrow sisters secretly hoped that one of them—Adele probably—would be asked to fill the envied role of godmother. They were bitterly disappointed when Caroline announced that she would have chosen Mignette had she been there. But having had no news of the blacksmith and his wife, she offered the honor to Minnie Forest, the daughter of a magistrate in Bayou Sara. Ed Barthew, for the first time in his life, was asked to be godfather.

Commenting on these peculiar choices, and the mistress of Bagatelle's astonishing fecundity, Adele Barrow said crisply: "That Caroline is all belly!"

During the following March, while Marie-Adrien, now a proud five and a half, chased by Félice, now going on four, watched Pierre-Adrien take his first steps around Julie's cradle, Mignette was jolting eastward toward Louisiana in a military wagon. Next to her wailed an emaciated infant. The baby's father lay with a few other pioneers under a small heap of earth in Chicachas country—home of the Indians called "Short Legs"—near a river at the foot of the Sangre de Cristo Mountains that the immigrants had named, not without reason, Purgatory. Their encampment, already grown to the size of a village, had been attacked by Indians. The inhabitants, with the blacksmith as their leader, had defended themselves like lions, but the "Short Legs" seemed to spring out of the very soil where their brothers fell. At the time of the attack, Mignette was doing her laundry in the river, her baby lying in the shade of a bush on the water's edge. Luckily, she was able to escape the massacre and the fire that destroyed their wagons and huts. Weeping, Mignette carried her baby and the bag that never left her up the river. She remembered having seen, a few days earlier, a detachment of troops escorting a geographer who was exploring the territory. She walked for over a week, surviving on the bitter berries on the shrubs and on river water. Her breasts dried up and she had nothing to feed the baby.

Near exhaustion, the young widow finally came upon the troops. Once she was restored to health, she asked to go back to the scene of the massacre and give Albert a decent burial. The soldiers dug a deep trench and buried the eighteen dead, already half devoured by vultures and lynx. An officer read two verses from the Bible, a detachment standing at strict attention fired a salute, and the convoy turned back, leaving the dead to the earth they had worked with such high hopes when alive.

The baby seemed to revive. Then he suddenly turned yellow, his urine took on the color of coffee and his stools had the texture of sand. "Your baby has jaundice, madam," the geographer announced. "He needs a lot of milk."

The soldiers forced Mignette to eat a nourishing diet, hoping this would bring back her milk. But she too turned yellow and was soon too weak to stand.

"It was all caused by fright," the geographer stated categorically. "The jaundice was brought on by fright which contaminated her milk and thus infected the child. Neither can be saved. It's too bad. Mrs. Schoeler must have been a pretty girl when she was healthy."

The learned man may have known his trigonometry and the identification of rocks, but he knew nothing about a woman with the will to live. A month later, when the convoy had reached Natchitoches, Mignette and her baby were still alive. The soldiers wanted to leave her with a family, but she pleaded with them to take her and her child to Pointe-Coupée. She didn't want to die among strangers. Her only friends were at Bagatelle and that's where she wanted to be. By mentioning Captain Templeton's name, she managed to get a wagon with a sergeant and two soldiers, but not before they had made her promise that she would reimburse the United States Army for the expenses of the journey.

That is how, one April evening, an officer in uniform riding ahead of a covered wagon appeared under the oaks at Bagatelle. Clarence and Adrien had been chatting on the gallery. They looked up with apprehension, called the dogs and advanced on the officer.

"Is this Bagatelle?" the officer asked.

"Yes, and I am its master," Adrien replied.

"I've brought you a very sick lady who asked to come here. She's in there, inside the wagon. She isn't in very good shape, nor is the child. We picked them up out west."

Caroline had heard the horses' hooves, the creaking of wheels and bits of the conversation.

"It's Mignette!" she exclaimed, rushing down the steps. "Don't you understand? Mignette is in there!"

Caroline had already reached the wagon and looked under the cover by the time the men caught up with her.

"Dear God. My poor Mignette, what have they done to you?"

Lying on a straw mat, the blacksmith's widow couldn't speak for her tears. Finally she managed: "Miss Caroline . . . I'm so happy . . . to be here . . ." and fainted.

As the men were trying to lift the dying woman out of the wagon, Caroline noticed a lumpy bundle on the mat. She opened it up and saw an emaciated baby the color of old shoe leather. She touched the child and at the feel of its cold skin, she let out a stifled scream. Mignette's baby was dead.

The soldiers set off the next day, stuffed with Anna's good food liberally washed down with Adrien's wine. They also carried off a wealth of provisions that amply made up for the detour. The sergeant, who came from Philadelphia and professed to be an abolitionist, found his convictions tempered by his experience of Southern hospitality. As he was getting ready to leave, he asked if he might express his thanks to Mrs. de Damvilliers.

"What a beauty! That Marquis is a lucky man," he said to his companions as they passed under the oaks. "She smells like a bouquet of roses and her skin's as soft as my horse's nostrils. If I ever find myself in these parts again, I'm going to stop by and ask after Mrs. Schoeler's health."

"She's going to die, like her kid," one of his companions said. "If we ever do come back, sergeant, your beautiful lady will be sending you to the cemetery."

Confirming the fact that the military's predictions are not always accurate, Mignette's health gradually improved. By summer's end, had the sergeant returned, he would have had trouble choosing between the mistress of the house and the blacksmith's widow.

Dr. Murphy took great interest in Mrs. Schoeler's case and finally cured her of her jaundice. Caroline's kindness and the Marquis's and Clarence's affection did the rest.

"Perhaps I should go back to France now," she said. "I've had no news of my mother for two years, and except for you, there's nothing to keep me here."

Caroline countered that Bagatelle was a heavy burden for a mother of four. A companion would be a great help in lightening her load. Mignette was easily convinced. So she stayed on at Bagatelle, basking in the warmth of its inmates' attentions and the lively presence of its children.

Julie's baptism brought Mignette and Ed Barthew together for the first time since her return. As soon as he had heard of her sad fate, he sent her the balance of the insurance on the smithy. But he refrained from appearing at Bagatelle himself while his "client" was convalescing. The ceremony gave her an opportunity to describe in detail the tragic adventure that had brought her back to Pointe-Coupée. Barthew was much moved.

"I have something to give you," Mignette said as she finished her tale. She opened her bag and handed the lawyer a snake-skin cigar case which he readily recognized.

"I lost it a long time ago," he said in some confusion, shaking the rebellious lock out of his right eye.

"My husband found it near the smithy on the night of the fire, Mr. Barthew. It made me realize the risk you had taken to prove your friendship. I always carried it with me, hoping I would someday be able to return it to you."

"It is doubly precious to me now, madam," the lawyer stammered. "I would have preferred that you and your family had found happiness in the West. But since the fates decided otherwise and you're now back, I want you to know that I'd gladly do it all over again."

Mignette took his hand. The first real smile since her return lit up her freckled face. In her black dress, she looked even prettier than before, less like an adolescent, more womanly. And Ed Barthew, who always discounted all claims of the heart, drew her hand to his lips and kissed it with fervor. The next day, he sent a scabious plant to Bagatelle. Mignette placed it on her windowsill and took great pains with it. When the countryside and the river grew faint in the purple mists of evening, she found comfort in the perfume of mourning's flower.

A child is graced with a wonderful innocence: He is completely ignorant of how short-lived his privileges are. He feeds on discoveries, responds to his whims, finds his rest in dreams. Unburdened by memories, regrets or remorse, he is propelled by his imagination. Life is conjugated in the present tense. He has no use for illusions, since nothing seems impossible. Cause and effect are meaningless. To him, the Good is what is agreeable, the Bad what causes pain. He is like Adam and Eve in the plenitude of Eden.

The earliest difference between rich and poor lies in the length or brevity of this heedless period. The poor learn early to live with that enemy of childhood called "reality." The rich meet it only later, screened by the protection of family and fortune.

Marie-Adrien, a handsome, curly-haired child, had all of childhood's usual privileges, plus those that came to him because of his station. Treated like an heir to a throne, he was soon aware of his importance. His nurse, Imilie, called him "the little Marquis" and when, at age seven, he learned what it meant, he began to act like a master. A learned old Jesuit priest with a yellowing beard and a rusty cassock came every day from Sainte-Marie to teach him French and Latin. His father asked Dandridge to teach him English and, through the history of the de Damvillierses, that of Louisiana.

These early studies gave the child assurance and a serious cast of mind. For her part, his mother taught him how to maintain his rank and subtly transformed his vanity into pride. One day, he astonished his father by announcing in the royal third person: "Marie-Adrien is second in rank at Bagatelle."

To Dandridge, who had never been near children, the Damvilliers brood was a caste unto itself. But he quickly learned to appreciate Marie-Adrien's intelligence and curiosity and talked to him like an adult. This purged the boy's vocabulary of the baby-talk nurses feel obliged to use. But his precocity masked certain impulses that some might have found disquieting. One day, when he was playing around the pigeon cote, he said to his mother, "I know how to put the pigeons to sleep."

Caroline and the boy went into the cote and there she saw four white pigeons lying motionless on the ground.

"How did you do it?"

"Like this." And he went up to a pigeon cooing in a hole, stroked its head, then squeezed its neck with his hands. "There. Now she's asleep!" he said in a tone of triumph.

Imilie, who had also witnessed the scene, was horrified.

"That's what he does, ma'm. The little Marquis chokes the pigeons."

Caroline told Imilie not to mention the incident to anyone and led the child back to the house. She didn't scold him; she simply explained that the sleep he had inflicted on the pigeons was definitive—it was called "death." And that because of what he'd done—because of simple ignorance, of course— those beautiful birds would never fly again, and that no one had the right to take another's life, except in the case of dangerous animals. Hands behind his back, Marie-Adrien listened to his mother's lecture with dutiful attention. But three days later, when James went to the cote to feed the pigeons, he found two more "asleep."

On being questioned, the child replied: "Now I do know what I'm doing. I am the pigeons' master!"

Two years later, he dismissed his nurse and asked for a valet. His father approved the manly request, so poor Imilie was replaced by Brent, a gentle young black who assisted James when the Damvilliers gave a party.

Marie-Adrien knew already that anyone with a black skin was his father's property. One day, he dragged Brent to the stables and asked Bobo to heat up the branding iron they used on the livestock. He would brand his valet so that everyone would know he belonged to him.

"But, little Marquis, you do that only to animals. It's not nice to do it to a Negro."

Marie-Adrien was adamant, his hand clutching Brent's wrist. "They gave me Brent. I can do with him what I like. I could even put him to sleep, like the pigeons."

Dandridge, who had come for his horse, arrived just in time to solve the two blacks' dilemma. Bobo, with fear in his voice, said, "Mister Dandridge, the little Marquis wants to brand Brent with the iron like he was cattle."

"That's a great idea," Dandridge said in deadly earnest. "Mr. de Damvilliers told me this very morning that he wanted Marie-Adrien branded so that everyone would know he belonged to him."

The child grew pale and fled. From that day on, he was terrified of Bagatelle's manager.

A few months later, while Adrien and Dandridge were having their usual late afternoon conversation on the gallery, the Marquis said, "Clarence, I'd like you to explain slavery to my son. Scientifically, if you can. It's time he understood it."

"Sorry, Adrien, but I think that kind of instruction should come from you."

"Why in Heaven's name?"

"Because I wouldn't know how to go about it, and he needs your authority to help shape his ideas. It's quite likely that your son will have to take on the abolitionists and their theories when he gets older."

"But look here, you know all this as well as I do. What are you lacking?"

"Conviction."

The Marquis's eyebrows shot up. "Because you don't believe we should maintain slavery in the South, is that it? You think the abolitionists are going to carry the day and we'll be forced to emancipate our slaves? Is that what you think?"

"I think that another civilization is on the march, Adrien. That what was good for yesterday won't be good for tomorrow, and we'd better get ready for it. The new era may not be better than the one we've known, but it will be different."

"All right then," the Marquis said, "I'll teach Marie-Adrien about the civilization we brought to this country. It's the only one I know and, as God is my witness, I'll do everything in my power to hold onto it. If we let it go, the South will end up in chaos."

And so it was from his father that the little Marquis learned everything that a slave owner, a good Christian and a master conscious of his responsibilities needs to know.

He learned that during the Old Kingdom in Egypt, prisoners

of war became the pharaoh's slaves and worked in the mines and quarries. In Babylon, the slave's master had him tattooed, his hair shaved off and an identifying tablet hung around his neck. The master had rights to the slave's children and was indemnified in case he died by accident. However, the slave could buy his freedom from his savings, or by borrowing money from the temple. Also, families were not allowed to be dispersed. Then Adrien moved on to the Hittites, where the slave had legal rights although insubordination was severely punished. Among the Hebrews, debtors were reduced to slavery for a maximum of ten years, and in the case of the Greeks and Romans, war provided them with prisoners to do the hard labor and housework.

Then the Marquis quoted Aristotle: "A slave is an animated instrument created to do what the master commands." Furthermore, the philosopher viewed slavery as a "natural relationship" which assumed the participation—even if passive —of the slave in his master's wishes. Although Aristotle stated: "It can happen that the souls of slaves inhabit the bodies of free men and vice-versa," he also maintained that "domestic animals and slaves are useful to about the same degree. By virtue of their physical strength, both are helpful in satisfying life's needs."

The Marquis then turned to the spiritual masters. He quoted Saint Paul as being in favor of "gentle slavery" in the patriarchal mode; Saint Augustine, who stated that slavery was "a punishment meted out to sinners"; Saint Thomas, who proclaimed that relations between master and slave lay outside the claims of justice and that a slave was private property. Then the Marquis took *De Rerustica* down from his library shelf and read his son Cato's observations on a slave's labor and nourishment: five pounds of bread from the time the slave begins spading until the figs are ripe, the remainder of the time, a ration of four pounds. Adrien concluded with an item from the "Black Code" promulgated in France in 1685 to fix the punishment to be meted out to slaves: "After the first escape, if it last longer than a month, cut off ears and brand with the fleur-de-lis; second escape, cut him off at the knees; third escape, put him to death."

Marie-Adrien listened to his father with the concentration of a knight on the eve of his dubbing.

"As you see," the Marquis said, sitting back in his chair, "all the great civilizations, all those that have left their imprint on man's history, have accepted slavery as a perfectly natural thing. Certainly there were barbarous times when slaves were mistreated and ill-fed. But we have grown more humane. You know that at Bagatelle, we never whip a slave, never break up families, and see to it that they have houses, a bit of land, domestic animals, a hospital, a church. Because, in the eyes of God, we are held responsible for their existence and good conduct."

"Why don't we brand them the way they did in Babylon?" the little Marquis asked.

"Because a good master knows his slaves and his slaves know him. There's no need for branding."

"I once wanted to brand Brent, but Mr. Dandridge came and wouldn't let me. He even said you'd brand me too."

"I probably would have."

"Why, please?"

"Because, Marie-Adrien, God in His infinite goodness has decided that whites and blacks share two things: pain and prayer. This equality willed by our Creator must be respected. And don't forget that Balthazar, one of the three Magi, was black, yet he was allowed into the stable in Bethlehem. As for Cham's story, I'll tell you that another time."

From that day on, Marie-Adrien viewed the slaves with a different eye. Brent, whom he had often bullied, was the first to notice the change. But contrary to what one might have expected, the boy didn't model himself after his father but after his father's manager, whose ease of manner and air of distinction he secretly admired. Aping Dandridge, he spoke sparingly to Brent and the other slaves, addressing them only when he wanted to issue orders, which he did with a tone that was both grave and casual. Before long, he was being accused of arrogance. Even in his games with his sister, big placid Félice, he made his authority felt. He demanded to be served before her at meals and made her stay behind him when Imilie and Brent took them on walks. In his words, "girls count for nothing in our family." Julie, who was just beginning to put one tentative foot in front of the other, was "Mummy's baby." With Pierre-Adrien he was more circumspect, for his four-year-old brother was still strangely fragile. He sometimes gave him a pitying look: "He's so small. He falls down all the time." His words conveyed a hint of satisfaction, even contempt.

His father countered: "You wait. When you're big, there'll be little difference between you. These small differences in age fade with time."

"There will too be a difference," Marie-Adrien replied heatedly. "I am the older and I'll be called 'Marquis' like you."

Only Dandridge sensed something disquieting in the boy's childish arrogance and his obsession with precedence—which the servants unconsciously encouraged. And there was another thing: the child's fascination with death. He had stopped putting the pigeons "to sleep" but he took excessive interest in all forms of death. When Mac died of old age and Mic had to be put away because she had become uncontrollable, he watched with rapt attention their burial in a corner of the park.

"How long does a dog live?" the young Marquis asked Dandridge.

"Oh, ten, eleven, twelve years. Sometimes more."

"And a man?"

"Some live to a hundred, or so they say."

"Then you'll die before me?"

"Probably," Dandridge said.

"And Mummy too?"

"If everything follows in the natural order, it could be."

"What does natural order mean?" the boy asked.

"It means the normal span of life, if there are no serious illnesses or accidents."

The child leaned down to stroke the two new Dalmatians,

puppies of the two just interred. Clarence had picked them out of his bitch's last litter.

"What are you going to call them?"

"Mic and Mac, like their parents," Dandridge said.

"How did you choose them?"

"I took the best-looking."

"What happened to the others?" Marie-Adrien asked.

"They were drowned. A bitch mustn't be made to feed puppies no one wants."

"You could do the same thing with babies. Keep the best-looking and let the rest die."

"Children are very different from animals, Marie-Adrien. They have souls and all human life is sacred. It would be a crime to choose among babies."

"I suppose so," the child said thoughtfully. "But it's certainly convenient that you can do it with animals."

"It isn't convenient. It's necessary, but it doesn't mean you don't love them," Dandridge said, hoping to bring the conversation to a close.

"But, Mr. Dandridge, you can't love everybody!"

Abraham Mosely celebrated his forty-fifth birthday at Bagatelle. On his arrival, he was full of praise for the new hotel in New Orleans—the Hotel de la Baie Saint-Louis—which was bound to steal customers from the Saint-Charles. It had spacious rooms, rooms "with baths," a billiard room, bars, a vegetable garden, a dock for pleasure craft, stables and a coach house. The Marquis wailed at the price: sixty dollars a month for an adult, twenty-five dollars for a servant! No, he had no intention of deserting the Saint-Charles. Let the nouveaux riches and Northerners stay at the Saint-Louis.

Mosely's trunk produced a quantity of presents: a rapier for the little Marquis, silk socks for Clarence, an ermine scarf for Caroline, pieces of lace for Félice and Julie, a fife for Pierre-Adrien and silver buttons for the Marquis's hunting jacket. Not knowing Mignette would be there, he apologized for not having brought her anything. In the end, he made her accept a bottle of Guerlain toilet water from his own toilet kit.

"What a charming man," Mignette said while she was helping her mistress undress. "It's too bad he eats so much. It's going to ruin his health and he'll end up as fat as a laundry tub."

Eighteen forty was a troublesome year for the jovial broker from Manchester. It looked as if Louisiana wouldn't be able to provide him with enough cotton, his mills having greatly increased their capacity since the depression of 1837. He had no desire to go to Alabama, where planters were producing the so-called "beau et fin" cotton grown on high sandy soil which sold for between 13½¢ to 14½¢ a pound. All this was due to Vincent Otto Nolte, the speculator who had disappeared after his bankruptcy ten years before and had now turned up as an associate of Nicholas Biddle, the president of the Bank of Pennsylvania. Together they were trying to buy up all the cotton in New Orleans. Nicholas Biddle, originally from Liverpool and now considered the outstanding financier in the United States, had sent a notice to all the planters proposing "liberal advances" on all the cotton they were willing to consign to him, also promising "to keep the cotton until the following summer in order that they be able to get the highest possible price." Business in New Orleans was suffering from this concerted speculation and the Louisiana press attacked Biddle, calling him "a vampire financier and enemy of the Southern states, a veritable Egyptian pasha who aspires to industrial supremacy which will be fatal to the prosperity and independence of the country." The Bank of Pennsylvania offered the planters sixty dollars for a four-hundred-pound bale, which put cotton at fifteen cents a pound, thus out of reach for European traders.

Mr. Mosely was full of inside information he had picked up from Washington agents. To the planters the Marquis had gathered together at Bagatelle, he disclosed that this was an underhand operation organized by the government. He explained how Biddle had calculated that the United States' commercial deficit could be wiped out if they succeeded in raising the price of cotton one or two cents a pound. To set this giant plan in motion, he was prepared to use all the financial means at his disposal. Nolte, back in America with his reputation intact, was sitting in New Orleans with unlimited credit for the purchase of all the cotton he could lay his hands on.

"I've seen Nolte's figures on cotton production covering the last twenty-four years," one planter put in. "Using these, he can forecast the rise in price for the next ten years."

"My advice to you," Mosely countered, "is to deal only in cash on available goods. Then when the price goes up—if it does—you make a profit and you're not at the mercy of the speculators for having bought on credit."

Mosely succeeded in convincing enough planters to resist the Northern financiers' tempting offers to the point where he was able to get all the cotton he needed in Louisiana after all.

Before Mosely left for England, events proved him right. Biddle's offer was circulated in March. By November of the same year, his efforts had been defeated, and in Pointe-Coupée, the British trader was hailed as a great economist.

"Mosely is a brilliant man," Caroline observed. "The planters who listened to him and followed my husband's example owe him a great debt of thanks."

The thanks proffered by Adrien's friends took the form of a cane with a gold knob weighing almost a pound. It was presented to him by Julie, who had just turned three, while Félice recited a poetic compliment written by Adele Barrow, who fancied herself a poetess, in which she likened the paunchy Englishman to Mercury, the God of Commerce.

Willy Templeton returned from his battles with the Florida Indians in time for the New Year. Brown as a pirate, he found Caroline more beautiful than ever, but it was Mignette he invited to dance. The captain's lively interest in the blacksmith's widow caused a number of comments among the young ladies and was especially displeasing to Ed Barthew.

"That swashbuckling Indian-killer has good taste," the lawyer muttered. Then, changing his tone, he said gamely: "I've never seen you look so well, Mrs. Schoeler."

"Are you jealous, Mr. Barthew?"

If he hadn't had several glasses with Dr. Murphy, who was at the moment down on all fours "playing horsey" with Pierre-Adrien, Barthew would never have dared say what he did: "Yes, I am jealous." He quickly looked away.

Mignette said nothing. The lawyer, tongue-tied, turned in the direction of the buffet. Mignette held him back.

"You've had enough to drink. I'd like you to dance with me."

"I dance like a bear."

"I like bears."

She pulled him into the big drawing room, where a quadrille was getting underway. As they crossed paths with Willy Templeton, Barthew shook off Mignette's hand.

"Please take my place, Captain. You're a much better dancer than I." He bowed in Mignette's direction and fled. A few minutes later, he was galloping toward the ferry to Bayou Sara.

Clarence had seen the lawyer leave from the gallery, where he was smoking with a group of guests. As the party was drawing to a close, he sought out Dr. Murphy who, as always, had a glass of whiskey in his hand.

"Why did Barthew leave so early, Murphy?"

"Something urgent."

"On New Year's Day?" Clarence asked, puzzled.

"An affair of the heart, my friend."

"Ah! So that explains his sudden departure . . ."

"That was no departure. That was flight. Our friend Barthew is in love with Mrs. Schoeler."

"Did she give him the air?"

"No, she asked him to dance," Murphy replied.

"Then I don't understand . . ."

"He doesn't either. Maybe he needs a lawyer."

The two men agreed it was best to stay out of other people's affairs. Then Murphy confessed that if he weren't a drunk, and old, and past all illusions, he might have sought the hand of the blacksmith's widow.

A few days later, Mignette queried Clarence on Barthew's odd behavior on New Year's Day. They were taking a morning ride along the levee. The weather was cold and dry and their horses' hooves rang out on the hard-packed earth. Skeletons of trees floated down the river and the smell of humus heralded nature's awakening.

"Is Mr. Barthew your friend?"

"Yes, he is," Clarence said.

"Life must have been hard on him."

Clarence guessed that Mignette wanted to know about Barthew's past, for there had been rumors going around for years. But his natural sense of discretion kept him from disclosing what he knew.

"I think he had some bad moments, but he always extricated himself with honor," Dandridge said.

"Is it true that he killed his wife?" Mignette asked abruptly.

Clarence stopped his horse, folded his hands on the pommel of his saddle, and looked at Mignette. Under the brim of his hat, his eyes looked as cold as the river.

"Yes, it's true. He killed his wife, and it was an act of courage few would be capable of. She had been horribly burned in a fire and was suffering agonies. At her request, he cut short a life that would have ended soon anyway."

Mignette's eyes filled with tears. Clarence went on, "At one time, Edward Barthew was perhaps the outstanding lawyer in Boston. He had married a beautiful English girl. They were very happy. After the accident, he appeared before a criminal jury and was acquitted because even his parents-in-law testified in his favor. He thereupon cleaned out his office, broke with all his relatives and came to live in Bayou Sara. And that is Ed Barthew's story. Since you seem to be interested in him, I might add that I consider him an estimable man, even if he did put a match to a smithy to provide a sentimental lady with the means to emancipate her slaves."

"So you guessed it?"

"It wasn't too difficult," Clarence said, spurring his horse. As he took the lead, he turned in his saddle and added: "It's no more difficult than guessing that in you he thinks he's found a companion who can bring him what every man needs, no matter what his memories: tenderness and understanding. In both your cases, it may be too soon to talk of happiness."

"Thank you for telling me all this, Mr. Dandridge. Albert was the first man I ever loved. It couldn't be the same with anyone else."

"It could be different," Dandridge said.

They didn't speak again until they'd reached Bagatelle. As they were getting off their horses, Bobo informed them that Dr. Murphy had been fetched from the hospital for a matter of greatest urgency. The Marquis was ill.

Apparently when Adrien returned from the cotton gins, he had collapsed on a sofa, unable to breathe. "I've had it once before," the Marquis said. "It's like a burning sensation in my chest. I had it after a gallop in the rain, remember?"

Dr. Murphy was reassuring. "A mild attack of congestion, perhaps. You must stay in bed for three days, keep warm, and no cigars! If things aren't better tomorrow, we'll apply the leeches."

Caroline's fears were eased but Dandridge thought the doctor's brusque indifference a bit forced. He accompanied him to his gig.

"So?"

"It's his heart, Dandridge. He mustn't have this kind of attack too often. He isn't twenty anymore."

That's all Clarence could get out of him, but he promised himself that he'd try to restrict his employer's activities. The Marquis was one of those vigorous men who can't do anything by halves. Whether on horseback, in the fields, directing the slaves' labors, hunting, at a ball or at table, he gave his all with a kind of obsessive vitality. Dandridge supposed he was the same in bed.

Two days of quiet were all the Marquis could stand. When his manager observed that he must discipline his energies,

Adrien was outraged. "What do you take me for, Dandridge? An old maid? The body may have its weaknesses but one mustn't attach more importance to it than absolutely necessary." And since Marie-Adrien had just been given a new rifle, he set off to initiate his son into the joys of hunting.

While the heir to Bagatelle was thus preparing himself for the role of a plantation gentleman, Clarence was becoming increasingly aware of his godson's intelligence and subtle mind. Pierre-Adrien, who was not yet five, had an insatiable curiosity. When he wasn't playing under his nurse's watchful eye, he would appear on the walkway connecting Clarence's apartment with the main house. Ilifet would sit him down in a large chair across from Clarence, and Clarence would put down his pen and close his books in anticipation of the questions he knew were coming.

"Why do the people giving orders have a white skin and those obeying a black skin? Where does the wind come from? Where is the river going? What happens to the soft white balls they call cotton that people are always talking about and that disappear into big bags? Does rain fall from the trees? Why can't we understand what dogs are saying?"

Dandridge applied himself to the answers with a patience that no one at Bagatelle would have thought him capable of. And so it was that as the months went by, it was the plantation's manager who initiated Adrien's second son into the mysteries of life. Pierre-Adrien, with his reddish-blond hair, pale skin, widely spaced intense eyes and the graceful body of a girl, was an apt pupil.

Caroline asked Clarence: "Doesn't he annoy you with his eternal questions? He's a curious child. He's always playing alone and spends hours telling himself the most incredible stories."

"Thanks to him, I've learned that children aren't interested in what adults do or in the problems of daily life. They go directly to the essentials we've long since given up considering. Pierre-Adrien often forces me to think. I dread the day he asks me for proof of God's existence!"

Caroline smiled with a hint of condescension. She much

preferred Marie-Adrien's more virile character and his growing air of assurance. Félice, totally impervious to her tutor's
instructions, was a lively and docile child occupied with dolls
and dresses and who gave every indication of growing up to
be the perfect ornament of a planter's family. Julie, a little
slow in walking, was given no more attention than a baby
deserves. This quartet of children was a challenge to Bagatelle's adults. More even than the Marquis and his wife, Dandridge was sensitive to the need for a certain equilibrium to
maintain the peace. But unlike the children's parents, he found
it hard to be spontaneous with them.

"It's funny. I can't remember ever having been a child,"
Dandridge remarked to the Marquis one winter afternoon
when they were watching the children play on the gallery.

"That's odd. I remember it so clearly. I'm constantly reminded of the way I played when I was Pierre-Adrien's age.
I'm sure if you returned to the place you spent your childhood,
it would all come back."

"I doubt it. When I think back to my father's house in
Boston, I don't see myself in it. If I do see a child, it isn't me.
It's a stranger."

Clarence was ready for a respite from the Damvilliers by
the time he boarded the boat for a business trip to New Orleans. He made his usual rounds, and at the end of ten days,
took the *Eclipse*, the river's latest pride, for the trip home.
As they stopped at Baton Rouge—he was in the act of shaving with a new cream whose label proclaimed it was used by
Albert, Queen Victoria's consort—he was handed a message
which had been waiting several days. It was from Dr. Murphy: "Come back as soon as possible. The Marquis has had
two new attacks. He's in very serious condition." Clarence
immediately packed his bags and gave them to a ship's officer
to drop off at Bayou Sara, where Bobo would pick them up.
Then he had himself taken to Port Allen by tug. One hour
later, he was galloping on a hired horse along the twenty-five
miles separating him from Bagatelle. Slaves bending over their
furrows looked up with astonishment as the cavalier dashed

past at breakneck speed. By the time he arrived in front of the house, the horse's chest was covered with foam. Young Mic and Mac, come to greet their master, didn't get so much as a pat. Alerted by the dogs' barking, James appeared at the door. From his expression, Dandridge knew he was in time.

"How's the master, James?"

"He's sleeping, Mister Dandridge. Anna and Rosa is with him. The mistress stayed up all night with him. She's resting now. We was sure scared!"

Clarence found Marie-Adrien sitting in the drawing room, leafing through an illustrated book on Roman history.

"Father asked for you several times. He'll be very happy to see you. He's very sick."

Just then, Caroline walked in. Her face looked unchanged. Only the dark circles under her eyes betrayed her fatigue. Clarence kissed her hand. From the gentle pressure of her fingers, he knew she was glad he was back.

"Leave us for a moment, Marie-Adrien. I want to talk to Mr. Dandridge."

The boy stalked out of the room with pursed lips as if he considered this tête-à-tête uncalled for. Walking out on the gallery, he told James in a commanding tone, "Let me know if anything happens. I'll be on the bench near the pigeon house, reading."

Caroline smiled wanly. Dandridge watched the child disappear, his stride as stiff as a cockerel's.

"Caroline, tell me what happened."

She explained how Adrien had twice been seized with agonizing pains on the left side of his chest. He had been virtually unconscious for an hour, and Murphy found his pulse weak and irregular. The night before, he had complained of paralysis in the legs and a buzzing in his head. His condition was visibly worsening.

"What does Murphy say?"

Caroline looked away. In a dull voice, she replied, "He says he will die soon, or live on a little while but completely paralyzed. It's too terrible."

Clarence led Caroline to a sofa. She sat down, rigid, her

eyes closed. When she opened them again, it was to look at Clarence with an expression of profound sadness.

"We were probably too happy at Bagatelle for it to last. If Murphy is right, paralysis would be more than Adrien could stand. Do you think we should get Dr. Berthollet to come from New Orleans, Clarence?"

"I've known Murphy a long time. He's the best doctor in Louisiana, but there's nothing wrong with getting another opinion . . ."

He said this to Caroline out of politeness, to add a measure of hope, but his remark was without conviction. He knew how brutal Murphy could be when he was sure of his diagnosis.

"Does Adrien know how serious his condition is?" Dandridge asked.

"I think so," Caroline replied. "He wanted to make his confession yesterday afternoon, then he called for Marie-Adrien. He kept him an hour. I don't know what he told him. Then he asked for you. . . . Actually, how did you learn of this?"

Clarence told her about the message waiting for him in Baton Rouge. This act on the part of the doctor confirmed her worst fears. She stood up and straightened the folds of her skirt.

"We're going to have to be very brave, Clarence. I don't worry about myself, or Marie-Adrien. But Pierre-Adrien troubles me. He hasn't eaten or slept for two days. For all his youth, he senses something calamitous in the air. He'll be needing you more than any of us."

"Adrien has such a strong constitution he may still pull out of it," Clarence said, again without conviction.

He went back to his apartment to wait until the Marquis was ready to see him. All the while he was washing and putting on a clean shirt, he was conscious that death was prowling around Bagatelle. Was it hiding under the oaks, or on the riverbank, its invisible bark tied up to a willow tree? Or was it stalking the gallery, waiting for the appointed hour?

At fifty-one, the Marquis had seemed so robust that it was difficult to imagine him laid low, yet there he was, lying on his bed, unable to move. The master of Bagatelle was no longer issuing orders. It was his turn now to obey, to submit to the inevitable.

James came for Clarence at the end of the afternoon. "The master is awake. He's asking for you."

"How is he?"

"He's better. His voice is stronger than this morning."

Clarence found the Marquis resigned, pale, shrunken, and his large brown eyes were bright with fever. With concentrated effort, he held out his hand, disfigured by bulging blue veins. He spoke slowly, using the words easiest to pronounce, the ones that took the least effort.

"I know I'm dying, Clarence."

Clarence made the expectable gesture of denial.

"No, no, I know it. I feel it. Murphy told me so. My affairs are in order. I'm . . . very sad to be leaving this life. . . . I was so happy . . ."

He stopped, his throat filled with emotion. Large heavy tears began to roll down his cheeks. Clarence took his hand and squeezed it hard as if to transmit some of his own life to him. The Marquis took strength from the touch.

"Caroline knows, too. She's very brave. It's Marie-Adrien who worries me. He's too arrogant, too avid, too hard. I want him to go to the Jesuits. They'll make a man of him. But Clarence, promise me you'll stay at Bagatelle and look after everybody. Pierre-Adrien loves you. He's a sensitive and gentle boy. As for the girls, their mother will know how to make young ladies of them."

He seemed to have come to the end. Clarence started to leave so that Adrien could rest, but the Marquis stopped him.

"Wait. I haven't finished. I've drawn up a codicil that completes my will, which the Mertaux brothers have. I did it after my first seizure, three years ago. You'll find it in the library, on the top shelf to the left, inside that book with the pictures—you know the one, the one we never look at. Everything is in it, and my instructions for my funeral. Go now, Dandridge. I hope your life . . . if possible . . . happy."

Shaken by the deep pathos of this conversation, Clarence avoided the others until he could pull himself together. He walked down through the park to the river's edge. The dignity and self-control of the man face to face with death, his eyes wide open, revealed a spiritual strength Clarence hadn't expected. The spirit of the Christian knights of long ago was alive in this burly awkward man. Perhaps this was the way his warrior ancestors had died on the field of battle, their backs against an oak tree, indifferent to their wounds, hiding the pain, relinquishing life in order to deny Death the satisfaction of rupturing the cord. Adrien would be surrendering a shattered body, a pathetic harvest worth little more than that of an anonymous slave. In its frustration, Death would gnash its teeth like the thief who finds that the coffer he's stolen is empty.

Dandridge then turned his thoughts to the living. Adrien had sized up his sons very accurately. Perhaps the approach of death had given him new insights—or perhaps circumstances had prevented him from expressing them earlier. And what would become of Caroline? A widow at thirty, reduced to dependence on a manager for the running of the plantation?

Or would her growing responsibilities become a springboard to new ambitions? With slow steps, his dogs at his heels, Clarence returned to the house, twilight bathing it in a cold sharp light. The lights were already on in the drawing room; James was closing the windows and Bobo was leading the horses to the drinking trough; on the gallery the rocking chairs were waiting in vain for the master and his manager and the ritual of the late afternoon punch. Clarence felt the deep sadness that foreshadows a permanent separation. Bagatelle was awaiting the visitor to whom all one can say is "Never again!"

Dr. Murphy came to see the Marquis during the course of the evening. Unusual for him, he seemed to wish to stay on with Caroline and Clarence, and Mignette, who had spent a wearing day with the children. Clarence guessed at the doctor's reluctance to leave. He edged him out onto the gallery.

"You think it's imminent, Murphy?"

"Before dawn, I fear. Tell the women to go to bed. You and I will keep watch. I don't know how to say this to the Marquise."

Mignette couldn't keep her eyes open, so she willingly went to her room. But Caroline had suspected the reason why the watch wasn't to include her.

"Stay with us, Murphy. I'm going to sit with Adrien. It's where I belong."

As she was getting ready to go to her husband's room, she caught sight of Marie-Adrien standing in the doorway, his hands behind his back, waiting to be noticed. Before his mother could speak, he said, "I want to be there too. I'm not afraid of death."

And, without waiting for a reply, he sat down in his father's chair. He was sound asleep when, at about three in the morning, Caroline appeared at the door with a stricken face.

"Come," she said. "I think it's the end."

Clarence and Murphy rushed out. The noise of Adrien's raucous breathing filled his room. His swollen fingers clutched at the sheet and his eyes had the blank stare of a drowning man. Caroline wiped his forehead with a cloth soaked in vinegar, then gently kissed his brow. Murphy took his pulse, his lips moving as if he were talking to himself. Finally he looked at Clarence with eyebrows raised to signify his helplessness before what was about to happen.

While they stood waiting for an unhoped-for sign of renewed life in the exhausted body, Marie-Adrien approached the bed and stood next to his mother, head down, his eyes fixed on his father's face. Adrien, occupied with his death, raised his eyes to the canopy above the bed and with his last breath, said the word he'd been determined to say before he died: "Adieu."

A heavy silence enveloped the room. The dying man's breathing ceased. Calmly and without a tear, Caroline closed his eyes, kissed him again and pushed Marie-Adrien toward the bed. The child contemplated the dead man's face, placed a kiss on the limp hand, then left the room so that no one would see him cry.

When the others returned to the drawing room, the boy was standing solemn and stiff in front of the fireplace. Dry of eye, his hands behind his back in his now-familiar posture, he announced crisply: "And so I am now the Marquis de Damvilliers."

Leaving his mother, Dandridge and Murphy speechless, he turned on his heel and went up to his room.

"So much strength so soon," Caroline exclaimed with pride. "No question but that my son has the blood of the Damvilliers. That will be my consolation."

The funeral of Jacques-Adrien, third Marquis de Damvilliers, took place on March 10, 1842. In accordance with the codicil Dandridge had found without difficulty, the ceremony was brief and sober. As the Marquis had expressly asked, every worker on the plantation took part in the Mass, which was celebrated in the wooden church usually used only by the slaves. The priest at Sainte-Marie was disappointed to be done out of such a distinguished service, and many of the planters attending could not be contained in the modest building. Under an early spring sun, long lines of landaus, barouches and gigs converged on Bagatelle. The governor of Louisiana dispatched his first secretary, and the commander of the French warship *Dunois*, who had been invited to visit Bagatelle a month before, attended with his chief of staff and an honor guard. Since he had been unable to meet the Marquis before his death, he wished to pay him the final homage due a French gentleman. The presence of the military, lined up behind their flag and marching on either side of the hearse, lent the service a pomp the deceased might have found in questionable taste.

Caroline and Marie-Adrien led the funeral procession, with Willy and Percy Templeton and two members of the parish council serving as pallbearers. Everyone commented on the brave and dignified bearing of the heir to Bagatelle in his black velvet suit. Caroline's face was hidden behind a veil. Clarence, whom Caroline had asked to sit with the family, looked even taller and leaner in his black suit. As they admired his rangy silhouette, several ladies wondered if he wouldn't make the young widow an entirely acceptable second husband.

Because Mignette was in charge of the three younger children, she couldn't walk in the procession. She had to comfort the weeping Pierre-Adrien because he hadn't been allowed to follow his father's coffin. Caroline had been about to give in when Marie-Adrien intervened, protesting that his brother "cried like a girl."

Conforming to Damvilliers tradition, the coffin was carried by slaves as far as the entrance to Bagatelle where it was placed in the waiting hearse—the Marquis's last trip under the oaks. At the cemetery in Sainte-Marie, the Damvilliers's great vault was open, a majestic monument visible from a great distance. The actual tomb was built of cut stone, surmounted by a small temple with eight Ionic columns. The roof was made of a single slab of granite faced on all four sides with the Damvilliers's escutcheon. On it rose a cross. Adrien was about to join his grandparents, parents, and first wife. The gravedigger, in the manner of a man loading a stagecoach, let it be known that "there was room for four more."

It is said that the funeral indicates the esteem in which the deceased was held when alive. Marie-Adrien learned that day that his father was respected everywhere, from the biggest landowners down to the lowliest "rednecks" from Fausse-Rivière. Once the ordeal of the condolences was over, Caroline told her older son: "It will be your duty to maintain the honor of the Damvilliers."

Telemaque and his choir sang a hymn after the closing of the tomb.

"Apparently the Marquis wanted it this way," Clement

Barrow commented to a neighbor. "Funny idea to want your niggers at your burial."

"Where he is now, sir, there are neither masters nor slaves," said the priest from Sainte-Marie with unaccustomed boldness.

"Are you quite sure, Father?" Adele asked dryly.

The priest held his tongue, ruminating on the fact that Christians didn't always know Christ's teachings.

At Bagatelle, life resumed. The earth couldn't wait, and no dead man, however loved and respected, could excuse the living from putting the seed in the ground. With Clarence Dandridge now in charge, the blacks saw no change in their condition. The hours of work were neither longer nor shorter, the sun felt as hot as it had other summers when it was time for weeding and the battle against the boll worm. Marie-Adrien, now riding a small Arabian horse, sometimes accompanied the manager and was always quick to note any sign of laziness. Dandridge was impatient for the day when he and Caroline would make the trip to New Orleans for the reading of the will. Praise God it would clear up a few questions and deliver the arrogant brat into the hands of the Jesuit Fathers!

Two or three incidents had cast light on the true character of Adrien's heir. There was the day, for example, when Clarence took in the fact that the servants were no longer addressing the boy as "the little Marquis" but simply as "the Marquis." He asked around and learned that Marie-Adrien had so instructed them, threatening them with the whip if they forgot his proper title. When Clarence reported this premature exercise in authority to Caroline, she said crisply, "I know all about it. Isn't that the way he should be addressed now?"

"But Caroline, to threaten servants with the whip?"

"Oh, it's just a childish expression. Don't take it so seriously."

Clarence was not of the same mind. His fears increased the night Marie-Adrien came to dinner in a strange state of excitement, his face on fire, his eyes glazed. Mignette, sitting next to him, suddenly exclaimed:

"Madam, he smells of wine. I think he's been drinking."

"Brent gave me some port," the nine-year-old stated with hauteur. "He told me that Daddy had some every evening."

When his servant was summoned, he gave a very different account. He had found "the Marquis" alone with a bottle of port and had had great difficulty separating him from it.

"He's a liar," the child said, unabashed.

But, suddenly seized with nausea, he had to rush from the dining room.

Caroline said with unflinching partiality, "Brent, if I ever see my son in that condition again, I send you right back to the cotton fields!"

Clarence was certain the servant hadn't lied. Anna, above all, knew the boy's gluttony. She had found him several times with his nose in the jam cupboard. "Everything here belongs to me," he had told her. She decided it was best not to report his harmless pranks.

These peccadilloes common to all children didn't accord with the extraordinary maturity he otherwise displayed. Clarence wasn't blinded by maternal love, as was Caroline. He saw the signs of a budding sensualist hiding under the boy's stern and insolent exterior. Very cautiously, he tried to convey his misgivings to Caroline. She was immediately on the defensive.

"I know you don't like Marie-Adrien, Clarence. You see more faults in him than he really has. Naturally, he isn't malleable like your godson, nor docile like Félice. Leave him to grow up and benefit from the advantages of his situation. I don't intend to let my son become an ascetic like you!"

Since her husband's death, the Marquise had kept both Dandridge and Mignette at arm's length. The days of the confidential talks seemed to be over. She often ate with Marie-Adrien in the breakfast room earlier than the usual dinner hour, leaving Clarence to sit alone with the blacksmith's widow. He began to feel like a kind of hybrid—as did Mignette —not quite a member of the family but not among the higher rung of servants either. He tried to give Caroline the benefit of the doubt by attributing it to the shock of her husband's death. But wasn't there also something of the early Caroline in her behavior?

When the letter from the Mertaux brothers arrived informing them that the two months stipulated by the Marquis before the reading of the will were over, Caroline appeared surprised and not a little put out by the fact that not only Dandridge but both her sons were to be present.

Marie-Adrien put on a long face when he learned that he wouldn't be taking his first trip down the river alone with his mother. Caroline had to explain that it must have been a request of his father's. So, reservations were made on the *Zebulon Pike IV* and Bobo drove the four passengers to Bayou Sara to board the boat. Pierre-Adrien, now six and almost as tall as his brother, was curious about everything on board, while Marie-Adrien, playing the blasé traveler, concentrated on the engines, the boilers and the speed of the boat.

Caroline undertook to teach the fourth Marquis—whom she introduced as such—the rules and etiquette of boat travel. Clarence took Pierre-Adrien under his wing, naming the birds, the trees and the big houses screened behind the trees. Fearing that Caroline might take his godson's affection for him amiss, he suggested that he join his mother and brother in the saloon or on the promenade deck.

"I think they like it better if I stay with you," the boy told him. "They talk about things I don't understand and laugh at me."

Clarence caught a note of sadness in his voice. The boy was well aware of the distinction his mother made between her two sons, for she made no effort to hide it.

If the river trip delighted the younger boy, it was the city that aroused his brother's enthusiasm. The people, shops, houses, carriages, restaurants and the bustle in the Saint-Charles lobby opened up a new and wonderful world.

"This is where I want to live. I want to see what goes on inside those houses, get to know the people, buy things in the shops . . ."

"Well, I like our house, our trees, our fields," Pierre-Adrien replied. "All these people look the same, wear the same clothes. I don't like them."

"You're stupid. You don't know anything. Mummy says there are even bigger cities in the North and they're all lit up at night. I'm going to go there, too."

But meanwhile, there was the appointment at the Mertaux's office. The two brothers in their black frock coats spoke in relays, taking over in mid-sentence:

"In a sealed letter he left with us . . ."

". . . and that he asked us to open as soon as we were informed of his . . ."

". . . death, Monsieur the Marquis de Damvilliers asked that you, madam, be present with your sons and Mr. Dandridge for the reading of his will which he left in our care."

The two brothers rose and, their movements coordinated like two dancers, approached the old strongbox hidden between two mahogany filing cabinets. Each brother took a key from his waistcoat pocket and prepared to open the box.

"You see," one of them said proudly, "we need the two keys to work the combination. It makes for greater security."

". . . double security," the other added.

From the box they extracted a large yellow envelope sealed with five globs of sealing wax. Like magicians demonstrating the innocence of their materials, they exhibited the envelope to show that the seals were indeed intact. Clarence, always amused by the brothers' duet, wondered if they would go so far as to read the will in unison. Although both put on their glasses, only one read:

"I, Jacques-Adrien, Marquis de Damvilliers, of sound mind and body, designate as the executors of my will, my widow the Marquise de Damvilliers, née Caroline Trégan, and Clarence Dandridge, my friend and presently manager of my plantation, Bagatelle, in order that they realize my wishes:

"I leave to my son, Marie-Adrien, all the property, furnishings and buildings, lands and dependencies, shares and cash in my possession on the day of my death, of which he will come into possession on reaching his majority, should I die before he has attained it. Until that time, and in that case only, the administration of my possessions shall be entrusted to my widow and my manager, who will exercise the right to dispose of them in the legatee's best interests. They must preserve Bagatelle's domain of ten thousand acres and maintain as good Christians the just treatment of the Negro slaves God has entrusted to them.

"On the day of my death, my older son, Marie-Adrien, shall take the title of Marquis de Damvilliers and the dynastic responsibilities this entails, but if he has not reached his majority, he may not oppose in any way the acts and decisions of the administrators indicated above. If by death or other reason, my older son finds himself incapable of guaranteeing my succession, the same provisions will apply to his younger brother, Pierre-Adrien.

"Once he is master of Bagatelle, it will be Marie-Adrien's duty to maintain as befits their station my beloved widow, née Caroline Trégan, his brother, Pierre-Adrien, and his sisters Félice and Julie, whom he shall dower at the time of their marriages.

"Pierre-Adrien, regardless of where he lives, shall have a life interest in a fourth of the revenues accruing from Bagatelle, and he may live there as long as he so desires.

"In addition, I leave my widow, Caroline, Marquise de Damvilliers, full possession of the gold and silver jewelry as well as the precious stones I inherited from my mother, which are now at Bagatelle.

"I also ask that small remembrances be given to my most intimate friends: Messrs. Templeton, Barrow and Murphy, as well as Mrs. Albert Schoeler, and I leave the choice to my executors.

"Finally, to my faithful manager, Clarence Dandridge, I leave my gold watch and chain, and ask him kindly to continue his history of my family so that future generations, issuing from my sons, will know what constituted the honor and glory of the Damvilliers.

"Having re-read, and holding to the above, I sign, Jacques-Adrien, Marquis de Damvilliers."

The brother who had not read the will spoke up first, "The wording of the will may not conform to exact legal terminology . . ."

". . . but it does clearly express the wishes of a man of warm heart . . ."

Caroline stood up and placed her hand on Marie-Adrien's shoulder.

"In short, until my son comes of age, nothing is to change at Bagatelle."

"That is correct," the two brothers said in unison.

"Should you at any time have need of our advice . . ."

". . . we are entirely at your disposal."

The Marquise and her sons excused themselves, leaving Clarence to discuss other matters with the two lawyers. They invited him to share their dinner, and since their cook had a reputation for her gumbo, he was happy to accept. Besides, he needed a respite from the Damvilliers.

Before leaving New Orleans, Caroline took Marie-Adrien to the Jesuit Fathers' school and enrolled him for the following term, scheduled to begin on November 1, when the boy would have turned ten. Meanwhile, Clarence was taking Pierre-Adrien for a walk through the city. As they approached the Stock Exchange, they could hear a slave auction going on in a hall nearby. The boy was curious to see how a slave was bought. Standing in a row on a platform, the blacks held their heads high. From time to time, prospective buyers asked to have a closer look in order to judge the men's muscles or the women's bodies, the latter ordered to undress with no thought for their modesty. A Creole woman began to weep when she saw the look of undisguised lechery on the faces of the men bidding for her. In the end, she was bought by a dried-up old man who wanted to provide his three sons "with some amusement at home."

Pierre-Adrien was silent, too mortified by the spectacle to look at Dandridge. To him, the blacks on the plantation were friends with whom he could laugh and play. He couldn't believe they could be disposed of, just like that.

"Where do you buy whites?" he asked as they were leaving.

"Whites aren't sold, Pierre-Adrien. They're free to do as they like." And he added, more to himself than to his young companion: "Even though they sometimes sell themselves."

"Papa bought Imilie?"

"Yes, Imilie along with many others."

Once they were out on the street, the boy remained thoughtful.

"We're lucky to be white, aren't we, Mr. Dandridge?"

"Yes, we are. That's why we have to be nice to the Negroes and not give Imilie any trouble. Later on, you must be a good master like your father."

"I don't want to be a master. Marie-Adrien's the master. I'd rather be a sailor and not buy Negroes."

The evening of that day—which Pierre-Adrien would remember for a long time—the four from Bagatelle boarded the boat for the trip home. Caroline appeared pleased with her stay in New Orleans. She had bought silk stockings at Abraham Trier's and had given the bishop twenty-five dollars for the victims of the recent earthquake on Martinique. For the first time since her husband's death, Clarence saw her smile. More beautiful than ever in her widow's weeds, she caused many heads to turn. Men doffed their hats as she went by, brought her a chair when she appeared on deck. In her role of the grieving widow, she exchanged a subdued word here and there with other ladies who would later be able to report that they had become fast friends with the Marquise de Damvilliers on board the *Oronoko*.

One night, when the boys were asleep, Clarence found her leaning on the railing, a dark silhouette against the mauve sky.

"I'm thinking back on the many trips I've taken on the river. Trips with Adrien, and the first one, just after I returned from Europe. I'm not the same person any longer, Clarence. I wouldn't be able to play poker or trictrac now. I feel as if life's intensity had been drained out of me. Nothing excites me the way it used to. Since Adrien's death, I've wanted only peace and silence. I'm tamped down. The old impatience is gone."

"I know it sounds banal, but with time you'll get your old self back. Surely your interest in people and things will return."

"I know that, Clarence, but I don't want it yet. My situation gives me the right to a period of isolation. I'm almost grateful for the emptiness Adrien's death has left. In a way it's a blessing, for I'm discovering that my grief is not the same as other people's."

"It's a stage, something we all go through. Your children will provide you with others, happier ones . . ."

They were silent for a moment as they watched the starlings swoop down to the river, the impact of their beaks leaving concentric circles on the water's surface. Then Clarence continued, "Our lives are a sequence of victories we're granted and defeats we must learn to accept. Adrien died during a victory, since death took him at a time of great happiness. I know, because I was a witness."

"I know it too. He took away a wonderful memory of me. But only you know, Clarence, that he gave more than he received. He loved me; I only tried to please him."

When she returned to Bagatelle, Caroline immediately set about satisfying her husband's instructions regarding the gifts to his "intimate friends." Old Mr. Templeton received a cane with a carved ivory handle, Clement Barrow a small bronze figure he had often admired on the Marquis's desk, Dr. Murphy a silver flask that Adrien had always carried when hunting—it still smelled of good whiskey, and Mignette a miniature of the Marquis as a boy.

"I can't locate the watch my husband wanted you to have, Clarence. It must be locked up in some drawer. But I'll find it."

Clarence assured her there was no hurry, and since the season of germination was underway, his thoughts were otherwise occupied.

Came the day when Marie-Adrien, accompanied by his mother, was to leave for New Orleans and the Jesuit Fathers. The boy came to say good-bye to Clarence.

"Work hard," Dandridge said, "for your father's sake."

"You work hard too, sir, for Bagatelle's," the boy answered back.

The remark brought a smile to Caroline's lips. For Clarence, it cemented his decision to leave Bagatelle the day the little Marquis took possession. He would have done his duty to Adrien, by God, and could depart with a clear conscience.

"You just wait until that brat asks you for an accounting!" Murphy, who happened to be there, said with a snicker.

"I'll give him an accounting," Dandridge said with a steely smile, "but that's all he gets."

Marie-Adrien's departure was a great relief to Clarence. It wasn't that the child's outrageous behavior really bothered him, but he was afraid that his instinct for mischief augured ill for the future. The same impatience Clarence had seen in his mother was multiplied tenfold in her son. It wouldn't be wise to find oneself crossing the path of his ambition.

Aged nine, Félice was painfully learning English and the piano. Except for desserts, her main preoccupation was her clothes. Left to her own devices, she would have changed her dress three times a day and had her hair brushed for hours on end. She liked nothing better than to watch her mother dress and, when she had been especially good, to receive a dab of perfume behind her ear. She hated Mic and Mac because, being puppies, they loved to get their teeth in the lace fringe of her drawers and put their dirty paws on her coat.

Julie, about to turn six, constantly mimicked her sister and liked to pretend she was "a lady serving tea" at the foot of an oak tree. The pale little girl was always catching cold and was out of breath after taking ten steps. The purple cast of her lips worried Dr. Murphy, who detected a weak heart that needed to be watched.

Her godfather, Ed Barthew, was full of attention and never came without bringing her a present. His visits, however, had been less frequent of late. He seemed to be avoiding Mrs. Schoeler. She, for her part, had attended no receptions or barbecues since the Marquis's death, as if adding her mistress's widowhood to her own. Clarence, ever watchful, observed that in this game of hide-and-seek, love was the loser. So he decided to give destiny a nudge—which had worked so well for Caroline Trégan. The propitious time came just before New Year's, which was to be purely a family affair this year.

"I have something to return to you, Ed," Clarence said, taking from his pocket a locket containing a strand of hair.

Barthew looked confused.

"It's a lock of hair that you once gave to brave Willy Templeton after a certain duel on board the *Prince du Delta.* He, in a manner of speaking, gave it to me."

"What do I want with Mrs. de Damvilliers's hair? Hadn't you better burn it, Clarence?"

"This is Mignette's hair, Ed."

This required some explaining, which Dandridge did.

"That Caroline! What a woman, hey, Clarence? She fooled everybody. But how can I accept this? What if Mignette knew . . ."

"She does know, since Miss Trégan gave it to you in the first place. What she doesn't know is that you now know."

"The simplest and most correct thing would be to give it back to Mignette," Barthew said. "The locket isn't bad-looking. She might like it."

"You do it, Barthew, and explain the locket's interesting itinerary. I have good reason to believe she'll ask you to keep it."

Barthew took the locket and put it in his waistcoat pocket.

"This is all very complicated, Clarence. And much too romanesque for a man like me. I know what you're up to. But your kindness can't produce the sentiments I'd like to have found in Mignette."

"You wouldn't know how to recognize them if they bit you, Ed. A woman who takes it upon herself to choose a partner for a quadrille, then sees him run off like a scared rabbit while offering her up to another man deserves an explanation."

"Clarence, I've given the matter a lot of thought. Even if Mrs. Schoeler were willing to marry me, I would feel I had to confess my past, which she either doesn't know or knows only in bits and pieces."

"She knows all about it, Ed. I told her—I hope you'll forgive my lack of discretion."

"I bet she was shocked. How could she want to become the second wife of a man who killed his first?"

"No, she wasn't shocked. She cried like a baby," Dandridge replied.

"All right, Clarence. I'll think about it," and Barthew left.

Clarence called after him: "Don't take too long, Ed. Captain Templeton will be visiting soon, bringing Seminole scalps."

Ed Barthew grunted, slammed his hat down on his head and leaped into his saddle.

"You're a damn good marriage broker, Clarence. Why don't you do something for Adele Barrow?"

Two weeks later, Mignette had a long conversation with Caroline during which she asked, with the pretense at indecision of a woman who has already made up her mind, if she should marry Ed Barthew. Her mistress showed little surprise and declared it would be a good thing for the blacksmith's widow, on condition that the eminent jurist gave up drinking.

"I'll see to that. A man drinks because he's unhappy. I intend to make him happy."

Only Murphy complained: The people at Bagatelle were in league against him and he would henceforth be reduced to solitary drinking—like a Yankee.

That year, 1842, Bagatelle's cotton crop was a good one, as were the crops throughout the state. New Orleans sent 749,267 bales of cotton to Europe and 68,058 hogsheads of tobacco. Ever since 1839, when a slave found a new method of treating tobacco, producing the "bright-leaf" with the honeyed taste, the more bitter Natchitoches had fallen from grace. The English traders were paying a high price for the bright-leaf and despite the financial crisis in the United States, local middlemen were making handsome profits.

The day after the first anniversary of the Marquis's death, which was commemorated without pomp in the little church in Sainte-Marie, Caroline announced she would accept her Aunt Drouin's invitation to spend a few months in Paris. With the mourning period over, she would be obliged to take up her social duties, reopen the house, organize receptions and barbecues. The prospect gave her little pleasure, and she told Clarence that a stay in Paris would allow her to "pull herself together." When she returned, Bagatelle would have shaken off its pall of gloom and life could resume its normal rhythm, bringing old memories into harmony with new expectations.

Before her departure, she made her first public appearance at Mignette's marriage to Edward Barthew. However, she did not go to the ball, thus disappointing a number of young men who were prepared to enter the lists for the hand of the young widow. During the wedding ceremony, her proud bearing, the smile of a wounded woman on her lips, the grace with which she wiped away a tear as the couple exchanged rings, excited pity in the men, morbid jealousy in the women. The mistress of Bagatelle carried her melancholy like an ornament, separating her from the common herd and making her all the more seductive.

Captain Willy Templeton took advantage of a short leave to attend the wedding. All his old desires were reborn. Perhaps a lone woman with four children would be more responsive to his advances than the ambitious Caroline Trégan of old.

"I've met many beautiful women in Charleston," he remarked to his brother Percy, "but not one of them can match Caroline's grace and distinction."

"And what a glorious body!" Percy put in, for he could claim with some pride that he was the only man present in a position to make that judgment with total certainty.

The following day, as Mignette and her husband were heading upriver to Saint Louis, Mrs. de Damvilliers was going downriver to New Orleans, accompanied by her maid, Rosa. They had reservations on the *Saratoga* for the trip to New York where they would board the *Great Western*, the fastest of all the transatlantic steamers. She would be in Paris in time to see her aunt's lilacs in bloom.

During her brief stay in New Orleans, Caroline went to the Jesuit school to kiss Marie-Adrien good-bye, and bought herself a green silk scarf at Bouvry d'Ivernais which set off her coppery hair.

With a timid smile, the salesman ventured: "Green is the color of hope."

Caroline knew it well. Having been an irreproachable wife, a good mother and an impeccable widow, she looked forward to her new independence with relish.

For the younger children left behind at Bagatelle, their mother's absence meant months of freedom. Under their nurses' indulgent eye, the little girls played all day. Félice invited Percy Templeton's daughters to endless lavish tea parties; Julie began to show an interest in animals and flowers. Her nurse, Imilie, having taught her some old Creole songs, she sang constantly, mimicking the black's accent. Pierre-Adrien drew even closer to Clarence Dandridge. Passionately interested in a wide variety of subjects, he read until his eyes were bloodshot, using up quantities of candles which obliged Brent, now his valet since his brother's departure, to spend part of each night watching to see that his young master didn't set the house on fire.

Pierre-Adrien was particularly concerned with the condition of the slaves. He kept asking embarrassing questions, sensing the basic injustice in a universally accepted condition. He was often seen talking to the young workers on the plantation, which old James didn't approve of. Like all the house servants, the butler considered the field hands as belonging to an inferior caste with whom a white child should have no truck. As his favorite playmate, Pierre-Adrien had singled out an orphan girl named Ivy who had been adopted by Anna and did small chores in the laundry to earn her keep. He taught her to play shuttlecock, and talked Félice into giving Ivy her outgrown dresses.

At the end of autumn when the cotton harvest was over,

Dandridge was summoned to New Orleans to consult with Mosely's local agent, the Englishman not being able to make the trip that year. Pierre-Adrien begged to be taken along and Dandridge agreed. Marie-Adrien had spent the summer with a schoolmate, Gilles de Kernant, whose father owned a large plantation near Saint-Martinville. He hadn't set foot near Bagatelle for a year, and Dandridge promised his mother to visit him at school. With Pierre-Adrien in tow, he fulfilled his mission. When Marie-Adrien, now eleven, was summoned into the school parlor, his younger brother exclaimed: "You look like a man!"

"I am a man," his brother said with cool disdain.

The young Marquis had in fact grown prodigiously. Also, he was wearing an impeccably tailored midnight blue suit made by the best tailor in town, where the Marquise had opened an account so that he could stand up to the other rich planters' sons. Pierre-Adrien was very impressed by his brother's elegance, although he was entirely indifferent to his own clothes.

Leaving the two brothers alone, Dandridge repaired to the rector's office to ask how the young Marquis was doing in his studies. Apparently not too well. With the unctuous assurance of an educator at ease in the high society that produced his pupils, the Jesuit noted that M. the Marquis had a tendency to treat the school as a club, that he was more interested in riding and fencing than he was in mathematics, and that he displayed an unchristian contempt for his schoolmates. Only the boys with titles were worthy of his attention. Everybody who wasn't of his class was put down as a commoner, and his teachers were treated with icy politeness. And last but not least, he had "gone over the wall" on two occasions—with Gilles de Kernant and Hyacinthe de Beausset—to buy cigars which the supervising father promptly seized.

"The boy has exceptional intelligence. He is arrogant to be sure, but he has a great appetite for learning. In time, we think we can make a perfect gentleman of him," the rector concluded suavely. Then he added as if it were an afterthought

that the Marquise de Damvilliers had been regularly informed
of her son's grades and escapades. Dandridge was relieved that
he wouldn't have to report the good father's comments to
Caroline.

As he and Pierre-Adrien were preparing to leave, Dandridge noticed a gold chain looped across Marie-Adrien's
waistcoat. He immediately recognized it as the one Adrien
had left him in his will.

"Can you tell me the time, Marie-Adrien?" Dandridge
asked.

"Ten minutes past six," the young Marquis stated after
consulting the watch. The boy looked straight at his father's
manager, waiting for the remark that didn't come. Dandridge
turned on his heels and left with Pierre-Adrien close behind.
So, the little Marquis was not only arrogant and lazy; he had
slippery fingers as well.

With the torpor of the summer months gone and business
picking up again, Maspero's Exchange at the corner of Rue
de Chartres and Rue Saint-Louis was full of planters and
merchants who dropped in after dinner to discuss the cotton
harvest, politics and local gossip. Feeling the need for company, Dandridge stopped by as soon as his godson was asleep.
This particular evening, some of the clientele were celebrating
the arrival of an Anglo-American commission come to study
the possibility of organizing a steamship line to connect the
Southern capital with London. Another group was discussing
the recent threat by the city's American sector to split off
from the old city. The American municipality, made up
mostly of Northerners speaking English, was now as large and
certainly as handsome as the French sector, and had snared
a larger share of the city's commercial activity into the bargain. As a result, middlemen were moving their offices and
retailers their shops from the old city into the new. Property
values were rising in the new in proportion to their drop in
the old. Encouraged by this migration, the Americans now
wanted a complete separation. Maspero's Exchange had become the headquarters of the resistance. Arguments were

traded back and forth, the diehards maintaining that, like it or not, and despite demolitions, fires and floods, the city retained the indelible marks of its early settlers. Perhaps most of its business was transacted in English and in dollars, but among themselves, the people of New Orleans dealt in either French or Creole—depending on their social station—and in piasters. Everything the Northerners knew they had learned on Rue de Chartres and Rue de Bourgogne. Their daughters were educated by the Ursuline nuns, their sons by the Jesuits, even though Anglicans, Methodists, Presbyterians and other sects were making inroads. The old French city had profited by its Spanish heritage. The marriage of the two cultures had created a Creole population, soon added to by the Santo Domingans fleeing the massacres of 1791. It could be said, therefore, that the people of New Orleans had been "at home" for over a hundred years by the time the United States took possession of Louisiana.

When his companions, many glasses of port under their belts, began to damn the Yankees and the discussion became increasingly noisy and incoherent, Dandridge decided it was time to go to bed. He knew that the American mosaic was still a long way from constituting a harmonious national whole. The rivalry between North and South was, as much as anything, a question of temperament. If the coming strains could be kept at the level of the bluster he had heard tonight, things might not be too bad.

It was in her Aunt Drouin's drawing room, peopled as usual with unpublished poets and rich wastrels, that the Marquise de Damvilliers met Colonel Charles de Vigors. The colonel had retired because he was unwilling to serve the present monarchy after his brief but glorious career under Napoleon. He was not a frequent visitor at Mme. Drouin's. He had come as a guide to a blind cousin out of an instinct of loyalty. At fifty-four, Charles de Vigors, a member of the minor nobility in Perigord, was considered a handsome man. Not unlike the late Marquis in general physique, his complexion was ruddy, and the points of his moustache reached all the way to his curly side-whiskers. Perhaps the hirsuteness of his face was designed to make up for the complete baldness of his head, which gleamed like a waxed floor, crisscrossed, alas, by a long fine scar, the result of a Russian's sabre before Smolensk. Were it not for his engaging smile and sly blue eyes, he would have looked like a Prussian. In any event, the ladies found him irresistible.

Born in 1789 while the patriotic farce at the Bastille was being played out, the colonel maintained he would serve only under a republic. "I'm waiting for the kings to pass," he often remarked.

"Oh, if the police heard you say that," cooed Mme. Drouin, who always quivered at the memory of the great imperial battles even though they made many more widows and orphans than heroes.

When Charles de Vigors saw Caroline enter, he rushed to kiss her hand. She vaguely remembered having met him at a ball in New Orleans, where he had been sent on some military mission, ten years before.

"My, my, what a small world," Caroline said archly, noting that the colonel's figure had withstood the test of time.

"And hasn't the Atlantic ocean shrunk," he answered in turn.

Mme. Drouin hurried to make introductions only to learn that they had already met.

"Naturally your husband is with you?" M. de Vigors inquired.

"Alas, sir," Mme. Drouin intervened with an appropriate tone of regret, "my niece's husband died over a year ago."

The colonel offered suitable condolences, then, recognizing the propitious moment at hand, promptly invited the Marquise to dinner. Caroline accepted with alacrity, from which he gathered that it was only conjugal fidelity that had made her keep him at arm's length at their earlier meeting in New Orleans.

"Tomorrow the sun of Austerlitz will rise again," he crowed

as he regained his apartment after taking his blind cousin home, grateful to him for an encounter as agreeable as it was unexpected.

Two days later, he escorted Caroline to Véry's in the Palais Royal. When the Marquise entered the restaurant wearing a sea-green dress with leg-o'-mutton sleeves and a matching velvet hat, all heads turned her way. The heavy "anglaises" framing her pale face may have looked old-fashioned to the ladies; to the men, she was the epitome of romantic charm and they envied the dashing colonel.

The couple started with breasts of chicken with truffles washed down with a bottle of Volnay. By the time they had reached the apple charlotte, accompanied by a Sauterne, Caroline knew everything about her dinner companion's life and he knew everything about Bagatelle and plantation life. When the colonel learned that this delectable woman was the mother of four, he complimented her on her figure and youthful freshness. Caroline protested coyly, "You are a flatterer, Colonel. I wonder how many times you've said that to a woman." This expected reply gave him a chance to play one of his favorite roles—that of the lonely and misunderstood male.

"Of course a man can always find women enough to listen to him or distract him, but if he places feeling above pleasure, what he looks for is a real woman. Well, madam, I've never met one to whom I wanted to give my name, with whom I wanted to spend the rest of my days. To be sure, I lead an agreeable life, I have enough money to spend on travel, at the antique shops or on whatever strikes my fancy—I have a passion for small bronzes—I have friends, I hunt with the best rifles, I spend three nights a week at the theater, but . . . but what I miss is someone with whom I can share the small joys of daily life . . . and I, the last of the Vigors, am without an heir!"

They talked long and late. When the colonel left Caroline at her aunt's, the bells of Saint-Sulpice were ringing midnight. The colonel was in love, and Caroline was not displeased.

They made a rendezvous for the next day at the Louvre, where the colonel wanted to show her three paintings by Jean-Antoine Gros, whom he considered the Empire's finest painter. After approving these rousing works, Caroline asked if she might see Géricault's "The Wounded Cuirassier" again.

"Colonel, I see you in that painting, waiting under a rain of bullets for the help that doesn't come. It gives me the shivers. War is so awful!"

The colonel grasped Caroline's hand and kissed it with fervor. Caroline responded with the sad smile of a lady bending over her wounded hero.

"War is like love, madam. It is the natural element of the male. Both demand the gift of the body and the commitment of the soul."

As they left the Louvre, M. de Vigors, like Géricault's cuirassier, carried an invisible wound. And why wouldn't the Marquis's widow be the ideal nurse to make it well? From then on, things moved at a brisk pace. "Not to dare is to do nothing when the moment is ripe, and one never dares unless one is convinced of one's good luck." Charles de Vigors liked to apply Napoleon's principles of war to his amorous conquests. Convinced of his good luck, he dared. He had armfuls of roses sent to the Rue de Luxembourg, showered her with invitations and gave her one of his favorite possessions—a drawing by Pils of the Emperor leaning against a gun carriage. Finally, one rainy afternoon when they had taken shelter in a café, he made his proposal over a steaming cup of chocolate.

"I have a request to make of you, madam, a delicate request that could change the course of my life. Please forgive my abruptness: Will you marry me?"

Caroline showed no surprise, thinking it useless to play the traditional scene of coy astonishment. So, she simply said: "Where can I send you a reply in, say, two days?"

She liked the man. He was vigorous and direct, a far cry from the libidinous bankers and pimply poets she met at her aunt's.

The colonel was taken aback by her businesslike tone. He

stammered: "You can send me a note . . . at the Jockey Club. I won't move from the place until I've heard from you. If I stayed home, I'd be like a caged beast."

As he left her at the shop where she was to meet her aunt, the colonel asked: "Have I reason to hope?"

She gave him her hand to kiss. "Isn't hope pleasure enough?"

Charles de Vigors ended the day at the club, not altogether sober, but with what he had won at cards, he could buy Caroline a handsome engagement present if her answer was in the affirmative. He slept badly, like all expectant lovers, and spent the rest of the day alternating between bouts of optimism and blackest despair. When, at the end of the afternoon, a footman announced that a lady was waiting outside in her carriage, he bolted down the stairs. If she was there in person, it must be that her answer was yes. Slightly out of breath and as silent as a convicted man awaiting his sentence, the colonel took the scented hand she held out.

"Please get in and sit down," she said. She didn't say another word until the gig was underway.

"I plan to return home to Louisiana at the beginning of March. It's the best season; the weather is beautiful. The sun is already warm, the magnolias are in bloom and they're sowing the cotton. Bagatelle is never more magical. We go for long rides along the banks of the Mississippi, and give large barbecues that always wind up with a ball . . ."

Charles rubbed the handle of his cane with impatience. Was this preamble a tactical diversion? He had expected an answer of prime importance and instead he was getting a tourist's brochure. When she saw the look on his face, Caroline broke into laughter.

"You see, Charles, I count on your liking Bagatelle, because as my husband, that's where you're going to have to live!"

The colonel dropped his cane, turned toward the woman who had in two minutes made him suffer more than all his battle wounds put together, parted the fox fur that hid the face that hadn't left his thoughts for three mortal weeks and kissed her with an ardor she hadn't expected. His thick moustache was silkier than it looked, and his lips were warm and soft. She answered his kiss with equal abandon, knowing immediately that she would have nothing to teach her second husband. The women of Austria, Germany, Italy and France had made eclectic lovers of the Emperor's officers. "It's a great advantage to choose a man who has lived," she said to herself as she straightened her hat.

"Now let's have dinner. I'm dying of hunger," she said.

To the accompaniment of fervent declarations and tender gestures on the colonel's part, and laughter and teasing responses on Caroline's, they finally reached an accommodation which they celebrated with pink champagne.

"When can we be married, Caroline? The sooner the better. I'm impatient."

"Whenever you like, Charles. My aunt's notary can take care of all the details. But," she added, "what's the need for impatience since everything is decided?"

At her last words, she had a look the colonel had never seen before. His heart beat faster. It confirmed the very agreeable sensation he had felt when they were kissing in the gig. The Marquis's widow was not one of those prigs who makes a great to-do in front of the bed. Enthralled and embarrassed at the same time, he said nothing, kissing her fingers for the hundredth time. The Marquise was an ardent woman with strong after-dinner impulses, but she knew the appropriate pretexts.

"If it isn't too late, Colonel, I'd love to see your apartment. I've heard that you've furnished it in exquisite taste, and before you pack your bronzes, I'd like to see them in their own setting . . ."

This time, there could be no doubt. The sun of Austerlitz would indeed be rising tomorrow morning—at the hour of toast and coddled eggs. M. de Vigors paid the bill, called for their coats, and swept Caroline off with the verve he formerly used in a cavalry charge. Mme. Drouin's gig, which was dismissed as soon as it deposited them outside the colonel's apartment, had harbored an exchange of caresses that promised more to come.

As soon as they entered the apartment, Caroline made the promised examination of the bronzes. Her fingers stroked the patina of a horse by Falconet, rubbed the back of an Etruscan warrior and delicately fondled the rump of a lascivious nymph. When Charles de Vigors started to take off her coat, she turned around, laced her arms around his neck and whispered, "Why wait, Charles?"

The scene that followed was a double offensive. The colonel, accustomed to bold cavalry charges, had to contend with a woman who knew all the evasive moves and feints of an adversary who delighted in the scrimmage for its own sake. The large bed sighed and shook under the stress of battle, Charles taking the initiative only to be discomfited by his companion's sly sallies.

"Charles, I'm not the Prussian Army," she said with a giggle. "I'm just a hapless female. You must treat me tenderly, Colonel."

"Hapless female indeed!" Charles retorted. "You're a naughty lioness and I'm going to give you what for!"

The "what for" reached a noisy climax and both fell back on the bed panting. But it wasn't long before the colonel's fiancée was caressing his body with feverish fingers and her partner was responding in kind. She moaned, and soon they were joined again. After an hour of tussle and a brief respite, Charles put on his dressing gown and went in search of a bottle of champagne which his manservant—well versed in his master's ways—kept chilled in his dressing room. Charles uncorked the bottle, brought it and two glasses to his bedside table and filled the glasses. As he was toasting his delicious new mistress, she blew the foam on her glass at her new and proficient lover. They quickly emptied their glasses. Putting them out of harm's way, Charles initiated a flanking attack.

When the sun penetrated the drawn curtains the next morning, it picked out an empty bottle of champagne, and a bed in vast disarray occupied by two spent bodies peacefully asleep in each other's arms. An hour later, the colonel's valet, formerly his orderly and now fully accustomed to civilian ways, noted that his master's latest conquest was the most beautiful and most distinguished of all the ladies to whom he had served breakfast.

That very evening, M. de Vigors informed his faithful servant that he was at long last getting married.

"Mallibert, would you like to go to America?"

"To fight the Indians? Colonel, I'm on my way."

"And to fondle mulattoes with breasts the size of melons, Mallibert?"

"I've left already, Colonel."

Caroline's letter, which Dandridge found at Bagatelle on his return from New Orleans, proved to him that peace and quiet are temporary at best. Her news stunned him. The Marquise de Damvilliers simply announced that she had been married in Paris in November and that she would be arriving in Louisiana with her new husband, Charles de Vigors, at the end of March —and that she was sure they would be the best of friends in no time. She asked the manager to inform Pierre-Adrien, Félice and Julie; she would be writing to Marie-Adrien herself.

Having read and reread the letter, Dandridge stood motionless on the gallery, his eyes wandering vacantly over the park. The rain was beating down on the gallery roof and gray clouds clung to the treetops. A cold north wind was puffing out the Spanish moss like petticoats, and Mic and Mac lay by the door waiting for the favorable moment to slip into the house. For all his self-control, Clarence felt a spasm of pain and regret. So Caroline was about to introduce a new man into Bagatelle. Would he get used to seeing him in Adrien's place even though, with no real power over the plantation, he would be only a kind of master-consort? The thought of telling the children about their mother's remarriage filled him with dread. He had no idea how they would take it, and tried to think of arguments that would reconcile them to the unknown stepfather. The fact that Caroline had chosen to tell Marie-Adrien herself was not in itself surprising. He had been aware of their complicity for a long time. In Caroline's eyes, the future master of Bagatelle by right of primogeniture—a right not recognized by American law—made him the only Damvilliers worthy of interest. On the one hand there was Marie-Adrien; on the other, "the children." And it was to him, Dandridge, she had delegated the authority of supervising their education as if it were some minor task.

Contrary to his expectations, the children took it very well. Félice clapped her hands: "Mummy is so good and beautiful, I want to see her happy." Then, as an afterthought, she asked, "What does a colonel wear?"

Julie, now six and a half, said nothing. Her large dark eyes in her chalk-colored face opened wide, as they did whenever she had to concentrate. Pierre-Adrien was very precise: "Should I call the man 'father,' sir?"

Clarence replied that that would be up to his mother, but he personally didn't think it would be required.

"I'd rather not. But I'll do whatever Marie-Adrien does."

Relieved by the children's reactions, Dandridge left them to discuss the news among themselves. As he dressed for dinner, he felt strangely unnerved. As he was a man used to analyzing himself coolly, this symptom irritated him. He had to tie his cravat three times. It couldn't be jealousy in the way ordinary men defined it. Caroline's letter had hurt him deeply but he couldn't define the nature of the hurt. Could it be simple egotism? That even when you didn't want a thing or person, you suffered to see them become someone else's? Caroline's marriage to Adrien had pleased him greatly; her second marriage had brought him a stupid and indefinable pain. He couldn't begrudge her wanting to find love and all its joys with another man. In fact he would have been unhappy to see Caroline continue as the inconsolable widow. Would he have preferred her marrying Willy Templeton or some other planter's son? He wasn't sure of that either. So what ailed him? Was it that Caroline was being disloyal to the special relationship they shared? That's what he eventually concluded, and he promptly decided that in ten years, when he was free of the responsibilities the Marquis had saddled him with, he could go live far away and perhaps find another life with new enthusiasms.

Colonel Charles de Vigors and Bagatelle made each other's acquaintance in early March, 1844. The hussar who had slept in the beds of fleeing Prussians, bivouacked in the snow under draperies snatched from Boyards' burning houses, and in retreat, had shared the straw with the livestock and requisitioned the rooms of Polish nuns, was immediately taken with Bagatelle's charms and the exuberant landscape burgeoning with impatient growth.

Vigors was adopted straight off by plantation society, whose loyalties more often than not remained Bonapartist, and made a quick conquest of Dandridge, who found in him many of Adrien's qualities. Of finer grain and more expansive than the late Marquis, he was less smug, less worshipful of Caroline, although not wanting in loving attentions. He mixed little in plantation affairs except to give advice when asked and moral support when needed.

The children welcomed him warmly. Pierre-Adrien badgered him to recount his military campaigns, Félice talked him into wearing his bedizened uniform to dinner one night, and Julie was ecstatic over the furniture he made for her doll's house. Marie-Adrien, whom the colonel visited with his mother at the Jesuit Fathers', was less receptive. Caroline explained to her husband that her older son wasn't given to demonstrations of affection.

It wasn't until several weeks after her return that Dandridge and Caroline had another one of their intimate conversations, the price of which each knew only too well.

"Clarence, I was afraid you'd disapprove of my remarrying so soon."

"I would disapprove if it hadn't made you happy, Caroline. But since that isn't the case, I'm delighted. You did the right thing, as always. The colonel is a charming man and you couldn't have found yourself a better companion—and Bagatelle a better regent."

"Bagatelle, Bagatelle! You're always talking about Bagatelle as if it were a kingdom. I wasn't thinking of Bagatelle when I married Charles. I needed a man. It was as simple as that. It makes me doubly happy to see that he's good for Bagatelle."

Caroline said this with heat and not a little irritation. Her tone took Dandridge by surprise.

"Look, whether you like it or not, Bagatelle is a kingdom and that's important to you as well as your children. I'm certain it crossed your mind when you accepted Mr. de Vigors as a husband."

"Not for a minute, I assure you," Caroline replied. "I'm not the vestal type. Bagatelle is part of my life and part of my happiness, but it's not all . . . and the true regent of Bagatelle is you, Clarence. What I needed was a husband or a lover. With your austerity, you can get along without affection and tenderness. All power to you. I wasn't made that way. I need to be loved."

"Everybody needs to be loved, Caroline. An empty heart is nothing to envy. It brings only a hollow peace."

"Forgive me, Clarence. I know you so little in spite of my affection for you. I have no idea why you keep so aloof from the way ordinary people live, but I do wish I could do something to make you happy."

"Just live according to your own lights, Caroline. That's enough. The rest is beyond your or my control. But I do want you to know that having accepted myself such as I am, I'm not unhappy."

"Nor happy?"

"It's a question of words."

Caroline knew that that was all she was going to get out of him today.

Had Adrien de Damvilliers been able to look through the

stone of the family vault on the third anniversary of his death, he would have seen only Dandridge and Pierre-Adrien at his grave. All the other Damvilliers were in New Orleans with Mr. and Mrs. de Vigors. At Bagatelle, Imilie was watching over a six-month old baby boy Caroline brought into the world just before Christmas. As with the dead Marquis's, the Vigors's lineage now seemed assured. Murphy had presided over the delivery alone, Planche having died a few days before the baby's birth. The colonel had felt little confidence in the plantation's blacks, finding it hard to get used to their indolent ways. He therefore saw it as a sign of a benevolent destiny that the old sorceress had been gathered before his son's birth. The Damvilliers children greeted their half-brother with joy. Félice, now boarding with the Ursuline nuns in New Orleans, looked forward to using him as her doll during the coming holidays.

The summer before, Marie-Adrien had been distant with his stepfather. Caroline had hoped for a strong bond between her husband and the future master of Bagatelle. Instead, the boy treated him like a guest and referred to him as "my mother's husband." It bothered the colonel not at all, for in his eyes, Marie-Adrien was no different from any other child and he had no intention of going out of his way to gain his affection. When the young Marquis realized that his stepfather's indifference was entirely real, he felt a certain resentment. To his friends at school, he attributed his mother's second marriage to the vulgar need of a woman for a man. Monsieur de Vigors's role was limited to that of a legally recognized lover. If Marie-Adrien owed his claim on the Damvilliers inheritance to what he considered the bestial embrace of his father and mother, at least it removed his stepfather from any position that might threaten him. Should the Marquise die after he became master of Bagatelle, he would send his stepfather packing, together with his issue.

Caroline made no further attempt to bring the two closer. Charles de Vigors didn't belong to the Damvilliers but to her alone, and he had enough money of his own to live without the plantation's revenues. It was gratifying to know that he wished to keep his financial independence. She made it clear to her older son that the colonel lived at Bagatelle but not off it. In fact, a few days after his own son's birth, Vigors had acquired a thousand acres of forest across the river in the parish of West Feliciana near Saint-Francisville in order to have some property that belonged exclusively to the Vigors and which he intended to enlarge with the years. His valet, Mallibert, promoted to overseer, had been given a team of slaves and was already clearing the forest so that the colonel's heir could eventually build his own house, should he care to.

Furthermore, the colonel had invested in land in the western part of Virginia where one of his old French friends, a former director of the Théâtre de l'Odéon in Paris, owned eighty thousand acres of oak trees. With a thousand trees to the acre, the land promised a good yield for exploitation. The colonel had obtained a contract from the French Navy and the two men were now its official suppliers of lumber. As a result, when Marie-Adrien became master of Bagatelle, his half-brother would be a landowner too, and equally rich. Charles had thus demonstrated that one could be a sound businessman and a farsighted father as well as a "saber-rattler," as Dr. Murphy affectionately called him.

Clarence liked him better with every passing day. Unlike Adrien, he made little of his nobility and never talked about his ancestors. One evening, when Clarence had shown him the Damvilliers family tree, he touched briefly on the origin of his own family. When the Damvilliers were still untitled peasants in Lorraine, the Vigors were taking part in the Crusades. Later, there had been a Vigors fighting at François I's side in Pavia, and another at Maestricht as a lieutenant with the Musketeers.

"We were never big on agriculture. As far as the land was concerned, we knew only how to defend it or conquer it, and most of my ancestors died—which seldom happened in bed —leaving more trophies than écus."

The untroubled future that Vigors was planning for his son

looked less sanguine to Clarence. The South's peace seemed increasingly threatened by the North's commercial aggressiveness and its expanding antislavery campaign. James Polk had been elected President in 1844, the Democrats thinking him a stronger candidate than Tyler in their battle against Henry Clay, the Kentucky Senator. Clay had been beaten by only thirty-eight thousand votes in spite of his electoral shenanigans. In Plaquemines, a small town near New Orleans, for instance, a thousand people had turned up to vote in a parish that counted only three hundred voters.

The new President, a former representative from Tennessee, had proclaimed his attachment to the Monroe Doctrine for having saved the New World from the Old, but his expansionist leanings threatened the fragile equilibrium between the pro- and antislavery states. Before leaving the White House, Tyler had signed the bill annexing the Republic of Texas and this act had produced an explosive situation vis-à-vis Mexico. General Zachary Taylor had been ordered to leave Fort Jesup in Louisiana and head for the Rio Grande. The government was also suspected of encouraging Frémont to take over California and fix Oregon's border at the forty-ninth parallel without a by-your-leave to the British.

At Bagatelle, cotton harvests and picnics came and went, and time followed its untroubled course. Caroline's beauty was at its peak. Perhaps Rosa had to pull the corset strings a little tighter, but her firm breasts and springing step still caused heads to turn. She seemed even more desirable than the day she put on the transparent dotted Swiss to seduce Adrien-Herod. No matter how irreproachable her décolletage, how muted the color of her dress, how unflattering its lines, it managed to mold her body and expose tantalizing glimpses of ivory flesh while her skirts fell in seductive folds. When she stretched an arm to accept a cup of tea, or picked up her skirts to climb the stairs, or bent over a gouty dowager slumped in her chair, or gave her hand to a gentleman to kiss, Caroline seemed totally unaware that these blameless gestures delineated her sumptuous body more than the most lascivious pose.

Next to his wife, Charles de Vigors cut a manly figure. Less stodgy than Adrien, more at home in the drawing room, he was a polished waltzing partner to the ladies and a good conversationalist with the men. With his contemporaries, he discussed De Tocqueville's new book on American democracy, the strange new sect that went by the name of Mormon, the network of railroads that was bringing ever more goods from the North, and he damned the Yankees with the best of them. To the rheumatic and wheezing old, he recounted his feats in the Empire's battles.

At the buffet table, he proved himself a gourmand "sans peur et sans reproche." He lunged at the turkey, speared a canapé, seized a bottle of wine by the neck as if it were a Prussian soldier, and always with an elegance of gesture and the hearty laugh of the warrior back at his bivouac unscarred. At last Murphy had a drinking partner of his stripe.

"Doctor, I've known what it was to be thirsty!"

"Not I," the doctor said with a wink. "I always managed to get a drink in beforehand."

Ed Barthew occasionally escaped Mignette's watchful eye to join the two. The doctor would be reeling and the lawyer spluttering, but the colonel would still be clearheaded and standing as straight as a ramrod, carrying on the conversation alone.

"You two would never have made it in the Hussars of the Guard. You couldn't have stood the shock. Your bourbon is a lady's liqueur compared to schnapps and vodka."

Caroline's husband brought an atmosphere of gaiety into their daily lives. They laughed over everything and nothing and something was always being celebrated. In his holster the hussar had brought a new measure of happiness to the plantation.

For Caroline's birthday, he commissioned Adolph Rinck, a New Orleans artist who had just had an exhibition in Paris, to paint portraits of each of her children. The pictures now hung on the four walls of the big drawing room: Félice in a long dress; Julie sitting on a piano stool, not knowing what to do with her hands; Pierre-Adrien in a studious pose at a table piled high with books; Marie-Adrien standing, one hand on his hip, the other on the mantel, in the earnest yet relaxed pose of a candidate for President of the United States.

The future master of Bagatelle was now riding a bay gelding, and the colonel complimented him on his seat.

"Next year I'm going to ride a stallion. Our ancestors rode only Anglo-Norman horses as slender as blades."

"Mine were more apt to ride percherons and drafthorses," the colonel said with studied modesty. "A delicate horse couldn't have stood the weight of a knight in full armor, let alone the brunt of a morgenstern."

Clarence, now in complete charge of the plantation's activities, wondered if the time hadn't come to initiate the young Marquis into its workings. After all, he was going on fourteen now. At the moment, the boy didn't seem the least bit interested, thinking perhaps that the knowledge would come to him in a vision when he reached his majority.

"There's plenty of time," Caroline said when he asked for her opinion. "And I have such confidence in his intelligence that I know he'll keep you on as manager. No one knows the planter's trade better than you. After all, you had the ideal teacher in Adrien."

"You might consider the fact that I could someday lose my enthusiasm for the job," Dandridge responded. "Perhaps I'd like to do other kinds of things. It's months since I've had time to work on the history of the Damvilliers. If you recall, that was supposed to be my principal task."

"You'll have plenty of time to scribble later on when we're all old."

Dandridge was becoming irritated. "Look, Caroline, has it ever occurred to you that once Marie-Adrien comes of age and takes over his responsibilities, I might wish to leave Bagatelle and lead my own life?"

"One doesn't leave Bagatelle. You know that."

"But I'm not a slave, damn it. And just as Marie-Adrien may wish to get rid of me, so I might like to leave of my own accord. I'm only a salaried man, Caroline—of a special kind, to be sure—but that's all I am."

It was the first time Caroline had looked at Clarence as something other than a member of the family. She was torn between conflicting emotions. Either she could say nothing and leave things as they were, or she could let herself go and say what she really felt—or thought she felt.

"If I told you I can't conceive of Bagatelle without you, would you believe me?"

"Certainly I'd believe you. I'm one of your habits."

"Don't be bitter, Clarence, and don't force me to say more than I care to."

She spoke these last words in a low voice tinged with regret, while looking at him sideways under lowered lids. Unmoved, Clarence wasn't going to let her think he was easy prey to her charms.

"I've never seen you play this role before, Caroline," he said maliciously. "You know, it doesn't suit you at all."

She went pale and there was a sharp intake of breath.

"You don't think I'm being sincere, or that my affection for you is real? That's a stupid insult, Clarence."

Dandridge was silent a moment. Then, trying to take the edge off his voice, he said more gently, "I don't think any such thing, Caroline, but neither do I exaggerate your sincerity or affection. My life has run parallel to yours for many years and we've taken a fair number of hurdles together. Also, I love Pierre-Adrien like a son. But I still remain an outsider, an observer, an element at Bagatelle that has its uses, even in the emotional sense, but that's all. Allow me to be an egoist from time to time, Caroline, and try to imagine how I might have other desires."

She understood what he meant. These "other desires" weren't women, not herself, even less money, but he had wounded her and she was going to play this game to its conclusion.

"To ignore your desires is to have none. What I don't understand is what makes you suffer to be here with us, with me!"

"Caroline, in Bagatelle's lulling atmosphere, I suffer from a pernicious malady called inconsistency."

"What in God's name does that mean?"

"It means that I sometimes feel like committing a cardinal sin, not one of the sins in the Ten Commandments, but one that remains to be discovered."

"Why on earth?"

"To prove to myself that I'm made of flesh and blood, like you. Simply to prove that I exist."

"How will you do that, may I ask?"

"I have no idea," he said, his voice suddenly weary. With that, he turned on his heels and strode down the gallery steps.

With an angry swish of skirts, Caroline stormed into the house.

"He's blind . . . blind," she muttered between her teeth.

Clarence was furious with himself for making such a to-do about an illusory freedom he wasn't even sure he wanted. On looking back, he felt he'd been more petulant than rebellious. That evening, Caroline pleaded a headache and didn't come down for dinner. But the next day she was all smiles as if she had completely forgotten the incident. And Dandridge, who was eager to erase all memory of the conversation, was more outgoing than usual.

The autumn rains had come and it was time for Marie-Adrien and Félice to return to school, this time accompanied by Pierre-Adrien, who was also now enrolled in the Jesuit school. Julie, just turning nine, was the only Damvilliers child left at Bagatelle. Her half-brother was not yet two.

The little girl was growing into a gentle, dutiful child fully conscious that she was different from other children—notably from the Templeton girls, who were her chief playmates. Julie stood in wonder as her friends jumped rope, climbed over barriers, ran, yelled, stuck out their tongues, quarreled, even had fights—all these delectable activities forbidden her by her mother because of her "weak heart." Her mysterious affliction could have made her feel deprived or, on the other hand, interesting. Instead, she simply felt resigned, and came to accept the condition to which the fates had assigned her. The blue circles under the large lusterless eyes might have led people to wonder if she indulged in solitary pleasures admitted only in the confessional. With her thin braids, angular shoulders and long fingers, she looked not unlike an emaciated saint dying of consumption.

One day, her godfather Ed Barthew asked her, "What will you do when you grow up, Julie?"

She answered simply: "I'll be sick."

Then she discovered a way to stop the commiserations of her mother's friends. When one of these ladies was announced, she ran to the mirror and frantically rubbed her cheeks until they became as red as those of a girl in ruddy health. It impressed the visitors, but her mother immediately jumped to the conclusion that she was running a fever.

In December 1846, Caroline and Charles de Vigors made a trip north to Philadelphia, New York and Boston. In their absence, Clarence read, played billiards, and spent long evenings talking to Ed Barthew while Mignette lent an attentive ear.

The Mexican War was a constant topic. With Taylor's troops in Monterey, Winfield Scott's in Vera Cruz and Kearny's in Santa Fe, the Mexicans were having second thoughts. In California, Frémont was waiting for Kearny and Stockton to join his offensive against Los Angeles. In the South, as elsewhere, the United States' "manifest destiny" was assumed to justify any inroads into Central America. The threat of war with Great Britain was removed when the two countries signed an accord fixing the Oregon-Canadian border at the forty-ninth parallel. Iowa was accepted into the Union while Taylor's troops occupied Mexico City.

Even though the Massachusetts legislature had declared the Mexican War to be "undesirable, unjust and unconstitutional," General Taylor had pursued his campaign brilliantly, only occasionally going beyond his orders. Driven to their knees, the Mexicans were forced to give up Texas, New Mexico and California. "Manifest destiny" was taking shape.

On his return to New Orleans from his Mexican triumphs, Zachary Taylor was given a hero's welcome. He was honored with cannon salutes, a torchlight parade, banquets and balls. Once the celebrations were over, however, the population had to cope with the ten thousand army volunteers who, now returned to civilian status, were trying to find employment. They filled the long empty hours at bars, often becoming vindictive when they felt their sacrifices or glory insufficiently appreciated. Jobs being scarce, another war appeared to be the logical solution to their unwelcome presence. As if these demobilized soldiers weren't enough, in a period of eight months, 130,000 new immigrants had moved into the Mississippi valley, among them 79,000 Irish, 44,000 Germans, 20,000 British, 5,600 Scots, 2,246 French, 1,414 Swiss, 1,048 Dutch, 353 from the Antilles, 251 Italians, 230 Spaniards, 11 Russians and one Chinese.

In the election of 1848, the South supported Taylor as candidate for the Presidency on the Whig ticket. Since he was a slave owner, Southerners assumed he would silence the abolitionists. Besides, it was becoming obvious that political lines didn't always conform to people's stand on this thorny issue. Party labels were losing all meaning: In the North, Whigs and Democrats called themselves abolitionists; in the South, Democrats and Whigs were proslavery; Northern Democrats were for the tariff, Southern Democrats against it.

Of equal importance in Louisiana was a paragraph in the state's new constitution prohibiting duels. This affront to a favorite local tradition had been brought to a head by the growing number of duels involving prominent personages. Noncompliance to the edict—which included seconds as well —removed the protagonists' right to vote or to accept salaried employment. Residents of New Orleans were particularly outraged because it applied only to citizens of Louisiana: Foreigners could elect to kill themselves with impunity. On the other hand, planters, merchants, traders and members of the professions who lived off their revenues had nothing to fear from the restriction on "salaried" people. The French consul, a man not without humor, noted: "If the Constitution had the power to suppress yellow fever, it wouldn't do it if it applied only to foreigners."

The new telegraph brought the news that another revolution had broken out in France. To the cries of "Hurrah for the Revolution, down with Guizot!", troops of the National Guard, mobilized to put down a republican demonstration, had to inform Louis-Philippe that the bourgeoisie had deserted him. A series of bad harvests which had caused widespread famine, the general corruption, the government's refusal to consider electoral reforms, the deficit of the Banque de France and the decline in the country's prosperity had furnished the opposition with more than enough ammunition. When the king heard the chant: "Hurrah for the Republic!" and "Down with the Ministers!", he quickly abdicated in favor of his grandson, the Comte de Paris, and fled from the capital. The constitutional monarchy lasted less than a day.

One spring day in 1848, Dandridge proposed that Caroline buy more land because their cotton was beginning to exhaust the soil. By alternating crops and leaving some fields fallow for a season, their cotton crop would improve substantially. Without telling her manager, she consulted her son, Marie-Adrien, who at sixteen was finishing his last year at the Jesuits'. He approved the decision, for he had heard from his friends' fathers that one should never miss an opportunity to add to one's holdings.

However, the oldest Damvilliers's interests lay elsewhere. His studies bored him, so he had wheedled permission from the Fathers to devote himself to the subjects that fascinated him and to disregard those that did not. Thus liberated, he pursued an anarchical course through European literature, music, history and philosophy. These satisfied his capricious mind and gave him the appearance of a serious student. He would shut himself up for weeks with his books, forgetting to wash or dress, forgetting even to eat. Then, for several nights in a row, he would go "over the wall" for mysterious assignations in town. He was seen in brothels in dubious company, getting drunk on strange mixtures he concocted himself, prodding prostitutes to describe the intimate details of their profession, and talking casual acquaintances into deals and speculations that the more scrupulous would have termed swindles.

Ever since he had read *Confessions of an English Opium-Eater*, by Thomas De Quincey, of whose existence the Jesuit Fathers were unaware, he had collected all the author's works and took morbid delight in his descriptions of the horror of opium's physiological effects. "On assassination as one of the fine arts," and "On the knock on the door in Macbeth" were revelations his temperament craved. The opium he bought at vast cost from sailors returning from London gave him a sense of intense lucidity and refinement of thought. All his faculties were brought into harmony, the way a well-constructed score blends all the instruments into a single voice with no one single instrument being ignored. The young Marquis tried to entice Gilles de Kernant and Hyacinthe de Beausset into his drug-induced ecstasies, but Gilles felt nauseous after his first drag on the pernicious amber pipe, and Hyacinthe was terrified by the "unbearable expansion of his brain." His friends' reneging increased Marie-Adrien's sense of isolation, as it did his arrogance; he drew the conclusion that only he was capable of pleasures unknown to the common herd. His taste in clothes also astonished his friends. His beleaguered tailor was goaded into producing garments that conformed to no known style: His trousers of velvety flannel had to have silk linings; his shirts were made of voile, his waistcoats of rainbow-hued moiré. He had a frock coat made from a cashmere shawl which he wore over riding breeches of almond-colored velvet and gray deerskin boots. He spent his evenings designing liveries in the Turkish style for Bagatelle's servants, indulging his fascination in the contrast of brilliant colors and gold on a slave's black skin.

To Caroline, these fantasies seemed eminently suitable to a moneyed heir, a prince of cotton, and indicated that her son was an aesthete of exceptional sensibilities. She readily gave him money to buy semi-precious stones. Eschewing diamonds, it was the play of light and color he was after, and so he bought lazulite, peridots, pink quartz, Australian opals, said and chrysoberyls from Ceylon and had them made into buttons by a jeweler on the Rue Saint-Charles. On his finger, he wore a deep black hematite on which he had had a broken cross engraved to demonstrate that he no longer believed in any form of redemption.

During his summer holidays at the plantation, his arrogance seemed to have turned into detachment. Clarence wondered if the young man had perhaps found interests he judged inaccessible to ordinary mortals.

To his always-attentive mother, he played Chopin nocturnes on the Pleyel. Caroline, reclining on a sofa, had the candles snuffed "the better to depart this earth," and gave herself to the music as to a lover's embrace. In exchange for these precious moments, she played the harpsichord. Instead of the ritornellos of Rameau which had so enchanted his father, he preferred the sophisticated architecture of a triple fugue by Bach, finding in its polyphonic labyrinths a mystical reflection of his thoughts. Were he not at home, he would have liked to add a ball of opium to his musical transports to lead him through the dense thicket of his soul toward a garden of rare flowers with petals of sumptuous and poisoned female flesh.

Later, perhaps, he would find a discreet companion with whom he could indulge the forbidden pleasure. But being an epicurean, he could put it off for the moment as if to hoard his appetites.

Félice, whose beauty already rivaled her mother's and who

could boast more admirers than Bagatelle had oaks, liked to play *My Old Kentucky Home* and *Oh! Susanna,* which her brother found insipid and vulgar. The colonel loved the songs and sang them with more enthusiasm than accuracy of pitch. Marie-Adrien would pinch his nostrils as if these songs conveyed the sour smell of army camps or the acrid stench of sweating men.

While he waited to set forth on his "grand tour" of Europe —the traditional culmination of the education of a rich planter's son—he became involved in several incidents that a few of Bagatelle's inmates found eccentric.

On the first occasion, he summoned Telemaque and his church choir to a place under the oaks, had the piano brought down, and ordered the slaves to sing; some accompanied themselves on their banjos made of cheese crates while others clapped. As their melancholy spirituals penetrated his soul, he used the piano to force a livelier rhythm. The blacks, always docile, became more animated, soon breaking into florid improvisations. Before long, under Marie-Adrien's authoritative direction, they approached a state of trance, their syrupy melodies becoming lascivious, their incantations turning into raucous shouts. From the piano, he nodded toward Telemaque to break into a solo that modulated a motif while the chorus accompanied him with murmurs and plaints. These soon grew into private confessions as if the music were a language that abolished the distinction between master and slave, joining them in a shared exasperation.

Caroline, Charles and Dandridge had listened to the performance from the gallery. Caroline was troubled by her son's audacity, her husband disapproved outright, but Dandridge was moved.

"That was beautiful. And very cleansing for the soul," he remarked to the young Marquis.

"It might seem scandalous to some," he said, glancing at his stepfather. Dandridge protested, "Not to me, in any event. I find it wholesome, although it does depend on the intention, perhaps?"

"I had only an instrumentalist's intention, Mr. Dandridge. I wanted to convince myself that blacks are intelligent instruments where music is concerned."

Clarence was less happy with the way Marie-Adrien was dressing his valet Brent in anticipation of their trip to Europe. The young Marquis summoned his tailor from New Orleans and kept him at the plantation for a month. The results included two suits of gray cheviot with pink shirts for the Marquis, and for Brent—as designed by his master—a pale blue frock coat with silk facing and a blood-red jacket with black lapels. To these were added a beige woolen cape held together at the collar by a silver chain, and as headgear, a honey-colored silk opera hat.

"With that get-up, you won't go unnoticed in Paris," the colonel said tersely.

"Sir, was your hussar's uniform any less showy? With your gilt frogs, varnished leather boots, white trousers, medal-strewn tunic and plumed shako?"

"We wanted to attract only glory's attention, young man," the colonel snapped back.

"Permit me, then, on a more modest level, to wish to attract the attention of people of taste. That is the limit of my ambition."

This verbal duel convinced the colonel that Marie-Adrien was a spoiled, vain and insolent brat. From then on, he refrained from showing the slightest interest in his activities.

If the hussar had known what transpired in Marie-Adrien's room at night, he would have felt still different emotions. Caroline, whom nothing escaped where her older son was concerned, knew that the young Marquis had chosen for himself a young black girl from among Bagatelle's laundresses. She let it go unremarked, for the girl arrived after the house was asleep and left before dawn. She too must have been very discreet, for Anna, who was in on all the servants' secrets, had told her nothing. Marie-Adrien's choice had fallen on a girl of rounded sculptural beauty with a velvety mat-black skin and dazzling smile. Taciturn and prudish, she had thus far avoided all involvements, and the young Marquis stood a good chance of finding her a virgin—a rare thing on a plantation.

But what was most astonishing was that Marie-Adrien did not ask of Bessy what was usually expected of young slaves. The pleasure he derived was both more innocent and more perverted, for it sprang from a warped aesthetic impulse joined to a nonviolent sadism. When Bessy entered his room at midnight, it was almost as bright as high noon. Five dozen varicolored candles in glass containers were scattered all over the room—in the ceiling fixture, on furniture, on the mantel. Obviously the poor girl had no idea of the care with which Marie-Adrien had placed each light according to the color of the wax, its reflections in the various mirrors, the way it glistened on crystal bowls and vases.

Sitting in a chair in his dressing gown, he would ask the girl to take off her clothes and keep her arms close to her body; then he would begin opening jars of paint and choose among his brushes. The first night, Bessy had wanted to run away; then she thought maybe he was going to paint her portrait—for she knew she was beautiful. When she learned that it was she who was going to be painted, she became frightened again. But Marie-Adrien stroked her gently the way one would a piece of polished marble, and she gave in to his bewildering whim. Hadn't her mother told her you never knew what to expect from white men?

Then Marie-Adrien set about painting her splendid body, starting afresh each night, trying new methods, his inspiration changing according to his moods. One night, he drew concentric circles in green, red and yellow around Bessy's navel, pasted stars to her nipples and powdered her pubic hair with gold dust. Then he painted interweaving stripes on her thighs and mauve and saffron arabesques on her buttocks, and affixed enormous green patches to her cheeks. To cap it all, he had her dunk her hands in a basin full of red paint to give her blood-colored gloves. Another night, having succeeded in mixing the chalky pink color so dear to Southern women, he covered Bessy with it from head to toe, then dusted her hair with yellow powder.

"Look at yourself, Bessy. You're a white woman now."

He led her to a mirror and she burst into tears. This gave him the idea of adding scarlet tears to the girl's cheeks.

As he worked with swift and precise strokes in a kind of cold rage, her skin quivering at the touch of the wet brushes, he talked to himself in words Bessy didn't understand.

"You're a carnal poem, Bessy. . . . Color is rhyme, to which you communicate the movement of life. . . . Your body is beautiful, but it's only that. . . . I'm turning you into something unique and ephemeral. . . . I want you to be a chameleon-goddess . . . or a panther. . . . Yes, a panther!" And he spent hours painting her body to look like the animal's spotted fur, then enlarged her eyes with violet-tinted white makeup. When he was done, he ordered her down an all fours and instructed her to move like a cat and curl up on the bed.

"Now what you need is a collar."

So he unfastened his heavy gold watch chain and tied it around her neck. Finally, like an artist adding the last sublime detail, he gilded her teeth and colored her thick lips with pink pomade.

"There. You're a panther with gold teeth. How beautiful and desirable you are, Bessy. The next time, I'm going to turn you into a female alligator with bumps and globulous eyes. You'll be superbly frightening."

After these sessions, Bessy was limp with fatigue. He carefully washed her with a soft sponge and dismissed her. But never a gesture she had expected and now craved. For Marie-Adrien had aroused frantic desires in her warm and healthy body. Her nipples grew erect; there was a forward thrust to her pelvis which Bessy, in her innocence, made no attempt to hide. But the Marquis paid it no heed, judging all this the mechanical reaction of a body which he wanted only as material for his fantasies.

Each night, Bessy left with a dollar and the injunction to tell no one about these "polychrome studies on black skin," as he liked to call them.

At breakfast, Caroline, with more a woman's curiosity than a mother's, tried to read in her son's face the signs of a passionate night spent between Bessy's thighs. In her view, the lush black girl must surely make a formidable bedmate. Her son's heavy eyelids were understandable. Had she known it was due to opium, she would have felt differently.

No one in the big house had any idea of Marie-Adrien's peculiar activities. Dandridge, however, had occasion to glimpse a dominant facet of the young man's personality. The house was always full of flowers—roses, gardenias, jasmine, seringa, laurel, cattleya, and many more. But never magnolia blossoms, because they lost their ivory color in a matter of hours, turning caramel, then a dull brown. One afternoon, when Marie-Adrien had invited Clarence to his room to look at a book of frescoes from the Sistine Chapel, he noticed a dying magnolia blossom in a crystal bowl. Seeing that Dandridge had noticed it, the young man picked up the bowl and said: "This flower is about to acquire a new beauty. Its normal pearly whiteness is too ordinary. But notice how it is slowly mummifying without losing its suppleness. Now its petals are the color of an overripe pear. Soon they will take on the warm tint of old cordovan leather, then one morning, they'll fall off. They'll become as rigid as a corpse, the sap gone, and stay that way, just like pharaohs in their tombs. Then I'll slip them between the pages of a book and some day, far away from here perhaps, I'll happen to open the book and find my magnolia, intact."

Dandridge objected. "To me, the beauty of these flowers is in the life they represent. Dead, they're nothing but compost."

"No, death stabilizes them. Their beauty becomes confidential. Life's evolution corrupts them. It reduces them to common humus. There, in my books, they're the immortal testimony to a summer and my choice."

Clarence came away from their conversation with a feeling of disquiet. Not that he couldn't follow the convolutions of Marie-Adrien's thought, but the morbid choice of mummified and corrupted beauty over the exuberance of life—however commonplace—struck him as deeply disturbing. By itself, this quirk wouldn't have bothered him, but added to the curious concert with the blacks, his style of dress, his strange collection of semi-precious stones with their weird colors, and what he had learned of his behavior at the Jesuits' suggested a secret if unconscious revolt against the role for which he was destined. In addition, hadn't he caught a whiff of something acrid and sweet in Marie-Adrien's room that emanated from no known flower? Opium didn't occur to him, for he had no idea how it smelled, but it hinted at some form of Mephistophelian alchemy.

Pierre-Adrien didn't share Clarence's reservations about his brother. He admired him, even though he worried that out of bravado or a sense of fun perhaps Marie-Adrien might someday place himself in a dangerous situation. Yet he had to admire his courage: It took a certain strength of character to follow his unusual inclinations, indulge his novel tastes, and fly in the face of the prejudices of their conformist society. They were discussing Marie-Adrien one day when his brother said: "Mr. Dandridge, Marie-Adrien has confided to me that he wants his life to be a work of art whose meaning may not be understood until much later—like an epic poem or a tragedy of Sophocles that will astonish the world. I know he'll never act like ordinary people. He'll always do what's least expected. So we must accept him as he is whether we like it or not, and love him without trying to understand him."

Unlike the young Marquis, Pierre-Adrien's eyes were open to everything and everybody. He was increasingly disturbed over the merits of the "peculiar institution" that had made the South a proslavery country. He read a great deal on the subject and collected clippings from Northern and European newspapers commenting on the anachronism of slave work in a democracy. Dandridge was the only person with whom he could discuss this issue. His own mother had said, when he suggested they employ freed blacks rather than slaves, "There's no reason for you to concern yourself with these problems since you don't want to be a planter. Besides, no Damvilliers should cast doubts on an institution that has been accepted by his ancestors for a hundred and fifty years."

What could he say?

There were two things he found especially shocking. First, the prohibition against teaching slaves how to read, which was, of course, the best way to keep them in the state of ignorance people accused them of. Then, there was the "breeding" of blacks organized by a group of Virginians. Since the importation of slaves was now illegal, the surest way to increase their numbers—and to keep the slave dealers in business—was to make them procreate.

Most planters were content to encourage normal procreation, which maintained their stock of slaves without further cost. Others demanded that the women produce a child a year. Some even practiced eugenics and crossbreeding to obtain the strongest slaves. When the "breeders" bought slaves, they examined their reproductive organs as if they were operating a stud farm.

"If they could find ways of making only boys, they'd really be happy," Pierre-Adrien commented bitterly.

Also, he couldn't understand why his kindness to the slaves at Bagatelle wasn't reciprocated. The nicer he was, the less they obeyed him. Marie-Adrien was the one the house servants respected because he addressed them only to give an order or to reprimand. Pierre-Adrien was mystified by this paradoxical behavior. Only Ivy, his childhood friend and now a nurse at the plantation hospital, responded to his overtures. All the others, from old James to the youngest stableboys, saw in him only weakness and an inability to command. The young Marquis's brother certainly didn't have the makings of a master.

* * *

After a long period without memorable events, the year 1850 was to pull Bagatelle out of its normal lethargy. That year, the Mississippi crested three months earlier than usual. The river ruptured the levees, devastated plantations, dug a trench two hundred feet wide and eight feet deep a few miles above New Orleans. In the city itself, several sections were inundated. Old Man River carried flotsam and uprooted trees right into its streets, and cholera swept into the best neighborhoods. Bagatelle was spared, although a dried-up pond behind the house was once again full of water.

Cholera was not limited to the Louisiana delta. It found a choice victim in President Zachary Taylor, who died in a matter of days. His successor, Millard Fillmore, was in office when Congress approved California's entry into the Union as a free state and the Missouri Compromise permitted all states acquired from Mexico to choose whether they would be pro- or antislavery.

Meanwhile, Marie-Adrien, who had begun his European journey, was writing long letters to his mother postmarked Paris, London, Venice and Rome. He liked Paris best, finding London too sooty, Venice too libertine, and Rome shockingly indifferent to its archeological treasures. What he didn't tell her about were the nights spent gambling, or the drunken bouts with whores and third-rate actresses. Nor did he share with his mother the spicier moments which the "Chinese Baths" provided to fanciers of young flesh, or the afternoons in private opium dens whose owners introduced a debauched elite to ever-more-powerful drugs. The young Marquis de Damvilliers—called Adri by his friends—included in one of his letters a daguerrotype showing him leaning on a sculptor's stand in the same pose he had assumed for the portrait hanging at Bagatelle. Fortunately, the print—which did make him look thinner than Caroline remembered—was too fuzzy to show the pallor of his face, its deeply etched lines, the violet circles under his eyes, the trembling hands and rigid neck, all stigmatas of an undisciplined life, of a body already racked with venereal disease.

* * *

At the plantation, the fourth of September should have been a day like any other. Félice was busy with dressmakers who were putting the finishing touches on the gown she was to wear to a ball at the Templetons' the following week. Julie was watching, full of envy at her older sister's poise and elegance. Their activities were interrupted by the sound of the breakfast bell.

Everybody sat down and Mr. de Vigors was unfolding his napkin when Caroline asked abruptly, "Where's Pierre-Adrien? Hasn't he gotten up yet? He spends the whole night reading, so naturally he oversleeps in the morning . . ."

At his mistress's bidding, James went up to wake the laggard. On his return, he announced, "Master Pierre isn't in his bed, ma'm. It doesn't even look as if he'd slept in it."

"Perhaps he's in the garden privy. Go have a look, James."

James came back and reported, "He isn't there either, ma'm. I called him everywhere, and Bobo and the gardeners haven't seen him neither. Maybe he's gone off somewhere?"

Caroline shrugged. "Clarence, have you any idea where your godson might be hiding?"

"No. I saw him go up to his room last night. He didn't even borrow a book, for once. I don't understand it. We should try to find him all the same. I'll have a look."

Clarence got up, leaving the breakfast room strangely silent. Félice and Julie exchanged glances while their mother took little irritated sips of tea.

"Maybe he went for an early horseback ride. It's such a beautiful day," the colonel suggested.

"But his bed is made up," Julie ventured timidly. "That means he hasn't slept in it."

Dandridge went to the stables. All the horses were in their stalls. He inquired of each gardener in turn, then walked down the alley of oaks to the levee, Mic and Mac at his heels. The big wooden barrier which was closed each evening hadn't been opened. He began to feel really troubled. When he returned to the house, there was general consternation. The colonel had sent the servants to search through the woods, the barns, the pigeon cote, and to ask the foremen if any of them had seen Pierre-Adrien. Caroline stood at the railing of the gallery trying to imagine what could have gotten into her son's head to keep him from coming to breakfast. After a quick consultation, the colonel and Dandridge decided to have their horses saddled, one to ride along the riverbank, the other to go through the slaves' quarters. Clarence chose the second, for it suddenly occurred to him that Ivy might know something. "Pierre-Adrien is fourteen and a healthy boy. Maybe he's already . . ."

He found the young black girl in the hospital, doing her usual chore—emptying the malodorous bedpans.

"Ivy, have you seen Master Pierre?"

"No, sir, not yet. Why are you asking me, sir?"

"We're looking for him. It seems he didn't sleep at the house last night."

The slave stood speechless and the look she gave the manager was both skeptical and questioning. Then she picked up her bedpans and turned to go.

"If you knew anything, you'd tell me, wouldn't you, Ivy?" Dandridge was insistent. "I know that Master Pierre is very fond of you."

"Yes, sir. If I knew where he was, I'd tell you. But I don't know."

When Clarence returned to the house, everybody was caught up in the same feeling of anxiety. Servants kept coming in with negative reports on their searches and it began to seem as if Pierre-Adrien had vanished like a phantom. Caroline, pale and tense, suggested a new approach.

"Let's collect a group of fifty slaves and methodically comb the woods and fields. Pierre-Adrien could have sprained an ankle or broken something and not be able to walk. He may be waiting for help."

By lunchtime, every inch of the plantation had been scoured and not a clue had turned up. The family was about to sit down at table when Anna signaled to Dandridge from the door. He excused himself and followed her into the kitchen.

"Mister Dandridge, I got to tell you . . . Ivy just come to see me. But don't say a word to the mistress 'cause Ivy's scared. Master Pierre went to Ivy's last night like he often do, but not for what you be thinking, she told me. Only to talk and show her books. But he left her before the middle of the night and went home. She hasn't seen him since."

Clarence thanked Anna, excused himself from lunch and went to the hospital. Murphy had just arrived.

"It looks as if the boy slept out all night," the doctor ventured.

"If that's all it was, it wouldn't be serious. I want to see Ivy."

The girl was summoned and Clarence took her to one side.

"Anna told me what you told her, but she said it only to me. What path does Master Pierre take when he comes to see you?"

The girl started to cry.

"There's nothing to be afraid of. I just want you to help us find Master Pierre, that's all."

She pointed to a path that went from the hospital past a field and toward the rose garden, skirting the pond.

Dr. Murphy joined them. "What's all this about, Dandridge? Is it serious? You look upset. The child couldn't have gone far."

"Come with me, Murphy. We'll follow the path. Something must have happened to the boy."

The two men, the dogs bounding ahead, took the path and soon found themselves by the side of the pond. The spring floods had filled it but much of the water had evaporated under the hot sun, leaving a wide, muddy bank. Even before Murphy had spotted the body, Dandridge knew that his godson would be there.

"Good God," the doctor cried out, "look at that!" and he pointed at two legs sticking out of the stagnant water. He slithered forward through the yellow ooze, followed by Clarence. Mic and Mac, yapping in the water, reached the body first, sniffed at the legs and, recognizing the odor of death, turned away. Breathing heavily, the two men dragged the body out of the shallow water. The boy had been lying face down in the muck. Murphy turned the body over, wiped away the mud, found the heart and wiped the eyelids with his thumb. Two sightless eyes looked out. In the sunlight, they resembled two carbuncles set in dirty clay.

"There's no hope, Dandridge. The child suffocated in this filthy muck."

Clarence stood motionless, his face drained of color, his jaw twitching. The dogs were trying to shake off the mud that clung to their hair.

"Go bring some Negroes and a stretcher, Clarence," the doctor said after a heavy pause. "We'll take him to the hospital. I'll try to clean him up. His mother mustn't see him in this condition."

Clarence obeyed like an automaton. On this bright summer morning, Pierre-Adrien's death struck him as obscene. Near the hospital he ran into Ivy and told her straight out what had happened. The girl dropped to the ground as if he'd struck her and broke into sobs. He left her there, remembering that he had to tell Caroline that her son was dead.

The entire plantation lay under a pall. Caroline locked herself in with her daughters and refused to see anyone. Only Mignette Barthew was allowed into her room. Her former mistress was especially bitter toward poor Ivy.

"That Negress has to go. I want her sold. Immediately. She's not to stay at Bagatelle another day. I could strangle that slut with my bare hands."

While funeral preparations were underway and the gravediggers were opening the Damvilliers vault once again, Dandridge went to see Ivy. She was prostrate, her whole body shaking, eyes bloodshot, her skin ashen. Murphy had given her time off, knowing she was stricken with a grief she didn't dare show.

"We didn't do what you think, Mister Dandridge," the girl

said between sobs. "You got to believe me. We just talked, that's all."

Dandridge was sitting on a stool next to the straw mat on which the girl lay like a beaten dog. He felt a profound respect for Pierre's friend. What could she be accused of beyond the affection he had felt for her all the years they played together behind the big house like two children who didn't give a damn about the color of their skins?

She went on between muffled sobs: "The mistress says she wants to sell me. I don't mind. I don't want to stay here where people will look at me funny."

"We'll see, Ivy. We have to wait a little. The mistress is very sad, you know . . . like you."

"Yes, I know. But if she knew what Master Pierre and me was doing, she might turn me over to the sheriff."

"What did you do that was so bad, Ivy? You can tell me. I won't tell anybody."

"Well, Mister Dandridge," and Ivy sat up with a glint of defiance in her eyes, "Master Pierre was teaching me to read and write."

For all his grief, Clarence had to smile. It certainly sounded like his godson, with his conviction that blacks were perfectible. To salve his conscience, Pierre-Adrien had embarked on an enterprise he knew was illegal.

Ivy, emboldened, showed the manager her notebooks in which she had painstakingly traced the outlines of letters and was just starting on syllables. He recognized his godson's well-formed handwriting on the facing pages. On the last page, she had written the same word on ten successive lines: "Bagatelle."

"This secret is between us," he said, giving her back her notebooks. "But you must keep doing it alone—to please Master Pierre."

This made her cry again. Dandridge, who had never touched a Negro's hair before, stroked her head and left the room with its smell of garlic that had bothered his godson as little as the color of Ivy's skin. He whistled for his dogs, whose delicate sense of smell had been more outraged than his, and went back to his apartment. On the Damvilliers family tree, he placed a black cross and the date after Pierre-Adrien's name.

A few days later, when Caroline had resumed her role as mistress of the house, she asked Clarence: "When are we getting rid of that Negress? We must sell her right away. I hope she's not expecting a baby."

"No, she's not expecting a baby, Caroline, and I intend to relieve you of her very soon."

"Only tell me after it's done."

"It will take me awhile to get in touch with the dealer, but I'll get to it as soon as the cotton picking is over."

"All right, but get on with it. The sight of the girl turns my stomach."

Dandridge had no intention of turning Ivy over to the slave dealer in Bayou Sara, where the pretty girl would have found many a taker. Such an act would have betrayed his godson's memory. And he didn't give a damn if he disobeyed Mrs. de Vigors. But the idea he'd hit on would take a few weeks. Through Ed Barthew, he had already made contact with a freed black who was working with Harriet Tubman, the famous black the Northern abolitionists called "General Tubman" and the runaway slaves called the "Moses of our people." Committed to helping her brothers and sisters escape, this ex-slave had organized a network known as the "Underground railroad." With the help of white abolitionists, Tubman made clandestine forays into the South to look for runaway slaves whom she helped across the Mason-Dixon line to the free North. Hiding by day and walking at night, the runaways achieved a liberty more theoretical than real, federal agents being everywhere on the lookout and authorized to return them to their masters. Luckily for Ivy, Barthew had found a Transcendentalist lady in Concord ready to take her in when she finally arrived. Dandridge didn't want Pierre-Adrien's friend to suffer for the liberty he was deliberately and perhaps highhandedly thrusting upon her.

When "General Tubman's" answer came, setting their meeting at Gallatin, a village in Tennessee, Dandridge used the pretext of a trip to Memphis to look at a new cotton gin an engineer had designed.

On a cold, rainy November morning, Clarence drove the gig to Bayou Sara—Bobo would bring it back later. In a small clearing by the side of the road, Ivy was waiting with her pitifully small bundle, a bouquet of wild flowers in her hand.

"What are you going to do with those flowers?" he asked as he helped her into the gig. She looked at him shyly.

"I'd like to leave them on Master Pierre's grave when we pass the cemetery at Sainte-Marie."

"It may not be wise for you to show yourself, but we'll do it anyway."

Ivy deposited the flowers on the freshly dug grave, crossed herself and, turning toward Dandridge, announced, "Someday, I'll come back and bring him the most beautiful flowers in the whole world."

On the boat going up the river, Ivy was registered as Dandridge's servant. He took note of the ladies' skeptical looks when they saw him with the pretty black girl. The men thought she had both grace and distinction—for a slave, that is. In fact, one man offered two thousand dollars for "the ebony filly."

At Memphis, Dandridge hired a four-horse carriage and, avoiding all the larger towns, bumped along side roads until he arrived at the clearing where Harriet Tubman and three escaped slaves from a Georgia plantation were waiting for the new recruit. Dandridge wasn't taken with "General Tubman." She was a pudgy woman in a black dress, wearing a flat bonnet that seemed to press her coarse features together. Furthermore, she carried a large revolver in her handbag.

"Who are you?" she barked at Dandridge, surprised to see a white man escorting a black and therefore suspecting a trap.

"That is none of your business," Dandridge said icily. "I'm depending on you to do what you're supposed to, which is to see that Ivy arrives in Concord safe and sound. If anything happens to her, I'll know where to find you."

"All right, all right. Let's go."

Dandridge surreptitiously slipped Ivy a purse, for he had little confidence in the other three blacks. However, he made a great show of handing the general a fistful of bills.

"It's for the cause," she said, stuffing the money in her handbag.

"No, it's so that you take good care of Ivy. She has no resources. For the moment, *she* is your cause. That's all I care about."

Then he turned to the young slave and, to everyone's astonishment, kissed her.

"Glory be to God and Jesus Christ, one more soul is saved," Harriet Tubman said in ringing tones.

She shook hands with Dandridge and he got back into the carriage, cracked his whip and, without looking back, took the road to Nashville where he slept for twelve hours before returning to Memphis. He took in Mr. Parkinson's cotton gins with half an eye, and was on the first boat going downriver.

Marie-Adrien had returned to his apartment after attending Frédéric Chopin's funeral at the Madeleine when he received his mother's letter announcing the death of his younger brother. His ears were still reverberating to the ardent pulse of the Prelude in E Minor, brilliantly played by the organist Lefébure-Wély before three thousand mourners in the crepe-draped church. Marie-Adrien read the letter several times. He pictured his brother staggering in the wet clay, his body gradually sinking in the mire, his sexual appetites appeased by this Ivy his mother held responsible for his death. He was sorry he had neglected the sensitive private person he was just now discovering in Pierre-Adrien. They shared the same precocious physical needs. He also realized that this meant he was the only male Damvilliers left and it was up to him to procreate in order to carry on the name—unless he refused and departed this life too.

In his long answer to his mother, he informed her that

he would be coming home in the autumn of 1851. When he told Brent of the sad news from Louisiana, the poor black burst into tears.

"Stop that bawling," Marie-Adrien snapped. "Now Master Pierre knows what's behind all the lies the priests keep drumming into our heads about the next world and the soul's immortality. You, Brent, are mewling over the great void, emptiness, nonexistence. Our brains are nothing but sponges for mopping up memories. When death squeezes them, they dry up and become dust, like everything else."

"Yes, Master," his valet replied, understanding not a word of what he had said. "But I'll never forget Master Pierre. You remember what Planche said when he was born? That he had the sign of water? That's why he drowned in the pond."

Marie-Adrien shrugged. To try to combat the blacks' superstitions was absolutely hopeless. Besides, weren't they just as valid as the Christians' who accepted the hocus-pocus of the Eucharist and ruined their lives worrying about the boiling caldrons of hell? "There is no such thing as sin," he said to himself. "There are only cowards too frightened to explore life to its depths."

"Go away. You bother me," he said out loud to Brent.

The valet didn't wait to be told twice. He went straight to the nice white chambermaid whose bed he had been sharing for some time now. She would understand and comfort his grieving soul.

It took Bagatelle several months to emerge from the deep depression that followed Pierre-Adrien's death. As if to aggravate their grief, business was in a general decline. New Orleans's commerce was in a slump; in fact, it might be a thing of the past. People blamed it on the railroads, which threatened to make the Mississippi useless. The Erie line was now 450 miles long, the New York line heading north 325 miles, and the Baltimore & Ohio 179 miles. Plans were underway for a line connecting Chicago and Mobile, and another crossing the Appalachians whose construction would cost

$10,000 a mile. Some Louisiana parishes had already bought $80,000 worth of shares, which would yield dividends of between 8 percent and 10 percent. This line would cross country that had shipped 110,880 hogsheads of tobacco, 193,000 barrels of molasses and 40,000 head of cattle to New Orleans. All this might soon bypass New Orleans. Moreover, by increasing the value of the land it traversed, only one fourth of which was presently under cultivation, the railroad would attract new farmers and planters, who would inevitably ship their produce directly north.

Old Mr. Templeton, however, was sanguine: "Someday, the railroads will go across Texas and then New Orleans will have a direct connection with the Pacific Ocean. It's only a matter of time." The Mertaux brothers were equally optimistic. New Orleans must accept the railroad, not as competition for the Mississippi but as a supplementary route for delivering the South's produce to its customers.

The wheat and flour shipped to Europe would go via New York only if the South failed to demonstrate the advantages of river transportation. A good third of the pork raised around Cincinnati—it filled three thousand boats a year—was destined for England and France, as were the 50,000 barrels of dried beef that went to Liverpool. The 410,000 ingots of lead now produced in the new state of Wisconsin and in Galena, Illinois, brought tidy profits to the middlemen in New Orleans. Sugarcane was a chancy crop in view of its susceptibility to changes in temperature, early frosts, late rains and sudden floods. But the twofold increase in its production between 1840 and 1850 testified that it was well worth the risk.

On the other hand, cotton was suffering from competition with India and South America. And the development of sugarcane had pushed up the price of slaves from $800 to $4,000. There were fewer now around the port or on the streets of New Orleans. They had been replaced by whites, just as Irish maids were taking the place of blacks in Southern houses. And for special types of work, like repairing the levees, digging canals and baking slate bricks, white labor was more dextrous. Still, Louisiana cotton sold well even though it had dropped from 1,142,382 to 837,723 bales in one year. But at $450 a bale, it was still a profitable venture.

New Orleans traders and merchants had finally come to terms with the tariff and were making good profits from European imports. From France alone, the city received arms, articles of brass and bronze, leather and skins, sheets, notions, gloves, hats, jewelry, porcelain, saddles and boots, trunks, wines, liqueurs, crystal and glass. In 1850, New Orleans received nearly half a million dollars' worth of silk and taffeta.

The young Marquis de Damvilliers was subjected to hours of this unsought information on board the *Belle Assise,* a large ship outfitted by the Messieurs Rothschild. Since Marie-Adrien had no interest in business whatsoever, he found his fellow passengers' conversation stultifying. Subject to increasingly frequent migraines, he couldn't keep his mind on where the new railroad lines were going, the need to build textile mills in the South to compete with the North, or the best way to fatten beef for slaughter.

By the same token, Marie-Adrien took little pleasure in the prospect of guiding Bagatelle's destiny. He was only too happy to leave all that to Dandridge so that he could spend his time on activities closer to his heart. Chief among these was the building of a new house, the plans for which he had with him in his bags. This would occupy him for at least two years. His mother and all the others would simply have to accept it. With his sizable fortune, he would not only build a manor house but would fill it with works of art and rare furniture. His mother and sisters could have Bagatelle. The Roman, Venetian and Florentine palaces he had seen had spoiled him for the planters' wooden houses with their parents' dreary furniture and the overabundant gimcrack. Among his cases, he already had a few priceless things he had found in European antique shops: a Louis XVI clock with a crystal bell and a clock face balanced between the curved arms of a gilded bronze lyre: a set of glasses blown to his order in Murano, Sèvres plates of extreme fragility, a pair of lapis lazuli vases commissioned from Bernardo Buontalenti by a Medici. His furniture was being made by a London cabinet-maker at that very moment. He had chosen lemonwood for its warm blond tones, infinitely preferable to the dark mahogany of Bagatelle.

While Marie-Adrien was sailing home, five hundred delegates attended a convention in South Carolina and voted unanimously to secede from the Union. A Convention of the People was scheduled for the following February to ratify the decision. Few planters in Louisiana understood the significance of this step. Much more interesting was the expedition mounted by General Narciso López and his band of adventurers to deliver Havana from the Spanish yoke. In spite of the fact that it was strongly condemned by the federal government, many greeted the enterprise with enthusiasm, using the call of liberty as the pretext for a profitable expansion of commerce. In New Orleans, it was firmly believed that the poor Cubans should be supported in their revolt against Spanish authority. But hadn't this always been the conqueror's way—to encourage real or alleged rebellions in order to move in as would-be liberators and appropriate the lands they coveted?

While New Orleans, with the frenzy common to cities in hot climates, mobilized for the war with Cuba, local Spaniards feared for their lives and fled the city, leaving houses and belongings behind. The cooler heads in the federal government tried to prevent the embarkation of three thousand volunteers on two ships bought through public subscription, one of them —the *Pampero*—considered so unseaworthy it couldn't make it across the Mississippi.

On landing in New Orleans, Marie-Adrien had the impression of a cramped, provincial backwater. He took a suite at the Saint-Charles and dispatched a courier to Bagatelle to announce his arrival. Although he could have booked passage on any one of the twenty boats leaving that day, he chose to wait for the *Croissant d'Or*, being the newest, most luxurious and fastest vessel now plying the river. Three hundred and sixty feet long and seventy-three feet wide, it boasted eight boilers forty-two inches in diameter and thirty-two feet long, plus seven more twelve inches in diameter and thirty-five feet long. Its paddle wheels were forty-two feet in diameter. All of this made it possible to carry fifteen hundred tons of cargo at over ten miles an hour against the current.

The interior was palatial and furnished accordingly. Its 190 passengers in First Class enjoyed white marble washstands, private toilets, and two life belts each. There were also baths for ladies and gentlemen, a barber-hairdresser, and the indispensable bar. The ship had cost the enormous sum of $135,000 and carried a crew of 125. The 1,415 miles separating New Orleans and Louisville were covered in five days. All in all, it was a suitable craft for a prince returning from exile—which is how Marie-Adrien saw himself. But he intended to make good use of his time on board to make up for the austerity of old Bagatelle.

During the two nights he spent in New Orleans, he had tried to bring back his exciting days as a dissolute student, going to the cabarets, the whorehouses and gambling rooms. But it didn't work. He had become used to stronger drink, more refined diversions. The octoroons with the apricot-colored skin and lascivious ways he used to find so irresistible now disgusted him. The oyster stew at Antoine's was tasteless and slimy, the champagne—at six dollars the bottle—too green. There was no one he could talk to. Only Hyacinthe de Beausset and Gilles de Kernant were worthy of his racy accounts of Parisian nights, yet they too seemed more interested in their law studies at Jefferson University. For their part, all they could muster were descriptions of midnight revels about as exciting as an evening on a showboat. Their idea of the summum bonum of debauchery was a dinner with lots of wine after which tipsy women unhooked their dresses for the men to judge the firmness and roundness of their breasts.

To Marie-Adrien, it all smelled of rice powder, tattered underwear, coarse laughter—"bourgeois," as they called it in Paris. All right for drunken notaries and libidinous politicians, but hardly tempting to an aristocrat who had been backstage at the Cyder Cellars in London where naked ballerinas danced with lords and unfrocked pastors. For anyone who had seen dukes disguised as Bacchus and ladies riding Godiva-style on broomsticks with a panting excitement so obvious it made the men doubt their usefulness, the delights of New Orleans resembled country hops. Not to mention the "tableaux vivants" and lotteries held in certain Paris salons, where the person buying a ticket won an hour with a woman picked by lot, unless it was his luck to get the young man who was always included in the draw and to whose caprices, like it or not, the "winner" had to submit. When Marie-Adrien looked at the distance separating him from his two old friends, he realized how far he had come.

After vague promises of future meetings, the young Marquis was relieved to say good-bye and board the *Croissant d'Or*, where he would at least be alone among strangers.

Brent, on the other hand, was thrilled to be going back to Bagatelle. To listen to him, compared to New Orleans, Paris, Rome and London were nothing but jerry-built villages, and compared to the Mississippi, the Seine, Tiber and Thames were refuse-strewn streams you could cross in a single jump.

To forget Brent's chatter and prepare for Bagatelle at the end of its alley of oaks, the young Marquis gave the key in his lock a turn and lit a pipe of hashish. Back in his private Orient, he forgot to go down to dinner. The next day, when he finally awoke, its effects had worn off. Outside, the warm golden sun of autumn and the limpid air brought out the smallest detail in the passing landscape. Marie-Adrien saw that the *Croissant d'Or* was racing another boat. He could just make out the smaller *Baltimore* about half a mile ahead, its stacks belching large clouds of black smoke. As always in these cases, and defying the new navigation law that forbade this form of competition, all the passengers were gathered on the forward deck, egging the captain on. The women, under their fringed parasols called out: "Faster! Faster! We must catch up with it, Captain!"

The male passengers were even more provoking: "Show us what your forty-two-inch boilers can do!" or "The *Baltimore* is an old tub. If it beats us, the *Croissant d'Or* is dishonored!"

Before such an elegant crowd, the captain had no choice but to preserve the reputation of his ship and take on all comers. He had given his orders to his machinists, but the connecting rod assembly was too new and stiff, and the pistons resisted the pressure of the superheated boilers. Casting a look of contempt at the raucous crowd, Marie-Adrien decided to take matters into his own hands.

"Brent, lead me to the machines."

The slave disappeared down a steep flight of stairs, the Marquis in his wake. The black stokers, their bodies glistening with sweat, were outdoing themselves to satisfy the chief mechanic who, his eyes on the manometers, shouted exhortations with a Cajun accent. Whole cords of wood were hurled into the raging fireboxes. As the resin in the logs exploded, it set off sparks and their reflection on the boilers' brass sides took on the aspect of fireworks. Marie-Adrien had to shout to make himself heard:

"Each of you gets two dollars if we catch up to the *Baltimore* before we reach Monte Vista." Monte Vista was a large plantation a few miles south of Baton Rouge.

The Marquis's offer fired up the stokers, actors in a spectacle they themselves couldn't see. The fireboxes had now reached a blinding incandescence, the brass sheathing on the boilers turning dark under the pressure of the boiling water. The hardwood connecting rods seemed stretched to their limits, one man trying to cool them with bucketsful of water while another watched the grease in the machines, ready to add more as needed.

Brent, now promoted to courier, shuttled between the bridge and the hold to report on the position of the *Croissant d'Or*. When the other passengers learned how the Marquis de Damvilliers—whom many knew by name—had encouraged the stokers, they sent their servants down to up the ante.

"Mr. Priestley has doubled the bet," Brent reported on one of his visits.

"How are we doing now, Brent?" Marie-Adrien asked, his face pale and dry despite the suffocating heat in the boiler room.

"We're creeping up, but not by much, Monsieur le Marquis."

"We've got to overtake that damn boat. We must get up more steam. See if all the valves are closed."

"They're all closed except for the safety valve," the head mechanic reported.

"Close it then. It'll give us a little more pressure."

"But, sir, these boilers are brand new."

"So, we put them to the test," the Marquis shouted irritably.

"The fireboxes would heat better if we had cypress wood," one stoker volunteered. "This wood starts too slowly, then burns up too fast."

On the deck, the excitement was getting out of hand. The *Croissant d'Or* was moving up on the *Baltimore,* but the smaller ship's paddles kept churning the water with effortless ease. It raced along like a buggy on a smooth road, gliding past the barges and steamers coming downriver. Knowing the Marquis had set Monte Vista as the finish line, the passengers were feverishly raising their bets. Brent informed his master that the odds on the *Baltimore* were three to one.

As he did whenever he was crossed, Marie-Adrien bit his lip with vexation. He had always been fascinated by fire. Its destructive force born of a tiny flame was like a sublimation of inert matter, the symbol of definitive obliteration. Even if this fire was a kind of sacrilege—making it serve the footling pursuit of one boat by another, like harnessing a god to a buckboard—it gave him a morbid pleasure.

The stokers had done all they could, and the long shuddering vibrations of the boat gave warning that its engines were reaching the limit of their capacity.

"What do the manometers say?" Marie-Adrien asked the mechanic.

"They're up about as far as they can go, sir."

"What about the superheater?"

"With better wood, we could easily raise it five degrees."

Marie-Adrien, who was no engineer, was pensive, then his face suddenly brightened.

"We'll get those five degrees. Brent, go get me two cases of whiskey!" When the stokers heard this sumptuous order, they exchanged winks and went to work with redoubled energy. That white man knew how to live. They might not get the promised dollars if they didn't beat the *Baltimore* but they'd get the whiskey and once that was drunk, nobody would even remember.

The Cajun put in timidly: "You're not allowed to give niggers anything to drink."

"It isn't for them. Leave everything to me."

When the passengers saw the Marquis's servant carry down two cases of ten bottles each, they let out a murmur of approval, and the odds on the *Croissant d'Or,* which had risen to five to one, now fell two points. So that little Marquis who looked as pale and thin as a girl hadn't played his last trump. He had come up with something that would really get those lazy good-for-nothing niggers off their butts . . .

With the stokers standing by, panting, parched and watching his every gesture, Brent started opening up the bottles. The Marquis seized the first two, turned his back on the expectant blacks, walked up to the wood about to be thrown into the fireboxes, broke the necks with a swift crack against a log and methodically doused the logs with the whiskey. There was a moment of stupefaction. No one had ever beheld such waste, and there were mutterings of disapproval.

"Here. Get these logs into the boxes fast. If we overtake the *Baltimore* before the whiskey's gone, you get the rest." Then he took two more bottles and splattered the next batch of logs.

The boilers acted like an exhausted man who has downed a large glass of whiskey. The fireboxes roared. Then blue flames started licking the outside of the boilers and the seams began to swell and crack. From the vibrations of the floor, they could feel the boat lunge forward like a horse that's been whipped.

Brent appeared again.

"We're doing better now, sir."

His voice could be heard over the captain's, which was asking through his loudspeaker what was going on down in the boiler room to make the boat act so strangely.

"Don't stop! Don't stop!" Marie-Adrien kept prodding the men, who were already half drunk on the alcohol fumes.

Brent had never seen his master in such a state. His frock coat thrown into a corner, his hair plastered to his forehead, his eyes bulging, his breath coming in spasms, he reminded the black of someone in a trance.

The mechanic was watching the governor, which was now going through frantic convulsions.

"Out of my way," Marie-Adrien suddenly shouted as the stokers were about to heave in more logs.

With studied precision, he threw an unopened bottle into the middle of the flames. For a split second, nothing happened. Then there was an explosion like that of a bomb hitting a target. A shower of shards threw a purple light over the hold. The last thing the mechanic saw was the distended whites of the stokers' eyes and the Marquis's rictus when his saturated waistcoat caught on fire. At the same time a boiler split open with a great crunch of ruptured brass, liberating a cascade of boiling water and white steam that quickly invaded the hold.

The passengers on the *Baltimore* later told how they had heard a dozen explosions and seen a large black leap from the deck into the water, his clothes in flames, soon followed by men and women who moments before had been squealing with joy over the excitement of the race. The captain barely had time to steer the boat toward the nearer bank; the *Croissant d'Or* was already engulfed in flames. Women's skirts were spreading out over the surface of the water like water lilies. The high-pitched sound of screams merged with the crackle of burning decks while a heavy acrid smoke seeped out of every opening. Suddenly, for no reason, the whistle blew, set

off by a final spasm of steam, the last breath of the river's
newest and proudest vessel.

When the bridge began to give way, the captain picked up
his ship's log and the spyglass the owner had given him when
he took command of the ship. With calm nonchalance, he
slid down to the deck where the barber, an old river hand,
was waiting for the propitious moment to jump into the water,
his box of razors in his hand.

"Shall we go?" asked the black.

"Now," the captain replied.

Brent reached Bagatelle that same evening, in a carriage
borrowed from Monte Vista, whose owners were the first people to arrive at the scene. Brent had received only superficial
burns. Mr. de Vigors was struck dumb by the sight of the
black at the drawing-room door, his clothes filthy and in
tatters, a large red lump on his cheek. When Caroline saw her
son's servant, she instinctively knew that a new calamity was
upon her. Before Brent could open his mouth, she sat up, pale
and fierce, and demanded, "Where is the Marquis?"

The black made a gesture encompassing everything he
couldn't put into words, then ventured:

"The boilers exploded, ma'm. Everything burned. The boat
is all burned, ma'm."

"What boat? Where is the Marquis?"

"The *Croissant d'Or,* ma'm. And maybe Monsieur le Marquis is dead. Maybe."

The slave's "maybe" was his attempt to soften the blow.
Clarence happened into the room and looked at each face
with bewilderment. The colonel had regained his self-control.
"But where is he, for God's sake? Speak up, boy!"

"At Monte Vista, sir. That's where they put all the dead they
found."

Clarence led Caroline to a sofa. She sank into it, her eyes
shut tight, her breathing labored.

"I'm going with you," she finally managed with little conviction.

"No," Clarence said gently. "It's no use, Caroline. We'll do what's necessary. You must be brave now."

James had told Anna that something bad had happened. She now came into the room, knelt at her mistress's feet, took her hands in hers and started to weep.

While the colonel and Dandridge were galloping toward Monte Vista, Caroline summoned the strength to listen to Brent's recital. When he had finished, she said, "Why didn't you stop him, Brent? Why did you let him pour that whiskey into the boilers? He was only a child. He didn't know what he was doing."

"Nobody knew it would make the boiler burst, ma'm. Monsieur le Marquis wanted the *Croissant* to beat the *Balti*'. That's how he got the idea for the whiskey. There're at least fifty dead, the master of Monte Vista said . . ."

Caroline dismissed the valet with a wave of the hand.

Anna put in, "Go get yourself looked after at the hospital, Brent. Dr. Murphy's there."

Brent left the room, trying to hold back the tears. In his fine clothes now reduced to dirty rags, he looked like a scarecrow left out in the fields all winter.

While the doctor treated his burns, Brent again described the catastrophe, adding an embellishment here and there, ennobling his master into a Mephisto stoking the infernal fire.

"They say Planche knew it, doctor. She said Monsieur le Marquis had the sign of fire. Do you remember that? Like she said Pierre had the sign of water. Planche knew whiskey made boilers burst."

"Planche was an old gossip, Brent," the doctor said gruffly.

"All the same, that's what she said."

"Maybe so, Brent. What sign did she see on you?"

"Well, she told my mother I had the sign of the magpie. You know, that black and white bird. My mother never understood what she meant."

Murphy smiled. "The magpie is the biggest talker of all the birds. Planche hit it right on the nose. I'll bet you'll never be done telling about what you saw in Paris, heh, Brent?"

"You're so right, doctor. I know lots of things. Everything I did with Monsieur le Marquis. The funny tobacco he smoked that made his eyes roll around in his head, and the funny houses where the ladies and gentlemen bathed together . . . naked!"

"A piece of advice, Brent. Wait a while before you go on with your stories. The dead don't like people telling everything they've done."

"Yes, doctor. I'll wait until the mistress has stopped crying. But maybe I'll have forgotten things by then."

"The more you forget, the better."

"Oh?" said the black, not understanding.

A year after his younger brother had drowned, Marie-Adrien was lowered into the Damvilliers's vault. Old Templeton, now seventy-five years old, dragged himself to the cemetery in Sainte-Marie. To Caroline, he remarked, "Marie-Adrien died just like Corinne."

"I have no sons anymore, Mr. Templeton. No boys."

"You still have little Charles, Caroline," the old man said, nodding toward the small blond boy of seven, lost among the tall people in mourning and trying not to cry as his mother had admonished him.

"He's not a Damvilliers. Bagatelle no longer has a master. If Adrien could see us now, how he'd suffer. To take two sons from a mother. It's too much."

She said all this quietly, dry-eyed, as if in a daze, with no thought for the husband who was holding her arm or how he might take the implied slur on his son.

This sad day belonged only to the Damvilliers. Charles de Vigors didn't question his wife's love, but today he felt like a stranger. Caroline belonged to this group of petty aristocrats and they had their own way of expressing their grief. Even Clarence was closer to these people than he was; they shared the same life and work. They may have adopted him yet he still felt like an extraneous piece added to a game whose rules he often didn't understand.

As his son grew up, the boy would probably feel the same sense of isolation, despite his mother's love and the friends he would make among the cotton nobility. All those lands, all the great plantations on the Mississippi were the fiefdoms of the pioneers who had originally cleared them. They remained dynastic holdings. When one of these dynasties died out and the land changed hands, the plantation didn't change its name. Whoever became the future proprietor of Bagatelle, the house would always be referred to as Bagatelle and never quite belong to him. The new master would probably be accepted by the other planters but they would continue to talk about the Damvilliers's lands, almost is if to rub in the fact that the new owner was enjoying a fortune amassed by someone else. He assumed that Caroline would leave the plantation to her daughters; as long as Clarence Dandridge managed the plantation, the absence of a master wouldn't be felt.

A few weeks after the funeral, Caroline discovered her first white hairs. She would soon be forty, but her beauty was intact. Now that she had finally stopped crying, her face had found its old luster that no amount of sorrow could tarnish. The stubborn character that refused to admit defeat was restoring her taste for life. Only these white hairs—which she soon found ways to dissemble—testified to the suffering she had gone through.

Marie-Adrien's death brought her still closer to Clarence. Together they had shared experiences whose significance her husband couldn't possibly comprehend. More than ever, she knew that whatever happened to her, her life depended on Bagatelle. The only thing she feared was that Dandridge, as he had suggested one day, might decide to leave the plantation.

To allay her anxiety, she summoned the courage to bring up the matter again. Clarence had just turned forty-four, but he was still the same lean "cavalier emeritus." Maturity had given him even more elegance and ease of manner. Under the white panama, his close-cropped side whiskers now tinged with silver added to the distinction of his narrow bony face and the green eyes that missed nothing. His frock coats were the same size as twenty years before, and few men half his age could leap into the saddle with equal grace.

"Now that Marie-Adrien is gone," she ventured, "you're Bagatelle's real master, as long as you wish to be."

"Legally," Dandridge said, "you're your son's heir, together with his sisters. I am and will always remain only your manager. But you must never doubt my loyalty. We'll harvest our crops this year, like every other year."

"But what about the future, Clarence?"

"I'll stay as long as Bagatelle needs me, Caroline. You know that."

"I need you too. Don't forget that."

Clarence bowed with just the right degree of courtesy and placed a kiss on the slender fingers that clutched his hand. She felt flustered but happy. The specter of solitude had been dispatched.

That night, Colonel de Vigors's wife was the ardent lover she had been at the beginning of their marriage. He was grateful for this tenderness, which suggested the effort she was making to shake off the tug of the grave and resume her place in the open spaces of life.

Clarence made a point of asking Brent how his master had behaved in Europe and more specifically how he had seemed on the morning of the disaster. It had taken this talented and neurotic boy's death to make Dandridge fully understand him. Having armed himself against disillusion with a pessimism that passed for philosophy, what could Marie-Adrien have expected of the future? Only a renewal of his unhealthy curiosity brought to a still more self-destructive level. The death he had provoked as one would a wild beast was, it would seem, the last and supreme curiosity for a boy who had exhausted all other possibilities.

As Brent described in detail his master's life, he couldn't possibly know that he was laying bare the pitiful loneliness of the last male Damvilliers. Even Caroline had had no inkling.

Pierre-Adrien had been as clear as crystal; his older brother was opaque.

Clarence stood by the side of the river which held so many painful memories for him. The faces of Corinne Templeton, Adrien de Damvilliers and his two sons ranged themselves in his mind like so many portraits hanging on a wall. That evening, he opened a book he had recently bought in New Orleans, a work by a drunken poet named Edgar Allen Poe who had died in Baltimore two years before. He happened on the last two lines of a poem embedded in a prose text that read as if Marie-Adrien's phantom had picked them out:

> . . . the play is the tragedy, "Man,"
> And its hero, the conqueror Worm.

Abraham Mosely was expected again at Bagatelle. After the buffeting of the past year, the plantation was like an old ship that has survived a storm and, come what may, goes out to sea again—but with little enthusiasm on the part of the crew. Their old friend hadn't been back for several years, and his visit would be both a distraction and a reminder that there was a world beyond the plantation's boundaries.

Félice had returned to the nuns in New Orleans. Julie's indifferent studies and "weak heart" had mitigated against her joining her sister. In the old days, when the other Damvilliers children had enlivened the house, her presence had gone virtually unnoticed. But now that she was there alone with Charles, she was more in evidence, like a minor character in a play once the leading figures have left the stage.

Whether embroidering napkins or painting porcelains, Julie shut herself up for hours in complete silence. Since earliest childhood, she had been told: "Don't run, don't jump, don't get too hot, avoid drafts." She wasn't allowed to ride or take long walks, or to dance but briefly—to the point where, while waiting for the illnesses that never came, she had no resistance or appetite. When she went on the endless buggy rides with her mother or on visits to the cemetery in Sainte-Marie, she was always enveloped in shawls even in the heat of summer.

In spite of, or perhaps because of her poor health, she had taken on an odd and fragile beauty.

When young people talked to her, it was as if to a child or invalid. Adele Barrow, who was addicted to floral metaphors, likened Julie to "a slow-growing lily on a crystal stem." One young man, bolder than his peers, ventured to tell her during the course of a picnic that he thought she was pretty. Astonished, Julie answered, "You think so? You must be mistaken, sir."

The next day, the boy sent her a book of poems. No one ever knew if she had opened it.

Because she so rarely voiced an opinion on anything or anybody, her stepfather thought her bland when she was only being secretive. Her mother found her lack of vitality irritating and often picked on her for no reason. Although she was considered to be without talent—her painted porcelains had no discernible merit and her letters to her sister were correct to the point of being platitudinous—the old Jesuit charged with teaching her the few essentials necessary to a planter's daughter maintained that she was intelligent, of sharp intuition and unerring taste. Mignette Barthew also admired the girl, who responded eagerly to her godmother's warmth.

Dandridge saw only an old maid in the making who would live on tea, English novels and embroidery. She might even become cheeky and sharp-tongued, for he had sometimes caught a wicked light in her eyes, but aimed at whom or what he had no wish to know. Meanwhile, like everybody else at Bagatelle, he put her down as a pleasant and inoffensive vegetable.

Since, Mosely's last visit to Bagatelle, death—that demanding shrew who always gave the joyous broker from Manchester the shivers—had taken Adrien and his two sons. So, as he started up the alley of oaks in his hired gig, he prepared himself for the worst, although everything around him appeared unchanged. He was happy to make Colonel de Vigors's acquaintance. A hearty, outspoken man like him, he seemed to enjoy life without dwelling on its sorrows.

As he did every time he visited Bagatelle, Mosely brought presents for everybody: silver embroidery thread for Julie, coloring books for Charles, a curious pen that contained a reservoir of ink for the colonel, six ermine skins for Caroline, and for Dandridge, *Le Dictionnaire de la Fable* in two volumes, printed by Le Normant in Paris. To his goddaughter Félice, he brought a length of shantung from India. Disappointed to learn that she was locked up with the Ursuline nuns in New Orleans, he promised himself he would visit her, if her mother gave him permission.

Abraham Mosely, as paunchy as ever, displayed a physical prosperity which, he maintained, reflected his country's. John Bull was triumphant, the British government had ensured the victory of free enterprise, conquered India, reestablished relations with China, extended its colonial dominion over the distant countries of Australia, South Africa and New Zealand, and proclaimed the industrial genius of a nation of twenty-seven million people who, through diligence and the superiority of their navy, dominated an empire that extended to every continent, inhabited by 240,000,000 people of every race and color. Abraham Mosely couldn't have been more proud of noble England if he himself had occupied Victoria's throne. He had quintupled his fortune in ten years and crowed at the very thought of increasing it still further. How he pitied the Americans for not having understood in 1776 that by choosing independence they had given up the chance to share in Albion's glory!

The presence of the large round man with the chubby hands and infectious gaiety broke up Bagatelle's gloom. Caroline organized receptions and played the harpsichord to while away the evenings. Mosely seemed especially interested in Julie. The pale, diffident girl intrigued him. A connoisseur of long standing in such matters, he appreciated her timid grace and the supple lines of her body in the same way that powerful and red-blooded men have a taste for miniatures, Dresden figurines and delicate bibelots which they handle with infinite care. Mosely showered Julie with attention and the girl, little accustomed to gallantry in any form, responded with delight. She was happy to accept Mr. Mosely's arm at receptions and he on his side was proud to be escorting this strange hothouse flower who looked as perishable as an orchid. He even managed to wheedle Caroline's permission to take Julie with him on a brief trip to New Orleans during which he would call on his goddaughter Félice. Imilie, of course, would act as chaperone, happy to see her little mistress smile at last.

On their return up the river, Mosely grew confidential. "You know, Julie, when your parents asked me to be Félice's godfather, I told your father, 'Maybe someday I'll do what you did . . . marry my goddaughter. I was joking, of course. But today, even though Félice is as beautiful as her mother, if I had to choose between the Bagatelle girls, I'd choose you."

"Oh, thank you, Mr. Mosely," Julie said, reddening. "But . . ."

"I know I'm now an old party, of course, and no one regrets it more than I . . ."

"That's not what I meant, Mr. Mosely. I was only thinking that Félice merits more attention than I do."

"I don't like young girls who merit attention, Julie. Most men don't know how to recognize real beauty, the beauty that hides itself and has to be revealed to its owner."

Naturally, it was all lighthearted talk. Thrilled with her trip to New Orleans, where Mosely had taken her to the theater to see the notorious Lola Montez, Julie had been astonished that she felt no ill effects, no fatigue, none of the dire illnesses Imilie kept expecting.

"You're going to bed too late," her nurse grumbled.

"Let her live a little," Mosely broke in. "Look at me. I've never gone to bed before midnight."

The English broker, whose visits had never gone beyond two months, showed no signs of leaving. Mr. de Vigors took the first step. "Would you do us the kindness of spending the New Year holidays with us, Mr. Mosely?"

The usually precise Englishman beat around the bush. "That depends, colonel, on an . . . affair I can't make up my mind about."

"Take your time. Consider yourself in your own home. And if I can be of any help in your 'affair' . . ."

"Oh, yes, you certainly can help. You and Mrs. de Vigors can . . . in fact . . . do everything in this affair, which isn't exactly an affair."

The colonel, who was sipping a mint julep sublimely concocted by Anna, put down his frosted goblet and laughed.

"If we can do everything, then this affair which isn't an affair appears to be settled. But do at least tell me what it's about."

"I'd like to say it in your wife's presence so that I don't have to blush with shame twice."

"Then let's get her here by all means," the colonel said, intrigued.

When Caroline arrived, she took her place on the sofa like a seasoned theatergoer waiting for the curtain to go up. Mosely cleared his throat, stroked the side of his goblet with a trembling finger, and began.

"It's a little difficult. And I'm as afraid of your laughter as I am of your anger. All right! I wish to marry your daughter!"

"Félice?" Caroline asked right off.

"No, not Félice. Julie, madam."

"Good Heavens, Mr. Mosely. You can't be serious. You know how Julie is."

"She's a child," the colonel blurted. "Even if she does look more mature than her age, she's only just turned fourteen."

"But I've always heard that girls here marry very young."

"That's true," Caroline conceded, "but I feel terribly embarrassed, Mr. Mosely. If you had asked for Félice, I wouldn't have been so surprised, but Julie. Really!"

Mosely, his face grown purple to the ears, launched on a long exposé of Julie's attributes, singing the praises of her grace, her bearing, her sweetness and the beauty which he, Abraham Mosely, had perceived. He concluded that with his fortune, Julie would be one of the first ladies of Manchester, and that so far as her delicate constitution was concerned, he would care for her as for a Tanagra figurine.

Caroline, less put out than her husband, was amazed to hear her sickly daughter described in terms men normally used in talking about grown women. Mosely had opened her eyes to the fact that her daughter was indeed a burgeoning woman and one capable of attracting a man.

Colonel de Vigors was not unaware of the attraction some older men feel for adolescent girls in whom the faintly acid freshness of youth is joined to the budding charms of a woman. But it was hard to imagine scrawny Julie in the arms of that funny round man whose eyes so easily turned concupiscent.

Mosely waited, embarrassed, for the verdict that seemed so long in coming.

"Well, you see that we didn't laugh and we aren't angry, Mr. Mosely," Caroline said, all smiles.

"But you don't approve either."

"It's hard, you know," the colonel put in. "You can imagine how a mother can be taken aback by such a request. Julie is so . . . such a peculiar person, and . . ."

"I am not taken aback," Caroline said heatedly, interrupting her husband. "Mr. Mosely is an exceptional man and if Julie accepts him, I would have no reason to oppose the match."

The colonel was startled, but he had had enough experience of Caroline's willful ways to know that if she had so decided, she would cheerfully deliver up her daughter to the Englishman. He hoped that Julie, for once, would explode with laughter when her admirer had gone, taking with him his shame and his filthy little thoughts.

The hussar was mistaken. When, that very evening, Mrs. de Vigors went to see her daughter in her room, she had made up her mind that Julie would marry Abraham Mosely. Astonished to see her mother at that hour, Julie prepared herself for another catastrophe. Caroline sat down on her bed, carefully rearranged the folds of her skirt, and stroked her daughter's hair.

"I have good news for you, my darling. Mr. Mosely has just asked for your hand."

"What! He wants to marry me! What a funny idea!"

"Why funny, for heaven's sake. Lots of people get married, my child."

"I know, but not me. I don't want to. Besides, Mummy, he's old enough to be my father."

"What of it? Your father was twice my age when I married him."

"But Mr. Mosely is four times older than me."

A little put out by her daughter's deft circumlocutions, Caroline moved on from the discrepancy in age, where Mr. Mosely was obviously not in the strongest of positions.

"Do you intend to be a spinster?" she said with a touch of malice.

"I don't know. But if I'm able to please Mr. Mosely, maybe I can please others too."

"Who, for God's sake. Look at you. Skinny, sad, stupid, who could possibly want you? Believe me, don't pass up this proposal. What will you do with your life when I'm no longer around?"

"Come on, Mummy. You've never looked so young and so beautiful."

Raising her eyes to the ceiling, Caroline said, "We've suffered enough in this house to know we can't depend on hopes of longevity. Isn't Mr. Mosely pleasant and thoughtful with you?"

"Oh yes, very pleasant and very thoughtful, but . . ."

"Well, then, you'd better learn, my darling. I've learned this from personal experience. A woman is never really happy and well cared for except by a man older than she is. Before I married your father, I refused a number of young men."

"Yes, I know. Willy Templeton, among others."

"And others . . . because I knew that young husbands

are hard to dominate. You can make of Mr. Mosely whatever you like. And he's incredibly rich."

This conversation was a rude test of Julie's delicate nerves. Under the nightgown, her small breasts palpitated as if she'd climbed the stairs too fast. Caroline sensed that her daughter was having second thoughts.

"You know you're sickly, my darling. You have to have lots of attention, you mustn't be taxed. I wouldn't give you to a man who didn't know that and who wouldn't have the means to provide you with a comfortable and carefree life."

The debate between mother and daughter lasted over an hour. With diabolical cleverness, Caroline divulged certain aspects of marriage that Julie had never suspected. Then she described Mosely's house in Manchester, his flat in London, English high society, the theaters, the refined comfort in which rich Britons lived, the horse racing, the museums stuffed with treasures, the countryside groomed like a park, and the freedom—unknown in the South—enjoyed by British wives.

As Julie began to weary, her parrying flagged. Using her indefatigable willpower, Caroline gradually persuaded her daughter to accept things she would have thought laughable the day before. Such was the lady of Bagatelle's influence over the pure and unarmed. When her mother finally left with her resigned acceptance, Julie fell back on her pillow, her large eyes open in the dark, asking herself if she wasn't delirious or running a high fever.

The following morning, Mrs. de Vigors had a long tête-à-tête with Abraham Mosely. She explained that the negotiations she had conducted the night before had every chance of success, but that he must be prepared to wait a little for the definitive reply.

"You see, Mr. Mosely, now that my daughter knows of your proposal, she wants to think it over calmly. The old days when a mother could impose a husband on her daughter are past. The decision has to come from Julie alone."

At the close of this conversation, the British broker suddenly remembered urgent reasons why he must make a precipitous trip to New England and Canada. Before leaving, he announced that he would be back in three months—at the end of March probably—before he returned to England. He kissed Caroline's hand, pumped the colonel's. Charles de Vigors was relieved to see the Englishman go, and with him, the prospect of a marriage that made him queasy.

Mosely did not see Julie before his departure. The girl had spent a sleepless night and let it be known that she would spend the day in her room. But through her mother, she sent the broker "affectionate messages." Caroline saw fit to add that her daughter sincerely regretted his sudden departure and looked forward eagerly to his return in the spring. And so it was that, light of heart and with a spring in his step, the visitor from Manchester took the boat for Saint Louis.

During the next few weeks, the subject of marriage was carefully avoided. Julie picked up her brushes and became absorbed in decorating powder boxes, her New Year's presents to the Templeton sisters. For Dandridge she made a watchcase and for her stepfather, she wove a book cover with thin strips of leather.

Christmas was a subdued family affair. Since Marie-Adrien's death, Caroline had refused most invitations and spent long hours at the piano playing the pieces her son used to perform for her. Then she would lock herself in the "little Marquis's" room, making sure that all his trinkets, his stones and lamps were in the places he had assigned to them. She too used as bookmarks the brown, dry magnolia petals her son had left between the pages of his books. Sometimes she opened his closet and felt the cloth of his clothes. Or she would sit in a chair and try to imagine pretty Bessy's black body on the white lace bedcover, waiting for the young master to take his pleasure.

Only young Charles seemed able to distract her. When the weather was dry and the winter sun brought into relief the wide stretches of brown earth and the woods half stripped of leaves, she took him for long rides in the buggy. These outings pleased the boy, and delighted his father even more as he saw his son gradually taking the place his mother had so long denied him.

During one of their rides, Caroline talked about the plantation, the master's responsibilities, the soil's needs, the happiness he would feel when he finally took charge of Bagatelle.

"But Daddy has already bought me a plantation at Saint-Francisville," the child said.

"Well, Charles, if you like, you can annex it to Bagatelle and you'll be the biggest planter in the country."

"I wouldn't mind, but first I have to learn a lot of things and go to school in France. Daddy wants me to become a lawyer, like Mr. Barthew. He says it's better to be in business."

"Of course. Your father is right. But I'll be very sad when you leave for school."

And Caroline, holding onto the reins with one hand, hugged her child to her breast, kissed him and pulled up the fur lap robe to keep him warm.

For the first time young Charles was discovering the tenderness in this wonderfully scented woman with the soft hands who, though maybe she didn't mean to, had made him suffer. The word "Mummy" began to have a new meaning, and he soaked up the smiles, the little attentions and caresses. He now said it with a different inflection. Caroline belonged to him the way he belonged to her. At long last, he was suffused with the warmth and security every child needs. He didn't realize yet—perhaps he never would—that it was to his two half-brothers' deaths that he owed the joy of being his mother's son in the fullest sense.

For his part, the colonel was preoccupied with what was going on in France. The coup d'état that Louis-Napoleon had plotted to coincide with the anniversary of the Battle of Austerlitz had apparently been successful. The politicians with their big mouths had been routed after their attempt to stage a general revolt. There had been a number of arrests, but a plebiscite had given the people a chance to be heard. A republican to the core, Charles de Vigors still believed in order and authority and approved of having the power in the hands of his idol's nephew. He thought, perhaps naively, that with such a man at the helm, France would recover its appetite for glory and grandeur. The results of the plebiscite were stunning: over seven million for and a little over half a million against the Prince-President. Thus had the country expressed its confidence in its leader.

Colonel de Vigors had almost forgotten about Mosely when a telegram arrived announcing the broker's return the following week. Caroline had not forgotten. If her relationship with young Charles was slowly filling an emotional void, her dealings with Julie were full of subtle strategies. She continued to paint in glowing colors the virtues of living abroad in luxury; she dwelt on the ill effects of Louisiana's climate on a girl of delicate health; she reminded her daughter that little by little all the girls her age were getting married and soon all the eligible young men would be taken, leaving only the dregs. This barrage left the girl in a quandary, increasing her fear that she belonged to that category of young ladies who get only those husbands nobody else wants.

During the course of the winter, Caroline shifted from treating her daughter as an adolescent to shoring up the idea that she was now a grown-up woman. When Julie couldn't make up her mind about what to wear, or gave orders haltingly, her mother gave her a verbal thrashing.

"Julie, it's high time you made your own decisions, that you learned how to organize your life. I won't always be around to do your thinking for you. What would you do, my poor darling, if you married a man who couldn't provide you with a staff of servants? There are lots of girls your age who are already running their own households."

As a result, when Caroline learned that Mosely was returning, she had no trouble getting Julie's assent. Ever since the Englishman's departure, the girl had increasingly had the disagreeable sensation that she was becoming a stranger at Bagatelle, a sort of supernumerary. She ended by coming to the conclusion that the time had come to turn over a new leaf.

"Mr. Mosely is coming back, Julie. What are we to say to him?"

Caroline asked the question with the exasperated tone of a mother who expects a stupid reply. Julie, sitting at her embroidery frame, was silent. She pricked her finger.

"Julie, we have to give him an answer. I promised him, as soon as he was back. If you refuse him, it's not worth his unpacking his bags. He would want to leave immediately, probably angry, for a man of his quality would be very upset at our refusal. Too bad. We'll have to find a new broker for our cotton. It won't be easy the way things are going. But I suppose Dandridge will work it out somehow."

Sucking on her finger, Julie saw the plantation with its storage houses full of unsalable cotton, all because of her; Mr. Mosely slamming the door; Dandridge and her stepfather looking at her balefully; the youngest Templeton girl marrying before she did.

Julie sat up, took a deep breath and said in a voice she hoped sounded strong and cheerful, "Mummy, you're not letting me get a word in. I accept. Yes, I'll marry Mr. Mosely whenever you like."

Caroline got up and kissed her daughter. "Julie, at last you're making a wise decision." Then she sighed: "It's always hard for a mother to give up a daughter, but it's a sacrifice we all have to make for the sake of our children's happiness. After all, the Bible tells us that a bride must forsake her mother and father for her husband."

Julie, bent over her embroidery, noticed a large tear clinging to a flower of yellow wool, like a drop of dew. It had fallen without her even feeling it.

When, two days before Mosely's arrival, Mrs. de Vigors told her husband that Julie had accepted the Manchester broker, the hussar reacted with vehemence.

"It's like throwing the Christians to the lions. If Julie were my daughter, I'd refuse to let that whoremaster into the house."

"But she isn't your daughter, and I happen to know what's good for her."

"She won't be happy, Caroline. It isn't possible."

"She'll be rich and protected. Love can come later."

"Caroline, can you picture her in the same bed with that flabby lecher."

"That isn't all there is to life."

"No, but that's all there is in bed."

"She has accepted him. Isn't that enough?"

"What you mean is she has submitted. That's very different."

The two men were out riding when Dandridge learned the news from the colonel. He was stunned.

"That's very strange," he said, being a man who kept his thoughts to himself. The colonel was less diffident.

"It's against nature. Is that what you're trying to say? I'd give a million dollars to have that Englishman finished off by an attack of apoplexy before he reaches Bagatelle. Dammit, it's so typically British. They have no sense of decency. When they feel the need to drink or fornicate, they stop at nothing. I've seen them at war—hypocrites, crafty, fondling the young girls—and always with the Bible in their pockets."

"Is it really decided, or is it still under consideration?" Clarence asked.

"It's all decided. You know Caroline. She liked the idea, I don't know why. And in two hours, the thing was done."

"Does Julie like the idea?"

"How can she know if she likes it?" the colonel replied. "She knows about as much as a spring chicken. Can you see her, mounted by that pig? Rape, that's what I'd call it."

Julie, whose imagination was more limited, was very nice to Abraham Mosely. After all, girls got married. It was their destiny. All novels finished with marriage. To be sure, the betrothed in books were usually young and handsome, but occasionally bearded kings married young princesses and they lived happily, surrounded by many children. What really bothered her was the sensation or feeling called love. Certainly she liked listening to Mr. Mosely talk about England, factories, horses, its shops and castles, but it seemed different from what prompted the looks of ecstasy on the faces of the couples she'd seen pictured in novels. And when, after breakfast the morning following his arrival, Mr. Mosely had taken her for a walk in the park and pressed his thick wet lips to her neck, she didn't swoon with delight like the lady in *Quentin Durward*. She even had to suppress a shiver of disgust.

For, now that he was authorized to pursue his courtship, ardent Mosely was eaten with impatience. Only his good breeding and the South's puritan conventions kept him from initiating Julie into less innocent games than shuttlecock, which winded him, or backgammon, which gave him a headache. So he pressed Caroline to set the wedding date for as soon as possible, arguing that business required his return to England before the fifteenth of May.

So, Julie and Abraham's engagement was officially announced on March 28, 1852, almost ten years to the day after the Marquis de Damvilliers's death.

The colonel noted that few people seemed to share his indignation at the extreme youth of the fiancée. Even Adele Barrow, known for her ferocious virtue, didn't find the disparity in their ages worthy of comment. She simply stated that "the late-blooming lily on the crystal stem must have fire in her belly, just like her mother."

On the other hand, the Barthews were firmly in the colonel's camp, as were Mallibert and Imilie. Ed Barthew had been stunned when Dandridge told him the news of his goddaughter's impending marriage. To him, she was little more than a gentle imbecile. Like his wife, who had vivid memories of Mosely's slippery advances, he detected Caroline's conniving hand.

"She saw only the money and the social success," he said to Dandridge. "I tremble for Julie. Nobody seems to realize how immature she is about the facts of life."

"It's possible that Mosely, as an old bachelor who has finally decided to make the big plunge, will do everything to make her happy. It may not be such a bad move."

"Happy?" Mignette sighed. "What conception of happiness can the poor girl possibly have?"

Little by little, the objections to Caroline's high-handed methods subsided. The couple gave the impression of a perfect understanding. They took long buggy rides, visited neighboring families, and spent long hours in conversation. Caroline had cajoled her daughter into dressing more austerely in order to look a little older. Now she supervised the trousseau, commandeering every seamstress on the plantation to pick up her needle. Caroline and the couple made a trip to New Orleans to buy fabrics suitable to the English climate, and Mosely took the two ladies to hear "the Swedish Nightingale," Jenny Lind, whom Barnum was touring all over the United States. He had had to pay out a hundred and fifty dollars a ticket, which impressed Julie and thrilled her mother.

The ceremony uniting Julie de Damvilliers and Abraham Mosely was brief and relatively intimate. Julie, in a white lace dress, had been lightly made up by her mother to camouflage her pallor, but she did not, as Mignette Barthew had feared, look like a child pretending to be a bride. Julie smiled and looked the picture of the happy bride. Mosely, bright of eye, his potbelly well corseted inside his waistcoat, made a perfectly presentable groom. Félice, in an organdy dress with many-layered flounces, was maid of honor. When Félice took the arm of Major Templeton, who came in his midnight blue dress uniform with gold epaulets, Adele Barrow remarked: "After courting the mother in vain all these years, perhaps he'll have better luck with the daughter"—an observation that, for once, Barthew and Dandridge found themselves supporting.

Handsome Willy, his face tanned by the Mexican and California sun, was approaching forty and awaiting his promotion to lieutenant-colonel. He was still as enamored of Caroline as ever, though Félice was certainly very attractive. But on this occasion, he envied Colonel de Vigors not only because he was the lucky husband of the woman he had coveted all these years, but for a typically childish reason that summed up his character: The Legion of Honor that hung between the gold frogs of the colonel's resplendent uniform, given to him by the Emperor, was evidence that he had taken part in real wars.

Willy's brother Percy was also in attendance, with his wife and six children. Watching his children dance, Caroline thought bitterly of how the Templeton dynasty had continued uninterrupted. And when she looked at the man to whom she had once given herself on a foolish impulse, she felt a vague sadness.

When Dandridge asked her for a waltz—then called "the marquise" by some—she gratefully accepted.

"You see, I was right, Clarence. Julie looks happy, doesn't she?"

"Well, she doesn't look unhappy."

"You know me well enough to realize that I did it purely for her sake. No mother likes to see her daughter go off on a husband's arm." Then she added with a malicious glint, "I'm going to marry you off too one of these days! Unless I find a mistress worthy of you!"

"I already have what I need," Dandridge replied.

"Good Heavens. Who is it?"

"Bagatelle."

The dance was coming to an end. Caroline broke off the conversation with a pronounced squeeze of her partner's arm and they exchanged smiles whose meaning they alone knew. At that moment, an observer unacquainted with the two could have taken them for old lovers.

The bride and groom could hardly spend their first night at Bagatelle, so Caroline had made arrangements with the Templetons to let them use a pretty little guest house on the edge of their property, quite close to Bagatelle. In fact, Mrs. Templeton had often used it for her own amours.

When darkness fell, and while the guests were still dancing in the big candlelit drawing room, Julie went to look for her mother. She seemed tired and nervous.

"Mummy, Mr. Mosely wants to take me away now."

"All right then, go. Haven't you danced enough?"

"Oh yes, I have. But I'm so tired. It's been such a long day."

Caroline gave her daughter a kiss to signify that the moment of parting had come. But Julie didn't move.

"I'm a little frightened, Mummy. I'd rather sleep here another night."

"Don't be silly, my darling. You know that a wife is supposed to sleep with her husband. Nothing terrible will happen. Just don't catch cold, that's all."

"All right, Mummy. I'll go."

"Good girl. But go quietly," her mother added, not wishing the inebriated guests to make a scene around the departing carriage.

Reluctantly, Julie went to meet her husband, who was waiting for her near the kitchen door. He also wished to avoid the off-color jokes that the departure of a newly wedded couple always provoked. He took Julie's hand and led her through the kitchen to the back door used only by the servants. Anna was sitting stiffly on a stool trying not to wrinkle her starched apron, a lace cloth wound around her head. As she watched the furtive couple pass, she muttered, "Go with God, child," having a good idea of the trial her little mistress was about to undergo.

With Mosely dragging her on, Julie turned to Anna and threw her the look of a chained animal. The depth of misery it conveyed made Anna wince. "Poor little soul," she sighed as she heard the carriage drive off.

The last guests had long since left Bagatelle and the servants had restored a semblance of order to the house while picking at the remains of the buffet, when Clarence's dogs started a furious barking. He got up without lighting a lamp, quickly put on the trousers and frock coat he had taken off only two hours before and went out onto the walkway. Shivering with cold, he tried to peer into the darkness. The big house was silent. No one there seemed disturbed by the barking. To be sure, his dogs were known to go into a frenzy over a family of armadillos or a venturesome muskrat crossing the park.

Sensitive to their responses, Dandridge knew they weren't barking out of anger but rather out of fear or confusion. He lit an oil lamp and, protecting the flame with his hand, walked toward the front of the house. Mic and Mac ran toward him, still yapping, but their heads turned toward the park. Having gotten his attention, they spun around and headed back to the alley of oaks. Clarence loped after them trying to quiet them. Then, in the halo of the lamp, he saw what had excited the dogs. A white shape lay spread out at the base of a tree. "Somebody's forgotten a shawl," Clarence said to himself. "Those idiot dogs." As he started to pick up what he thought was cloth, he saw that it was a body in a white lace dress. Wondering what guest could have come to this pass, he shook the sleeping figure's shoulder. The gesture only made the body rock back and forth. Bringing the lamp closer, he saw that it was Julie. The dogs had calmed down. With infinite care, Clarence righted the body. It was then that he realized from the gaping mouth and large staring eyes that she was dead.

For a moment, he stood motionless. Then, with the foolish hope that she had only fainted, he felt for her heart. There was no beat. As he stood up, he heard the sound of footsteps coming down the alley. It was Bobo, a hatchet in his hand, the whites of his eyes huge in the lamplight.

"Oh, it's you, Mister Dandridge. When. I see the light, I thought it was robbers."

"Look, Bobo," Clarence said, lowering the lamp.

"It's Miss Julie, sir. Is she sick?"

"Go wake up your masters, Bobo, then harness the buggy and go find Dr. Murphy. And get a move on."

While the groom was banging on the front door of the house, Clarence rearranged Julie's dress and, after a second's hesitation, decided it was wiser not to wait for Caroline's arrival and closed her eyes.

When the lights of the house came on, Dandridge walked toward the gallery and climbed the stairs with a heavy tread. On the doorsill, he ran into Anna, enveloped in a blanket, come to find out what was amiss. He was trying to explain when Caroline appeared, followed by the colonel, both in their dressing gowns. When she saw the manager's face, she didn't dare speak, not knowing what to expect but suspecting the worst.

"Julie . . . is down there," was all Dandridge could bring himself to say. He pointed toward the oaks.

Caroline flew down the steps, followed by Anna. Dandridge detained the colonel as he was preparing to follow the women.

"She's dead. I've sent for Dr. Murphy, but I'm afraid there's nothing he can do."

Caroline bent over her daughter's body, then stood up, her eyes wide with horror, her jaw trembling. When her husband joined her, she had yet to say a word. In the faint light of the oil lamp, she looked like a madwoman, her chin twitching with a convulsive tic. Julie lay inert, her arms close to her body, her palms turned up as if offering herself to the spirits of the night, the resigned expression of the martyrs on her face.

Anna knelt beside her, sobbing, "Miss Julie, Miss Julie . . . she's all cold, ma'm, she's cold all over."

The colonel led his silent wife back to the house. Clarence gave Anna the lamp and gathered up Julie, her long train brushing the ground. The house servants had assembled on the gallery and made way for the manager and his burden. Brent, old James's replacement as butler, crossed himself as the two went by.

Julie was laid out on her bed and that is where Murphy found her when he arrived an hour later, his kit in his hand. Caroline was sitting at the foot of the bed in a stupor, the colonel standing helplessly by the door.

"Her heart gave out," he said laconically to Dandridge as they were leaving the room. Then, he added in a voice loud enough for everyone to hear, "That girl wasn't made for marriage. It's exactly as if she'd been murdered."

"Be quiet, Murphy!" the colonel shot back. "Caroline might hear you!"

"So what? Are you afraid of the truth?"

This reference to the marriage reminded the colonel that Julie had had a husband.

"Where is Mosely? Has anybody seen him?" Then, nervously, "I'm going to go find him."

"Leave it to me," said Dandridge. "You stay with Caroline. She needs you."

The colonel gave in. Murphy picked up his kit and left with Dandridge. The night was exceptionally cold, the pale dawn picking out the hoarfrost covering the fields and the horses' breath coming out in large white puffs.

"I'm going with you," Murphy said to Dandridge. "That fat bastard might try to attack you when he learns what happened."

"He doesn't seem to be overly worried about his wife. Wouldn't you think he would have noticed she was gone?"

"I'll bet you that pig is fast asleep," Murphy said between his teeth.

"Because you think she ran away after . . ."

"I don't think anything. I know. I examined the child. She didn't die a virgin, my friend."

Dandridge felt a spasm of revulsion. He had avoided thinking about the bestial side of this marriage. Now it hit him with full force. He snapped his whip and galloped toward the Templetons' guest house.

As the doctor predicted, Abraham Mosely was sound asleep. His visitors had to wait five minutes before he opened the door. On waking up, he had taken in the fact of Julie's absence.

"What's going on? Where is my wife? I don't understand."

In the wan light of early morning, the dashing broker was not a handsome sight. With his flowered silk dressing gown and embroidered slippers and the sparse dyed hair falling over his ears, he looked like an obese satyr.

"Julie is at Bagatelle, Mosely," Dandridge said.

"Why so early? It's barely daylight!"

"She's dead," said Murphy, who had no intention of protecting Mosely's feelings.

"Dead. It can't be. Why, it's impossible. Why do you say such a thing?"

"Because it's true," Clarence said, taking over. "She ran away while you were asleep. She ran all the way to Bagatelle but collapsed before she could reach the house."

Under the scrutiny of his two visitors, Abraham Mosely suddenly crumpled like a punctured balloon. The color drained from his face; he slumped into a chair and broke into sobs. The folds of his dressing gown parted, exposing a pair of puny calves etched with varicose veins. Dandridge looked away.

"You would do well to go over there right now," Murphy said icily.

"Of course I'll go, in a minute, but I'd rather not see her . . . you understand . . . I want to keep my beautiful memories. She was so pretty, so good, and . . . everything . . . went very well. Why did she go like that, in the middle of the night?"

"Because you disgusted her," Murphy spat out. He nodded to Dandridge and the two men went out, leaving the bewildered widower weeping, his face buried in his chubby hands.

Abraham Mosely was never seen at Bagatelle again. A few hours after receiving the news of Julie's death, he had sent a letter to Colonel de Vigors expressing his despair, his grief, but no remorse. He had left forever "this country where he was about to find happiness." While the colonel was reading the note, Mosely was already on the small steamer he had hired to rush him to New Orleans as if he feared pursuit.

"What a cad!" said the colonel.

"Mosely had a horror of death," Caroline put in, as if to excuse the runaway broker.

"I hope it catches up with him, and soon," the colonel exploded.

Julie's sudden and shocking death plunged Bagatelle into a stupor once again. When Caroline finally took in the scope of the tragedy, she spent long hours prostrate by her daughter's bed. She too had seen the blood smeared between the girl's thighs while Dr. Murphy was examining the body. The sight of it stirred her deepest emotions. So love could be something other than the exuberance of the flesh, the celebration of naked bodies she relished so keenly. Her first lover had spared her the male's selfish brutality; he had initiated her with great tenderness. But on later occasions, she had had to suffer, and still later, she had come to desire her partner's sometimes unsparing impetuosity.

Poor Julie was clearly not prepared for the violence of male desire. In delivering her innocent daughter into Mosely's hands, Caroline had trusted in the tact and sensibility of this man of refined tastes and courteous bearing. His sudden passion for Julie, his many attentions during their brief engagement, his particular attachment for a girl whose delicate nature he well knew should have made him a patient and restrained lover. Instead, he had treated Julie like a soldier's whore without a thought for what was happening to her. Perhaps her heart hadn't given out until she reached the oaks, but wasn't the rape she had endured in the Templetons' guest house enough to kill her? To the unbearable grief of losing a third child, Caroline now had to add the secret guilt of being—she tried to confine it to "seeming"—responsible for her daughter's death. For the first time in her life, she knew the shame of the criminal at the sight of what he has wrought. Her ears throbbed with the accusations her husband would have leveled at her if he'd been less smitten. Dandridge's reserve confirmed the reaction she read in the servants' faces, in Anna's grief, in Murphy's pitiless candor.

Face to face with the dead girl, she gradually took hold of herself. She would face the gossips with her old arrogance and close her mind to the insinuations of her conscience. No one would be permitted to say, let alone think, that Julie had died through her mother's fault. By the time she joined the silent company in the drawing room, she was once again mistress of herself, her nerves under control and ready to take command.

"I don't want any ceremony. We will bury Julie here, not

in the cemetery. At the foot of the oak where Clarence found her and in her wedding dress."

The colonel nodded in agreement. Dandridge gave her that frozen, paralyzing look she detested. "He knows what I'm going through," she said to herself.

Early the next morning, a grave was dug as ordered, at the foot of the first oak on the right side of the alley. The narrow coffin was lowered between two large roots, the Jesuit father who had been Julie's tutor officiating. No Barthews, Templetons or Barrows were invited and no servant was allowed to leave the house during the burial. Clarence gave his arm to Félice, the last of the Damvilliers. Death, Bagatelle's insatiable and methodical visitor, seemed bent on annihilating this family.

At the house, young Charles pulled aside the curtains in the room where he had been left in Brent's care and watched the two borrowed slaves raking the soil over the grave.

"Julie is now an angel," Brent said with a sigh.

"But you can't see angels," Charles said, "and I want to see Julie."

"Sometimes you see them at night, Master Charles, when they come back to their houses."

Later on, at the foot of the oak now overgrown with grass, the colonel and his wife placed a stone chiseled into the shape of an open book. On it was engraved: "Julie de Damvilliers (1837–1852)" and a phrase picked out by Dandridge: "Everyone owes me this shade."

When the news of Julie's death reached the parish, people began to talk about the evil spell on Bagatelle. In the four deaths—three children in less than ten years—the less superstitious saw a divine malice directed at one of Louisiana's oldest families. Search as they would, nothing in the Marquis's past revealed anything that justified or even explained this relentless obsession on destiny's part. Nobody dared say it, but many people thought that Bagatelle's bad luck had come with the arrival of Caroline Trégan. Perhaps it would be wise to avoid the woman in the future, especially since the slaves reported that after Julie's burial, a white shadow had been seen walking under the oaks. Others maintained they heard moans, still others said that the dogs circled the tree under which Miss Julie was buried and often howled at the turn of midnight.

Without actually believing these stories, Colonel de Vigors began to feel uncomfortable in the big silent house. Also, Caroline's health worried him. After seeming to recover, she had taken to displaying an exaggerated and smiling resignation that wasn't like her. Her excessive sweetness, abnormal graciousness, and the lapses in the middle of conversations made him think of a woman under the effects of a soporific or perhaps a spell that drained her of her will. She wouldn't let Félice or Charles out of her sight, eyeing them intently and shaking her head as if she were looking for their time to come.

"We must leave Bagatelle for a while, even if it looks like flight," the colonel announced one day.

Eight days later, without having seen a soul, Colonel and Mrs. de Vigors, Félice, Charles, Brent and Rosa embarked for Europe. As Dandridge helped her into the big landau, Caroline said, "We have no idea when we'll be back. You do whatever you think best. The living and the dead entrust Bagatelle to you."

Clarence bowed without speaking, kissed her hand, shook the colonel's, hugged Félice and Charles, then signaled Bobo to set off. When the carriage, preceded by a wagon piled high with luggage, turned down the river road, Caroline looked back. Under the long tunnel of oaks, the Spanish moss waving a bleak farewell, Dandridge stood as motionless and rigid as a sentinel. Turning on his heel, he walked briskly back to the house. First he warmed his hands over the drawing-room fire, then, one by one, he examined the portraits of the children. "I'm nothing but the guardian of a cemetery," he muttered to himself.

However, the plantation's work had to go on. The cotton

was over a foot high; it was time to begin cultivating. Dandridge had his horse saddled and set forth to inspect the fields. The soil looked dry, hard, unyielding, like a sleeping person who refuses to wake up. But the rains finally came and the earth awakened. He made a trip to Saint-Francisville, where Mallibert had begun to cultivate the colonel's land and was always in need of advice. Dandridge had given him the cotton seed to sow on the newly cleared earth. He had had a good harvest and was now an enthusiastic planter. Clarence's only objection was that Mallibert treated his slaves as if they were a battalion of infantry. The former orderly was categorical: "You follow the same methods whether you're turning out good soldiers or good laborers. Discipline is what's called for, discipline and coordination."

Thus, in a few years, the former intransigent republican had become a typical Southern slave owner. The notion of liberty, of which he proclaimed himself a passionate supporter, did not apply to slaves, who were of no use to society beyond the rigid boundaries of the plantation.

Meanwhile, the number of freed blacks in Louisiana had grown to twenty thousand. Some families enjoyed well-earned reputations. The men had become carpenters and masons and earned good money. The more intelligent or gifted went into business and lived in a degree of comfort the rednecks and Cajuns might well envy. Still, although accepted in business, they couldn't penetrate white society. And they held themselves aloof from the slaves they had once been, viewing them with even more contempt than did the whites.

But in the country, slavery was still the rule. Louisiana had a slave population of 250,000 working 1,200,000 acres of land. And many of the blacks on the plantations had some of the same blood as the families that owned them. Even though neither would admit it, the whites out of shame and the blacks out of fear, there was a certain complicity between them which the former expressed in indulgence and the latter in devotion.

People who knew the North, like Willy Templeton, explained that in the antislavery states, the freed blacks were at the bottom of the social ladder whereas the freed blacks in the South were on the second rung. With the privileged white class above them, these blacks consoled themselves for their inferiority by comparing it to the "ignominy of slavery."

All these distinctions came to a head with the publication of *Uncle Tom's Cabin* which, thanks to abolitionist efforts, was widely distributed in the South. Handed from family to family, it raised a furor: Who did she think she was, this author in skirts, a Puritan born of a Congregational minister who was making a fortune off the planters' backs! Dandridge discussed the book with Barthew and Murphy and they all agreed that it would do more for the abolitionist cause than all the politicians and philosophers put together. These men touched only a limited and already convinced public; Harriet Beecher Stowe reached into people's homes and stirred their deepest feelings.

Much more affecting to Dandridge was Thoreau's *Walden*, where he found so many of his own convictions confirmed, and the author's belief that trees and men shared the same attributes: If prevented from living according to their natures, they died. The Sage of Concord also put his finger on what had unconsciously brought Caroline and Dandridge together —the desire "to suck life to the marrow"—although they had naturally taken different paths to reach their goals. She had chosen ambition, power, social success and the money that can buy everything; he, an almost Spartan existence "to bypass everything that wasn't life"—in other words, the daily and superficial. Thoreau had written: "I went to the woods because I wished to live deliberately, to front only the essential facts of life, and see if I could learn what it had to teach, and not, when I came to die, discover that I had not lived."

Since he'd been living alone at Bagatelle—in a degree of comfort the sylvan philosopher would surely have condemned —Dandridge had given this much thought. He recalled something Adrien de Damvilliers had once told him: "The soil, Clarence, nothing but the soil. Everything comes from it and everything returns to it. A man can find happiness only in the middle of his field, no matter how small."

In the Paris world that Colonel and Mrs. de Vigors frequented, few cared a fig for Mrs. Stowe or Mr. Thoreau. But when they learned that the pretty lady who rarely smiled and her gregarious husband actually owned slaves, they found this fact exciting and exotic. Caroline's friends liked to borrow Brent for their parties. To be served by this stylish black, who could be whipped by his mistress if she so desired, enraptured the ladies.

The Vigors were gratified to find Paris in the full bloom of prosperity. After the great scare of 1848, the rich were no longer afraid to show off their wealth. Those who had feared disorder in the streets—always bad news for commerce—saw the specter of vandalism and violence recede. As it turned out, the common herd was equally eager for peace and order.

As old age caught up with her, Mme. Drouin consorted more often with bankers than with hungry poets. Early in their visit, she gave Colonel de Vigors pointers on the best way to infiltrate Paris society and high finance.

While Mrs. de Vigors cultivated old friends and new admirers, her husband found his way back to the Jockey Club. Between the club, restaurants, cafés, theaters, not to mention financiers, journalists, writers and officers back from Algeria —and all the places where the best and most expensive call girls were to be found—Colonel de Vigors, husband and father, rediscovered his old bachelor pleasures. It even happened that he sometimes returned to the Rue de Luxembourg quite late, having followed some tart to her malodorous garret in Belleville. As he grew older, the hussar craved what passed for young flesh. Caroline looked the other way, for she didn't lack for admirers ready to comfort her should the need arise.

Young Charles was sent to board with the Jesuit Fathers and Félice enjoyed the role of only daughter, going from ball to ball and spending a small fortune at the dressmaker's. A banker's son soon won Caroline's permission to act as her daughter's official escort and embarked on a methodical and circumspect courtship. A graduate of the École Polytechnique, his emotions were subjected to the logic of the exact sciences. Félice, outwardly frivolous but basically a realist in the manner of the Damvilliers, took a fancy to his declarations.

"You talk of love as if it were a form of geometry," she said to her admirer one day.

"If love were geometry, it would be a vicious circle," replied the young man, who wasn't altogether lacking in wit.

While Dandridge, on the banks of the Mississippi, was working to furnish the income necessary to the family on the banks of the Seine, time sped by at a prodigious pace.

"When do you expect your Parisians to return?" Willy Templeton asked him one summer evening in 1854.

"I receive a monthly letter from either the colonel or Caroline, but neither speaks of returning. In his last note, Mr. de Vigors mentioned his connections at the Tuileries and that the emperor had invited them to Compiègne. Félice is as good as engaged to the son of a big banker and Dubufe is painting a larger-than-life portrait of our Caroline. That's all the forgotten man of Bagatelle can report, Willy."

Clarence smiled wryly as he said these words, for he did wonder if Caroline had any real desire to come back to Louisiana.

Caroline was in fact entirely caught up in the whirl of the capital's social life. Perhaps, Clarence speculated, her several brushes with death made her avid for distraction, flattery, the giddy world. But that wasn't where the marrow of life was to be found. Had she given up trying to look beyond the appearance of happiness—was she now satisfied with its outward signs? Yet Clarence never doubted that she would return, like the prodigal child, knowing that the true values and the resolution of her destiny lay on the banks of the Mississippi and nowhere else.

The Vigors finally returned, in the spring of 1855. Dandridge went to meet them in New Orleans and recognized Caroline's familiar silhouette from afar. The colonel, with his white moustache, cane and lumbering gait, looked like an old man. Caroline flung herself in Clarence's arms. He drank in her perfume, noticed the few gray hairs visible under her hat, the few fine lines at the corner of the eyes and mouth.

"We married Félice off before taking the boat. Goodness, but it's nice to be back."

The colonel, who admitted to a gouty foot, was equally cheerful. He boasted that Charles, about to be eleven, was carrying off all the top honors in his studies. "So the children are safe from the curse of Bagatelle," Dandridge said to himself.

While they sailed up the Mississippi on the *Eclipse*, Mr. de Vigors exchanged the news of the day with the other planters in the smoking lounge. Caroline sought out Clarence and found him, as usual, leaning against the railing.

"We were gone a long time, Clarence. I hope you don't hold it against me."

"Why should I, Caroline? You had some bad times to get over."

"When I think that I've spent a quarter century going up and down this river with you. What was I then? A pretentious girl who thought she had the world by the ear."

"And you did."

"Are you sure, Clarence? Or was I the victim of a great illusion that made me think I could always make the decisions?"

"You can't order death around, if that's what you mean."

"Nor life. We're all dogs on leashes. We run freely until the leash is taut and stops us dead in our tracks. Our leashes are not all the same length, of course, but there always comes a time when ours holds us in check."

"So we're back where the leash is attached to the collar. Is that it?"

"Yes, Clarence, we're backing up a little, but in order to make a fresh leap."

"Which will be cut off, like all the others?"

"Perhaps someday the leash will break," Caroline said.

"What then?"

"Then we'll run free . . . to the very end of the road."

"But we know what awaits us there, Caroline."

"Yes, but think of what can happen along the way!"

They parted, and Dandridge headed for the smoking lounge, thinking: "She is still capable of surprising me."

Not long after his return, Charles de Vigors learned that he had been promoted to general, the happy result of his intimacy with the emperor and the friendship of certain influential people in the court. Of course the rank was purely honorific, being paired with the title of "Counselor-Extraordinary to the Imperial Chief of Staff"—none of which meant a thing. "One day we may need to call on your experience," Napoleon III had said to him as he changed the rosette of an officer in the Legion of Honor to the badge of "commander." A great ball was given in New Orleans to celebrate the event, and the French ambassador came all the way from Washington.

At the same time, in distant Ontario, a man by the undistinguished name of John Brown was holding secret meetings with twelve white abolitionists and thirty-four blacks during which he delineated his plan for a general insurrection of all slaves. Brown used as pretext a recent decision of the Supreme Court that showed conclusively that blacks were deprived of legal protection and so he proposed a revision of the Constitution, which the abolitionists were quick to adopt.

A few weeks later, during his campaign for senator from Illinois, Abraham Lincoln, a former Whig now turned Republican, took sharp issue with the "peculiar institution" which up to that time he had tolerated. When the Democrat, Stephen Douglas, a man of known proslavery sympathies, won the election, the South gave a sigh of relief. But not for long. Early that fall, Brown suddenly turned up at Harpers Ferry in Virginia, which happened to have a federal arsenal. With eighteen men, among them five blacks and his own two sons, they seized the arsenal, killing four men and taking several hostages, one of them Colonel Lewis Washington, a grandnephew of the first President.

Bagatelle learned of the incident through Willy Templeton, who had been dispatched to the scene of John Brown's execution with a troop of cavalry. Charles de Vigors invited a group of planters and their wives to dinner at Bagatelle to hear the lieutenant-colonel's stirring tale. When he had finished, his host remarked, "I wonder if John Brown isn't more dangerous dead than alive."

Caroline put in: "Willy, what will come of all this hatred Brown has provoked?"

"I don't think anything serious," Willy replied. "Everybody will calm down. Naturally, the Virginians are very angry that he was tried in a federal court, for they wanted to get their hands on him. Now they want to break off all commercial relations with the North. They say they're going to build their own factories, their own railroads, start their own shipping companies and deal directly with Europe, buying nothing from the North. They also talk of starving the North and setting up a government for the South. Boys and old men want to be soldiers and the women have sworn they'll wear sackcloth rather than cloth manufactured in the North."

Willy looked around at his audience and sensed they'd heard enough for one evening. With a debonair smile, he said, "I'm sure that our Southern ladies would now like to dance. I appreciate the interest and courtesy you've shown my speech and I now release you."

The guests moved into the big drawing room, the musicians took their places and the champagne corks began to pop.

Clarence held himself aloof, as usual. Watching all this inane happiness and superficial splendor, he instinctively sensed that it was fatal. But like a spectator at an engrossing play, he didn't want the curtain to come down and force everybody back to cruel reality.

When Caroline came and asked him to dance, he gave a small bow and took her arm.

"What a magnificent couple," Adele Barrow commented

to her neighbor. "There's no better dancer in the parish than Clarence Dandridge."

And that night, he was dancing well. Twirling with Caroline to the sound of her swishing skirt, his face wore the ironic smile which she knew masked his reserve. They moved in perfect rhythm as if waltzing was the natural movement of their bodies. For the first time, Clarence felt the memory of desire, and Caroline knew that this man was more important to her than any of the men she had loved. The younger couples began to retreat to the sides, leaving the center of the dance floor to Clarence and Caroline.

When the dance came to an end, Clarence made a deep bow to his partner and the guests broke into applause. As he leaned down, Caroline took in the silver-streaked hair, the slender neck and the broad shoulders inside the well-cut coat and, as if they were a couple taking a curtain call, she gave him her hand to kiss. He touched it lightly with his lips, straightened up and escorted her back to the ladies' corner. As they were parting, Caroline said under her breath:

"Clarence, I'm afraid . . . of tomorrow."

"The leash is taut, Caroline."

"What do you think is going to happen?"

"Everything and nothing. The end of splendor."

When Abraham Lincoln was elected President on November 6, 1860, the Southern planters feared that this moderate politician whose real intentions were unknown and who, as head of a minority party, would have his difficulties with Congress, was certain to be manipulated by the abolitionists.

"We committed a tactical mistake," Clement Barrow said the day after the election. "Had we voted for Stephen Douglas, admittedly a Northerner but willing to go along with the 'peculiar institution,' he would have been the candidate of all Democrats and would be President today. By choosing an intransigent proslavery man like Breckenridge of Kentucky, we took the shadow for the substance. The die is cast; from now on the North is in command."

While the South was waiting for the other shoe to drop, General de Vigors was packing his bags. He had just received by Pony Express a confidential dispatch from Napoleon III, via the French ambassador in Washington, in which the emperor asked—"if he had the appetite and desire to serve"—to go to Vera Cruz to assess the mood of the population and to make contact with the enemies of Juárez, who had just reconquered Mexico. Mr. de Vigors liked the idea of being a secret agent and Mallibert was eager to be on the move again. Using as his cover that he was "a planter on a business trip," the newly minted general nevertheless packed a uniform and a pair of Colt revolvers. Always the gallant husband, he asked Caroline's permission to leave and she gave it with the casual air of a mother allowing her child to play next door.

Before his departure, Vigors sought out Dandridge to explain—and justify—the reasons for his departure.

"Fateful events are about to take place in the South in which I neither can nor wish to take part. Some may think my leaving Bagatelle at such a time is an act of cowardice, or at least indifference. But you and Caroline know that isn't the case. What I fear is that men of goodwill are going to have to choose sides. And I cannot make up my mind. I despise slavery from the bottom of my heart, but I would be betraying the country that gave me such a warm welcome and the wife I love if I exposed my true feelings. I therefore want to avoid having to choose. So I take the middle road which, because I am still French, is open to me. But believe me, Dandridge, I'm deeply troubled and unhappy."

"I understand, Charles," Clarence said. "For me, the choice is clear only in appearance. At this particular moment, my feelings lead me to think you're wrong. But my conception of justice for the long term, of justice beyond present circumstances, makes me think you're right. I may have to fight the Yankees, but with my conscience as well. And that may be one of the more difficult aspects of the conflict."

The general had no sooner left than the Louisiana legislature voted half a million dollars to buy arms for its regular militia and the volunteer corps it had just authorized. There was also an announcement that early in the new year, Louisiana voters would be asked to elect delegates to a convention which would decide what measures to take to protect the state from the dangers incurred by Lincoln's election.

A week before, South Carolina had taken the initiative and seceded from the Union. All hopes for reconciliation between North and South were gone. At its convention, one hundred thirteen Louisiana delegates voted for immediate secession with seventeen against. It had thus followed the example of Mississippi, Florida, Alabama and Georgia, which had all seceded during the preceding three weeks. Delaware, although a slave state, voted to stay in the Union, and Texas, against Sam Houston's better judgment, joined the secessionist states three days later.

The Confederacy was born on February 4, 1861. It brought together the seven secessionist states and elected Jefferson Davis, the Mississippi Congressman, president. On adding up the population it represented, the Confederacy found that it numbered 2,623,147 whites and 2,350,607 slaves. But the North's twenty million gave it a very large edge in manpower.

When Lincoln was inducted on March 4, a French journalist describing the inaugural parade filed the following story: "The Republican Party, now triumphant thanks to the election of the 'rail-splitter,' decorated a float reminiscent of our own first revolution. On the float, pulled by four white horses bedizened with gold trappings, banners and trophies, stood two fifteen-year-old girls holding each other by the hand. One, wearing a blue tunic covered with fur, symbolized the North; the other, wearing a white tunic and reclining on a bed of flowers, represented the South. Thirty-four ten-year-old girls —the thirty-four states of the Union—each carried her state's flag."

It was as if Washington were trying to pretend that national unity was still alive, as if by putting on blinders it could exorcise the danger of civil war. In his address, Lincoln specifically addressed himself to the South when he said: "In your hands, my dissatisfied fellow-countrymen, and not in mine, is the momentous issue of civil war. The government will not assail you. You can have no conflict without being yourselves the aggressors."

Despite his suggestion that the responsibility for what might come to pass lay in Southern hands, Lincoln made two moves three weeks later that the South considered flagrantly hostile. He sent troops to Fort Sumter in South Carolina to support Major Anderson, and an expedition to Pensacola to protect Fort Pickens from possible Southern aggression. When Jefferson Davis dispatched General Beauregard to Fort Sumter with four thousand men and demanded that Anderson evacuate the citadel and Anderson refused, the Southerners opened fire. That first shot by one of Beauregard's militiamen was to have the gravest consequences for the destiny of the Union. Anderson, with his eighty-five officers and forty-three laborers, resisted for thirty-eight hours, but when his powder kegs exploded, he had to give in. As Anderson surrendered his sword to Beauregard, the latter said he couldn't bring himself to disarm such a brave officer. Perhaps the timid goddess of peace was trying to give a final signal, for despite all the cannonades and rifle fire, not a drop of blood was shed. This miracle went unnoticed and from that moment on, violence had free rein.

In quick succession, Arkansas, North Carolina, Virginia and Tennessee joined the Confederacy, and the federal government countered by calling up 75,000 militiamen. The South immediately sent six thousand men marching toward Washington, which was separated from the South only by the Potomac River. When a Massachusetts regiment rushing to the scene was stoned by the citizens of Baltimore, it opened fire. There was no turning back now. The war was on.

Lieutenant-Colonel Willy Templeton, like most Southern officers in the federal army, resigned his commission. Before offering himself to General Beauregard, he ordered a new uniform, and although his tunic had changed from blue to gray, he still retained the two silver maple leaves on his collar.

Willy was convinced the war would be over soon.

"We'll give those Northerners a good lesson, teach them to respect our borders, then we'll be back."

Clarence was less sanguine. To be sure, the South could boast the finest West Pointers, the best cavalry, the most enthusiastic volunteers, but the factories and the munitions makers were in the North, and if the Federalists managed to blockade the Southern ports, how would the South be supplied?

By May 27, six Union warships had taken up positions at the mouth of the Mississippi and forced all foreign ships to turn back. For all that the Confederate government tried to encourage Southern shipowners and ships' captains to play pirate, it couldn't prevent New Orleans from feeling the effects of the blockade.

Meanwhile, the sons of the cotton nobility were rushing off to join the Confederate cavalry, taking with them their best horses and assembling all their own equipment. In the main, these young men were not only excellent horsemen, but knew how to use a hunting rifle as well as a sword. To the applause of the girls and the prodding of their own mothers, they went off to war as if to a great ball they didn't want to miss. Many also took their black valets, now promoted to orderlies, in order to be spared the soldier's more irksome tasks.

"Dandridge, aren't you tempted to go with me and shoot a few Yankees the way we used to shoot deer?" Willy asked as he was about to leave.

"What would happen to the plantation without Clarence?" Caroline asked before Clarence could reply.

"True," Willy observed, "and who would look after you?"

Clarence thought he caught a hint of malice in Willy's tone, but said nothing.

The first real battle took place at Bull Run in Virginia. It was a brilliant victory for the South and augured well for the future. Lincoln's response was to replace the defeated general, McDowell, with McClellan and to authorize the recruitment of half a million volunteers. In August and October, the North suffered two additional reverses, and the government set up a federal committee to inquire into the passivity of the Union armies and their too-numerous defeats.

The South was naturally ecstatic. If Beauregard's soldiers needed equipment, schooners from Cuba, Europe and the Antilles forced the blockade and unloaded at Bayou Vista. But because the blockade was still a serious hindrance to New Orleans commerce, an expedition was launched on the night of October 11 against the Union ships which, owing to bad weather, had had to anchor outside the sandbar at the mouth of the river. As night fell, a strange armada put out to sea: eight fireships, preceded by vessels armed for the occasion with cannons borrowed from various forts, and in the middle, a curious ship that resembled a tortoise. It had a single large chimney that stuck straight up out of its iron dome like a tree, and it could make thirteen knots an hour. Christened the *Manassas* after one of the South's recent victories, this carcass of a former tugboat had been completely sheathed with metal, including an iron beak. Under this carapace, men and machines were fully protected. The Union ships, well armed with cannons, watched the flotilla advance without undue anxiety. But as it drew nearer, their confidence evaporated. The engagement was brief and confused but the South was the victor.

As the Northern frigates tried to flee, the *Manassas* rammed the *Preble* and sank it after opening a gash twenty feet long on its flank. A shell hit a troop ship and it too went down. What federal ships remained chose to withdraw. This was the first time in naval history that an ironclad ship had been used. The *Manassas*'s brave sailors were welcomed in New Orleans as if they were the heroes of Trafalgar. The Confederate government immediately ordered two more ironclads like the *Manassas*. Meanwhile, Jefferson Davis floated a loan of $100,000, organized an army of 400,000 men and levied a tax of fifty cents on every hundred dollars' worth of property, houses, slaves, supplies, livestock, jewelry, silver, etc.

It was at about this time that Willy Templeton was sent to

New Orleans to speed up the manufacture of munitions. The thirteen hundred rifles and one thousand carbines recently shipped from England—since the start of the blockade, five hundred and ten ships had gotten through—were not nearly enough for the struggling army. On a visit to Bagatelle he complained that the three factories in New Orleans weren't capable of producing weapons of sufficient quality.

"To be sure, rudimentary rifles are good enough for young recruits, but if we had more Minié cannons and Infield carbines, we could certainly use them. I sometimes wonder if our suppliers in Paris and London aren't spending all their time at balls."

Clarence smiled. Wasn't this what the front lines always said of those in the rear, that they weren't furnishing them with the means to fight? This complaint was as old as war. William the Conqueror's archers must have complained that they weren't getting enough arrows.

Caroline had been following the conversation with half an ear. Now she suddenly grew very interested.

"About these weapons, Willy. You must have them. I will see that you get them."

Dandridge and Templeton looked at each other with bewilderment.

"How will you do that, Caroline?" Willy asked.

"I'll simply go to Paris and London and buy rifles, cannon. I don't know. Whatever you say you need. Write me up a list, and it's as good as done!"

"But you'd be a fool to try to get through the blockade," Willy said. "The Federalists are capable of anything . . ."

"I'm married to a French general, who happens to be serving his country in Mexico at the moment, I have a son in Paris, we have business affairs there. Who can stop me from going?"

Dandridge knew when Caroline had made up her mind. Nothing on earth could stop her now.

"But it would be very dangerous," Willy insisted.

"What if I want to fight for the South too?"

"Clarence could go in your stead, Caroline."

"No, his place is here. I can buy arms the same way I buy petticoats, but I can't supervise four hundred slaves and make the cotton grow. I've said my piece."

Lieutenant-Colonel Templeton spent three hours making out a list of weapons and ammunition. As he gave it to Caroline, he said, "Even if you can only get a quarter, it would be a big help."

After Willy had gone, Clarence returned to the subject. "Are you sure this makes sense, Caroline?"

"Of course. War has its reasons. In any case, it makes as much sense as the trip you're plotting with Barthew."

"So you know about it?"

"Yes, Mignette told me."

"But there's nothing dangerous in what we're doing. Load our bales of cotton on a steamer, go down the river, transfer them to wagons I've already hired and transport them to Bayou Vista. That's hardly a challenging exploit. And it will make us a tidy sum of money."

"Who is buying the cotton?"

"A shipowner from Rouen, a friend of the Mertaux's," Clarence replied. "The best blockade runner of them all, according to them."

"Why didn't you tell me about this?"

"Because I thought it was part of the manager's responsibility, not the mistress's."

"I could go with the cotton," Caroline said. "When do you expect to ship it?"

"In a week. But I'm afraid the wagon ride from Oak Alley to Bayou Vista won't be very comfortable. Much of it is across swamps."

"I'm going with you, Clarence. It's much the best solution."

That is how, a week later, a steamboat loaded with five hundred bales of cotton floated down the Mississippi. Two and a half miles from a village called Vacherie, near Oak Alley, the boat was tied up to the bank. The slaves of the nearby plantation had been mobilized to transfer the cotton onto the wagons, which Dandridge and Barthew had assembled not without effort.

As the master of Oak Alley welcomed Caroline and her manager and invited them to spend the night, he commented on the fact that there wasn't a wagon left in the whole parish.

"Without Edward Barthew and his connections," Dandridge said, "we would never have been able to get up such a convoy. But if everything goes well, we'll have proved that we can ship our cotton despite the Yankee blockade."

The next morning at dawn, the long line of eighty wagons started off through a forest of cypress. Clarence and two overseers from Oak Alley led the convoy, with Caroline immediately behind in a gig loaned by the master of Oak Alley. From time to time the Bagatelle slaves had to use shovels and lengths of board to free the wagons from the deep muddy ruts, but even so, they were able to reach Bayou Vista by nightfall. The captain of the *Volontaire*, a wide-beamed brig, was astonished to find that a lady of quality had been added to the expected load of cotton. Because he was a Frenchman, and therefore gallant, he straightway offered her his cabin.

As the South became aware of its inferiority in food supplies, textile and metallurgic factories and its troops' lack of discipline—a brave lot but not trained for mass maneuvers—they realized that a quick end to the war was essential. The North had had reverses to be sure, but thanks to its vast resources in manpower and its armaments potential, it was clearly capable of sustaining a long-drawn-out resistance.

The blockade was taking its toll, not only in Louisiana but in the other Confederate states, where prices were rising alarmingly. To make up for its deficiencies, the South organized a conscription, built factories for the manufacture of cannons in Richmond and Selma, and in regions where up to then only cotton, sugarcane and tobacco had been grown, they started cultivating cereals and fodder. And they comforted themselves with the illusion that the Northern government would surely tire of a war that had so far produced only reverses and whose citizens were less than enthusiastic.

At long last, Clarence had a letter from Caroline, timed to arrive with the news that Grant had taken Fort Henry, which meant that the North now commanded the road south via the Tennessee River.

In her letter, Caroline announced she would be back in March "at the same place where I embarked and bringing a few toys that should please the young Templetons." And she hoped to be met by Dandridge "with the same equipage as before."

"What do you think she means?" Clarence asked Barthew.

"That she is coming to Bayou Vista with the weapons and that we must assemble the wagons to transport them here."

"That's what I make of it. We'd better warn Templeton in Richmond."

After the Southern defeats at Roanoke Island and Fort Donelson, Templeton was relieved to learn that more weapons were on the way, but he warned Dandridge to be on the alert for Northern spies who, under the leadership of the famous detective Allan Pinkerton, were becoming very active.

The wagons had to wait a week at Bayou Vista for Caroline's British brig and its load of "toys." Caroline looked worn from the rough crossing and the tense maneuvers necessary to get past the Union frigates patrolling the coast.

As the cargo was being transferred from ship to wagons, Caroline listed its contents: from France, ten thousand Minié rifles, thirteen cannons with ammunition, medicines, shoes and blankets. France had been less generous than she had counted on, even though Napoleon III was hoping that the United States would break up into two independent entities because it would facilitate his imperialistic plans for Mexico. Realizing that this explained her husband's role in Vera Cruz, she made much of his devotion to the emperor. Result: the ten thousand Minié rifles.

To complete the shipment as listed by Willy, she had had to go to London. There again, the officials were courteous but reluctant to satisfy her needs. The year before, the British government had proclaimed its neutrality; the actual effect was a de facto recognition of the Confederacy. Despite its obvious sympathy for the secessionists, England wanted to see peace between North and South rather than to furnish arms to the Confederates. All the same, Caroline had been able to bring back a fair number of rifles.

That was the end of their conversation, for the convoy was now ready to set off. It wasn't until they reached Oak Alley, where Templeton was waiting with a navy steamboat, that Clarence was able to ask how she was able to get the British rifles.

"I went to see Mosely in Manchester."

Clarence looked at her wide-eyed.

"You may find it in doubtful taste, but I did it all the same. When Mosely saw me, he began to shake like a leaf and his face broke out in sweat. He kept eyeing my bag as if he expected me to bring out a pistol. I told him: 'I am offering you a way to make up for the unspeakable evil you did my family and to prove that you don't always behave like a coward. I need twelve thousand Infield rifles!' "

"Did he come through?" Clarence asked.

"He beat around the bush for a while, saying that he had nothing to do with munitions. So I said, 'If you don't give me what I've asked for before the week is out, I'll kill you like a dog,' and I pretended to open my bag . . ."

"What happened then?"

"Well, as much a cad as ever, he did what he had to. I moved into his house and waited."

"Would you have killed him?"

"Certainly."

"How did you pay for the rifles?"

"I didn't. I told him the government in Richmond would reimburse him in cotton as soon as peace was restored."

"He was willing?"

"He had no choice. And he couldn't wait to see the last of me!"

* * *

"Look at what that amazing woman was able to cadge!" Dandridge exclaimed when he and Templeton took in the size of the cargo the next morning.

"But what's this?" Templeton asked, pointing to an enormous thin rectangular case of far better quality than the rudimentary crates containing the rifles.

"That's mine," Caroline said. "It's my portrait by Edouard Dubufe. I'm taking it back to Bagatelle."

When, later on, the slaves unpacked the eleven- by six-and-a-half-foot canvas in its elaborately carved frame weighing over two hundred pounds, Clarence was stunned not only by its size but by the quality of the painting. The artist had posed Caroline standing in a dark grayish silk dress that showed off her smooth, rounded shoulders. Her right forearm rested on the back of a chair on which an ermine scarf had been casually draped, her two hands lightly clasped together. Her face turned three-quarters toward the viewer, she wore a vague and solemn smile. Dubufe had caught the perfect oval of her face with its mother-of-pearl complexion framed by the strict "à la Sevigné" hairstyle, the slightly upturned nose, the full lower lip. Only the expression in her eyes seemed more subdued and conciliatory than Dandridge was accustomed to.

"It's an excellent portrait," Clarence said, "and not just its physical likeness. I see you as you were, as you are, as you will be. Time won't affect it because it will always reflect what you really are."

"Why, Clarence, you're being positively lyrical. Félice and her husband think it flatters me and that I look rigid and frozen."

"The effect of a painting is in the eye of the beholder," Clarence replied. "To me, you look the way I imagined you when you were away from Bagatelle." Then, to lessen the intimacy of his tone, he quickly added, "But I don't suppose that matters to you."

Caroline cocked her head, folded her hands and said in the coaxing voice women sometimes use with the timid, "It matters more than you can possibly know, Clarence. If I told you that all through those exhausting sessions, I was thinking of Bagatelle and you, perhaps you'd understand the portrait better."

Clarence made a small bow but remained silent.

To make room for the picture, the various Marquis de Damvilliers had to close ranks. Then it turned out that the walls weren't strong enough to support its weight. So in the end, the portrait was left standing against the wall until a better solution could be found.

After a good night's rest, Caroline recounted to Dandridge the details of her stay in Paris, how Félice seemed to be very happy, cosseted by a husband who was getting richer by the minute. She had carriages, footmen in blue and gold livery, a "hôtel particulier" off the Boulevard Saint-Germain, a country house in Senlis, and her wardrobe—together with her beauty—was making her one of the most elegant young women at the court. Charles, just turned seventeen, was proving to be a exceptional student and intended eventually to return to Louisiana and open a law office.

"Both children begged me to stay in Paris until this stupid war was over, but I couldn't do it. I've had the Paris life. I was in a hurry to get back to my house on the river. I wanted to be here for the end."

"It may not come tomorrow, Caroline," Clarence ventured.

"I don't care," she said. "Time no longer means anything to me. All that matters is what happens, what time brings. I know now that whatever time is left to me mustn't be wasted. This is the only place where the present has the intensity I'm looking for."

"I gather you haven't lost your appetite for life, then?"

"No, but my tastes have changed. I've learned that serenity is inside us. That's where it's to be found, not in our childish desires. And the value I attach to your confidence in me tells me that you will warn me when I'm about to take a false turn."

"If I see it coming too," Dandridge said. "But I'm fallible like all men . . ."

"No, Clarence, you're not like other men. You recognize

what's essential and know how to overlook what isn't. You've always understood that life is lived beyond the ordinary daily concerns. You never speak of God and you doubt if he's anything like what the various religions would have him, yet I'm certain that you believe in some kind of power that keeps us in balance, that controls us."

As he so often did when trying to cover up his feelings, he tried to think of a quotation and naturally happened on *Childe Harold*:

". . . whatsoe'er thy birth,
Thou wert a beautiful thought, and softly bodied forth."

"All right, Clarence. Put me off with one of your quotations if you like. But someday you'll consider me worthy of sharing your certainties. Someday, you'll give me your hand . . ."

Then she left the drawing room, leaving Clarence face to face with the woman in the portrait, the only living creature who seemed made of something other than common clay.

Then came the battle of Shiloh, which failed for all Caroline's rifles, and General Grant forced the Southerners out of Yorktown: Thousands were killed, tens of thousands were wounded or missing in action. No sooner had Louisiana recovered from this setback than it had to face its own Armageddon.

Thursday, April 24, 1862, would always remain a shameful memory in the minds of all New Orleans. At dawn, the fourteen federal frigates and gunboats under Farragut's command, which had been idling at the mouth of the river, started north. Because he considered it impossible to pass under the guns of Fort Jackson and Fort-Saint-Philippe, Farragut had decided to take advantage of the dense fog usual at that time of year. Almost immediately two Confederate frigates rammed and sunk a Yankee gunboat, but they went down too with all hands lost. The *Hartford*, Farragut's ship, barely made it after a fireship was driven against its side. Finally, with shore batteries firing blind at the dark silhouettes gliding past, a part of the federal fleet managed to get through. Its purpose, then unknown to the people of New Orleans, was to protect the unloading of General Butler's troops at La Quarantaine.

As they came abreast of the camp at Chalmette a few miles south of New Orleans, the invaders thought they were safe at last. Suddenly, they found themselves under General Lowell's fire. From their ships, the Federalists raked the camp; Lowell, lacking heavy guns, was unable to answer back. Deciding that any resistance would result in a bloodbath, Lowell ordered his soldiers to disperse. The imminent arrival of the federal troops set off a general panic in New Orleans. By noon, the Northern ships were ranged in battle formation in the crescent of the river facing the city. Lowell and his three thousand soldiers withdrew to Camp Noor. The forts on Lake Pontchartrain were evacuated, all ships on the lake having already been sunk to prevent them from falling into Yankee hands. That same morning, Lowell ordered all warehouses containing cotton or tobacco to be set on fire, as well as loaded ships tied up at the docks. Flames encircled the city and thick black smoke rolled over the housetops. The city seemed destined to go the way of a Hindu widow on her husband's funeral pyre.

On Friday, Farragut sent his chief of staff to the mayor of New Orleans to demand the city's surrender. His ultimatum: that all federal buildings be turned over to the Northerners, including the customs house, treasury, forts and all ships in the harbor. To soften the blow, he guaranteed that all property would be respected and citizens could continue their normal occupations. But the governor and his staff fled, leaving the population to fend for itself. Had it not been for the Foreign Legion, the looters would have taken over. The following day, two hundred Union Marines disembarked with two cannons and Farragut had all Confederate flags removed. On May 1, the troops of General Benjamin Butler took command. The once-proud city was now under the Northern yoke.

Adding insult to injury, Butler acted as if he were the proconsul of a defeated nation. A short, dumpy man with long, dishevelled hair and a scraggly moustache, he had shifty eyes but spoke in dogmatic tones. His draconian measures soon earned him the title of "Beast of the Mississippi." All New Orleans could hope for was that Butler's troops would begin to feel the effects of the heat and fall prey to yellow fever.

It soon became evident that Butler didn't give a rap for Northern interests; he was interested only in lining his own pockets. Eight hundred thousand dollars disappeared from the Dutch consul's office, he fined all merchants who didn't keep their shops open, he exacted loans as "contributions to the war effort" for the upkeep of his army and staff. He had the finer houses searched "for Southern spies" and more often than not, their owners found their most precious possessions gone. And under threat of imprisonment, he extorted funds from traders who had managed to import or export merchandise during the blockade.

With New Orleans safely under the Northern thumb, the scene shifted to the Mississippi. What the South feared most was that with the mouth of the river sealed off, the Yankees would tighten the noose farther north. The invaders had tried to do this without success when two Union navies converged on Vicksburg. But Farragut realized that the banks of the Mississippi between Vicksburg and Port Hudson were firmly in Southern hands. Port Hudson, a tiny fort set into the cliffs on the river's left bank, was only ten miles from Bagatelle. Inexorably the war was creeping toward the plantation and Dandridge never doubted that Farragut would try to take Port Hudson in order to cut communications between the Confederates on either side of the river.

As it waited for the fateful day, Bagatelle was living in increasing penury. Provisions were dwindling, port was only for special occasions, food was limited to what was grown on the plantation: salt pork, chickens, eggs, dairy products, corn bread and Anna's preserves—for they did not lack for sugar. Caroline had to resort to remodeled clothes, for cloth was unobtainable.

In the evenings, when Brent had served Clarence his mint julep—for, God be praised, Tennessee bourbon was still available—Caroline would join him on the gallery. May was triumphant in the heat. Never had the magnolias bloomed with such opulence or the jasmine with such heady perfume. Not too far away, nature was offering up its copses, fields and clearings to combatants and its forests to ambushes. Here at Bagatelle, it had maintained its innocence and neutrality. War might come soon and shell the oaks, gun down the reeds on the banks, churn up the grassy paths. Therefore it was imperative to enjoy the peaceful evenings where only one's soul felt anxiety, where only words could convey the threat that hovered over this tranquil world.

"Clarence, what will we do if the Northerners come and emancipate our Negroes?"

"We'll suggest that they accept some sort of salary. But the ones I know well have no desire to be emancipated against their will."

"Percy Templeton told Isabelle that in Southern Louisiana, Butler was forcibly freeing the slaves and that Lincoln was ready with a declaration of emancipation. He's only waiting for a military victory to make it public."

Clarence had picked up even more explicit information from Barthew and Murphy; he withheld it from Caroline for fear of adding to her anxieties. In point of fact, Butler was already "practicing abolition": In every parish his troops entered, the slaves were offered their freedom. It was reported, although impossible to verify, that over forty thousand slaves were following Butler's troops and were helping the Federalists devastate the plantations in their path. Also, Butler had given them rifles, in contempt of Congress, which had prohibited the use of slaves except for public works.

Instead, Clarence simply counseled Caroline to hide her silver and anything of value, but not to fall into the trap of stashing them in the hollow of a tree or digging up a section of the rose garden, as many planters' wives were doing. Caroline suggested the trumeaux over the doors and windows.

"Those would be good hiding places behind the painted panels," she said. "If I hear the Yankees coming, I just climb a ladder and stuff everything up there."

Without much faith in the inviolability of the trumeaux, Clarence approved her plan. Before the Northerners decided whether to dismantle the house or burn it down, other events would surely occur.

The year 1862 ended with the South's stunning victory at Fredericksburg: 12,633 Northerners dead to 5,309 Southerners. But in September had come Antietam where for once, McClellan had been decisive. Confederate losses: 25,000 killed, wounded or missing; Yankees, 12,000. This gave Lincoln the victory he was waiting for, and the Emancipation Proclamation followed five days later. Beginning on January 13, 1863, all slaves in the rebel states would be free men.

The slaves at Bagatelle greeted the news with mixed emotions. This liberty everybody was talking about didn't seem so very desirable. They already saw themselves abandoned and forced to find their own food and lodging. And without work, no money . . . and without money—nothing!

But for Louisiana, the year's end also brought the welcome departure of General Butler, relieved of his functions by President Lincoln. His replacement, General Nathaniel Banks, immediately took possession of all Butler's archives and files, which revealed to the government the extent of his depredations. General Banks also ordered Butler's officers to evacuate all the houses they had commandeered, lifted the embargo on all the sugar Butler's henchmen had seized at Bayou Lafourche and had it returned to its owners, set up a military police to control the disorderly soldiers on leave, and welcomed the population's complaints. To be sure, his purpose was to rally the war-weary South to the Union, but his methods were not unwelcome.

With New Orleans reassured, Banks marched on Baton Rouge with fifteen thousand men while Farragut sailed up the river with a flotilla of gunboats. North of Vicksburg, Porter, with another fleet, was preparing to attack while McClellan's army advanced by land. The big operation that would make the North master of the Mississippi from Saint Louis to the sea was about to begin.

Bagatelle knew that war was inching toward the plantation. All field work had stopped, most of the slaves having been turned over to the army. The slaves' quarters was down to perhaps thirty men, the rest being women and children.

"This will be the first spring in a century that Bagatelle will have sown no cotton," Clarence observed. "The fields are covered with weeds. In a few years, nature will have reclaimed the soil."

"But you wouldn't prepare a harvest for the Yankees, would you?" Caroline said with defiance. "What do you plan to do with the cotton in the warehouses?"

"All the planters around have decided to throw their bales into Fausse-Rivière. And we're going to set fire to the sugarcane."

"I want the Yankees to find Bagatelle barren and empty," Caroline said. "We must destroy all the wagons, wheelbarrows, and give all the horses—except our own—to the army."

Clarence told her, "I've had the big church bell taken down and we're sending it to the foundry in Richmond along with the bell at Sainte-Marie and a few other churches. They're short on bronze for making cannons."

"What about our provisions?"

"They're very low."

"I won't have the abolitionists drinking our wine and champagne." Her mood changing, Caroline said brightly: "Let's give a big barbecue and celebrate! I'm going to invite the entire parish."

"Don't you want to keep a few bottles to celebrate our victory?" Dandridge asked with a forced smile.

"You still believe in victory, Clarence?"

"The war will end the day one or the other capital falls—Richmond or Washington."

"You didn't answer my question."

"Everything depends on what happens on the eastern front," Clarence said. "As far as we're concerned here, I'm afraid we'll have to await the final decision with the Yankees on our backs."

"But you know that the population of Richmond is hungry, there have been uprisings, and the fifteen million dollars Europe loaned our army will be quickly spent."

For no apparent reason, the battle for the river seemed to be at a standstill. Banks had gone only as far as Springville, just east of Baton Rouge, and Farragut's ships seemed content with routine reconnaissance missions. The tension was becoming unbearable. Rumors spread like wildfire. Somebody had seen Yankee cavalry; somebody else ships unloading scouting parties; a third announced that Banks was using kite-balloons to observe the plains, and that spies came at night to incite the blacks to kill their masters.

"The time has come to give the barbecue," Caroline said one morning. "Everybody is going to go mad waiting for the sky to fall."

The party was a great success, although there were three times more girls than boys, many women were in mourning for a husband or son, and the old men had the closed faces of the defeated.

When Brent announced, as was the tradition, "The last waltz, ladies and gentlemen," a heavy silence filled the drawing room, lit by a shocking profusion of candles. Everyone was aware that with the waltz's last measures, all that constituted their happiness was coming to an end. The dancers solemnly took their places. Caroline looked for Clarence. He too wanted one more chance to put his arm around her waist, the mistress of Bagatelle's hand lightly poised on his shoulder. The violins seemed to be playing more slowly than usual, as if the musicians wanted to prolong the penultimate party. When the last note died away, the dancers remained stationary, and a few women broke into sobs. Clarence noted the tears running down Caroline's cheeks. She wiped them away and, standing as if at attention, called out: "The party is over."

The guests took their melancholy leave. Caroline and Clarence saw them off at the gate, then walked slowly back up the alley of oaks. The freshness of the night, the stars suspended like unattainable fruit among the topmost branches, the cries of the birds, the silky rustling of the bats, and the house standing white and majestic at the end of the alley, all conspired to make this moment a memory time could never efface.

Caroline stopped in front of the last oak, where a small moss-covered stone marked Julie's grave.

"Do you think I killed her, Clarence?" she asked quietly.

"No, Caroline. Perhaps you were the instrument, but her death was determined at the beginning of time. Forces beyond our control elected her, as they did your sons. Our day has already been set."

Before he could finish the sentence, Caroline grasped his arm and looked at him, a look of fixed intensity in her eyes.

"Clarence, please don't leave me alone tonight."

He took her gently by the hand. "Let's go back. You're shivering. Ask Anna to make you a cup of her fake barley coffee."

"Clarence, don't you understand what I'm trying to say," she said violently, moving back a step. "What I mean is . . . take me to your house and hold me in your arms . . . I need love."

"Caroline, stop. Do you realize what you're asking me—in front of this grave!"

He had the cold expression she dreaded.

"Haven't you ever desired me, Clarence? I've desired you, often."

"Yes, Caroline, I have desired you but I can't take you."

"Aren't you a man?" She almost shouted the question, like the desperate appeal of a woman in love.

He strode off toward the house. She walked slowly back and climbed the steps, her hands gripping her thighs like a weary old woman. She was humiliated, and for the first time in her life, she felt the intensity of her solitude.

The next morning, there was a letter on her breakfast tray. "Mister Dandridge told me to give it to you," Rosa said. "He left this morning before sun-up without saying where he was going."

Caroline tore open the envelope and read:

"My very dear Caroline:

"When you read these words, I shall already have left Bagatelle. I hate to leave the plantation at such a time but I trust you will understand that after last night's conversation, I would be ashamed to appear before you.

"Don't think for a minute that I'm scorning you. Of all the people in the world, you are the one to whom I feel closest. But your suggestion, a flattering one to anyone else—casting conventions aside—was a cruel one for me.

"Ask Murphy to tell you my story. I can't do it myself. I've authorized him to do so in a note he will receive today.

"Everything is in order at the plantation. No one will know how to receive the Yankees better than you, if they come. I doubt we will ever see each other again. But please know that I leave a part of my soul at Bagatelle, and for you, the ardent feelings others call love.

Clarence Dandridge"

Caroline read the letter twenty times, caught between the emotions of a love-sick girl and stinging curiosity.

She had thrown herself on Clarence like a bitch in heat. He could have attributed her behavior to her husband's absence —she had heard nothing from him for months even though the French troops had landed at Vera Cruz. Yet she didn't think he considered her a woman who couldn't control her sexual impulses. And she knew that it was an urge beyond mere sensuality that had made her thrust herself at this man who had been privy to the great events of her life.

She spent the day wandering about the house, hiding her silver and jewels behind the trumeaux, tucking bottles of wine in various caches. By evening, she couldn't hold off any longer and sent for Dr. Murphy.

"Who's sick?" the doctor asked on arriving.

"You know why I've asked you to come. Didn't you receive a letter from Clarence?"

"Yes, I did," he said, abandoning all attempt at nonchalance. "I received a note a while back. I don't know what could have passed between you two, but this is some mission he's laid on me. I've just come from Port Hudson where they're getting ready for battle. Between now and tomorrow the whole country could be devastated and he chooses this moment to give me this assignment. Dear lady, if by any chance you still have a bottle of whiskey around, I wouldn't mind a drop before I embark on the Dandridge case."

Brent brought in a tray and the doctor helped himself to half a glass, which he downed while looking fixedly at Caroline.

"Well. Clarence Dandridge, whom I love like a brother, has given me the task of explaining why he isn't a normal man where women are concerned. It's not a pretty tale to tell a lady and I hope I don't shock you."

"You can tell me everything," Caroline said impatiently. "I've been married twice and had a certain number of lovers. I know all about men's bodies, and in Paris they don't put skirts around piano legs the way the Quakers do."

As he was about to begin, Dr. Murphy glanced at the bottle of whiskey on the tray. "Forgive me, Caroline, if I pour myself another nip. It takes a little fortification to tell this story." Murphy filled his glass and, with his eyes on Caroline, started in. And this is the story the doctor told.

The first time he saw Clarence Dandridge—who was about twenty then—the boy was in a very sad state indeed. The Marquis had happened on him, lying half dead in a dugout canoe that had come aground in the rushes near the foot of the alley of oaks. Adrien got a couple of slaves to carry the boy up to the house. They stretched him out on a bed in a guest room and sent for Dr. Murphy. He gave Clarence a thorough examination and came to the conclusion that he was basically all right—just suffering from exhaustion, lack of food and exposure to the elements. And in due course, with the right food, a warm home and a lot of attention from the whole household—he was a very attractive lad, though on the shy side—Clarence came around. But even though he was physically well, Murphy sensed that something troubled him. Adrien of course thought that Netta's food and riding around on a horse was all he needed. But the doctor was worried. Clarence would get a faraway look in his eyes and seem to drop off into another world. Murphy tried to get him to talk about his youth in Boston, his education at Harvard, why he'd gone west to study Indian ways and his experiences with the Indians. Clarence was skimpy about his youth but he told him a lot about the Indians, how the various tribes differed, and so forth. Murphy was very interested, but behind all those earnest observations he guessed that something had happened to the young man that he couldn't put into words. Couldn't or didn't want to.

Then one night, they returned home from a ball—it was at the Templetons' if he remembered correctly—and Murphy began to tease him about his timidity with the girls. Clarence was such a good-looking lad and the young women showed great interest in the Marquis's young protégé. Murphy poured each of them a drink—the Marquis had gone up to bed—and put it directly to him. "Why are you so scared of our local damsels?" he asked him. "I assure you they're as harmless as a bunch of rabbits."

Clarence looked at him for a moment and said: "I can't be natural with girls anymore. They fixed that for all time."

The doctor was puzzled and asked him who "they" were and what "they" had done to him. Then the story poured out. As Clarence told it, he cried, although his voice was steady most of the time.

Where Clarence had always talked in general terms about the Indians, he now became specific. After visiting several Indian tribes, moving always westward, he had arrived one day in Pawnee territory near the Platte River. He explained how in those days, they were powerful warriors who shaved their heads, leaving only one long lock in the middle of their scalps. But, most of the time, they were a peaceful and hospitable people, and they made him feel very much at home—so much so that he took a mistress, a young girl of great beauty named Menthe. But it also happened that Menthe was the daughter of the tribe's chief, Lone Eagle. Morals were pretty free among ordinary Indians, but not so for the daughter of the chief. Clarence's love affair with Menthe created a scandal, and he was informed by the tribal council that once a white man had known the daughter of a chief, he would never be able to know another woman. Clarence was terrified, especially since they kept referring to his punishment in such ambiguous terms.

When Clarence had gotten to this point, he seemed unable to go on. Dr. Murphy said quietly: "Don't stop, Clarence. Keep going. Get to the end."

With a sigh, young Dandridge continued. It appeared that in his case he was doubly unlucky. The man chosen to carry out the tribal council's sentence—a man named Buffalo Mane —had, unbeknownst to Clarence, been promised Menthe by her father. So when this spindleshanks from the East arrived (here Clarence's face broke out in a bitter smile) and robbed him of his bride-to-be, he was naturally a very angry man. But in addition, Buffalo Mane was a very astute man. He guessed that "the pale face with the foreign ways" would suffer more if Menthe were hurt than if he was—that his soul was more vulnerable than his body. And so Buffalo Mane figured out a way he could get even both with his fiancée's seducer and the faithless Menthe.

One morning as dawn was breaking, Clarence and Menthe were led up a ravine to a tent a good mile from the camp. Menthe was taken into the tent while Buffalo Mane lit a fire outside and started to heat up a poker. All he said to Clarence, who was being held by two Indians, was: "Where the white man's member has been, no other man's will ever enter."

Clarence went rigid with terror. When he tried to protest, they gagged him with a smelly piece of rawhide. He saw them stretch Menthe out on a plank and four men pin down her arms and legs. Then they closed the flap of the tent. When the poker was red-hot, the Indian went into the tent and Clarence heard a bloodcurdling scream. He tried to make a lunge for the tent but his captors held him in a vise-like grip. At this point in his tale, Clarence began to sob and the words tumbled out in an incoherent jumble. He went on about how he had loved Menthe with all the ardor of a first love, how it had been a profoundly romantic experience for him, so far from home in a strange land, released from the bonds of staid New England. And here his beloved was being mutilated in the very place where he had experienced the first transports of love. Clarence's whole body was racked with sobs. Murphy got up, went to him and gently stroked his head as if to calm an hysterical child. Then he returned to his chair and waited.

Finally Clarence regained some measure of self-control and went on. The two Indians led him back to the camp. They allowed him to take his few possessions, gave him a supply of corn cakes and directed him to the path that led east toward the Missouri River. After two days, he met up with some friendly Indians who sold him a canoe in exchange for the fob on his father's watch, and he drifted down the Missouri and into the Mississippi, not caring whether he lived or died. After two, maybe three weeks—he had lost all track of time —the canoe caught in the reeds in front of Bagatelle but he didn't have the strength to extricate himself. That's when Adrien happened by. Clarence paused and, throwing his head back and closing his eyes, said: "You know the rest."

Murphy tried to suggest that perhaps the Indian, Buffalo Mane, hadn't really done what he said he was going to do— after all, she was the chief's daughter and promised to him— that he'd said it merely to scare Clarence and get rid of him. But Clarence wouldn't hear of it. Murphy let it go at that, helped him out of his chair and saw him up to his room. Clarence seemed to have calmed down, but to be on the safe side, the doctor spent the night in an adjoining room. By morning, Clarence was himself again, although he was very quiet for the next few days.

Dr. Murphy's eyes, which had been fixed on the fire in the hearth, came to rest on Caroline. "In short, dear lady, Clarence's body survived the ordeal but his psyche was dealt a blow from which it never recovered. I think the reason he refused to accept my version of the punishment was that he wanted to feel guilty. You and I both know that there's always been a strong strain of the Yankee Puritan in the man. Perhaps it fit in with the need for solitude which I've long felt was the central core of his character. I don't know. It's hard to tell which was the cause and which the effect." Murphy shook his head and sighed. "Anyway, it's a very sad story."

Caroline started to weep.

"You love him, don't you?" Murphy observed.

She nodded sheepishly.

"You could have realized this sooner. It's hardly fair for a man his age to have to leave the house he's lived in most of his life."

"What should I have done, Murphy?"

"Given him the chance to put distance between you when he was still young. Now he has nothing, not even a woman's compassion."

"If only I hadn't said what I did. I behaved like a fool . . ."

"What did you say that made him run away?"

"I asked him to spend the night with me."

The doctor raised his eyes to the ceiling and shook his head as if he had just been told of a child's foolish prank. Then he poured himself another glass of whiskey.

"Just like that, on the spur of the moment, you opened your bed. Your appetites are going to play you tricks, Caroline."

"Don't make fun of me. I'm very unhappy and furious with myself."

"If you had talked to him about feelings, his reaction would have been very different, believe me. Love, for Dandridge, is a form of disembodied tenderness. Adrien was right when he said: 'With Clarence, everything happens in his head.' But since I'm not really sure you love him, it may be just as well this way. Women often confuse love with desire. He can't. He has the most prodigious clarity!"

"Have you any idea where he's hiding?" Caroline asked.

"No, I don't, but if I did I wouldn't tell you. He needs peace and quiet."

Murphy stood up, emptied his glass and picked up his kit.

"I've done what he asked. You now know his story. If I were a woman, I'd view it as a hellishly big proof of love."

A few days later, the offensive against Port Hudson got underway. For the next six weeks the Northerners went back and forth to Baton Rouge, taking their battle-wounded and damaged ships down, then returning to the fray. General Banks's troops gained a foothold on the right bank of the river, near Fausse-Rivière, facing the Confederate infantry at West Feliciana. On the road next to the river, there was a daily file of cavalrymen gray with fatigue, sent to relieve the foot soldiers, and from the other direction, wagons carrying the wounded to the church at Sainte-Marie, now converted into a hospital. It was there that the mistress of Bagatelle and the other planters' wives served as nurses, assisting Dr. Murphy, who in turn assisted the military surgeons. The war was right there, lying on the porch of the church, with its gaping wounds, the moans of the dying, the amputees, the men found dead in the morning, the putrid bedpans that needed emptying, the filthy bandages, the overpowering stench of blood and sweat. The devoted blacks, promoted to stretcher-bearers, looked with bewilderment at the whites— their defeated masters.

As Caroline returned to Bagatelle after an exhausting day at the hospital, dreaming only of a warm bed and clean sheets, she found a man in dirty clothes and a four-day beard waiting for her in the drawing room. Sent by the French consul in New Orleans, he had spent five days dodging soldiers of both armies before reaching Bagatelle.

"I bring you what I'm afraid will be painful news, madam," the messenger announced. "It concerns your husband. The consul asked me to give you this," and he handed her a sealed envelope. Even before she had read the first line, Caroline knew it contained the news of her husband's death. In a few terse lines, the note explained that the general had died during an attack on Puebla, a Mexican fortress.

Caroline fought to control her emotions. "Charles had the death he wanted—a soldier's death," she said to herself. And she thought of him lying under the hot sun like the heroes of the Napoleonic wars in the paintings they had looked at together at the Louvre.

After the usual condolences, the messenger asked, "Do you wish the general's body brought back to Louisiana, once the situation is stabilized?"

Caroline made a vague gesture and replied, "It's hard for me to decide right now. We have a son in school in Paris. I have no way of getting in touch with him. I wonder if you could see that he's informed? We can decide later about the general's final resting place."

The messenger couldn't help but admire the self-possession of this woman who was still beautiful despite her look of weariness.

As he was about to take his leave, she said, "Please stay and rest for a day or two. Anna will show you to your room and give you some fresh linen. We dine at nine o'clock, if that suits you."

Once in her room and after a hot bath and a prolonged hair-brushing by Rosa, she sank into a chair. From now on she would be alone. Her children in Paris, Clarence gone, Charles dead, what was left of the universe she had so tenaciously put together? Dry-eyed, she drew up the balance sheet of her life and looked askance at what the future held. She felt as if she were hanging over a void, the rope about to snap. Never had she needed Clarence so much. All she had left was this old house and the devastated cotton fields. She had so desperately wanted to reign over Bagatelle. And now her wish had been granted by an ironic fate which, in exchange for satisfying her ambition, had taken everything back. She was like a miser clinging to her useless hoard.

Enough! Rapping the arm of her chair, she ordered her depression to be gone. There was a man waiting for her downstairs, a man with the secret ambitions and high expectations of youth. How she envied him. She picked out a black faille dress, patted some rice powder on her nose and went down to the dining room, ready to engage in the usual banalities. The mistress of Bagatelle knew her duty.

Somewhat to her surprise, the young man turned out to be an ardent liberal and launched into a tirade on liberty and the right to human dignity. She fought back with the zeal of a Damvilliers. When he left the next morning, the young man took away the image of a proud and obstinate woman who commanded one's respect even though she attached an almost voluptuous fervor to a lost cause.

At Port Hudson, the situation was becoming untenable. Bombarded from the river by Farragut's cannons, threatened from the rear by Banks's soldiers, the little fortress was on the point of having to choose between surrender and certain death. The Southerners were down to their last shells, their last cartridges.

Lieutenant-Colonel Templeton, a stray cavalryman among a handful of foot soldiers, was firing with the best of them. His horse, together with a few others, was safely tethered in a ruined redoubt. He was all ready for the retreat, if the attackers gave him half a chance.

The captain commanding the fortress, wounded in both arms, was a fire-eater. "They'll get our battery only by climbing over our corpses."

"That would be a useless sacrifice," Willy observed calmly. "Even if this fort is lost—and I realize it's the last stronghold on the Mississippi—we must preserve the largest number of soldiers possible for the Confederacy. I suggest that we get all the able-bodied men and those with superficial wounds out of here tonight. If we can get them down to the water's edge, they'll be protected by the cliffs."

"Me, I'm staying," the captain said flatly, carried away by the prospect of his supreme sacrifice.

"I can't forbid you, but you are taking the easy way out. Your wounds can be healed and you'll be more useful on other fields of battle than as a dead hero behind a silent cannon. Your duty, our duty, is not to get killed but to fight the enemy."

By nightfall, the captain was finally convinced and helped prepare the evacuation. One by one, the men slid down between the rocks, giving a hand to those wounded able to walk, while the men behind the cannons stood ready to answer any fire from the Yankee ships.

Willy supervised the evacuation. At dawn, the men would regroup on the riverbank, out of sight of Farragut's sailors and Banks's soldiers. They would then proceed to Bayou Sara, which was still protected by the Confederate infantry in West Feliciana, and thus avoid encirclement. He was soon alone with the gunners.

"We have eight horses left, but you are thirteen men . . ." Templeton said.

"That's an unlucky number," commented an old bearded veteran.

"No, a lucky number," a young sergeant answered back.

"Lucky or not, you've got to get thirteen men on your seven horses. Of course, if any of you would prefer to stay with the wounded and be taken prisoner by the Yankees, you have my permission. There's nothing dishonorable about it, for our escape won't be without risks."

As he spoke, Willy was eyeing the old gunner who didn't like the number thirteen. The soldier looked away. After all, life had given him enough of pleasure and pain so that he wouldn't hesitate to risk it one more time. He immediately set about grouping the gunners according to their weight.

"You, sergeant, have the right to a horse to yourself," the old man said, "then we'll be two each on the other six horses."

"No, sir. I leave you my horse. At your age, you deserve a little comfort."

Willy had to smile. Of course, it was what the old gunner had reckoned on.

When a pale yellow light finally broke through the mist on the river, Willy summoned his orderly, a black he had stolen from Percy on his last visit to The Myrtles.

"While I'm shaving, I want you to polish my boots, brush my uniform and make coffee for everybody, hear?"

"After that, I go with you, master?" the black asked, visibly nervous.

"No, you're staying here. The Yankees won't hurt you. You'll be freed. When we've gone, you take this handkerchief"—Willy took an unexpectedly white and dainty cambric square out of his pocket—"and tie it to the end of your rifle and wave it from behind the rampart. But don't let your head show! Then the Yankees will come and you say 'welcome.' Understand?"

"Yes, but I think I'd rather go with you, Colonel."

"You can't. Blacks have no business getting killed in this war. This is strictly a matter between whites."

"All right, Colonel. I'll go back to The Myrtles and I'll tell Master Templeton that everything's going just fine."

"That's a very good idea."

The group's departure was a great success. If Willy's servant hadn't been in such a hurry to wave the handkerchief—he didn't like finding himself alone with the wounded and dying —the Yankees might have shown greater interest in their flight. By the time the foot soldiers had awakened the cavalry, Willy and his men were already well on their way.

And so it was that on a hot morning in July, Sainte-Marie learned that the decimated garrison at Port Hudson had raised a white flag over the ruined ramparts. The Mississippi's southern bastion had finally ceded.

That day, Caroline returned to Bagatelle earlier than usual. Rosa informed her that the cavalry in blue had passed by the house and that one of the men had written something down in a notebook before the group set off along the river road toward Sainte-Marie.

"They're here, ma'm. Praise be to the Lord, what will happen to us now?"

"Nothing, Rosa. Don't worry. Get my bath ready."

At the end of the afternoon, there was a great noise of galloping hooves under the oaks. Caroline, who was resting naked on her bed, got up and peered through the voile curtains at her window.

Below her she saw a group of officers on horseback. They seemed to be discussing something before approaching the house. Suddenly they parted to make way for an older officer, a man of proud bearing but weary and visibly preoccupied. From the double row of gilt buttons on his blue tunic, the black facing on his collar and sleeves, and the three silver stars on his epaulettes, she knew he was a general of the Union armies. He brought his horse to a halt at the bottom of the steps and a major quickly dismounted. When the general started to speak, Caroline thought she recognized a Massachusetts accent.

"We'll spend the night here. Have the entrance guarded. The men will bivouac in the park. Major, go see if there's anyone left in the house."

As the officer climbed up the steps, Anna rushed to her mistress, shouting, "They're here, ma'm. They're here."

"Calm yourself, Anna," Caroline said through the closed door. "Tell the men that your mistress will be down in a minute."

Caroline went back to the window. The general must already be in the drawing room. She could hear the officers' voices coming up from the gallery.

"Whose turn is it to set the house on fire tomorrow when the general's left?" one of the voices said.

"It's my turn, Captain. This one is built of wood. It should go fast."

The mistress of Bagatelle had heard enough. She opened her wardrobe, examined several dresses, then came to a dotted Swiss she hadn't worn since before her marriage to Adrien. She slipped it on over her lace chemise, rubbed a little pink salve on her cheeks, dusted her nose with powder, smoothed her hair and joined the men in the drawing room.

The general and his three officers were standing admiring the portraits, hands clasped behind their backs like so many tourists. They turned when they heard her enter. It was as if the large portrait of the handsome woman they had been examining a second earlier had suddenly come to life.

"Gentlemen?" Caroline said, unruffled.

"Major Coster," one of the officers said, bowing. "This is General Banks of the United States Army. Although the idea may be displeasing to you, madam, it's our intention to spend the night here."

The general made a stiff little bow, his eyes on the Southern lady's flimsy dress.

"Since it's quite impossible for a lone woman to throw intruders out, I suppose I have to accept your presence as I would ordinary guests. Please sit down. My butler will show you to what rooms are available. May I offer you a glass of port?"

The general sat in the middle of the sofa, the colonel and the lieutenant on either side. The major left the room.

When Brent came in carrying with trembling hands a silver tray with a bottle and crystal glasses, the general's eyebrows shot up with astonishment.

"We're not accustomed to being welcomed in this manner, madam. Believe me, we are touched by your consideration."

"What would you have me do, General? I'm the widow of a French general recently killed in Mexico where he was fighting for his country. I therefore know that soldiers are also men, and that victorious or vanquished, they always appreciate a glass of port—if it doesn't upset you to be waited on by a slave," she added with a touch of irony.

Banks smiled, savoring the attitude of his reluctant hostess. When Brent had filled all the glasses, Caroline was the first to take a sip.

"You see," she said, cocking her head, "my port isn't poisoned."

Everyone relaxed and the conversation became animated. The general asked about General de Vigors, the plantation, cotton, molasses, indigo.

"I don't concern myself with these matters. We had a manager who disappeared a few months ago, our Negroes are dispersed, our fields neglected. This plantation is a poor thing, general, and I'm afraid you won't find much of use to you. And this old wooden house will burn quickly. Am I not correct in thinking it's your custom to burn the houses in which you've spent the night?"

Banks and his officers looked embarrassed.

"We're not obliged to, madam," the general replied, "but you must understand that with the enemy—that is, with the troops opposing ours nearby, our duty as soldiers is not to make things easier for them. When we do destroy houses like yours, it's not for the pleasure of it but because we don't want to leave sanctuaries for those hostile to the United States Army."

"In any case, General," Caroline said, "the results are the same for those who live in them. It's a fact that your war is a civil war, isn't it?"

The general suppressed a look of pain and Caroline moved on to other subjects.

As the hour for dinner approached, the sound of angry voices suddenly erupted from the kitchen. The door flew open and Anna stood with a rolling pin in her hand.

"There's a man in there who's trying to take over my ovens to feed the Yankees, ma'm. If he doesn't get out of my kitchen, I'm going to bash his head in."

Behind her stood an ungainly soldier, dumbfounded at the sight of his general conversing with a "slave owner." Everyone in the drawing room smiled.

"Anna," Caroline put in quickly, "I think it would be simpler if you prepared dinner for everybody. If those gentlemen don't mind keeping me company in the dining room."

The colonel was about to protest, but the general acquiesced. Caroline asked to be excused. Fifteen minutes later, while the general and his officers were finishing off the port, the general's cook was plucking two chickens under Anna's baleful eye.

The meal was pleasant. Caroline had thought it wise to produce a few bottles from her cache of wine to help the men forget they were fighting a war and sitting at table in enemy territory. Better that they remember only that they were dining with a hostess in a transparent gown who was as gracious as if she were entertaining her own friends.

In the middle of dessert, Brent burst into the room to announce that he had just caught a soldier rummaging through a room on the ground floor and he'd given him a good thrashing. The general burst out laughing. He summoned the soldier and told him smartly that all looting was forbidden. Caroline gave him a smile that conveyed unimaginable promises.

"General, I'm glad to see that the United States Army isn't like the band of pilferers Butler had around him."

"Madam, our mission is to win a war we didn't want and to hold the Union together, not to steal from citizens manipulated by slave dealers."

Once coffee was drunk, the general discreetly signaled his men to retire, leaving him alone with the mistress of the house. The house servants were no less surprised than the soldiers bivouacked in the park to see General Banks and the mistress of Bagatelle rocking together on the gallery.

Caroline was full of amiable chatter, sometimes cajoling, sometimes ironic, as she described life in the South and inquired about its future. Little by little, the talk became more intimate, and when Brent came in to serve the sassafras infusion, he was horrified to see the general's hand caressing his mistress's arm.

When reveille sounded at dawn, sending the cardinals and

waxwings wheeling into the sky, General Banks tiptoed back to the room he had been assigned. When his orderly brought him his hot water, he took in the unused bed and the general's unusual gaiety, and surmised that he must have spent, somewhere in this house, one of the better nights of the war.

Standing at her window, Caroline watched the men prepare for their departure and finally caught what she'd been hoping to hear. "The general doesn't want this house burned, or a single thing taken from it. Search your men, gentlemen. You'll answer for their infractions before the Council of War."

Then she saw the general leap into his saddle and, accompanied by his chief of staff, head toward the alley of oaks. Before disappearing under its branches, he looked back toward the house as if hoping for a last glimpse of a woman's figure. Caroline quickly stepped back from the window.

As the group set off, it broke into the song so fervently hated by all Southerners:

"John Brown's body lies a mould'ring in the grave,
John Brown's body lies a mould'ring in the grave,
John Brown's body lies a mould'ring in the grave,
But his soul goes marching on . . ."

"Yes, marching toward hell . . . like all those men," Caroline muttered bitterly.

But Bagatelle was saved. She rang for Rosa, had her sheets changed, and went back to sleep.

As the days wore on, the old field hands started dribbling back to Bagatelle. They had deserted from the Southern army and wanted "Mister Dandridge" to put them back to work. They were emaciated and heartsick. Caroline had no way of putting them back to work, for not only was Clarence gone, but her German overseers had enlisted in the Confederate army. All she could do was see that the slaves were fed and wait for some miracle to occur.

"They all want contracts, mistress," their spokesman said.

"They want to plant cotton, they want to be voluntary slaves
. . . have everything the way it used to be."

The North had in fact decided that every effort must be
made to get the plantations producing again. To that end, they
had formulated contracts between masters and freed slaves in
which the blacks exchanged submission, diligence and respect
for food and shelter, a twentieth of the harvest at year's end,
and a monthly salary fixed at three dollars for coachmen and
general workers; two dollars for field hands, whether men or
women; one dollar for house servants. Those blacks who
couldn't find work would be employed in "public works." To
the planters, the flagrant contradictions in the various laws
applying to freed blacks proved the abolitionists' total inca-
pacity to determine the future of Southern agriculture.

Exactly as General Banks had appeared at Bagatelle after
the fall of Port Hudson, General Richard Taylor, former President Zachary Taylor's son, arrived one November evening.

"It's the grays," Anna cried out. "They must have killed all
the blues."

The cook was laboring under a delusion. The general, accompanied by a few officers as exhausted as he was, had just
attempted an attack on Banks's rear guard as it worked its way
up the banks of the Mississippi to join General Grant at Vicksburg. Caroline, alert at her window as always, observed that
the Confederates were in a much more pitiful state than the
Northerners. A noisy young lieutenant was shouting from the
gallery that the Federalists had had a feast in this house, aided
and abetted by its mistress, and they would therefore do the
same, then hang the traitor and set fire to the plantation.

"These are our men," Caroline said sadly, "yet they seem
far more dangerous than the Yankees."

She could already hear the sound of boots in the house and
furniture being moved around. Without a moment's hesitation,
she slipped into the dotted Swiss and went down to the drawing
room, where she found a group of disorderly soldiers.

"Gentlemen," she said, "what are you looking for? There are no Yankees here."

"They may not be here now, but they were here before, weren't they? Right now, we're looking for something to drink," said the lieutenant.

"You'll get something to drink when you've put back what you've just stuffed into your pockets and have introduced yourselves properly. I am the wife of General de Vigors and unruly soldiers do not scare me."

General Taylor, who had been sitting slumped in a chair, got to his feet, clicked his heels, introduced himself, and dismissed his staff.

"Please forgive this intrusion. We've been fighting for two days and we need rest."

"You are entirely welcome, General, but do please see that your men behave. Everything I own belongs to the Confederacy but you mustn't treat this house worse than the Yankees did."

Taylor made a slight bow. "We were told that you gave them a warm welcome. They happen to be our enemies."

"General, what would you have me do, alone and unarmed? Claw their faces? Why weren't you here to defend me, dear general? All I had in mind was saving my house and my skin."

"Between that and dining and wining them, there's quite a difference."

"Believe me, they served themselves without my permission, just as your men were about to do a moment ago. My friend, Colonel Templeton, will be eager to know how the Confederates comport themselves."

"Colonel Templeton was promoted to general a few days ago. I know him well."

"When you see him again, please ask him what he thinks of Mrs. de Vigors and he'll tell you if I'm really capable of the villainies you accuse me of."

Contrite, the general replied, "It's the war, ma'm. A bad war, and we have a tendency to forget our manners."

"The son of a former President of the United States

shouldn't forget them, General. But I forgive you. I'll have the servants prepare you a bath and Anna will provide a suitable meal. I just managed to save some bottles of port and wine from the Yankees. I'm sure your officers will behave themselves at my table."

The lieutenant reappeared with two majors, one of whom had his arm in a sling. This time Brent served the port without trembling. The grays—now tending toward khaki after years of campaigning—were his friends, after all. And Anna went to work with dispatch.

"I toured the place as far as the hospital," the wounded major said while the general was upstairs taking his bath. "My sergeant recognized some blacks who deserted from a company of laborers in the Third Regiment. We'll hang them tomorrow morning."

Caroline started. "What did you say? You are under my roof, Major, and those Negroes belong to me. They came back to be treated at the hospital. They plan to return to the army as soon as they're well. You must be out of your mind."

Washed, brushed and shaved, General Taylor returned just in time to silence the overzealous major.

"Be good enough to send your slave-hanging sergeant to the kitchen, Major. There are chickens that need plucking."

Paradoxically, this dinner was less gay. Caroline knew that in his heart, Taylor was an abolitionist and she felt sympathy for the melancholy general. His tragedy wasn't that he was fighting on what his conscience told him was the wrong side, but that as a loyal soldier, he knew that his enemies weren't always in the wrong.

When his nodding officers retired for the night, Caroline invited her guest to share a cup of sassafras in front of the drawing-room fire. Watching the leaping flames, the general savored this brief return to domestic peace.

Caroline got up to snuff out a smoking candle, and as she passed in front of the hearth, the musing general's eye caught the transparencies of the dotted Swiss. Now over fifty, Caroline still had a desirable body, and the deprivations of the last few

years had taken off a few superfluous pounds. When the last
log broke up in a shower of sparks, casting a purple glow over
the darkened room, she wasn't altogether surprised to feel the
general's hand on hers. She smiled. The officer had the gentle,
sad expression of the gravely wounded lying in the church of
Sainte-Marie.

She stood up, placed a kiss on his brow and said in a whisper, "Come. I want this night to be one of peace for you, peace
and love."

When morning came, Caroline had to wake up the weary
warrior buried in the bedclothes next to her.

"I'm not Calypso," she whispered in his ear. "It's time Ulysses took up his sword again."

On this occasion, she parted the curtains to wave at the
general as he and his small band disappeared under the oaks.
But, a little shamefaced at having succumbed to the ardent
embrace of an unknown woman, the general spurred his horse
on as his men broke into the first stanza of *Dixie*.

As Mrs. de Vigors began to dress, she considered how she
had twice persuaded the war to spare Bagatelle. Walking
across the big drawing room, she thought she caught a hint
of a smile on the faces of the several Marquis de Damvilliers.

A few days later, Ed and Mignette Barthew and their small
son moved into Bagatelle. Their house had been destroyed,
as had most of the houses in Bayou Sara following a Yankee
bombardment. Caroline was grateful for their company and for
old friends with whom she could share her anxieties.

"I'm tired, Ed," she said one evening. "So terribly tired. I'm
so alone in this big house. I'll soon be out of money. I'll sell
my jewelry, of course, but how long can that put off the evil
day? If only Clarence were here."

In the evening, and despite the winter cold, Caroline often
wrapped herself in shawls and walked down to the river. She
would suddenly be seized with the desire to pack her bags,
leave this country for good and return to the easy life in Paris,

to Félice, but especially to the long-neglected Charles. The Damvilliers family was extinct. For whom had she saved the plantation? Why had she given herself to soldiers like a common prostitute if it wasn't for her son? But would he really come back? And as she did every time she walked back to the now-peeling house, she stopped before Julie's grave. And each time, she picked up a little more courage. The presence of her daughter's decomposed body lying under this trampled earth justified her clinging to Bagatelle.

Mignette and Ed worried to see her wandering around the plantation, a mournful, silent shadow. Murphy, always watchful, saw her slowly sliding into melancholia. She no longer changed her clothes, her hair was unkempt, and to any suggestions about anything, her answer was always: "What's the use . . . now."

"Our Caroline had too big a dose of disappointment," Murphy said to Barthew one night as they were emptying the last bottle of bourbon. "I'm afraid she's losing her sense of reality, that she'll go gently mad and we'll have to treat her like a child."

"What can we do to give her back her will to fight? Is there no remedy? What good is your science, Murphy?"

"I can heal sick bodies, not sick souls, my friend. Look, I have to make a quick trip to New Orleans to try to find medical supplies. We're running dangerously low. I'll also try to bring back a few cases of whiskey—to my mind the best remedy for many a complaint. But while I'm away, take good care of Caroline. Don't leave her alone if you can help it. I'll be back as soon as I can."

While he was in New Orleans, Murphy spent his evenings at his favorite bar, a not-too-savory spot where the river men liked to exchange stories. Murphy loved to hear about their exploits in the wilder reaches of the Mississippi and its tributaries, and he sometimes picked up some interesting medical lore in the process. One evening, he got into conversation with a weather-beaten old fur trader who had accompanied a bargeful of buffalo hides to New Orleans to get a taste of city life. The doctor asked him where his hides had come from and the old man told him he'd been dealing with various Indian tribes along the Platte River. At the mention of the Platte River, Murphy pricked up his ears.

"Have you had any dealings with the Pawnees?" the doctor asked.

"Sure, many times," the trader replied, "but what with the smallpox epidemic the trappers brought in and the Indian Wars, there's little left of the tribe now."

"How long have you known the Pawnees?" Murphy asked. "Does it go back as far as the time when Lone Eagle was their chief?"

"Not quite," the trader replied. "Actually, my first contact with them was soon after Lone Eagle's death. The new chief was his son-in-law, Buffalo Mane."

Murphy swallowed twice to control his excitement and asked as casually as possible: "Is it common practice for a son-in-law to be made chief?"

The trader explained that old Lone Eagle had had no sons, just one daughter. He couldn't remember her name except that she was very beautiful—for an Indian. The good doctor swallowed again. This was news indeed, but he needed just a little more. Praise be to the Lord the old fur trader would be able to furnish it. Dr. Murphy put it to him: "Do you remember if Buffalo Mane had any children?"

Squinting into the past, the trader thought for a long moment while Murphy's heart pounded in his chest.

"Yes, as a matter of fact," the old man said. "I remember one time when Buffalo Mane was very proud because his youngest son—a boy of ten or so—had shot the biggest buffalo that year. It was a monster of a beast, a real prize specimen."

As the fur trader rambled on about how much such a hide brought in, Murphy's thoughts began to spin wildly. So this confirmed what he had originally suspected: Menthe had not been tortured after all. The whole performance in that tent had been a farce put on to scare the bejesus out of poor Clarence. He was so dumbfounded by this discovery that he abruptly excused himself, leaving the trader in mid-sentence.

It didn't occur to him until he was undressing for the night that this information had probably been around for the asking for three decades. Admittedly, as the years passed by, he had filed Clarence's macabre tale in a back corner of his mind. Murphy was not one to dwell on the past; the present was as much as he could handle. And he had come to accept Clarence's peculiar but intensely likable personality as it was, without reference to its origins. Besides, had he been able to lift the curse on Clarence's sexuality when he was young, he might have married that simpering Corinne Templeton. Would that have made him happier? Murphy doubted it. No. Some superior intelligence—something the doctor usually viewed with profound skepticism—had saved the revelation for this particular moment, the moment when it would do the most good, when it could salvage the lives of two desperately unhappy people and bring them the serenity and love that had eluded them so long.

The next morning, he quickly dispatched his business and took the next boat north. But he wouldn't be getting off at Bayou Sara; his destination was Morganza and the Mertaux's plantation a little farther up the river, where Clarence had been in hiding since his precipitous departure from Bagatelle.

During Dr. Murphy's absence, Caroline had taken to spending hours at the harpsichord, playing with vacant eyes, an otherworldly smile on her lips. Because of the music, Mignette, who was sitting near her with her mending, failed to hear the sound of horses' hooves coming up the alley. But when she heard the creaking of the gallery steps she looked up, and what she saw caused her to let out a stifled cry.

In the doorway stood the familiar figure of Clarence Dandridge. At the sound of Mignette's exclamation, Caroline swiveled on her stool and looked toward the door. For an instant she didn't move. Then she crumpled to the floor. Murphy, who was standing close behind Clarence, rushed to her side.

"It isn't anything serious," he said. "I expected something like this to happen . . ."

An hour later, Dandridge was sitting by her bedside. She had finally begun to speak. She told him about her husband's death, then asked how he had spent the time while he had been gone.

"I was at Morganza, where the Mertaux's have a plantation. We lived as best we could, trying to help Taylor's men when there was a Yankee attack."

"Did you actually meet General Taylor?" Caroline asked, not without anxiety.

"Yes. He said you were a great lady, accepting adversity with dignity."

"But you've come back!" Caroline said for the hundredth time. "You can't imagine what it was like here. But I don't hold it against you for leaving. Murphy told me. And how I regretted . . ."

Dandridge looked down. He wasn't ready yet to meet her gaze. There was too much to absorb. In the few months he'd been away, the mistress of Bagatelle had wilted like a parched flower. Her beauty was still there, but only as a faded memory of what it had been. The lifeless hair was streaked with gray and her skin was wrinkled and dry. The pulse of life was only a faint murmur in the tired body. What moved him especially was the way she seemed to search his eyes for any sign of compassion, of caring. For the first time since he'd known her, the mistress of Bagatelle was pitiful, like someone dragged from a shipwreck. He knew she was yearning for the support he alone could give, for a denial of her conviction that all was lost.

He hesitated before saying the words that were on the tip of his tongue, the words she longed to hear. He wondered if she wouldn't once again mistake the only challenge that would give her another chance at life.

"Tomorrow we'll talk about the serious things," he said at last. "You must rest now, and don't torment yourself over questions that will solve themselves."

He got up carefully, like someone leaving a dying patient's side.

"But you're staying, aren't you? Oh, Clarence, tell me you're staying with me?"

"Yes, Caroline, I'm staying . . ."

Her lips quivered and tears of humiliation rolled down her cheek, and with them flowed her pride. Clutching his hand, she looked at him questioningly.

"No, Caroline, I'm not staying out of pity. Rest now."

Before joining the others in the drawing room, Clarence went out on the gallery and breathed in the air saturated with the familiar smells of Bagatelle. He nicked off a piece of peeling paint with his thumbnail. In the distance he could hear the sound of the river meandering through the rushes while a bat swooped over him and flew back to the branches of an oak, where it hung in the folds of its silken wings, waiting.

When Caroline woke up, Clarence had already inspected the slave village. The blacks made great demonstrations of welcome and Telemaque offered him a glass of his undrinkable liqueur.

"Are we going back to work, Mister Dandridge?"

"You're the ones to decide now. You're free men, or so I hear."

"We'll work whenever you like, Mister Dandridge."

"I'll be back, Telemaque. Tell the others I have to think it over."

Caroline had Rosa do her hair, then she put on a light-colored dress and went down for breakfast—something she hadn't done for a long time.

"It's a resurrection!" Mignette said, clapping her hands.

Caroline made a vague gesture as if to disparage the

metamorphosis. As soon as the meal was finished, Mignette and her husband excused themselves so as to leave Clarence and Caroline alone.

"I've had the gig harnessed. Perhaps we could take a tour of the plantation and see what condition it's in."

Caroline acquiesced like a docile child.

"Take a shawl. It's still cold this morning."

Under the oaks, a young groom Dandridge didn't recognize was holding the old mare's bridle.

"Where's Bobo?"

"In the hospital. He had rheumatism and I don't know what else. He's old now, like me . . . like you . . . like everything."

His panama down over his eyes to keep out the sun, Dandridge prodded the mare into a trot, then, once they reached the river road, left her to her normal gait, a walk.

Caroline sat silent and upright, her eyes half closed against the bright light. Now all decisions would come from the man sitting next to her. His elbows resting on his knees, he held the reins loosely, his eyes on the horizon.

"Well, now," he said at last. "We'll get Bagatelle back under cultivation. It'll be work, hard work, but if we hurry, we may still have time for a cotton crop this year. I have money enough to buy some new iron plowshares and we have the seed. We'll offer the slaves, I mean Negroes, good contracts and get them interested in the harvest, to encourage them."

He turned toward Caroline. Her shawl had slipped off her shoulders and he casually replaced it. Then he continued: "The South as we knew it is dead, Caroline, no matter how the war turns out. I don't think the secessionists will win, and nothing will ever be the same again. Slavery will never come back. We have to get ready for a new kind of life and we'll have to take a big step to catch up with the Northerners we've despised for so long. The landed aristocracy doesn't make the laws anymore. It's the needs of the masses—an entity I deplore —that will make the economic decisions. In exchange for our democratic and materialist compliance, I think they'll at least leave our spirits free. It's the only way the South will survive."

He was quiet for a while, but since Caroline remained silent, he went on: "Perhaps you wondered why I didn't fight in this war that so many people thought inevitable and just. I didn't fight because the rights of man are on the side of the hypocritical Yankees we view as barbarians. We cavaliers of the South, we inheritors of the pioneers' honor, committed the grave sin of enslaving a people with black skin and uneducated minds. We took from them what is given to every man and woman from the moment of their birth: to be your own master. Pierre-Adrien knew that. We're now paying the price for our stupidity, our specious justifications, the instinctive egotism of our race. The God in whom Adrien believed and who recruits his mercenaries wherever he can, is on the side of the Yankees. It's up to us now to be the Just . . ."

Caroline timidly slipped her arm through Clarence's. "I know you're right, that our cause wasn't the best, and that real courage can sometimes look like cowardice to others."

They had stopped before a vast field covered with dwarf shrubs with here and there a small tree showing its head. Freed of man's control, the earth had surrendered to anarchy.

"How sad," Caroline said, remembering the long disciplined rows of cotton.

Dandridge got down from the gig and held his hand out to Caroline. Together they walked toward the dense undergrowth. Without thinking, he put his arm around her shoulder and pulled her close, leaning down toward the face that looked up to his with adoration. From that instant, she knew what she had so longed to know: that whatever happened, whatever the results of the war or the color of the sky tomorrow, they were joined together and Bagatelle would be their land until they died.

Striking out, he led her through the high grass humming with insects. There, in the thick scrubby growth, the sucker of a half-suffocated cotton plant had put out a yellow blossom. Clarence picked it with ceremonious respect and presented it to Caroline.

"There. A present for today and my commitment to forever."

They slowly walked back to the river. The old mare, whom Dandridge had forgotten to tie up, had gone back to the stable trailing the empty gig.

"Did you know, Clarence, that General Templeton—Willy, I should say—has asked me to marry him again? I haven't given him an answer yet."

"And what will your answer be?"

"That it's very late. And that there's nothing more beautiful under the sun than a field of white cotton when the man to whom you've given your soul has made it bloom."

Dandridge smiled at Caroline with great tenderness, bent down, took her in his arms and kissed her long and deeply. Inside him something gave way: The feeling he had cast out of his life now welled up in him. At last he let her go and, hand in hand, as if they were going toward a new world waiting to be discovered, they took the narrow path along the river that led to their house.